Georgia Spearing

Spearing Publications

© 2024 by Georgia Roberts

All rights reserved.

No part of this manuscript may be reproduced, distributed, or transmitted in any form or by any means, including photocopying, recording, or other electronic or mechanical methods, without the prior written permission of the publisher, except in the case of brief quotations embodied in critical reviews and certain other noncommercial uses permitted by copyright law.

This book is a work of fiction. Names, characters, businesses, places, events, and incidents are either the products of the author's imagination or used in a fictitious manner. Any resemblance to actual persons, living or dead, or actual events is purely coincidental.

Published by Independent Publishing Network

ISBN: 9781836540144

Cover Design by Andrew Spearing

For permissions, contact: georgiaspearing.writer@gmail.com

Printed in United Kingdom

thegirlwiththemark.co.uk

Dedications

Thank you to my handsome hubby, Andrew Spearing, whose unwavering support and encouragement have been the driving force behind my journey as a writer. Your belief in me has fueled my passion and guided me through every chapter of this novel. Thank you for always being my inspiration and my biggest cheerleader.

I would like to express my heartfelt gratitude to Martin Spearing, my father-in-law, whose consistent support has been helpful in my writing journey. I want to express my love and admiration for my wonderful daughter, Iris. May you always hold onto your dreams and never let go.

A heartfelt thank you to my editor, Precious Durham. Your support has been invaluable on my journey as an author, and I am truly grateful for all your help.

And to all of those who suffer from chronic pain, keep going. You are doing great.

Author's Note

In "Soul," our heroine undertakes a journey marked by encounters infused with symbolic significance. These symbols, interwoven throughout the story, are designed to enrich the story and offer deeper insights into her experiences and personal growth.

I have provided an index at the end of the book to assist you in exploring these elements. I encourage you to use it as a guide to enhance your understanding of the narrative's symbolic layers as you read.

* Trigger Warning

This book addresses themes and content related to loss and miscarriage. Reader discretion is advised, as these subjects may be sensitive and evoke strong emotional responses.

Playlist

Breathe - Tommee Profit, Fleurie
Stronger Than Ever - Raleigh Ritchie
Live More & Love More - Cat Burns
Soulmate - Chainn
Give Me Love - Ed Sheeran
Outnumbered - Dermot Kennedy
Extrordinary Being - Emeli Sande
Breathe - Seinabo Sey
Hurts 2B Human - Pink, Khaild
Lost - Dermot Kennedy
Candles - Daughter
The Ending - Wafia, FINNEAS
Heaven's Not Too Far - We Three
Never Let Me Go - Florence & The Machine
Looking Too Closely - Fink
All That Really Matters - Teddy Swims
I Don't Miss A Thing - Karis
Prison - ADMT
If You Could See Me Now - The Script
Be On Your Way - Daughter
Stand By Me - Bootstraps
Shadow - John Mark Nelson
Lying To Myself - Portrait
How Do I Say Goodbye - Dean Lewis
Way We Go Down - KALEO
Breathe - Asgeir
Water - Jack Garratt
Weightless - Natasha Bedingfield
Undone - Haley Reinhart
An Eveining I Will Not Forget - Dermot Kennedy
Half Light - Banners
Tired of Healing - Noah Henderson
The Other Side - Ruelle
Let it All Go - RHODES, Birdy

Prologue

Although I've never been particularly religious, certain pivotal moments in your life compel you to seek comfort in something greater, someone who might answer the call in times of need.

I wasn't ready for mine.

Shattered

 My vision blurred and my thoughts scrambled to make sense of what was happening. Glass shattered against my skin, the tiny shards cutting into me like a thousand needles. The deafening sound of metal twisting as the car collided with a tremendous force. The seat belt snapped, its last grip on me vanishing as the impact thrust me forward. I crashed through the windshield, the sharp edges grazing my flesh and leaving a trail of stinging ache. The bitter taste of blood filled my mouth, metallic and warm, as the world spun in a chaotic blur. Pain flared, sharp and immediate, a searing agony that radiated through every nerve. I knew this pain was different. It was acute, fierce, but fleeting. It lacked the relentless, grinding nature of my chronic pain. But as quickly as it came, it vanished, replaced by the sudden coolness of water on my face.

 I found myself lying on the damp ground in a forest as I opened my eyes. Raindrops fell softly, their gentle patter blending with the rustling leaves. The scent of fresh rain filled the air, a comforting aroma surrounding me. I felt nature's embrace, grounding me in the forest's calm. Above, the canopy formed, and each leaf glistened with droplets. The rain was a delicate drizzle, its touch cool on my skin, mingling with the earthy scent of wet soil and the subtle scent of pine needles. All around, the forest was alive with the sound of nature. Birds cooed softly from hidden perches, their songs harmonizing with the rhythm of the falling rain. A gentle breeze whispered through the trees, causing branches to sway and leaves to flutter. The ground beneath me was of moss and fallen leaves, their textures soft and spongy against my fingertips. I could feel the dampness seeping through my clothes. I rose from the forest floor, the crunch of withered leaves beneath my bare feet. My gaze fell upon the white fabric covering my body, a dress unfamiliar and out of place against my skin. The dress clung to me, damp and translucent in places, its delicate lace and flowing material bare against the earthy surroundings. My long, curly red hair hung loose around my shoulders, the damp strands sticking to my skin and adding to the strangeness of the scene.

The coolness of the ground sent shivers up my legs, reminding me of my bare feet, which felt liberated and vulnerable against the forest floor. The wet moss was soft, almost velvety, under my soles, while the occasional twig or stone pricked sharply. The change of clothing raised more questions in my mind. How did I get here? Why was I wearing this dress, and where were my shoes? The dress felt alien, almost otherworldly, its pristine white fabric a mystery against the backdrop of my surroundings. I stood disconnected from reality, struggling to understand what had happened for me to end up here. The forest seemed to hold its breath, the only sound was the soft patter of raindrops and the gentle rustle of leaves, as if waiting for me to uncover its secrets.

I turned around in the forest, taking in the sights around me, until something caught my eye—an anomaly. There, where no door had stood moments before, now stood a solid wooden door. It was ancient and weathered, its surface covered with detailed carvings that seemed to pulsate faintly. Approaching cautiously, my bare feet sinking softly into the moss-covered ground, I couldn't help but feel a surge of curiosity. I hesitated before the door, my fingers trembling as I touched the cool wood, feeling the rough texture under my fingertips. The carvings seemed to shift subtly, almost imperceptibly, as if responding to my presence. My heart pounded in my chest, a mixture of curiosity and apprehension stirring within me. How did this door appear? What secrets did it hold? Was this a way out of this strange place? I couldn't shake the feeling that this door held answers to questions I hadn't even thought to ask.

As I stood there, a wave of anticipation washed over me—a faint whisper of cool air brushing against my skin, carrying with it a distant scent of must and age. Goosebumps prickled along my arms, and a shiver ran down my spine. I could feel the pull of the unknown, the promise of something extraordinary beyond this door, something that defied my understanding. The forest around me seemed to fade into the background, the sounds of nature muted as my focus centered on the enigmatic portal before me. I took a deep breath, steeling myself for what lay ahead, and placed my hand on the weathered handle. It was cold to the touch, yet oddly comforting, as if guiding me toward an unknown destiny.

With a hesitant push, the door slowly creaked open and a chill swept through me as I stepped inside. Blinking against the sudden brightness, I found myself standing in the middle of a vast hallway. The walls, painted in rich shades of brown, were decorated with intricate carvings that seemed to dance in the dim light from the old-fashioned fixtures overhead. The air crackled with an otherworldly energy, making my hair stand on end. Rows upon rows of doors, each a unique masterpiece, stretched out before me. Some were plain, others a riot of mesmerizing patterns, but all pulsed with a promise of unimaginable adventures. The buzzing of the fluorescent lights above mingled with the faint echo of my breath, creating a surreal ambience that left me momentarily paralyzed.

The scent of aged wood and musty air filled my nostrils, mingling with the faint aroma of something indefinable yet strangely familiar. The texture of the wooden floor beneath my feet was smooth yet slightly uneven, bearing the marks of centuries past. Each step echoed softly, the sound reverberating down the seemingly endless corridor, blending with the faint hum of the flickering lights above.

I stood in the middle of countless possibilities, unsure which of the doors to approach first. Each seemed to whisper a different promise—discovery, peril, fascination. I was overwhelmed by the beauty and mystery of this unexpected corridor, captivated by the magical and surreal nature. Standing amidst the rows of doors that stretched before me, I felt a surge of conflicting emotions. Curiosity tugged at me, urging me to explore what lay beyond each threshold so that I could uncover the secrets within each of the portals. Yet, fear gnawed at the edges of my resolve, whispering doubts and uncertainties about the consequences within my choices. What if these doors led to places from which I couldn't return? What if the mysteries they guarded were more than I could comprehend? As I turned around to look at the door I had come through; my heart skipped a beat—it was gone, somehow, it had vanished into thin air. A cold dread settled in my stomach and I felt trapped. The walls closed around me, forcing me to face the endless hallway. My breath quickened and my hands trembled but an unexplainable pull urged me forward. Fragmented images flickered through my mind, inaccessible and out of reach, leaving me grasping for the memories that weren't there. How did I end up here? Was this some kind of limbo? Each step through the hallway was heavy with uncertainty and the endless stretch of doors offered no answers. My eyes darted from one door to the next, my thoughts swirling with unanswered questions. Where was Luke? Why couldn't I remember anything from after the crash? What had caused the crash? While I tried to clear my mind of all the racing thoughts, a door suddenly stood out, its strange familiarity tugging at me. I stopped abruptly; my chest began to tighten as I grew more and more anxious.

The door stood before me, its weathered oak surface was casting a sight of timeless endurance. Each knot and grain in the wood seemed to pulse with life, whispering their secrets of resilience and steadfastness. As I traced my fingers over the intricate carvings, I felt the smooth and rough textures dance beneath my touch and I couldn't help but smile. Two elegant curves carved into the wood twisted and wove around each other, their paths forming into a mesmerizing embrace. They moved like graceful dancers frozen in time, their entwining forms creating a delicate space at the center where an unspoken connection hummed with energy. These distinct yet inseparable curves seemed to breathe with the silent promise of unity and understanding. The silver handle gleamed softly, catching the light in a way that seemed almost exquisite. It beckoned to me, its cool touch sending a tingle through my fingertips and up my arm. With each step closer, my heart drummed louder, suspense and longing mingling in my chest. This wasn't just an entryway but an entrance to a sanctuary where hearts beat in unison. The air around me seemed to hold its breath, filled with the unspoken promise of reunion and love. As I reached out and wrapped my fingers around the handle , excitement and hope surged through me. The door seemed to hum under my touch, resonating with the silent call of my soulmate, Luke. In that moment, every carved line and gleaming curve spoke to the eternal bond that transcended time and space, drawing me into a place where dreams and reality converged.

   I turned the handle and pushed the door open, its hinges creaking softly as it swung wide. But before I could react, I stumbled forward as if an invisible hand had pushed me through. As I gained my footing, the darkness wrapped around me like a suffocating cloak. My breath hitched, each inhale feeling tighter, it was as if the air itself was thickening. A dense silence pressed down on my ears, muting even the sound of my own heartbeat. I clenched my fists, my palms growing clammy, as my fingers trembled. My thoughts began to race, each one more frantic than the last, a wild fluttering that made my chest constrict. My throat compressed and my pulse pounded in my temples, a relentless beat echoing the creeping panic that threatened to engulf me. Just as I felt the fear threatening to overwhelm me completely, a flickering light pierced the darkness, casting a light upon the space before me. A holographic image materialized, shimmering and wavering like an illusion. As I adjusted to the sudden light and the image sharpened, I realized it was a video projection. There, on the screen, was Luke, his smile radiant and infectious as he gestured excitedly at something just beyond the frame. Suddenly, I was no longer in the room. The scene shifted, and I was back at the fair, Luke's laughter echoing in my ears. I was no longer an observer but an active participant, my hands moving smoothly and with familiarly in the holographic display.

   It was a memory, vivid and haunting. Its weight descended upon me like a heavy cloak, stirring up emotions buried deep beneath layers of time and distance. I had been transported back to a moment frozen in time, experiencing it again with such intensity that I felt breathless and trembling. Emotions bubbled inside me like sparkling champagne, a tornado of joy, happiness, and laughter. I watched as Luke and I met in the park, taking a brief break from our workday's demands and engaged in playful banter about the people surrounding us. Why was this happening? Was any of it real or was it merely a cruel mirage? Despite the beauty of the memory I was reliving, a creeping unease gripped me like icy fingers; goosebumps pricked my skin. The park dissolved into darkness around me, leaving me standing alone with the lingering echoes of our laughter.

"Where am I?" The question slipped from my lips, a desperate plea for clarity. I hoped my voice would reach someone, anyone, in this limbo. "Where is the real Luke?" I murmured, my voice faltering as the words lingered unanswered in the air. The holographic image flickered faintly before me, a reminder of what I had lost. "Why is this happening?" I repeated, my voice firmer this time but tinged with a deepening sense of isolation. The silence that followed echoed loudly, each unanswered question adding to the weight pressing down on me. Before I could gather my thoughts, another holographic image flickered to life on my left. Approaching cautiously, I hoped it would clarify the swirling questions in my mind.

I neared the projection and found myself thrust back into another memory from years ago—Luke and I at fifteen, embarking on our first date. The memory flooded in and how uncomfortable it felt to be alone together for the first time. Colorful lights danced against the darkening sky, lighting up the scene below with an ambient glow. Laughter and excited chatter filled the air, mixing with the cheerful melodies of carnival music. A maze of stalls and attractions filled with promises of thrills and delights, towering Ferris wheels stood brightly lit against the nighttime backdrop. The smell of sweet treats wafted through the air. Kids dashed around, joy lighting up their faces as they had fun on the spinning rides and found their way through the mazes. Stalls with stuffed prizes caught their attention, while attendants urged them with inviting voices. The fair pulsed with energy and life, a temporary glee and wonder amidst the ordinary world. Although Luke and I shared the same circle of friends, this was uncharted territory. Standing before this scene, I could almost feel my heart echoing the rapid beats of that distant moment.

"How about I win you a stuffed animal?" Luke suggested, breaking the silence. I grinned as we strolled to a tin can alley stall, its shelves decorated with stacked cans and stuffed animals dangling above.

"Which one do you want?" Luke asked, sweeping his hand towards the array of prizes. I pointed to the tabby cat perched on the shelf, its eyes seeming to beckon me. Luke handed over the money and picked up three small balls, determined to knock down the cans. With his first two throws, he missed completely. I couldn't contain my laughter at his failed attempts, and soon enough, he was left empty-handed. Giving him a gentle pat, I took charge and handed the money to the man.

"Now it's my turn," I declared with determination, while Luke simply rolled his eyes in response. I took the balls, and on my first throw, I knocked down four cans in one go. I could practically hear Luke's jaw hit the floor, but I remained focused. With my second throw, I sent all the cans tumbling down. The stall attendant retrieved the tabby cat from the shelf and handed it to me.

The stall attendant chuckled heartily as he handed me the tabby cat. "Well, well, looks like your lady friend here's got quite the arm! Don't worry; practice makes perfect!"

"Thank you," I said and turned to face Luke, his expression a mix of shock and pride. I couldn't resist teasing him." Well, someone had to show you how to do it," I quipped with a smirk, handing him the tabby cat. He

15

accepted the tabby cat from my outstretched hands with a playful remark. "I'll treasure this forever," he teased, but his eyes revealed his gratitude.

We left the stall behind and continued our stroll through the fairgrounds. Memories flooded back to me, especially the anxiety I felt when we first held hands. Looking back on those moments, it all seemed so innocent and amusing. Holding hands as we walked, we came across a young girl in tears; she had dropped her ice cream in a puddle on the ground. Her father struggled to comfort her. Luke glanced at me, a silent understanding passing between us. He approached the troubled little girl with a sudden spark of kindness and handed her the tabby cat. Almost instantly, her tears ceased, and her father's face filled with relief as we walked away. As the memory faded, I felt a force yank me back into the darkness again. The sensation was like being dragged underwater, the weight of the void pressing down on me.

****

"Why is this happening? I don't understand." I murmured, my voice barely audible. I realized that I wouldn't receive the answers I sought no matter what I asked.

A shooting pain seared through my head and bright flashes overwhelmed my vision. My senses reeled, and my feet seemed to lose touch with the ground, propelling me into another memory. As the disorienting shift subsided, a chilling scene unfolded before me. Sirens wailed in the distance, their piercing cries slicing through the chaotic air like a desperate plea for help. Adrenaline surged through my veins, a bitter taste of fear lingering on my tongue as I stood amidst the wreckage. In the distance, I saw myself and Luke's motionless bodies in the front seat of his copper red, beat-up car; my heart pounded in my chest as tears streamed down my face. The scene was surreal, almost as if I had witnessed it from a bystander's perspective and could not intervene. The sound of metal groaning echoed in my ears, intermingling with the distant cries of pain and the urgent commands of first responders. My heart surged, each beat hammering against my chest like a warning. *Is this real? How did I get here? What happened to us?*

I took a shaky breath, trying to steady myself against the onslaught of emotions threatening to overwhelm me. The metallic scent of blood tickled my nostrils, mingling with the acrid smoke that stung my eyes. *Stay calm,* I urged myself, *focus.* But the scene before me refused to make sense, leaving me abandoned in a nightmare that felt all too real. I touched the twisted wreckage with trembling hands as if grounding myself in its cold reality. *There must be a reason for this. Someone must know.* In a moment suspended in time, eerie and unbearable, I walked through the wreckage, wrestling with the reality unfolding before me. The smell of smoke and burning debris filled the air, stinging my nostrils as I struggled to breathe. The taste of grit and dust coated my tongue; the sight of twisted metal and shattered glass met my eyes, a jumble of fragmented images that refused to make sense. Each step I took sent tremors through the ground as the upheaval and chaos gripped the world around me. An invisible barrier blocked my path as I attempted to reach Luke, leaving me stranded in the chaos.

Pounding on the invisible barrier, I screamed Luke's name, my fists beating against the unseen wall that separated us. The urge to reach him consumed me, but some unseen force restrained me. I couldn't hold back the tears, overwhelmed by the surge of frustration and fear.

"Why can't I remember anything?" I sobbed, my voice cracking with emotion, the words torn from me in a desperate plea for answers. Memories of the crash flashed through my mind: laughing with Luke moments before the sudden impact, the chaotic blur of shattered glass and screeching metal. Then, a void—nothingness enveloped me. I found myself back in the darkened room, collapsing to the floor under a rush of emotions. As the memory diminished, determination surged forth, pushing aside the suffocating despair.

The answers weren't behind me; they lay ahead, beyond these enigmatic doors. I had to find them, no matter the obstacles. I wasn't sure how we had got into the crash, but I felt something was urging me to uncover the truth.

The Labyrinth Unraveled

As I sat defeated on the cold and gritty floor, the sudden creak of a distant door pierced the stifling silence; its faint sound vibrating through the darkness like a beacon. I wiped the tears that streaked down my cheeks, feeling their salty sting on my skin. The chill of the floor seeped through my dress, sending a shudder through my spine. As I drew in a deep breath, I summoned every ounce of strength I had to stand, my legs trembling like fragile reeds in a gust of wind. As I paced the hallway, my footsteps echoed softly against the worn wooden floor. My brow furrowed in frustration as I scanned each closed door, desperately seeking answers. Clenching my fists at my sides, I felt tension building within me. The urge to find Luke, to unravel the mystery of my existence here, surged through me like a relentless drumbeat. Each unopened door heightened my frustration, compelling me to press on in my quest for clarity and reunion.

I craved the comfort of certainty, needing to know he was safe. As I continued down the hallway, my senses were alert for any door that seemed to call to me. Every door represented a piece of my past that I wasn't sure I was ready to face. With every step, I sensed a heaviness bearing down on me, mingled with a growing urgency to uncover the truth about Luke's destiny. My eyes scanned the doors, searching for any sign, any clue that might lead me closer to the answers I sought. And then, among all the doors, I spotted a door that drew my gaze like a jagged shard of glass in a field of smooth stones. It was the door to Luke's worn-out car, I would recognize it anywhere. Its bright copper red was boldly contrasting with the muted tones around it. As I approached the door, memories rushed back with an overwhelming force. The echoes of our screams pierced my ears, mingling with the sickening sound of glass shattering and tires squealing. The scene unfolded vividly in my mind, causing my heart to race and my breath to quicken. Despite the rising anxiety and dread, I couldn't turn away. I hesitantly stretched out my hand, driven by a desperate need for closure that outweighed the fear threatening to consume me.

With a fierce tug, I wrenched the door open, expecting to face the grim reality of that fateful night face-to-face. But to my surprise, nothing but a solid brick wall stared back at me, mocking my futile efforts. Defeat washed over me, bitter and relentless, as I returned from the false promise of finding answers. The car door dissolved into thin air, taking with it the hope of any answers. As doubts gnawed at me, I wondered if fate would consign the truth to remain hidden beneath the labyrinthine layers of my memories. Desperation gripped me as I hurried towards three more of the doors, each slipping away just as my fingers grazed them. Agitation gnawed at me as I tried to grasp something real, something more substantial within the confusing labyrinth of memories. Then, a shift in the atmosphere caught my attention—the joyful melody of birdsong filled the air, halting my frantic search. My gaze was irresistibly drawn to an archway at the end of the hallway. Dressed with vibrant flowers and twining vines, its magnetic allure captivated all my senses.

As I traced my fingers over the hidden sunflower nestled within the arch, I sensed a strong tug drawing me forward. Stepping through, I felt the delicate brush of hanging flowers against my skin, their petals whispering secrets as I descended onto the soft, grassy ground below. Lifting my eyes, I was greeted by an unbelievable sight—a forest of towering trees and vibrant blooms that painted the air with their intoxicating scents. The path ahead flowed forward with an ethereal grace, adorned with flowers of unearthly beauty, each blossom radiating hues that defied nature's palette. The cool grass cushioned my bare feet with each step; beside the path, the mushrooms softly glowed in several shades of luminous purple, casting an otherworldly light that danced across the forest floor like mystical fireflies. As I continued, I came upon a withered playground, its structures barely visible beneath the foliage that had grown over it. Rusted swings hung motionless, their chains intertwined with creeping vines. The merry-go-round was almost unrecognizable, now a mound of green and brown where plant life had reclaimed it.

A broken slide, partially buried in the earth, hinted at the laughter that once filled this place, now long gone and replaced by the hushed whispers of the forest. The contrast of the decaying playground against the vibrant, otherworldly garden created an eerie yet mesmerizing scene that lingered in my mind as I moved into the unknown. It made me feel like I had stepped back into a moment from my childhood, a moment where I was innocent and naive; the only time in my life when the world seemed full of possibilities and magic. I wasn't sure what it meant but being here made me feel safe. I followed a stream's path and crossed a scenic bridge before I nearly bumped into a young girl and boy on the other side of the stream. Relief flooded through me at the sight of fellow explorers in this enchanted garden.

"Excuse me, can you tell me where I am?" I called out to the children. They darted across the bridge, giggling and oblivious to my query. With a flower crown reminiscent of those I used to make, the girl briefly turned, her eyes twinkling with a familiarity that tugged at a distant memory.

The boy, clutching an old, weathered red teddy bear that seemed oddly familiar, waved for me to follow. "Come on!" he shouted, echoing my brother's playful tone from years past. Uncertain whether they could hear me, I followed them, hoping to encounter more people in this enigmatic place. Their pure and joyful laughter intertwined with the rustling leaves and the gentle babble of the stream, creating a symphony that felt strange and comforting. As I trailed them, I noticed subtle clues that this place was intricately connected to my childhood. The path weaved through scenes that felt like fragments of forgotten dreams. The children led me deeper into the garden, their presence a beacon of something significant, something I knew that I needed to remember. This enchanted place seemed to hold the keys to my past. With every step, the lines between memory and reality blurred, urging me to uncover more of the secrets this magical realm held. A bright orange flower caught my eye. As I got closer, the flower's color seemed to shift before my eyes, transforming into a vibrant crimson hue with each step I took; its petals changing as if they were responding to my presence. As I reached out to touch its petals, the flower suddenly closed as if repelling my touch. Startled, I recoiled but as it reopened, I couldn't resist peering inside, where I glimpsed movement within.

Determined, I reached out once more, gasping aloud as my fingertips tingled, drawn to the vibrant petals of the flower. Suddenly, the twisted vines coiled around my wrist, their firm and insistent touch pulling me deeper into the heart of the floral labyrinth. Each tendril seemed to pulse with a life of its own as its grip tightened more and more with each passing moment. The sensation was as thrilling and unsettling as if I had stumbled upon a secret world hidden within the innocent beauty of the bloom. A shockwave of impact reverberated through me as my body collided with the ground. The gritty texture of the pavement was pressed against my palms and the sting of broken skin momentarily distracted me from my surroundings.

As I rose to my feet, I could still feel the cool roughness of the asphalt beneath my fingers, each grain telling a story of years gone by. Dusting myself off, I took a moment to absorb the sights and sounds of my childhood street, once filled with innocence and adventure, now tinged with the bittersweet nostalgia of time.

"Don't be out too long, Dee!" I heard a faint woman's voice call down the street. As I turned, I spotted a little girl joyfully skipping along the path, her curly red hair bouncing with each step. It was me, back when I must have been around six years old. The younger me carried a colorful crossover bag decorated with stickers and her eyes were filled with youthful exuberance as she danced down the street. She looked as happy as if she didn't care about the world. Suddenly, a loud crash followed by the piercing cry of a child broke me out of my thoughts. Without hesitation, we hurried towards the source of the commotion. The street seemed to stretch endlessly before us, the cobblestones cool beneath my feet. The sight that awaited us was heart-wrenching: a little boy lay sprawled on the ground beside his overturned bike, his face contorted in pain as tears streamed down his cheeks. The metallic tang of blood filled the air.

"Why don't I remember this?" I mused aloud while my younger version rushed over to the boy.

"It's okay, let me take a look. Where does it hurt?" little Dee asked.

The boy pointed to his knee. Carefully, little Dee lifted his trouser leg and saw a nasty gash. She then retrieved a small first-aid kit from her bag. I couldn't help but smile at the sight and reminisce about how cute I was back then.

"I'm going to clean it and then dress it, okay?" little Dee asked the boy as she began to work on cleaning the cut.

Unlike the vivid memories of Luke, these fragments of my childhood puzzled me. Why were these particular moments surfacing now and what did they signify? I leaned against the nearby streetlight, absorbed in the unfolding scene; when a sudden jolt surged through my body, throwing me off balance. I tumbled backwards, my arms flailing to regain stability but it was too late. With a startled gasp, I landed heavily on the soft grass. The impact knocked the wind out of me, leaving me breathless and disoriented as I lay there, staring up at the cloudy sky.

As I turned my head to assess my surroundings, the gentle rustling of leaves overhead caught my attention. The park stretched out before me, bathed in the warm glow of the afternoon sun. Sitting up, I furrowed my brow; the grass was cool and slightly damp beneath my fingers as I tried to piece together my current location. However, before I could make sense of it all, the air was filled with the sound of joyful laughter; carried on the same breeze that also carried the scent of freshly cut grass. Two young girls came running over, their giggles were echoing through the open space and their footsteps were crunching lightly on the gravel path as they raced toward the tunnel slide.

Once more, I found myself deep within the scene. My curly red hair was catching the light like the first rays of sunlight in the morning but this time I appeared slightly older. The girl beside me was my best friend, Evie, her skin radiant in the warm daylight. I recognized her instantly, her laughter echoing a sense of familiarity deep within me. I had always found it funny how when you're young, all you wish for is to be older but when you're older, you yearn to be young again. It's a universal feeling shared by many. Yet, time needs to align with our desires. I observed my younger self and Evie running around the park, inventing imaginary adventures like being pursued by a dragon or embarking on quests through magical realms in search of a charming prince. If Evie could see me now, I knew she would probably find it amusing.

As the two girls vanished into the tunnel, I followed, drawn in by their echoing laughter. Kneeling, I squeezed through the narrow opening, feeling the rough edges of the tunnel walls brushing against my arms. The dim light within cast eerie shadows, heightening my anticipation. Gradually, their voices faded into silence, leaving me alone in the oppressive quiet. Emerging on the other side, I landed in an unfamiliar place, the cool earth damp beneath my hands as I steadied myself. The forest enveloped me in its dense embrace, towering trees casting elongated shadows across the mossy ground. The air was crisp and tinged with the scent of pine needles, a sharp contrast to the warmth I had left behind. Descending the worn steps leading away from the tunnel entrance, I felt the chill settle deeper within me. Each step echoed with the creak of aged wood, amplifying the solitude that surrounded me. The barren forest loomed ominously in the darkness, its skeletal trees reaching up like gnarled fingers clawing at the sky. Wisps of mist slithered between the skeletal branches, casting eerie shadows that danced on the forest floor. The air was thick with an oppressive silence, broken only by the occasional creak of a branch or the distant hoot of an owl. The mist hung heavy, obscuring what little moonlight filtered through the canopy, turning the forest into a labyrinth of shadows and half-seen shapes. Each step forward made me feel like I was trespassing into an unknown realm, where every rustle of leaves or snap of a twig echoed loudly in the unsettling stillness. The ground beneath was soft and damp, a carpet of fallen leaves and tangled roots that seemed to writhe in the dim light. The forest emitted abandonment and decay almost as if nature itself had turned its back on this desolate place. Shapes moved in the mist, fleeting glimpses of phantom figures that vanished as quickly as they appeared, leaving behind a lingering sense of unease.

In the woodland, time seemed suspended where fear and uncertainty mingled with the cold tendrils of mist. Every sense was on edge, heightened by the primal instinct that unseen eyes watched and waited in the heart of darkness. Other trees loomed in the distance, their forms barely visible through the heavy mist that enveloped the area. Faint whispers seemed to drift from every direction, growing louder with each step I took.

"Am I worth it?" A whisper called out, so close that it felt like a breath on my neck.

I recognized the doubt it had stirred within me, echoing the same words as the whisper. Traveling further through the eerie woods, each whisper grew louder and closer, foreshadowing every doubt I had ever had.

"Do I even have what it takes?" Another whisper, questioning my abilities, echoed through the mist.

"Do I look okay?" Doubt about my appearance crept in, a subtle jab at my confidence.

"Am I wise enough?" A nagging voice, undermining my intellect, joined the chorus of doubts.

"What if I make the wrong choice?" Fear of failure whispered in my ear, casting shadows on my decisions.

"Can anyone truly care about me?" Loneliness and insecurity intertwined, leaving me feeling isolated.

"Do I have a future?" Ominous uncertainty about what lies ahead cast doubt on my path.

"Will they accept me?" Anxiety about acceptance gnawed at me, a constant worry in my mind.

"What's my purpose in all of this?" Existential questions loomed large, leaving me feeling lost and adrift in the darkness.

The doubts chewed at my confidence, my breath quickening as I fled from the voices that echoed through the hazy woods. The trees seemed to close in, their shadows twisting into grotesque shapes that mirrored my innermost fears. Shrouded by the mist, the weight of each whisper pressed down on me like a smothering veil. My heart pounded in my chest, my footsteps frantic and uneven. Every rustle of leaves and every snap of a twig sent a jolt of fear through me. Each step was a desperate attempt to outrun the relentless whispers that clawed at my mind, dragging me deeper into a spiral of panic and dread.

Are they just pretending to love me?

Will failure always be my fate?

Do I even deserve to be okay?

Why am I not as good as them?

Am I doomed to never truly accept myself?

Am I a good person?

The voices followed me like shadows, their sinister words fueling my fear and uncertainty. The more I ran, the closer they drew, their presence suffocating me with doubt. My heart hammered against my ribs and I could feel my hair whipping back and forth as I sprinted through the forest. Each breath burned in my lungs, matching the frantic rhythm of my footsteps. Branches littered the forest floor and I stumbled, my dress catching on the fallen twigs and leaves. Panic surged as I nearly tripped over the tangled undergrowth but I regained my balance just in time. I dared not look back but I could sense their proximity, their whispers were now almost physical against my skin.

The rustling of the leaves behind me echoed their unseen pursuit and it took everything in me not to succumb to the overwhelming fear coursing through my veins. I pushed harder, my legs straining against the uneven ground, desperate to outrun both the voices and the encroaching darkness that threatened to engulf me. As I passed each tree in a frantic search for a way to escape, I knew my insecurities were swallowing me whole but I didn't know how to stop them. How could I escape something that had been woven into the very fabric of my being? However, amidst the chaos, my eyes locked onto a tree resembling the one I had emerged from earlier. Its gnarled roots sprawled like steps, beckoning toward a dark tunnel, promising refuge. Without hesitation, I veered towards it, propelled by a desperate yearning for solace, my senses alert to every crackle of underbrush and the earthy scent of moss as I ascended the root-stairs toward the mysterious tunnel. Refusing to glance back at whatever lurked behind me, I pressed on. The tunnel swallowed me into its darkness. The air grew cooler and carried a faint earthy scent, a clear departure from the suffocating whispers of the woods I had just escaped. Anxiety corroded my thoughts but there was no turning back now. As I walked deeper into the darkness, my hands trailed along the rough, textured bark of the tunnel walls. Each step echoed softly against the stone floor, the sound echoing through the narrow passage. I stopped briefly, leaning against the cool wall for support and closed my eyes, trying to calm the emotions within me.

The rough bark scraped against my fingertips and as I continued forward, my hand suddenly encountered something cold and smooth. I gasped aloud and yanked my hand back, startled by the sudden change in texture. Doubt crept in once more, weighing my options in the darkness. Should I continue blindly forward or retreat into the familiar uncertainty of the whispering woods? The decision was made for me as memories of the haunting whispers echoed in my mind. With a resolve born of necessity, I pushed forward. My feet, now my only guide, sensed the subtle shift in the ground beneath me. The texture from the soft earth underfoot changed to something rugged and chilling, a reminder of the unknown path ahead. A feeling in my gut urged me to run, but I had ventured too far ahead with no option to turn back. As I moved forward, a light emerged at the tunnel's end, yet it appeared neither welcoming nor warm; instead, it seemed cold and alarming. Despite my hesitation, I had no choice but to continue forward. As I emerged from the other side, the cave's cool, damp air enveloped me, causing goosebumps to ripple across my arms and a shiver to trace down my spine. I hugged myself tightly, my fingers digging into my forearms as if trying to ward off the unease creeping through my stomach. Every breath felt shallow, each exhale a shaky release of tension. My gaze darted around the dimly lit cavern, searching for some sign of familiarity amidst the shadows that danced across the walls. I glanced at the ceiling, hoping for another light source but found only a rugged surface above me. Hundreds of stalactites hung menacingly, their jagged forms casting eerie shadows in the dimness. The air around me felt cool and motionless, carrying a faint mineral scent. Turning back to what lay ahead, I hesitated, my fingers tracing the rough texture of the tunnel walls for reassurance. The darkness seemed to press in from all sides, its weight almost tangible against my skin. Summoning all the courage within me, I took a tentative step forward, the silence broken only by the soft shuffle of my footsteps on the rocky floor.

Suddenly, my vision was overwhelmed by a bright, searing light. Blinking against the glare, I shielded my eyes until they adjusted. Gradually, I realized the light emanated from a hole in the cave floor, its beam shooting upwards towards the distant ceiling. The warmth of the light bathed over me, a clear difference from the coolness of the tunnel's depths. Above me, the stalactites loomed like ancient sentinels, their sharp points catching glimmers of light. Curiosity piqued, I was about to investigate further when a shadowy figure darted across the light, causing the hairs on the back of my neck to stand up. Without hesitation, I made a beeline for the tunnel, only to see it had disappeared.

"Why bother even trying?" A deep voice sounded behind me, almost in my ear. I spun around, heart pounding with fear, as I searched for the source of the grim voice but found nothing but an empty and dimly lit forest.

"Who's there?" I called out, my voice trembling despite my attempts to put on a brave face. "Show yourself!"

"You'll be back," the voice echoed, now distant yet unsettlingly clear. As I strained to locate the speaker, my eyes caught a glimpse of a dark figure standing ominously near the edge of the light.

"Stop hiding!" I shouted, taking a step forward, my breath quickening as my anxiety levels soared. "What do you want from me?"

The figure remained silent, its form blending in with the shadows. I could barely make out its silhouette, but the eyes... those eyes seemed to burn with an unnatural intensity.

"You can't escape," the voice whispered, chillingly calm. "Not from me, not from this place."

"Who are you? What do you want?" My voice was a mixture of fear and frustration, each word posed a challenge to the unseen presence. I stepped back, my foot catching on a root, that nearly sent me sprawling. "I'm not going to let you scare me."

"Scare you?" The voice chuckled, sounding like the noise of a pickup truck driving across a gravel road. "You're already scared, Dee. And you should be. Because the real question is, are you brave enough to face what you fear most?"

"Enough of this! Show yourself!" I demanded, my voice breaking with desperation.

The figure stepped forward, the darkness around it parting like a curtain. I could see its eyes now, cold and penetrating, like twin pits of void. "You don't have a choice, Dee. You're already part of this. The past is catching up with you and it won't be denied."

"Stay away!" I screamed, stumbling backwards. "Whatever you are, you can't have me!"

"Can't I?" The figure's voice was a mere whisper now, almost a breath against my ear. "You've always been mine, Dee. You just didn't know it. And now, you have to decide. Will you face the darkness, or will you let it consume you?"

Panicked, I frantically scanned for any other exit, desperate to escape this unknown presence. I dashed in any direction, attempting to distance myself from the figure. However, as I moved away from the glaring light, my visibility lessened, making it difficult to see.

The figure's silhouette faded into the darkness, its voice a mere echo in the distance. "You will be back, Dee. You can't run from your fate."

And with that, the darkness seemed to close in around me, every shadow a looming threat, every sound a sinister whisper. My only choice now was to keep moving, to find a way out before the darkness swallowed me whole. I stumbled over the uneven ground, desperate to escape this abyss. It wasn't until I fell to the floor that I noticed a small hole nearby, with scant water trickling through. The faint glimmer caught my eye in its reflection, drawing me cautiously closer. As I peered into the shallow puddle, mesmerized by its gentle ripples, I felt a strange, compelling force, as if something unseen was beckoning me. Without warning, the surface of the water began to shimmer and distort. With a sudden rush, I was pulled into the puddle's depths as if plunging into a mirror's reflection. Emerging on the other side, I stood in awe within a vast temple of mirrors. Each surface reflected and refracted light in mesmerizing patterns, creating a kaleidoscope of colors and shapes that danced around me.

The temple stood ancient and weathered, its grand ceilings embellished with intricate patterns that hinted at a message lost to time. Despite my efforts, I couldn't decipher its meaning. Yet, there was a clear impression that the temple sought to communicate something profound. Moving deeper into the temple, the ground beneath me transformed into a mosaic of water and glass, shimmering with a celestial sheen. Each step I took sent delicate ripples spreading outward, creating a symphony of movement beneath my feet. Walking on this ethereal surface was surreal and mesmerizing, adding to the enigmatic ambience that permeated the temple. Each mirror within reflected different iterations of myself, spanning various ages and expressions. They mirrored my movements with an eerie precision, each version carrying a subtle nuance of emotion. Intrigued by the spectacle, I approached a mirror showcasing a younger version of myself, perhaps around twenty-one years old, and tentatively reached out to touch its surface.

Instantly, as my fingertips made contact, the mirror's surface rippled and transformed, reshaping itself into the familiar setting of an office.

****

"I assume you know why I've asked you to come in?" Mr. Sevens, my boss, said as we settled into his office.

"I'm hoping it's regarding the editorial assistant position?" I responded, a glimmer of hope audible in my voice.

"Unfortunately, yes," he replied, gesturing for me to sit across from him.

"That doesn't sound promising," I remarked, taking a seat.

"Sadly, you didn't submit your application in time, so we had to offer the position to someone else. I'm truly sorry,

Dee. I did try to advocate for you but the decision was out of my hands." I sat stunned, his words echoing as I tried to comprehend where I had gone wrong. The opportunity of a lifetime slipped through my grasp, leaving me on the brink of securing my dream job.

Regret flooded through me like a rising tide, pulling me under with its weight. Each memory of carefree outings with Evie became a sharp pang of guilt. If only I had prioritized preparation over those leisurely moments, maybe things would be different now. The weight of responsibility settled heavily on my shoulders, a burden I couldn't shake off. I automatically recoiled from the mirror's reflection as regret flooded over me for the missed opportunity, the memory still vivid as if it happened yesterday. Every day, the weight of what could have been gnawed at me, leaving me to wonder about the path I might have taken if I had secured that job and where I would be now.

As I turned to face the reflections of myself, a mosaic of regrets and choices confronted me. Each mirror held a different version of who I had been, moments frozen in time, each whispering of decisions made and paths untaken. In the midst of these haunting reflections, a determination took root. This room, unlike the others I had passed through, beckoned with the promise of clarity. It held answers I yearned for in my pursuit of Luke—a chance to unravel the tangled threads of regret and uncertainty that had woven through my life. Amongst the myriad reflections, one caught my eye—an earlier version of myself, younger and less burdened by the weight of consequences. There was a hesitation in her eyes, a silent plea for understanding. The reflection was of myself at six, clutching a familiar red teddy bear in my small hands. Memories flooded back, transporting me to the enchanted garden where I first met that same teddy bear. Approaching it, I extended my arm to touch the mirror. Before my eyes, it once again began to ripple, and I was pulled back into another memory. I stood in the familiar surroundings of my childhood home, enveloped by the hushed atmosphere of mourners draped in somber black attire. The air carried a blend of faint floral scents and the subtle murmur of whispered condolences. Each person's solemn gaze mirrored the weight of sorrow settling in my chest.

As I observed the scene unfolding before me, memories surged forth, each moment melding into a quilt of heartfelt memories. In the center of the room, my younger self stood, clad in black, holding my cherished red stuffed bear tightly against my chest. The sight stirred a bittersweet ache within me, a reminder of the unbreakable bond I had shared with my nan. My nan was more than a grandmother to me; she was my confidante, a source of unwavering comfort; she was the steadfast anchor of our family. Together, we had spun a web of tales, laughter, and tender moments, now etched in the recesses of my heart like cherished heirlooms.

But then came the day of her funeral. The weight of guilt washed over me in unyielding surges. Memories of the week before haunted me — the choice to spend a carefree night at Evie's instead of visiting my nan, who was alone and ailing. The news of her passing arrived the next morning, crushing me with the weight of unspoken words and missed chances. Surrounded by the mournful crowd, sorrow and remorse enveloped me like a heavy shroud. I couldn't escape the self-blame that ate away at my heart. The ache of regret intensified with each passing moment, knowing I never got to say goodbye and never had the chance to tell her how much she meant to me.

I remembered how, in the aftermath, I distanced myself from Evie for a week, unable to confront my feelings of guilt and grief. Despite knowing deep down that I was responsible for my actions, I couldn't shake off the haunting sense of not being able to say goodbye to my beloved nan. I wiped at my cheeks, but fresh tears replaced the ones I had wiped away. Returning to the temple, the weight of each memory became increasingly difficult to bear, prompting me to question whether continuing was indeed what I desired. However, as I was surrounded by inner conflict, a determination stirred within me. I needed closure and to understand my role in the events that led me to this point. The temple held answers, and I was certain of it. With a steadying breath, I pushed through the hesitation and pressed forward into the temple's depths.

Eventually, I reached a staircase where the water ceased, and atop stood a mirror framed in intricate gold detailing, practically beckoning me closer. As I ascended the steps, each one echoing in the hollow expanse of the temple, a surge of hope and urgency gripped me. The mirror's reflection beckoned, promising answers that could lead me closer to Luke. The anticipation coiled tightly in my chest, mingling with the relentless thud of my heartbeat, amplifying the ache of longing that had plagued me since our separation. Before me, the mirror sparkled with a mystical shimmer, revealing a vision of Luke and me standing together. His presence in the reflection was both comforting and agonizing—a reminder of the distance between us, both physical and emotional. Driven by a desperate need to bridge the gap that separated us, I extended my hand towards the mirror's surface. The cool glass met my fingertips, sending a shiver of anticipation through me. In that moment of connection, I hoped to uncover the truth that lay hidden, to grasp any clue that might lead me to him.

*****

As I stared at the GPS app on my phone, attempting once again to pinpoint our location, frustration simmered beneath the surface. "Luke, it's the other way. I've told you this already," I insisted, my voice laced with exasperation.

Luke's response was immediate and sharp. "I'm sorry, but who's driving here? And that GPS is the reason we got into this mess," he shot back, his tone defensive and accusatory.

His words filled the silence with a suffocating presence, a barrier between us thickening with each heartbeat. The tension crackled, palpable in the terse silence that followed, punctuated only by the low hum of the car engine. My fingers tapped impatiently on the dashboard, mirroring the rapid pace of my thoughts. I could feel his frustration, a tightly coiled spring ready to snap, and it mirrored my own. Outside, the road stretched endlessly, a metaphor for the distance growing between us in this moment. We were supposed to be heading to a cosy cottage to celebrate our first wedding anniversary, but instead of anticipation and joy, our journey had spiralled into a battlefield of words and stubbornness.

"I can't believe you're blaming the GPS for your terrible driving!" I shot back, my frustration boiling over. "Maybe if you paid attention to the road instead of arguing with me, you wouldn't have missed the turn and we wouldn't be in this mess!"

Luke's face flushed with anger as he gripped the steering wheel tighter. "Oh, so now it's my fault? Typical," he spat out bitterly.

"You always have to be right, don't you? Well, guess what? You're not!" I shot back, my voice tinged with frustration and hurt. The words hung heavy in the air between us, each a dagger piercing through the already strained atmosphere of the car. Our first-anniversary celebration had turned into a battleground of hurtful words and wounded pride. As the tension peaked, our voices grew louder, and our tempers flared, I failed to notice the car veering dangerously close to the edge of the road until it was too late. I emerged from the memory, my steps faltering on the worn stone steps of the ancient temple. The echoes of our argument rang out in my mind, each word a sharp pebble that had set off an avalanche of consequences. Regret enveloped me like a suffocating fog. Images of the crash flashed before my eyes, the sound of screeching metal and shattering glass echoing in my ears. Luke's face, twisted in anger and frustration, haunted me. Guilt mingled with my worry for him; each thought was a knot tightening in my stomach. Where was he now? Was he safe? Questions plagued me with their silence. Tears threatened at the corners of my eyes, held back by a stubborn resolve. I stood amidst the solemn grandeur of the temple, its ancient walls a silent witness to the uneasiness raging within me.

"I can't believe it... It was that argument," I mutter to myself, my voice trembling with a mixture of disbelief and regret. "We were so caught up in our disagreement, we didn't see..." I pause, my gaze distant as I replay the scene in my mind. "I never thought it could lead to this," I continued, my voice filled with sorrow. "If only I had been more understanding, if only I had listened..." Taking a deep breath, I steady myself against the ancient stone walls, my fingers gripping the rough surface for support.

Was I dead? Or was there a chance to find my way back to Luke? And how was I meant to leave? "I need to find him," I murmured, determination flickering in my eyes. "I need to make things right."

I gazed back at the reflections of my past selves, acknowledging the regrets that haunted me. While I couldn't change the past, I understood the importance of accepting what I couldn't change and embracing whatever the future held, whether it led to life or something beyond. There might still be a path forward, a chance to find peace and perhaps even redemption. The mirror surface that had once displayed Luke's reflection shimmered like a tranquil sea suddenly stirred by a storm brewing beneath its surface. At first, the ripples were subtle, gentle waves that distorted his image. But as I watched, mesmerized and hopeful, the ripples intensified, growing in frequency and strength. It was as if the mirror itself responded to the stormy emotions swirling within me, its reflective surface vibrating with an unseen power. The distortions began to coalesce and shift, the edges of the mirror blurring and reforming into a new shape—a shape that gradually took on the recognizable form of a door. The transformation was gradual yet unmistakable, like witnessing a painting come to life with each brushstroke.

The once-clear reflection of Luke faded as the mirror door solidified, its contours becoming sharper and more defined. I could feel the tension in the air, charged with anticipation and the promise of revelation. A threshold between worlds, its mirrored surface reflecting the ambient light in colorful bursts of color. As I stood before the mirror door, my breath caught in my throat caught between trepidation and exhilaration. It wasn't just a door; it was a marvel of craftsmanship, its surface composed entirely of mirrored panels. Light danced and refracted off its myriad surfaces, creating a kaleidoscope of colors that painted the walls with shifting hues of blue, violet, and silver. The reflections twisted and warped, distorting the space around me in mesmerizing patterns. The door beckoned like a portal to another realm, promising secrets and revelations beyond its shimmering threshold. With a steadying breath, I extended my hand, fingers trembling as they hovered just above the smooth, cool surface of the mirror handle. My fingertips made contact, sending a jolt of electricity through me as if the very essence of the door responded to my touch. It yielded beneath my touch an invitation and a challenge wrapped in one. I hesitated for a moment as I prepared to step through, eager to discover the mysteries that lay beyond—a room bathed in starlight, waiting to unveil its celestial wonders. As I stepped through, the familiar sensation of the hallway embraced me once more, leaving me eager to discover what awaited beyond its threshold.

Starry Skies

As I crossed into the hallway, my eyes darted from one door to the next, each whispering hidden wonders. Yet an insistent urgency spurred me onward, urging me to hasten my search, to reunite with him, and to find my way home. With each step, my thoughts raced ahead, imagining scenarios where each door might reveal his whereabouts. The temptation to turn, to explore every avenue of possibility, tugged at my will. Images of Luke flashed through my mind, his face etched with concern, his absence a gaping void in my heart. I reminded myself of the need to stay focused, to heed only the call of a door that called to me on a deeper level.

As I passed each door, I was amazed by its variety of shapes and sizes. Some doors were tall and imposing, their ancient wood carved with intricate patterns that seemed to tell stories of ages past. Others were small and unassuming, their simplicity belying the potential depths of the memories they held. Each door had its own unique presence. Some gleamed with polished brass handles that caught the dim light, inviting a touch. Others were weathered, with rusted hinges that creaked softly as if whispering secrets of forgotten times. The colors varied from rich mahogany to faded pastels, each hue evoking different emotions and memories. As I walked, my fingertips brushed against the cool surface of a smooth marble door, its surface illuminated with delicate engravings that shimmered in the faint light. Amidst the array of doors and memories, my heart raced with suspense, each door a potential gateway to a fragment of my past. The labyrinthine corridors stretched endlessly before me, their walls echoing with whispers of forgotten moments and untold stories.

Despite the emotional rollercoaster of reliving past experiences, I recognized the hidden blessings. Each memory, even the most challenging ones, allowed me to reflect and grow. In that sense, I was fortunate to have the chance to revisit them, knowing that they held the key to unlocking the path forward. I spotted a door that seemed to shimmer and sparkle like a distant star, its surface radiant with a glow that danced and flickered with a heavenly luminescence. As I approached, the door thrummed with a vibrant energy, casting a mesmerizing array of light and shadow across the hallway. Each glimmering speck on the door seemed to tug at my very being. It was as if the door held the secrets of the cosmos; the tiny stars embedded within the door twinkled and danced, casting supernatural light across the hallway. With each step nearer, its brilliance intensified, its surface shimmering like a galaxy brought to life. The light was so dazzling that it seemed to blur the edges of the door, giving it an almost dreamlike quality. I reached out, my hand trembling slightly. Goosebumps rose on my skin, a signal of the concern coursing through me. The handle glowed brightly, resembling a tiny star promising wonder and danger. My fingers hovered, hesitant, expecting a fiery heat to sear my skin.

Drawing in a deep breath, I finally grasped the handle. The unexpected chill shocked me, a cold so stark it made me gasp. The icy touch sent a shiver up my arm, snapping me back to reality and grounding me in the moment. With a quick intake of breath, I twisted it, the mechanism turning smoothly under my hand. The suspense reached a fever pitch as the door began to open, revealing the starry expanse that lay beyond. The light spilled out, enveloping me as I stepped through, eager to uncover the adventure on the other side. Drawn by curiosity and bewilderment, I ventured through the doorway unknowingly. The door shut behind me, sending a loud echo reverberating through the space. However, I couldn't shake the feeling of whether this vast expanse was indeed a room or something else entirely.

I was stunned to find the entire room enveloped in complete darkness, yet it was not a suffocating void. Instead, it felt like I had stepped into the vast expanse of the night sky. Countless stars were suspended around me, twinkling and shimmering with an ethereal glow. They cast a soft, silvery light that danced on the edges of my vision. I stood in awe, unable to comprehend how such a sight could be possible; it felt as though I had entered a realm beyond space and time. The air was cool and crisp, carrying a faint hint of something otherworldly, like the scent of ozone after a storm. The vastness of the room defied all scientific expectations. It wasn't a scene from a science fiction tale; it had the enchanting, surreal quality of a fantasy realm. The stars stretched endlessly in every direction, creating a sense of infinite depth. As I took tentative steps forward, the ground beneath me felt solid yet yielded slightly, like walking on a surface that defied traditional physics. Despite the impossibility, I was mesmerized by the sight. My breath caught in my throat, and my heart pounded with wonder and disbelief. The silence was broken only by the soft, almost invisible hum of the stars. Each step I took sent gentle ripples of light across the dark expanse, enhancing the sense that I was floating in the galaxy itself. I inched ahead, my foot hovering before each step, unsure if the floor would hold beneath the darkness that coated it. My breaths came shallow and quick as I strained to see the ground. To calm my racing mind, I lifted my gaze to the stars, their brilliance drawing me in and steadying my nerves. Their soft, shimmering light wrapped around me like a comforting blanket, momentarily easing the worry and fear that coursed through me. Each star seemed to outshine the last; the dazzling starlight pulled me in, impossible to ignore. The light was so pure and mesmerizing that I felt a deep yearning to reach out and touch it.

My fingertips tingled as I outstretched my hand, unable to resist the urge any longer. The moment my skin made contact with the star, a jolt of energy surged through me, like an electric current charging every cell in my body. My heart raced, and my breath caught my throat. My chest tightened, and my pulse quickened as waves of heat coursed through my body. The star's light surrounded me, a comforting warmth that felt like a soft, glowing blanket. It was as if someone had swaddled me in pure, radiant energy, each beam of light hugging me closer, making my skin tingle with a pleasant intensity. The room around me began to blur and fade, the darkness replaced by a flood of color and light. I felt myself being lifted and transported through time and space. The stars' light seemed to melt away the present, pulling me deeper into a vivid memory. My surroundings morphed into familiar shapes and scenes, the sensation of being both here and elsewhere enveloping me. I was no longer in the star-filled room; instead, I found myself in the first house Luke and I had shared, transported back to that significant moment. It was the day Luke proposed, nine months after we moved in together. Despite sneaking suspicion of what was unfolding, the proposal left me speechless, with only two choices: yes or no. I stood frozen in place, staring down at Luke as he knelt before me. My palms grew clammy, the sweat making them slick against my trembling fingers. My heart thundered in my chest, each beat echoing in my ears like a drumroll. The weight of the moment hung heavy in the air, a tension that enveloped us both. It was surreal, almost too much to comprehend. Luke was looking up at me with eyes full of hope and nerves as he held out a small velvet box in his trembling hand. Inside glinted a delicate ring, its band embellished with a sparkling diamond that caught the light and shimmered with every movement. This memory seemed to hold the entire universe. A rush of emotions flooded over me—joy, disbelief; deep down, I knew this day would come, but the reality of watching it happen again left me breathless.

Time seemed to stand still as I struggled to find my voice and form words that could match the importance of what I felt. I wanted to capture every detail, every sensation, and etch it into my memory forever. This moment changed everything, a moment I would carry with me for the rest of my life. My eyes brimmed with tears as I looked into his tender eyes. I felt his hand trembling as he reached for mine, and in that moment, everything seemed to fall into place. There was no doubt in my mind, no hesitation. My heart whispered one word, echoing through my entire being: yes.

"Dee," Luke's voice was soft yet filled with determination.

"Luke," I replied, my heart fluttering in anticipation.

I watched as Luke took a deep breath, his chest rising and falling slowly. His eyes, filled with a mixture of determination and tenderness, never wavered from mine. I could see the slight tremor in his hands and the faint sound of his breath in my ears. The subtle scent of cologne mingled with the crisp evening air, grounding me in the reality of the moment. His warm and unwavering gaze seemed to penetrate my soul, creating a connection that made my heart beat faster

"From the moment we were young, I admired you," he began, his words washing over me like a warm embrace. "Your strength, the love you hold in your heart… it's what drew me to you. And from our first date, where you showed off your skills at the fair and how confident you were," he chuckled softly, "I knew I would fall head over heels for you. That day, I promised myself I would marry you." His confession left me speechless, my heart teeming with emotion. I knew he was the one I wanted to spend the rest of my life with.

"Yes." Tears poured down my cheeks, warm and salty. I choked out my answer, the word catching and trembling on my lips. As soon as it left my mouth, I felt a wave of certainty wash over me. This was the beginning of our forever. Luke's face lit up with joy as he sprang to his feet, pulling me into a tight embrace. The warmth of his body against mine was a comfort like no other. He tilted my chin up and pressed his lips to mine in a tender kiss, sealing our promise with a spark of magic. The world around us seemed to blur, leaving just the two of us in a moment of pure bliss.

****

As the star's heat intensified and seared my skin, I instinctively released my grip, pulling my hand back.

The vision dissolved instantly, and I found myself back in the starry dreamscape. It dawned on me that this ethereal room was revealing my deepest hopes and dreams. The memory of Luke's proposal was evidence of my heartfelt desire—marrying him and starting a family was a dream I held dear, one that represented my vision of a perfect future.

The stars around me seemed to twinkle with renewed clarity, reflecting the depth of my yearning and the promise of the life I wished to build with Luke. Eager for more, I extended my hand, grasping for another star. Suddenly, I found myself in what appeared to be a baby store, the air filled with the sweet scent of baby powder and the soft cooing of infants. Shelves decorated with colorful baby grows, plush toys and tiny shoes lined the walls. Each item shared the joy and wonder of parenthood. The gentle hum of chatter filled the air as expectant parents browsed the aisles, their faces alight with anticipation and excitement.

"What do you think of this one?" Evie's voice broke through my reverie as she held up a bright orange onesie, her swollen belly visible beneath it.

I blinked, tearing my gaze away from the baby's clothes. My fingers fidgeted with my engagement ring, twisting it nervously around my finger as I tried to focus on the onesie in front of me. "Sure, looks cute," I replied, my voice absentminded. My thoughts drifted away, imagining the day I would dress my own baby in such tiny clothes, the longing for that future tugging at my heart.

"Earth to Dee," Evie exclaimed, waving her hands before my face to snap me out of my daydream.

"Sorry," I apologized, refocusing my attention on Evie.

"Are you okay, sweetheart? You seemed a bit off today when I came to pick you up," Evie asked, her tone filled with concern and warmth as she placed the onesie back on the shelf.

I took a deep breath, my shoulders slumping as the weight of my worries pressed down on me. "Luke and I haven't talked about trying for a baby lately," I admitted, my voice barely above a whisper. I wrapped my arms around myself as if to hold the pieces of my breaking heart together. "He seems to be avoiding the subject, and I'm just worried that we might miss out on the chance to become parents." My fingers toyed with the engagement ring, spinning it round and round as if the motion could somehow bring me comfort. Tears threatened to spill from my eyes, and I blinked rapidly, trying to keep them at bay. The anxiety ate at me, a constant, uneasy presence that I couldn't shake. The thought of not having a child with Luke, of never becoming a mother, was a fear that loomed large and menacing in my mind. I looked at Evie, my eyes pleading for understanding, hoping she could see the depth of my longing and the intensity of my fear.

"Oh, sweetie, these things happen. You can't rush fate. Enjoy the moments you have with Luke, and things will fall into place when the time is right. It took Theo and me nearly two years to have a baby." Evie reassured me, pulling me into a comforting hug.

"Thanks, Evie. What would I do without you?" I quipped, giving her a playful side bump with my hip.

"You'd be utterly lost, Dee Dee," she teased back with a grin.

I knew she was right. We shouldn't be putting pressure on ourselves because it strained our relationship. I just wanted a baby so bad; I wanted nothing more than to be a mum. I imagined the joy of holding a baby in my arms, feeling their warmth and hearing their laughter fill our home. The idea of being a mother had always been a cherished dream, a vision of nurturing and creating a loving family with Luke. It wasn't just about wanting a baby; it was about the desire to experience the journey of motherhood, to witness a new life grow and thrive. I pulled back from the memory, the thought of being a parent moving further away. Now, I wasn't sure if I would ever have the chance to be a mom because I wasn't sure if I was dead or if there was still a chance to make my way back.

Moving further into the starry dreamscape, the air shimmered with a faint, celestial hum, as if the very fabric of space and time whispered secrets in unseen tongues. Each step resonated softly against an unseen floor, the ground beneath me cool and smooth, like polished marble underfoot. The faint scent of distant galaxies tickled my senses, a blend of cosmic dust and the faintest trace of starlight. I found a star calling out to me. It wasn't as bright as the rest, but something about it was calling my name. It begged me to touch it, so I did, and as soon as my fingertips brushed against it, I was transported to another memory. I was sitting next to Luke in what looked like an office waiting room; the soft hum of air conditioning filled the air, mixing with the faint scent of paper and ink that seemed to cling to everything. On the wall across from us, a sign in bold, black letters read 'Book Bee Books Publishing,' its surface gleaming under the overhead fluorescent lights. A low murmur of voices drifted from an open doorway nearby, blending with the occasional sound of footsteps echoing down the hallway outside.

"What happens if they don't like it, Luke?" I muttered, the edges of the manuscript in my hands crinkling under my nervous grip. Rubbing my palms on my jeans, I glanced around the waiting room, my movements restless and uneasy. "I don't think this is a good idea."

Luke took hold of my hand firmly to stop my nerves, "They will love it, Dee; what you have written is incredible; try not to doubt yourself. You have wanted to be a writer for as long as I have known you; it's your dream to share your stories with the world. Don't let anyone stop you from reaching that; people deserve to hear what you say, even if it is fiction. I love you, and even if they say no, which they won't, there will be other places to try. Don't give up, okay?" I looked at him, and I could see the determination reflecting back, and I knew his words were genuine. I felt a surge of courage as I nodded my head,

"Miss Dee Harris," called out a middle-aged man in a tailored charcoal suit, his neatly trimmed beard adding a touch of seriousness to his demeanor. His glasses perched on the bridge of his nose glinted under the office lights, and his voice carried a hint of authority softened by a professional courtesy.

"Here," I began, rising to my feet, but Luke gently pulled me back down, his hand squeezing mine encouragingly, before leaning in for a slow, reassuring kiss.

"You've got this," he whispered in my ear.

"Miss Harris," the man called out once more.

"Yeah, sorry," I hurriedly, rushing to follow him. I glanced back briefly, catching Luke's wink before disappearing after the man.

****

As I watched the star float away, Luke's words echoed in my head, bringing me back to the present. He might have intended his encouraging words for something else but hearing him say not to give up gave me the boost I needed. I knew it was time to leave when a wooden door materialized before me. I had learned what I needed for my journey and was ready for what was next. Taking a deep breath, I reached out; my fingers brushed against the cool, smooth wood, and the starry dreamscape began to dissolve around me. The stars dimmed, their light fading into the void, replaced by the warm, muted glow of sconces lining a long hallway. The transition was seamless, like stepping from one dream into another. Stepping through the threshold, I found myself in the hallway once more.

As I walked through the seemingly endless hallway, the distant sound of crashing waves caught my attention, prompting me to pause. The rhythmic roar and gentle hiss of the surf filled my ears. Peering down, I noticed a tiny puddle of water on the floor, its surface reflecting the dim light from the sconces. As I ventured closer, the sound of waves grew louder; I observed that the puddle emanated from behind a door. The door, covered with stunning sea shells of varying shapes and colors, revealed a glimpse of sand behind its intricate design. Each shell seemed meticulously placed, creating a collage that captured the essence of the ocean. As I extended my hand to touch the surface, the grains of sand began to crumble beneath my fingertips, indicating that the door consisted entirely of sand, fragile and mesmerizing.

Positioned at the center of the door was a giant starfish, serving as the knocker, intricately intertwined with what appeared to be brass metal. The starfish sparkled as if dusted with fine, shimmering sand, and its texture felt rough yet fascinating under my touch. But as soon as my hand rose, the door faded, dissolving like sand caught in the wind, revealing a breathtaking view. Stepping through, I was placed on a mesmerizing beach with an endless stretch of golden sand and crystal blue waters crashing rhythmically against the shore. Each wave rolled in with a soothing roar, leaving behind a frothy white line that quickly disappeared into the sand. Seashells, each unique in shape and color, were scattered along the beach, glinting in the sunlight like tiny treasures. The sky and the sea merged seamlessly at the horizon, making it impossible to discern where one ended and the other began. The sun shone brightly, its warm glow caressing my skin, while a gentle breeze carried the salty scent of the ocean, mingling with the faint aroma of sun-warmed sand. Seagulls called out overhead, their cries echoing across the vast expanse, and their shadows flitted across the ground as they soared gracefully above. The constant and calming sound of the waves created a natural symphony that harmonized with the occasional rustle of palm fronds swaying in the wind.

As I dug my toes into the sand, its warmth and grainy texture brought a slight shiver of delight up my spine. My shoulders relaxed, and the tension in my body slowly unwound. The serene beauty around me seemed to hold me in a gentle embrace as if time itself had paused to let me savor the moment. The scene evoked a sense of déjà vu, a familiar comfort settling in my chest despite the mystery of its origin. *Where have I felt this before? Why does this place feel so right, so comforting?* I stepped forward onto the sand, feeling its comforting embrace between my toes with each step, drawing me closer to the inviting water. My breaths became slower and deeper, matching the rhythmic lull of the waves, and a soft, contented smile tugged at my lips. *Maybe I've been here in a dream, or perhaps this place is a part of my forgotten memories. It feels like home, like peace. If only Luke were here to share this with me.*

I wanted to touch it and feel it against my skin. Was it cold? Was it warm? The sensation was comforting, like reconnecting with an old friend after a long absence. *This beach feels so familiar, like a memory just out of reach.* As I continued forward, my eyes scanned the sandy shore and noticed footprints imprinted in the sand. One set was more significant than the other, and suddenly, it all clicked into place - this was the same beach where Luke and I had taken a trip to Cornwall. Tucked away from crowds and civilization, it was our little hidden paradise. *I remember now, that day when we walked along this shore, laughing and talking about our future. The way the sun reflected in the water and the seagulls danced on the breeze.* The memories came flooding back - spending an entire day with Luke, just the two of us, without any worries or cares. The warmth and comfort of his arms wrapped around me, his laughter echoing in my ears, and his smile brightening up my world.

But now, those memories only brought sadness as I felt alone without him. *We were so carefree then, so hopeful. If only he could see this now. If only we could return to that time when everything seemed so simple and full of promise.* Finally reaching the water's edge, I gazed at the sea and realized it was anything but mundane; I felt its cool embrace tickle my toes. The waves crashed against the shore with a fierce intensity, almost surreal in their power; I caught glimpses of the people I loved most reflecting in the water- Luke, my mum, and Evie. Seeing their faces brought a sense of calm and comfort amidst my overwhelming emotions.

Sitting on the soft sand, I felt every grain beneath my feet and between my toes, creating a comforting sensation. As my feet dipped into the water, it felt cool and refreshing against my skin. Each wave's touch was refreshing, sending a gentle thrill through me. The waves grew more powerful, climbing up my leg with a playful energy that left me feeling alive and free. The rhythmic ebb and flow suddenly changed as I began playing with the water. The water swelled and shimmered, turning into a hazy image. My heart quickened as I recognized the memory. It was showing me a kiss I shared with Luke. We had been sitting on this very spot, watching the sunset. The sky had blazed with hues of orange and pink, casting a warm glow over us. The sound of the waves had created a serene background as Luke leaned in, his eyes searching mine for a sign. His lips met mine gently, a kiss filled with nervousness, excitement, and love. The memory was so vivid I could almost feel the warmth of his hand in mine and hear the distant calls of seagulls overhead. The waves returned to their natural rhythm as the image faded, but the emotion lingered. Tears welled up in my eyes, a blend of joy and sorrow. I felt the loss of that perfect moment, its tenderness and promise now just a beautiful echo in my heart.

We had been sitting on this spot, watching the sunset, when he leaned in and pressed his lips gently against mine. It was a moment filled with nervousness, excitement, and love. Tears formed in my eyes as the memory faded, blurring the shimmering water before me. I missed the warmth of his lips, the soft pressure that had once made my heart flutter. Unconsciously, I brought my fingers to my lips, hoping to recapture even a trace of that fleeting sensation. The gentle saltiness of the sea air mixed with the taste of my tears, a bittersweet reminder of what once was. The ache in my chest deepened, a longing for the love and connection that had filled that moment.

"Remember the first time we sat here?" I turned and saw Luke sitting next to me, a soft smile on his lips and a voice filled with nostalgia. I was unsure of what was happening and whether Luke was there; I was almost sure it was real, so I decided to play along in the fantasy.

I nodded, my heart swelling with the memory. "How could I forget? It was our first holiday together," I said, trembling slightly. "We were watching the sunset, just like now."

He reached out, gently taking my hand in his. "I was so happy," he admitted, his eyes locking with mine. "I couldn't resist kissing you and how the sunset hit your skin and how beautiful you looked."

A smile tugged at my lips, "And you did," I said softly. "You leaned in and pressed your lips gently against mine."

Even now, the memory was vivid, almost real, and I yearned for that touch again. The corners of my mouth lifted in a bittersweet smile.

Luke chuckled, a hint of nervousness in his laugh. "I was afraid I'd mess up the holiday, as I had never been away before," he confessed. "But it felt perfect."

"It was perfect," I whispered.

Seeing the tears in my eyes, Luke's expression softened. He reached out, brushing them away with his thumb. "Hey, don't cry," he said gently. "It was a beautiful memory."

I tried to smile, but the reality of the situation made it difficult. "I know," I said, my voice breaking. "It's just… I miss it. I miss you."

Luke pulled me into his arms, holding me close. I could hear his heart beating, a steady, comforting rhythm that almost made this feel real. "I miss you too," he murmured against my hair. "But we can build new memories, Dee. We're still here, and we still have each other."

I looked up at him, his face blurred by my tears. "I want that to be true, Luke," I said, my voice steadier now. "But, I'm not sure anymore. Are you even here?"

He smiled, leaning in to press a tender kiss on my forehead. "You have got this, Dee," he promised. "Don't give up." He ignored my question, his focus entirely on encouraging me.

Just as he appeared, he soon faded like a breeze whisked him away, leaving me alone. Pulling my legs in close as I leaned my head on my knees, something miraculous happened—the water began to change again at my feet.

****

I couldn't help but smile as I watched the scene unfold. The room glowed with the soft, twinkling lights of the Christmas tree. Evie's infectious laughter filled the air, a symphony of pure delight that echoed off the walls. Luke's eyes sparkled with joy; his cheeks flushed with excitement as he watched Evie tear through the wrapping paper with unrestrained glee. Mum moved slowly, her steps gentle and deliberate.

She paused occasionally, her handkerchief pressed to her mouth as she stifled a cough, a quiet reminder of the winter chill lingering outside. Despite this, she bustled around the room with purpose, handing out cups of steaming hot cocoa. The mugs radiated warmth in contrast to the cool evening air, their rich aroma mingling with the scent of pine and cinnamon that hung in the room. Her face beamed with happiness, a mix of love and contentment evident in every smile she shared with each family member gathered together.

"Look! It's the foot spa I wanted!" Evie exclaimed, holding up the gift for everyone to see.

Luke grinned, ruffling her hair. "I knew you'd love it, Evie. You've been talking about it non-stop."

Evie batted Luke's hand away and rolled her eyes. "Stop messing with my hair, Luke!"

Mum handed Luke a cup of cocoa, her movements slow and deliberate. "It's wonderful to see you all so happy. This is what Christmas is all about."

Luke took a sip of his cocoa, savoring the warmth. "You always know how to make the holidays special, Mrs. Harris."

Mum smiled, her expression softening, though a brief coughing fit interrupted her response. "It's not just me, Luke. It's all of us together. That's what makes it special."

I joined the conversation, placing a comforting hand on Mum's shoulder. "You're right, Mum. It's all of us. And it's so nice to see everyone enjoying themselves."

Evie looked up at Mum, her eyes wide with concern. "Are you okay, Mum? You've been coughing a lot."

Mum patted Evie's hand gently. "Oh, don't you worry, sweetheart. It's just a little tickle in my throat. Nothing to worry about. This has been lovely." She coughed again into her hanky, the sound muffled but noticeable in the quiet pause that followed.

Luke glanced around the room, "I couldn't agree more, Michele. This is the best Christmas ever."

Evie hugged her new foot spa tightly, her face glowing with happiness. "It really is!"

I smiled at everyone, feeling a surge of gratitude. "Let's cherish these moments. They're what make the holidays truly special."

Mum nodded, her eyes glistening with unshed tears. "Absolutely, hunny."

It was a moment of pure bliss, love, and family that I had almost forgotten during everything that had happened since. I watched with a warmth spreading through my chest, filling me with melancholy. Maybe, just maybe, we could find our way back to this happiness again. But as quickly as it came, the memory faded away, and the water returned to its calm state. Looking back it made me wish I had paid more attention to my mum and spent more time enjoying those little moments. I sat back and took in everything around me—crashing waves. There was nothing I could do to change that now; I just had to move forward, and I was unsure how or if I could. The door to the room appeared once again, its wooden frame weathered and slightly worn from countless openings and closings. And as much as I didn't want to leave, I knew it was time to go. With a sigh, I rose from the warm sand, feeling its fine grains cling momentarily to my skin before slipping away. I brushed myself down, my fingertips tracing the residual warmth of the sun that had kissed my shoulders.

Each step towards the door seemed to echo softly against the backdrop of crashing waves and distant seagull calls, a reminder of the peace I was reluctantly leaving behind. As I walked through, the hallway felt like it was expanding, with more doors and memories to explore. The smell of something burning filled the air, a pungent aroma that hung heavy and foreboding. It carried hints of scorched wood and melted plastic, mingling with the sharp tang of electrical components overheating. The acrid scent prickled at my senses, triggering a sense of urgency and caution. Conflicting desires tore at me, urging me to run for safety while also compelling me to investigate the source of the smoke. The instinct to flee clawed at my chest, each heartbeat echoing the urgency of escape. Yet, curiosity gripped me—could this seemingly safe haven truly be in flames? With my energy levels draining and hope fading after seeing Luke, I made the decision to move closer to the smoke.

Each step forward was deliberate yet tinged with apprehension, my senses heightened to detect any signs of danger. As I cautiously walked through the hallway, the air grew thicker with smoke, reducing visibility to a hazy blur. The fumes stung my throat and eyes, making each breath a struggle. I coughed, the sound muffled by the swirling haze around me, and desperately searched for something to cover my mouth and nose. Amidst the swirling haze, I noticed dark, charred marks etched into the carpet and walls. They seemed to converge towards a particular door, their presence ominous against the backdrop of the smoke-filled hallway. The heat radiating from the direction of the marks served as a reminder of the urgency of the situation, urging me to find a way out or towards safety, even as uncertainty clouded my thoughts.

The door appeared almost charred, its surface marred by blackened streaks and blistered paint. Once sturdy brass, the handle now melted and drooped towards the ground like a wounded soldier. A faint, pungent smell emanated from it, a reminder of the intense heat that had scorched its surface. Smoke billowed out from under the door in thick, swirling tendrils, creating an eerie barrier that made me hesitate to open it. Despite my hesitation, a persistent feeling urged me towards whatever lay beyond. It was as if this charred doorway held a crucial clue, a sign pointing me towards my next destination.

A chill raced through me as I reached out to grasp the handle. The metal felt icy cold against my fingertips, a vast difference from the heat radiating from the smoke-filled room beyond. I pulled the door open. A rush of smoke poured out, thick and disorienting, obscuring everything in its path. I raised my hands to shield my face and began to cough, the acrid taste of the smoke clawing at my throat. The smoke enveloped me, its tendrils brushing against my skin like icy fingers digging into flesh. Panic surged, tightening my chest with each labored breath. But gradually, as the smoke cleared, the tightness eased, and I could breathe normally again. As my vision returned, I realized I was no longer in the hallway. Before me stretched a surreal landscape; towering trees loomed like giants, their leaves glowing ember-like as if perpetually ablaze. The air was thick with the scent of wood smoke and the crackle of flames dancing across the foliage. Fear and wonder intertwined within me, a tight knot in my stomach that tightened with each breath. The forest before me blazed with an otherworldly intensity, its trees towering like sentinels of flame against the dimming light. Heat radiated in waves, prickling my skin and sending a shiver down my spine despite the warmth.

The trees arched overhead like flaming sentinels, their branches reaching towards each other to form a cathedral of fire. Upon closer inspection, I realized they had deliberately intertwined, creating a pathway that beckoned me forward with a subtle but undeniable allure. It was as if nature itself had conspired to guide me onward, each branch and leaf whispering, "this way." My footsteps echoed softly on the ground, a symphony of crunching charred leaves that clung lightly to my bare toes. The air, still and heavy with the scent of smoke and distant crackling flames, I marveled at the spectacle above me—the canopy of fire casting intricate patterns of light and shadow on the ground below. The warmth radiating from the flames was both comforting and unsettling, a reminder of the fragile balance between beauty and danger in this surreal landscape.

As I circled the stump, my eyes were drawn to a figure within the heart of the fire—Luke. His presence amidst the inferno seemed both impossible and inevitable. Without thinking, driven by an instinct I couldn't comprehend, I reached out towards the flames. The fire engulfed me within seconds, wrapping around my arms and spreading through my body with a fierce, burning sensation. A fiery pain lanced through my skin, a white-hot agony that ripped a scream from my throat. The flames licked hungrily at my flesh, their scorching heat relentless and all-encompassing. My vision blurred, the edges of the world dissolving into a searing brightness that blinded me.

Darkness began to encroach on the periphery of my vision, a creeping blackness that promised release from the excruciating pain. My screams faded into a dull roar, the world around me disintegrating into a swirling vortex of heat and light. The last thing I felt was the unbearable heat, then everything went black, the flames snuffing out my consciousness like a candle extinguished in a storm. When I awoke, I was standing inside a house, its familiarity tugging at the edges of my memory. I looked around, disoriented, and found myself in what appeared to be a kitchen. The air was thick with the scent of old wood and faintly lingering spices. I sank to the floor, the cool tiles a stark contrast to the burning heat I had just experienced. The room, bathed in soft, natural light, held a comforting familiarity, even though I couldn't quite place why it felt so known to me.

*****

"What are you talking about?" I heard Luke's voice, and soon after, I saw him walk into the room, with a version of me following behind.

"All I'm saying is we must think about it before committing. It's not that easy to buy a house, Luke. We've only rented this place, and now you're considering buying it. I don't see the rush. We're both doing well, so why do you suddenly want to use all our money for this house?" I asked.

"I just want us to be comfortable," Luke said as he took my hands, his voice filled with warmth and seriousness, "I want to provide for you and create stability. And if, down the road, we have a baby, then it's even better."

I squeezed his hand, "I know, but there is no rush. I know you want what's best for me, and you always do, we are in this together, okay? Let's enjoy our time now."

He breathed out slowly, his lips brushing softly against my hand. A scorching pain ignited within me, spreading until it felt unbearable. My vision blurred, the room twisting and turning. Without warning, I was hurled from the inferno and slammed onto the ruin floor with a jarring thud.

"What the hell!" I exclaimed, looking around, confusion and disorientation clouding my thoughts as I tried to wrap my head around what had just happened. I paid closer attention to my surroundings, my eyes scanning the charred remains and broken fragments.

The ruins were eerily familiar—the jagged outlines of walls, the charred remains of a once-cozy living room, and the twisted metal frame of what had been our front door. Memories flooded back as I noticed the remnants of our old bookshelf, its wood blackened but still bearing the faint outlines of the carvings Luke had made. Nearby, the shattered pieces of our coffee table lay scattered, the glass glinting faintly amidst the ashes. A lump formed in my throat as recognition set in. This was our first home, the place where Luke and I had built our life together. The realization hit me like a tidal wave, the weight of the past mingling with the present. The familiar details, now cloaked in ruin and decay, left no doubt in my mind. This was what remained of our shared dreams, now reduced to haunting memories amidst the ashes. *Each room has led me closer to something important. This is all connected, I just need to piece it together,* I pondered to myself. Stepping towards the fire, I was ready for what else it would show me. As the flames licked at my skin, I was pulled in once again. This time, I stood in what looked like a doctor's office.

"I'm sorry to say this," a man in a white coat said as he sat in the leather chair across from me and Luke. The room was cool, a faint antiseptic smell lingering in the air. The fluorescent lights above cast a harsh, clinical glow on the polished, white-tiled floor. We waited patiently for the results, the ticking of a wall clock amplifying the tense silence.

"Your test results show that you have hypothalamic dysfunction." His voice was calm but carried an undertone of gravity. My heart sank, the sterile scent of disinfectant suddenly feeling overpowering. The leather chair beneath me creaked as I shifted uncomfortably, the coldness of the room seeping into my skin.

"What does that mean?" Luke asked worriedly, his voice breaking the quiet tension. He reached over and took my hand in his, his grip warm and reassuring against the backdrop of the stark, impersonal office.

"The hypothalamus makes a special hormone that signals to another part of the brain, the pituitary gland, to release two important hormones. These hormones help your ovaries grow and release eggs."

"Okay, but how does this relate to my situation?" I asked, squeezing Luke's hand for support.

The doctor glanced at my medical records, then back at us. "I see that you have fibromyalgia and you suffer with irregular periods. This can make conceiving more challenging. The chronic pain and stress from fibromyalgia can disrupt your hormonal balance, leading to irregular menstrual cycles and ovulation issues, which can make it harder to get pregnant."

"Does that mean I can't get pregnant at all?" I asked, my voice cracking with a mix of desperation and disbelief. The lump in my throat felt like a barrier, threatening to choke back the flood of emotions welling up inside me.

"It's not impossible, but it might be more difficult," the doctor said gently, his tone softened with empathy. He leaned forward slightly, his eyes meeting mine with a sincerity that eased some of the weight from my shoulders. "I suggest we consider alternative ways to help you conceive, such as fertility treatments or lifestyle changes. We can explore these options together to find the best approach for you."

Luke squeezed my hand reassuringly, and I felt a glimmer of hope despite the challenges ahead. The thought of me with a swollen belly, sitting in a rocking chair, and singing to my small bump flashed through my mind; now, someone was ripping it all away. I stared into the crackling fire; I felt numb and empty, as if someone had drained all feeling from me. Sitting in the doctor's office, hearing the news about my condition haunted my thoughts: Guilt and doubt clouded my mind, their presence unshakeable. I watched the doubtful ember flicker and fade, its uncertain glow mirroring the turmoil in my own thoughts. As I sat there, the warmth of the fire offering little comfort, my mind wandered to Luke. *What thoughts were swirling through his mind in this moment of quiet uncertainty? Did he, too, wrestle with blame, with unspoken fears and shattered dreams of parenthood?* The crackling of the fire seemed louder now, each snap and pop echoing in the hollow space around us.

The silence felt heavy, pregnant with unspoken words and unanswered questions. *Was he silently blaming me for our struggles and the impossible hurdles? Did he carry the weight of disappointment and longing as heavily as I did?*

I imagined his face, etched with lines of concern and weariness, his eyes reflecting the flickering flames that danced before us. In that fleeting moment of solitude, I longed to bridge the distance between us, to break the silence that threatened to suffocate our hopes. Doubt churned within me like a stormy sea, each wave crashing against the fragile shores of my willpower. Hot and unrestrained tears streamed down my cheeks, tracing salty paths down my face. My fingers clenched into fists, nails digging into my palms in a silent plea for strength. The flames flickered and danced, casting erratic shadows that mirrored the chaos within me. They leapt higher, mocking my pain with their relentless dance.

The fire exploded in a sudden burst of intensity, a roaring storm that sent shockwaves rippling through the air. Heat surged, a clear wave wrapped around me, threatening to engulf everything in its path. I staggered backwards, my body colliding with the hard ground, the impact jarring against my senses. As I lay there, the flames surged forward, a persistent tide eager to consume. Yet, in the chaos, I felt a peculiar detachment, as though I had slipped into an alternate reality. The swirling vortex of fire danced around me, a mesmerizing display of raw power and beauty. Despite the inferno raging inches away, I remained oddly shielded within a cocoon of stillness. It was as if time had slowed, stretching each moment into an eternity. Within this bubble of protection, the fire's dance painted vivid pictures of my doubts, fears, and insecurities in brilliant hues of orange and red. Each flicker illuminated the darkest recesses of my mind with painful clarity, exposing vulnerabilities I had long buried. A scream tore from my throat, the sound raw and primal, echoing against the roar of the inferno. I squeezed my eyes shut, desperate to shut out the haunting images that flickered behind my eyelids.

The searing heat licked at my skin, a relentless assault that seeped through my defenses. The roar of the flames that had threatened to consume me moments ago now seemed distant, a memory fading into the background. The searing pain that had licked at my skin, leaving a trail of fiery discomfort, had dwindled away, leaving behind a tingling numbness. Every breath I took felt fragile, as if the slightest movement might shatter the fragile peace that had settled over me. Slowly, I dared to pry open my eyes, half-expecting to find myself still engulfed in the inferno's ruthless embrace. Relief washed over me as I took in my surroundings. I found myself back in the hallway; Confusion clouded my thoughts as I struggled to make sense of how I had ended up here, away from the consuming flames that had mirrored my inner turmoil.

Gratitude flooded through me like a warm current as I realized I was no longer trapped in the relentless cycle of doubt and fear that had plagued me moments before. Gathering my breath, I closed my eyes once more, savoring the stillness that enveloped me like a protective cocoon. When I reopened my eyes, a vibrant red door stood at the end of the corridor, immediately capturing my attention. The door was a striking shade of crimson as if it had been painted with the very essence of passion and life. Intricate carvings of delicate roses adorned its surface, each petal and thorn meticulously etched into the wood. The craftsmanship was exquisite, with every curve and twist rendered in stunning detail, giving the roses an almost lifelike quality. Weaved among the carvings were Polaroid photos of Luke and me, capturing moments from our shared past. Some showed us laughing, and others caught in tender embraces, each photograph a snapshot of our journey together. The images were slightly faded, their edges curling, but the memories they held were vivid and heartwarming.

Handwritten engravings intertwined with the floral designs, words and phrases etched into the wood in both my and Luke's handwriting. Love notes, shared dreams, and our promises to each other were etched on the door. The air around the door carried the sweet, intoxicating scent of roses, a rich and heady fragrance. The floral aroma mingled with the lingering scent of smoke that clung to my dress, creating a bittersweet symphony of scents that tugged at my emotions. The scent of fresh roses grew stronger, embracing me as I reached out and grasped the ornate brass handle. My breath caught in my throat, a tightness forming in my chest as if the scent itself was squeezing my heart. I pushed the door open, suspense tingling in my veins.

    I stepped into a room resembling a library. Bright red bookcases lined the walls, their surfaces intricately entwined with vibrant roses. The air was perfumed with the heady scent of roses, so intense it seemed to seep into my very soul. Hardcover books filled the shelves, their spines hinting at the intriguing stories within. The titles glimmered in gold and silver, catching the light in a way that beckoned me to pull them down and delve into their secrets. As I moved further into the room, rose petals drifted gently from the ceiling, fluttering like delicate butterflies before settling on the floor and my shoulders. The petals created a soft, whispering sound as they landed, adding to the dreamlike atmosphere. Water covered the floor, cool and clear, shimmering ripples reflecting the room's rosy glow. The gentle movement of the water created an ever-changing array of red and pink tints. My footsteps caused small splashes, sending ripples outward that distorted the reflections and added to the ambience. The unconventional nature of the room was both enchanting and calming. Each gentle splash and delicate whisper of petals landing around me coaxed my tense shoulders to relax, the tightness in my chest easing as I breathed in the sweet, floral air.

    My racing thoughts slowed, the chaotic swirl of worry and fear giving way to a calm curiosity. My hand froze when a book titled "Fragments of Us" caught my eye. Its cover was a deep, velvety blue. As I reached for it, the holographic image on the front shimmered, catching the light and changing as I shifted my perspective. The image depicted a younger version of Luke and me in our teens. Luke's arms were wrapped protectively around me, and my head rested comfortably on his chest. The hologram flickered slightly as I moved, bringing the memory to life with an almost magical quality.

A lump formed in my throat as a wave of nostalgia washed over me. I only realized tears were streaming down my face when a teardrop fell onto the book, causing the holographic image to shimmer briefly. I quickly brushed the tears away, leaving faint streaks on my cheeks, and took a deep breath to steady myself. With trembling hands, I opened the book. The pages were thick and slightly rough, emitting a faint, musty smell of aged paper mingled with the sweet scent of roses from the room. I was drawn into the memory, standing in a serene park landscape. As my eyes scanned the first few lines of familiar handwriting, the words seemed to ripple and blur, as though the ink was alive. The room around me began to fade, and I felt a curious pull, as if an invisible thread was winding around my heart, drawing me in. The book seemed to emit a soft, warm glow, and the text started to swirl, creating a vortex that enveloped me completely. I felt a rush of air and a strange sensation of weightlessness. Suddenly, the ground beneath my feet felt solid again.

"Why do you do this all the time? I'm trying to help you, and you keep pushing me away. Why?" Luke shouted, his voice carrying frustration and hurt. Luckily, it was dark, and there weren't many people around. But as I was pulled into the past version of myself, I could feel the weight of fear, detachment, and emptiness. We stood on a narrow, winding path in the middle of the park. The faint light of streetlamps stretched and contorted shadows across the pavement. The park, usually bustling with activity, was quiet, the only sounds being the distant rustling of leaves and the occasional chirping of crickets. The trees on either side of the path formed a dense canopy overhead, their branches swaying gently in the cool night breeze.

"I'm sorry," I said, my voice barely a whisper, barely audible above the sound of the wind.

"Don't," Luke's tone softened, but the hurt was still evident. "I'm tired. I can't keep up with you. We were doing so well, and then you say it's not working. Why? Tell me why you think it's not working." He stepped closer, his hands reaching out to cup mine, almost begging for an answer.

I couldn't give him an answer. I felt like I was a burden to anyone who got close as if my presence was a poison that destroyed everything it touched. The weight of my fibromyalgia hung heavy on my shoulders, a constant reminder of the limitations it imposed on my life. It wasn't just physical pain—it was the mental and emotional toll. This neverending exhaustion drained me of vitality and joy. My mind replayed all the moments I had missed because of my chronic disorder—romantic walks in the park, spontaneous adventures, and even simple everyday activities that others took for granted. Each missed opportunity felt like a dagger in my heart, a sharp pang of guilt and inadequacy.

I didn't want Luke to feel trapped with me and sacrifice his happiness because of my limitations. It felt like my fault as if I was failing him and our relationship by not being the partner he deserved. The thought of causing him more pain and holding him back from the life he deserved, tore at me. I felt a desperate need to protect him from the burden of my illness, to spare him the frustration and disappointment that inevitably came with it. At the time, I thought ending things seemed like the only solution, a painful sacrifice that I believed would free Luke to find someone who could give him everything I couldn't. The guilt and self-blame consumed me, overshadowing any hope that things could ever be different.

"I think we need space," I managed to cough out, on the verge of tears, as I watched his face fall. I could see the defeat in his eyes, knowing I had caused him this pain again.

"Please, don't leave me," he pleaded, his voice trembling with desperation, his eyes pleading for understanding as he watched me walk away.

I shut the book, the pages whispering against each other in a finality that felt too heavy to bear. I dropped the book to the floor, the sound of water splashing echoing loudly in the quiet room. It was a slight, insignificant noise that highlighted the enormity of the moment. Every fiber of my being screamed to turn back, to run into his arms and bury myself in his embrace. But fear held me captive, chaining me to the painful reality of my limitations and doubts

"Why show me this?" I asked, my voice shaking with emotion. It was only then that I got an answer. I realized that the petals were slowly shifting and rearranging themselves. The water on the floor gently nudged the petals, causing them to glide and rotate. The movement was subtle yet purposeful as if guided by an unseen hand. Some petals would drift closer together, forming the curves of letters. The petals slowly revealed two words.

Keep Going.

****

I had spent so much time trying to move on, to heal from the scars that those memories had left behind. Why was I being asked to confront them again? What purpose could it serve to dredge up the past? Loneliness and heartache churned within me. I wasn't sure I wanted to go through the heartbreak again. It was in the past, so why did it matter? Why should I reopen those old wounds? Torn between the desire to listen to the mysterious message and the instinct to protect myself from further pain. I retrieved the book from the floor, wiping off the water with the end of my dress before returning it to its place on the shelf. Ready to face my heart, I perused the shelves, eventually coming across a book titled "Tears in the Silence." Its cover was a deep shade of blue, with intricate silver filigree that seemed to shimmer under the soft library lights. The title was embossed in elegant, flowing script, catching the eye with its subtle yet poignant allure. The holographic image on the front was of myself standing, a look of pain etched across my face. The depiction was hauntingly vivid, capturing not just the visible anguish but also the invisible weight of chronic pain that I carried.

As I delicately cracked open the book, a feeling of nervousness washed over me like a cool breeze. The aroma of freshly ground coffee beans and warm pastries enveloped me, transporting me back to the old cafe we visited as kids. I found myself in the cafe's cosy atmosphere, with its worn leather booths that creaked softly under my weight and the tables anchored firmly into the floorboards. The wooden floors echoed with the soft murmur of patrons chatting and the clink of ceramic mugs.

"So, there's a party this weekend if any of you are interested," Evie said, her eyes scanning the menu as the lunch rush buzzed around us.

"Oh, is this the one for Valentine's? I'm surprised they went with it this year, especially because of what happened last year," Liam said, lifting his gaze from the menu. He was an old friend from when we were all together. We don't talk much these days.

"You in, Dee?" Evie asked, nudging my arm gently to get my attention.

"I'm not sure. I've not been great these past few days," I said, keeping my voice neutral and avoiding eye contact, not wanting to make it evident that my breakup with Luke and the emotional stress had caused my fibro to flare.

"Hey," Evie said softly, setting her menu down and giving me a side hug. "Everything will be okay. You two will work through this. It's fate that you belong together." She pulled away and picked up her menu again, trying to lighten the mood.

"She is always right, Dee. You and Luke are like one of those classic love stories," Emily chimed in, her warm smile offering reassurance.

"Thanks, guys," I said, grateful for their support.

"Yeah, and who knows? Maybe this party will be the start of something new," Evie added optimistically, always the one to see the silver lining.

"Speak of the devil," Liam said, nodding towards the glass window. I turned to see Luke walking by, and he wasn't alone.

"Who is that skank?" Evie said sharply, her eyes narrowing. I squeezed her hand, appreciating the support.

"It's okay, Eve. We're not together anymore. He can do what he likes," I said, forcing a calm tone.

"But it has only been four days," Evie stated, her concern evident in her voice.

Luke strolled over with his arm draped around the waist of a girl who wore tattoos all along her arms and striking bright red hair with black undertones. She seemed like the complete opposite of Luke's usual type. I needed clarification, trying to understand the message he intended to send. However, the more I attempted to determine his motives, the more I became consumed by a hollow, carefree sensation. Who was I to dictate who he could date? Even though I had broken up with him, it was still painful to witness him with someone else. The sight tugged at my heart, but I knew I had no right to influence his dating choices.

"Hey, guys, I would like you to meet Skye," he said, his eyes locking onto mine as if gauging my reaction.

"Hi," Emily greeted, cheerful but guarded.

"Hello, Skye," Liam echoed, his tone friendly yet cautious.

"Hey, guys, I think I will just head home. I'm not feeling too great," I said, sliding out of the booth quickly.

"I'll walk you out," Emily offered, sensing my discomfort.

I headed straight to the door, not looking back. As I pushed it open, I heard Luke yelp out in pain.

"What was that for?" Luke's voice echoed behind me.

"You are such a dumbass," Evie's voice followed, tinged with frustration.

A small smile crept onto my face as I walked into the street, grateful for friends who had my back. As I closed the book gently, I couldn't help but think about my friends and how incredibly supportive they had been. The memories of our time together made me miss them even more, especially Evie. After gently kissing the book, I placed it back on the shelf. I noticed a hidden bookcase tucked away in the back corner. Roses decorated the shelves, but one book caught my eye amidst the floral display: "Torn Hearts and Broken Dreams." Its cover displayed a haunting image of myself, tears glistening in my eyes. At the same time, Luke lingered in the background, kissing somebody else.

I stood in a secluded wooded area, bathed in the soft glow of a large bonfire crackling at its center. The scent of burning wood permeated the air, mixing with the earthy aroma of pine needles. Around the fire, a circle of teenage partygoers laughed and chatted animatedly, their voices blending with the gentle crackle of the flames. The clearing felt like our secret sanctuary, a hidden refuge where we could escape the constraints of everyday life. Seated on a sturdy tree stump near the fire, I could feel its warmth against my skin. The sound of clinking glasses and the rustle of bodies moving about added to the lively ambience, interrupted by bursts of laughter and shared stories.

As I gazed into the flames Evie handed me a flask, "Come on, you need this," As we stood surrounded by towering trees, the night sky barely visible through the canopy. The campfire cast flickering shadows, creating a cocoon of warmth and light in the chilly darkness. "We're going to have fun tonight, I promise."

I stared at the flask, the cool metal cold against my skin. "I don't know, Evie. I'm not really in the party mood."

She sighed, rolling her eyes with a mix of frustration and determination. "Do you really want to stay here and let Luke's latest conquest be the highlight of your thoughts? You deserve better than that."

My heart tightened at the mention of his name. "I saw them together all day," I muttered, setting the flask down on a nearby log. "He knows what he's doing."

"Exactly why you need to show him you're unbothered. Let's enjoy the fire and the company and forget about him for one night." She gently squeezed my shoulder, her voice softening. "Please, for me?"

I bit my lip, considering. "Fine," I said, picking up the flask again and taking a tentative sip. "But only because you're not giving me a choice."

A grin spread across her face. "That's the spirit! Now, let's toast to new beginnings and better days ahead." I drew in a deep breath, silently vowing not to let Luke's actions break me. Tonight was about reclaiming my strength, even if it was just for a few hours.

"Hey, you okay?" Liam asked, handing me a beer bottle as he settled into the seat beside me.

"I'm not sure, honestly," I admitted, swaying my beer. "Everyone thinks my fibro and Luke are simple things like I should just know how to feel. But these days, I feel like I'm losing my sense of self. Like I'm fading away. Did he tell you why we broke up?" I asked, curiosity tinged with a hint of worry.

"Not really," Liam replied honestly. "He didn't say much at all. Just mentioned that you needed space."

"I'm poison," I muttered out, the words escaping before I could stop them. "My chronic pain makes me feel like I don't deserve to enjoy the little things." I said, my voice devoid of emotion, "Like this is all I'm made for.'"

"Hey," Liam said gently, reaching for my hand. "That's not true, you know that, right? You can't help your fibromyalgia, and you shouldn't let it dictate your life. You're a beautiful and talented person. I've read your short stories; you have so much to offer. That's worth fighting for," he said, brushing away a tear that had escaped my eye.

As Liam's comforting words washed over me, a sudden commotion interrupted our conversation. Luke stormed over, his jaw clenched with jealousy. Without a word, he threw a vicious punch at Liam, catching him off guard. The force of the blow sent Liam sprawling backwards onto the forest floor with a thud.

Liam shouted, 'Hey, what the hell, man?' as he scrambled to his feet, blood streaming from his nose.

Luke stood there, his chest heaving with rage, his eyes blazing with fury. "Stay the hell away from her," he growled, his voice dripping with possessiveness.

I leaped to my feet, my heart pounding with shock and fear. "Luke, stop!" I cried out, but the chaos of the fight drowned out my voice. Ignoring me, Luke launched himself at Liam again, fists flying as they grappled in a whirlwind of violence, drawing a crowd amidst their fight.

Desperate to intervene, I pushed through the crowd, my heart racing with adrenaline. "Stop it, both of you!" I yelled, my voice trembling with emotion.

Finally, the chaos subsided as two teens rushed in to break up the fight. Luke and Liam were pulled apart, both breathing heavily, their faces twisted with anger and pain. Blood now dripped down both of their faces. I stood there, shocked and concerned. This was the final straw: two people close to me were fighting each other for no reason. I couldn't continue allowing the chaos to tear me apart. It was time to break free and reclaim my sense of self, no matter how difficult it may be. I shut the book, burdened by guilt. The look on Luke's face as he walked away, filled with betrayal, was unforgettable. Although I knew Liam was being a good friend, it must have seemed different from Luke's perspective. I didn't hate Luke for it; it was comforting to know he still cared, even though he was kissing someone else. I hated that Liam got hurt, but I remembered later that night he had told me that it was okay. He understood that Luke didn't mean it and believed we would get through this. I slipped the book back onto the shelf and moved on, my eyes scanning for the next find. Suddenly, I spotted a title: "The Art of Letting Go." My heart quickened—I knew this was it. As I drew nearer, a soft glow seemed to emanate from it.

I pulled the book out slowly, delicately treating it like glass. I made my way over to the small velvet chair in the corner. As I sank into the velvet chair, the soft fabric enveloped me, offering luxurious comfort as I admired the front cover. The book's cover was rough and textured, its surface embossed with intertwining vines that seemed to ensnare me in their grip. As I held it, the weight of the book felt solid and satisfying, grounding me in its presence. The texture of the cover prickled against my fingertips, evoking a sense of entanglement akin to being caught in a trap. Embossed images portrayed Luke and my family, their figures reaching out towards me with desperation, their expressions etched with concern and longing. I gazed at the image, my heart racing with a potent mix of emotions—fear, hope, and longing intertwined, swirling within me. The unnerving image left me questioning what memory it held and whether I possessed the strength to confront it.

Carefully, I opened the book.

****

Standing in the same park where I had broken up with Luke, I watched my past self seated on a bench under a streetlight. That's when it hit me.

"Hey," Luke said, walking towards me and stopping at the bench, his hands tucked into his pockets. "I wasn't sure you would come because of what happened with Liam," he added, his gaze flickering nervously.

"You do know I wouldn't do that to you; Liam was just being supportive," I said, gesturing to the space beside me. Luke sat, his leg bouncing and his fingers fidgeting with the edge of his jacket. I could see the nervous energy radiating off him. I place my hand on his leg to help stop his nerves.

"I wouldn't do that, Luke," I said as I stared him in the eye, hoping that he would see how genuine my words were. I felt the warmth of his hand covering mine.

"I understand," he murmured, gently cradling my cheek. The warmth of his touch seeped through my skin, sending a comforting shiver down my spine. "I spoke to Liam. He told me everything, including what you said." His eyes softened, drawing closer to mine, reflecting a flicker of candlelight that danced across the room. "You know you're not poison," he whispered, his lips brushing feather-light against my cheek, leaving a trail of warmth in their wake. The scent of his cologne, a blend of cedar and sandalwood, lingered in the air. He kissed the other side of my face, each touch imprinting a tender affirmation: "Beautiful," he murmured, his breath a gentle breeze against my skin, then my forehead, "talented," his voice barely above a whisper, before finally meeting my gaze. "Captivating," he breathed, his warm breath mingling with mine as we stood intimately close.

All I wanted was to kiss him. So I did.

As our lips touched, warmth spread from my core outwards, permeating every inch of my being with a tingling sensation that spoke of deep happiness. Tears brimmed at the corners of my eyes, a mixture of relief and joy that threatened to overflow, yet I held them back, wanting to savor every second of this perfect moment. My fingers, driven by an instinctive longing, found their way into his hair, weaving through the strands that felt like silk beneath my touch. I gently pulled him closer, feeling the slight resistance of his stubble against my skin, which only added to the intensity of the sensation. In response, he emitted a soft, involuntary sound, a deep murmur that rumbled through his chest and into mine. A sound stirred me to my core; goosebumps danced across my skin, amplifying my desire to be closer to him.

The world outside faded away, leaving only the sensation of his lips on mine, the beating of our hearts in perfect sync. Luke pulled away and took hold of my hands, his eyes filled with sincerity and concern. "I wish you had told me how you were feeling," he began, his voice soft yet firm. "Your fibromyalgia doesn't bother me at all. What really upsets me is seeing you in pain all the time and feeling so helpless because I can't do much to help."

He squeezed my hands tightly, his expression filled with remorse and pain. "I hate that you're going through this," he murmured, his voice thick with emotion, "I wish I could do more to help. Your condition doesn't change how much I love you." His thumb gently traced circles on the back of my hand as he spoke. "I'm sorry if I didn't make that clear before, and for the Skye incident, too. I thought maybe... I thought it might make you jealous, but as soon as I went along, it felt wrong. I want you to know that I love you, all of you, and that will never change."

His words wrapped around me like a warm embrace. He hugged me tenderly, his arms offering the comfort and reassurance I desperately needed. I almost didn't want to close the book; this moment was too vital to miss, but I knew I had to continue. I placed the book gently on the small table beside me and turned towards the door. As it swung open, a rush of cool air filled the room, and I took a deep breath, feeling the tension ease from my shoulders. All the challenges seemed worthwhile, filled with memories of Luke's support and genuine care for me. I knew I needed to find him and to not let him go. The door to the library room swung open, telling me it was time to leave. I stepped out into the hallway, and everything had changed. The familiar surroundings were now different, and I didn't know what to expect next.

4

Mourning Tree

Despite my confusion, I found relief in the sense of change that filled the air. The hallway stretched before me, dimly lit by sconces casting soft, golden glows that danced across the walls. The subtle shifts around me—the faint rustling of unseen breezes, the gentle creak of floorboards underfoot—offered a strange but comforting reassurance. It was as if the very fabric of this place was alive, shifting and adapting in response to my presence. As I continued my journey along the hallway, I paused before a particularly old door; unlike the others, it was not made entirely of wood or metal but was a mesmerizing fusion of nature and craftsmanship. The frame was formed from tree vines intertwined with glistening crystals, each vine pulsing with a life of its own, gently swaying and curling as if aware of my presence.

Embedded into the wood were delicate teardrop crystals glistening like dew drops in the morning sun. These crystals refracted light in various colors, projecting dancing rainbows on the walls. The wood itself was embellished with an intricate carving of a tree, its branches stretching outwards, entwining with the living vines, and its roots diving deep into the door's base. The carving was so detailed that it seemed almost alive, the grooves and knots forming a rough and smooth texture under my fingertips. I felt a faint hum in the air, vibrating within my chest. The combined elements of wood, vine, and crystal created an aura of ancient magic, a sense of timelessness and mystery. I couldn't resist the urge to touch it. My fingers brushed over the teardrop crystals, feeling their cold smoothness, before moving to the carved tree, tracing its intricate patterns. Each touch amplifies the door's gentle hum as if responding to my curiosity, urging me to discover what lay beyond. Holding my breath, I inched my fingers closer to the handle—a twist of vine and crystal—feeling a surge of readiness. As I turned it, the door swung open with a soft, welcoming creak, revealing a warm light that spilled out, enveloping me in its embrace. For a moment, I hesitated, standing at the cusp of the unknown, then stepped forward, crossing the threshold into the promise of new beginnings.

Stepping through, I found myself in a room unlike any I had ever seen. It was vast and empty, the walls stretching into shadowy obscurity, except for a single tree standing at its center. The air was cool and still, carrying a faint, earthy scent that hinted at age and forgotten stories. The tree was ancient and twisted, its bark gnarled and dark, exuding an aura of both strength and sorrow. My breath faltered, and a chill raced along my back as the scene unfolded before me. I hesitated, my heart pounding with a blend of fascination and unease. Its branches were long and strong, reaching out like bony fingers, casting eerie, dancing shadows on the floor. Hanging from its branches were teardrop-shaped crystals, each glowing faintly with an inner light that pulsed softly, like the tree's heartbeat. I stood there, mesmerized by the sight, feeling the room's coolness settle on my skin.

Despite its eerie appearance, the tree exuded a strange sense of beauty. The crystals swayed gently, catching the dim light and refracting it into a spectrum of colors that danced across the room. Their movement produced a delicate tinkling sound, like wind chimes in a silent breeze, filling the room with a hauntingly beautiful melody that echoed softly around me. The floor beneath my feet was cool and smooth, amplifying the sense of otherworldliness. As I walked closer, the faint hum of the crystals grew louder, harmonizing with the soft rustle of unseen leaves. The combination of sights, sounds, and sensations created an atmosphere that was both unsettling and captivating, urging me to explore further and uncover the secrets this mysterious room held.

As I watched, I felt connected to the tree, as if it were sharing its ancient wisdom and secrets with me. My initial fear gave way to a deep sense of ease. The teardrop crystals seemed to hold fragments of memories and emotions; each one held countless stories witnessed over the years. I moved closer to the tree like an invisible force guided my steps. The room's cool air deepened around me, amplifying the silence. My fingers trembled as I reached out toward one of the teardrop-shaped crystals hanging from the gnarled branches. As my fingertips brushed against the crystal, a warm pulse surged through my hand, radiating up my arm and settling in my chest. The sensation was like the gentle warmth of sunlight on a cold day, yet it carried an undertone of melancholy. My breath hitched, and my eyes closed tightly as vivid images flickered behind my closed lids—scenes of desolate landscapes and weeping figures. Each vision was brief but intensely emotional, filling me with an overwhelming sense of sorrow and loss.

The bark beneath my other hand was rough and cool, its texture contrasting sharply with the warmth of the crystal. I pressed my palm against the tree's trunk, feeling the uneven ridges and grooves like the skin of an ancient being. The wood was alive with the echoes of its long history, whispering through the tiny fissures and knots. A tremor shuddered through me, not from the cold but from the intense emotional presence that seemed to seep from the tree. The room around me felt as if it were closing in, the air heavy with unspoken stories. Each breath I took was shallow, my heartbeat erratic, as if the tree's history was intertwining with my own. The warmth from the crystal lingered, a bittersweet reminder of the visions that had invaded my senses, leaving me both awed and deeply unsettled. Standing beneath the tree, I felt a sense of renewal. The changes I had sensed earlier were now more apparent. The subtle shifts in the air, the allure of the doors, and the call of this mystical tree were all part of a journey toward understanding and growth. I realized that embracing these changes, however daunting they seem, was essential for my transformation. As I reached out to grab a teardrop crystal hanging from the tree, my heart clenched with anticipation and dread. With trembling fingers, I touched the crystal, and suddenly, I was engulfed in a memory.

I stood in a nursery, bathed in soft sunlight streaming through lace curtains. My eyes were drawn to the empty cot in the corner, to the dreams that had been shattered repeatedly. Tears began to form in my eyes as I remembered the hope, the anticipation, and the crushing disappointment of loss, each one more heartbreaking than the next. And then, piercing through the silence of the memory, came the sound of a baby's cry. It echoed through the room, a haunting melody of longing and loss. The pain of grief consumed me, washing over me like a tidal wave. I cried out, a raw, guttural sound torn from the depths of my soul. The weight of sorrow bore down on me, threatening to crush me beneath its unbearable burden. How many times had we hoped, prayed, and endured to be met with heartbreak? Collapsing to my knees, the crystal slipped from my grasp and shattered on the floor. The sound of it breaking echoed through the room, mirroring the shattering of our hopes and dreams. But even as tears streamed down my face, there was a glimmer of something else—resilience, determination, and a quiet strength born from despair. I realized that each loss, each heartache, had shaped me in ways I couldn't yet comprehend. They tested my faith, courage, and ability to love. With a deep breath, I pulled myself up, drawing courage from the memories that threatened to consume me. Reaching out, I grabbed another teardrop crystal from the tree, its surface shimmering with unshed tears. Holding the crystal, I felt a familiar longing and sorrow. The scene before me shifted again, and I found myself face-to-face with my mother. Her smile was gentle and hopeful, her eyes filled with warmth and love.

But as I reached out to touch her, a wave of grief washed over me. It had been five years since she passed away, yet the pain of her absence still felt raw. Every time I saw her face or heard her voice, I felt a part of myself break down as if her absence had left a permanent hole in my heart. My vision blurred as I gazed at her, longing for just a moment more, just one more chance to tell her how much she meant to me. But even as the pain threatened to overwhelm me, I knew that her memory would always be a source of guidance. With unsteady fingers, I traced the outline of her face in the crystal, committing every detail to memory—the curve of her smile, the sparkle in her eyes, the way her laughter filled the room. At that moment, I felt a sense of peace wash over me, a reminder that even in death, her love would always surround me.

Taking a deep breath, I returned the crystal to its place among the tears on the tree. The memories, pain, and love were all part of who I was and the journey that had brought me to this moment. She taught me that love is more powerful than death, that memories are more precious than gold, and that we are never truly alone as long as we carry the love of those who came before us in our hearts. It dawned on me that this was nothing but a room filled with grief, and I wondered if I was strong enough to face whatever else it had in store for me. I stood gazing up at the tree, I let out a long, shaky breath and felt the dampness spreading across my cheeks. I closed my eyes, allowing myself a moment of vulnerability. As each tear escaped, it carried a flood of emotions that I struggled to contain. I was strong; I just had to believe it.

As I reached out for the last time to choose another crystal, I felt another tear lingering on my hand. I observed it as it swirled and glistened in the dim light, revealing a familiar face that gazed back at me – it was Evie. I stood frozen, my eyes widening in disbelief as my hand flew to cover my quivering lips. At that moment, a choked "No" escaped my throat, breaking the heavy silence. As I tried to withdraw from the overwhelming memory, an unknown force seemed to tighten around my hand, anchoring it to the crystal. My fingers felt like they were ensnared in a vice, a cold pressure gripping them with an unyielding firmness. The crystal's surface was smooth but unnervingly warm, and the heat seemed to seep into my skin, intensifying the sensation of being held captive. The more I struggled, the more the force seemed to strengthen, like invisible chains wrapped around my wrist and fingers. My pulse raced beneath the skin; each beat throbbing painfully with the crystal's glow. The warmth from the crystal was a stark contrast to the icy tendrils of the unseen force that gripped me, creating a jarring sensory clash. Despite my frantic attempts to pull away, the crystal's heat only seemed to deepen, sinking into my bones and anchoring me further. I could feel a faint, almost imperceptible vibration traveling from the crystal up through my arm, a hum of my beating heart that seemed to sync with the unfolding scenes before me. The vividness of the memory played out with an almost oppressive clarity, filling my vision and my mind. I was compelled to watch, unable to break free, as the memory unfolded with a haunting intensity. Each detail was rendered with a vividness that left me breathless, my senses overwhelmed by the force of the experience that held me captive.

The scene solidified, pulling me into its vivid reality. I stood at a small, round table outside a charming café on a bustling corner. The café exuded an unmistakable French elegance, its exterior decorated with delicate wrought iron railings and intricate scrollwork that framed the windows. Each table was a quaint, bistro-style round, draped in checkered tablecloths of red and white that added a touch of rustic charm. The warm sunlight cascaded over the outdoor seating area, casting a golden glow that made the entire setting feel inviting and cozy. The air was filled with the soft hum of conversation and the occasional clink of cutlery, harmonizing with the gentle rustle of leaves in the light breeze. The breeze carried with it the mouthwatering aroma of freshly baked pastries—crisp croissants, buttery pain au chocolat—and the rich, robust scent of freshly brewed coffee that mingled and danced around us. I could feel the sun's warmth on my face and the chairs, with their intricate designs and cushioned seats, added to the café's authentic French allure. The clinking of porcelain cups and the soft murmur of the conversations around us blended with the occasional distant laughter, creating a symphony of sounds that enhanced the café's welcoming atmosphere. Evie and I sat at one of the tables, savoring the rich, aromatic coffee that warmed our hands as we lifted the cups to our lips. The coffee's bold flavor and velvety texture complemented the delicate sweetness of the pastries, making each bite and sip an indulgent pleasure.

"I don't know what to do, Evie," I said, my voice tinged with frustration and sadness, "Luke's been so distant lately. Every time we try for a baby, it pushes him further away."

Evie considered my words carefully. "I get it, Dee. Believe me, I do. Getting pregnant wasn't easy for us either. It's a struggle but you have to keep going. You need to talk to each other. Communication is key to any relationship. Without it, everything falls apart."

I nodded, though I didn't feel entirely convinced. "It just feels like Luke's shutting me out. I'm scared, Evie. What if we never have a baby? What if this ruins us?"

Evie reached across the table, squeezing my hand reassuringly. "You won't know unless you talk to him. Really talk to him. Tell him how you're feeling, and listen to what he says. You're in this together, remember?"

A small smile tugged at my lips. "Yeah, you're right. As always."

Evie glanced at her watch. "I hate to cut this short, but I have to pick Atlas from my sister's."

I grinned, astonished by how Evie had become a mother. "It's hard to believe he's three already. Time really does fly, doesn't it?"

She laughed softly. "It really does." As she stood to leave, she added with a teasing glint in her eye, "And hey, give Luke a kiss from me. He's still a catch, even if he is a bit of a pain right now."

I rolled her eyes playfully, waving me off. "Will do, Evie. Be safe."

I watched Evie as she turned to cross the street, the warmth of our earlier laughter lingering like a gentle embrace. The sun glinted off the smooth pavement, and the city chatter seemed to fade into the background. But then, the tranquility was shattered—a blaring screech cut through the air, a high-pitched wail that pierced the calm. My heart leapt into my throat as my gaze snapped to the source of the noise. In an instant, the world lurched into chaos. The metal of the car glinted menacingly as it hurtled toward her, tyres spinning violently against the asphalt. Time seemed to stretch, each second dragging painfully as I watched Evie's body lift off the ground, her movements eerily slow. Her expression was utter shock, her eyes wide and unseeing as she was flung through the air, a ragdoll in a cruel, invisible wind. A gut-wrenching thud that shook me to my core.

Everything around me blurred—screams from the crowd, the clamor of distant sirens, the harsh scrape of the car's tyres against the road. I stood frozen, rooted to the spot, my breath coming in ragged gasps. My mind raced in frantic confusion, struggling to piece together the horror before me. No. This couldn't be real. Not Evie. Not like this. A sharp pang of dread struck me as I thought of Atlas, her small, innocent three-year-old. The image of his expectant face, waiting for his mother's comforting embrace, cut through the haze of shock. A sob caught in my throat, the unbearable weight of reality pressing down on me. How could I ever find the words to explain this tragedy to him? The world seemed to collapse inward, the chaos and sorrow closing in like a suffocating fog.

People started to rush around the scene, their movements frantic and confused. The sound of sirens wailed in the distance, growing louder, yet everything felt muffled, as if I were underwater. My senses were numbed, and my body was paralyzed with shock. I wanted to scream, to run to her, but I was rooted to the spot, my legs heavy as lead. I could see people bending over Evie, trying to help. Still, all I could focus on was the stillness of her body and the unnatural angle of her limbs. Tears flowed freely down my face, my breath coming in ragged, shallow gasps. Everything around me blurred, the world spinning out of control.

As the memory's grip on me began to loosen, I felt a surge of panic and disorientation. My fingers, still clenched around the warm, pulsating crystal, seemed to lose their strength. The crystal, now a blinding light source, slipped from my grasp, its heat fading abruptly from my skin. It fell with a soft chime, the sound echoing like a distant, mournful bell as it hit the ground and rolled away. In that instant, the vivid images from the past shattered like glass, scattering into fragments that disappeared into the air. I was yanked violently back into the present; I stumbled backwards, my legs weak and unsteady as if the very ground had shifted beneath me. My heart pounded violently.

"Evie," I whispered, my voice trembling, the weight of the vision bearing down on me.

My knees gave out, and I sank to the floor, unable to hold back the sobs that wracked my body. The image of Evie's lifeless form lying in the street was seared into my mind, a nightmare that I couldn't escape.

She was gone. Evie, my closest friend, was dead.

****

The memory hit me like a tidal wave, crashing over me with an overwhelming force that drowned me in a sea of grief and despair. Each time the impact replayed, it was as if I were witnessing it anew, the details sharp and unrelenting. My heart pounded in a frantic rhythm, each beat a painful reminder of the horrific scene that seemed to stretch endlessly before me. I clutched at my chest, my fingers digging into my flesh as if to anchor myself to reality. The effort to breathe was a struggle, each inhalation a desperate gasp against the crushing weight of sorrow that enveloped me. The pain felt as though it were physically tearing at my insides, a relentless force that made every breath feel like a battle. It was as if a part of me had been violently ripped away, leaving behind a gaping, bleeding wound that throbbed with raw agony.

"Why?" I choked out between sobs. "Why show me this?"

The crystal hung from the tree, silent and still. It showed the past I desperately wanted to change. Evie was gone, and I was left to pick up the shattered pieces of my heart. As the minutes ticked by, I became dimly aware of my surroundings. The room was unmoving, the air heavy with an overpowering silence. I could hear my ragged breaths, the sound echoing in the quiet. I needed to move, to do something, but I felt paralyzed by the weight of my misery. Thoughts of Atlas swirled in my mind, the sweet, innocent boy who had lost his mother. How did he cope? How did we manage without Evie's warmth, laughter, and uplifting spirit? The thought of his father telling him, of seeing his face crumple in confusion and sadness, was almost too much to bear.

I forced myself to stand, my legs shaky and weak. I had to be strong for Atlas, Luke, myself, and Evie's memory. She wouldn't want me to fall apart. She would want me to fight, to find a way to move forward, even in the face of this unimaginable loss. She would want me to locate Luke and be happy, cherish our love, and not let it slip away. I gazed at the crystal. The vision I had just witnessed left me with an overwhelming guilt. It felt as if the vision had forced me to confront something I had long buried within myself, something I had tried to ignore for so long. Now, it was time I had to face it finally.

"It's not your fault, Dee." The words pierced through the haze of my shock, making me freeze in place. My breath caught, trapped somewhere between disbelief and hope. Before me, by the ancient tree, stood a figure that was unmistakably Evie—or at least someone who looked strikingly like her. The resemblance was uncanny, with her familiar features and the same warm, gentle demeanor I remembered. Evie's presence was both comforting and bewildering. Her eyes, usually so vibrant, were now a deep, luminous shade that seemed to reflect sorrow and reassurance. The gentle sway of her hair in the breeze and the way her voice floated through the air created a surreal juxtaposition with the horror I had just witnessed.

My heart pounded violently in my chest; each beat a frantic reminder of my racing thoughts. The sight of her was like a jolt of electricity, sparking a whirlwind of fear, hope, and skepticism within me. I could feel my pulse quicken as my mind struggled to grasp the impossible—was this really Evie, or a figment of my imagination conjured by the trauma? My breath came in shallow, uneven gasps; each exhale was a shaky attempt to steady myself. I tried to focus on the figure before me, my vision blurring with the intensity of my emotions.

The world around me felt unreal as if I were standing on the edge of a precipice between reality and a dream. My thoughts raced, colliding in a chaotic storm as I desperately sought to understand this surreal encounter. The sense of disbelief was a heavy weight pressing down on me, mixing with a flicker of hope that refused to be extinguished. I stood there, paralyzed and disoriented, my entire being caught in a tumultuous tide of emotions as I faced the hauntingly familiar yet impossibly strange figure of Evie.

"How? You're dead. Am I dead? Is that why I can see you?" I asked.

"It's a little more complicated than that. I'm not allowed to say much. You have to do this on your own," Evie said as she pushed away from the tree.

It had been over a year since she had died, and the grief felt like an unshakable shadow. As I stood before her now, my heart raced with fear, hope, and skepticism. *Was this real, or just a cruel illusion?* My arms ached to hold her, to feel her warmth and confirm that she was truly here. The overwhelming desire to reach out and embrace her clashed with the sinking doubt that this moment might be a figment of my longing. I needed to touch her, to chase away the constant ache that had settled in my soul, but for now, I was caught between hope and disbelief, unable to fully grasp if this reunion was real or just a fleeting dream.

"I miss you, Evie," I said, my voice breaking. The words felt insufficient, too small to contain the depth of my sadness. All I could do was cry, the pent-up grief and heartache spilling out uncontrollably.

"I know, I miss you too," she said softly, her voice carrying the same warmth and love I remembered. She reached out to me, her hand extending toward mine. For a moment, hope flared in my chest. But then her hand passed straight through me like a ghost. The cold, empty sensation sent a shiver down my spine, and the flicker of hope was extinguished, replaced by a crushing sense of loss. There was so much I wanted to say. "Atlas has become a handsome little man," I said, trying to lighten the mood despite my teary eyes. "He's so bright, so full of life. He reminds me so much of you."

Evie's eyes sparkled with a mix of pride and sadness. "I know. I've been watching."

I nodded, the lump in my throat growing tighter. "We're all doing our best to ensure he knows how much he's loved and you loved him."

A radiant smile spread across Evie's face, her features illuminated with an ethereal glow that defied the darkness surrounding us. Her eyes, always so full of life, now held a serene, almost otherworldly light. "Thank you, Dee Dee," she said softly, her voice imbued with a warmth that felt like a balm to my aching soul. "That means everything to me. But there's something I need to tell you—something important." Her smile faltered slightly but only gave way to a look of profound sincerity. "You have to keep going, no matter how hard it gets," she continued, her tone firm yet gentle. "I don't blame you for what happened. It isn't your fault."

Her words, though comforting, were laced with an urgency that I could not ignore. I could see in her eyes that she was trying to say something more. "There's someone else who needs you," she said, her gaze turning wistful. "Luke—he's lost without you. I know you've been through so much, but you have to find him." The weight of her words settled over me like a heavy mantle, but I felt a spark of hope ignite in my chest. Evie expressed heartfelt concern and deep affection, and she clearly wanted more than to reassure me. "Luke deserves to be happy," she said again, more firmly this time. "And you do, too. Life is still waiting for both of you, and it's important that you find each other."

Her gaze was steady, her eyes full of a love transcending even death. It was as if she was imparting a final piece of wisdom, urging me to move forward not just for myself, but for the both of us. "But Evie, there's so much I need to know. So much I need to tell you—"

She began to glow brighter and brighter, her form radiating an intense, almost blinding light. It was as if the very essence of her being was being drawn upwards, illuminating everything around her with a soft, golden hue. Her features, once so clear and distinct, started to blur and meld with the light until she became a shimmering silhouette. "I know; I'll always be with you in every memory, every moment we shared. I love you," she said, her voice growing fainter but still warm and reassuring. The light surrounding her intensified as she spoke, making it difficult to look directly at her. Gradually, her form dissolved into the brilliant glow, her edges melting away until she was no more than a flicker of light. The glow grew so intense that it became nearly impossible to distinguish her from the radiance. Then, just as abruptly as it began, the light began to fade, leaving behind a lingering aura of her presence. With a final, gentle shimmer, she vanished completely, leaving me standing alone beneath the mourning tree. I had to find a way to move forward and ensure that Atlas knew just how much his mother loved him. And I would fight for the future she wanted for Luke and me, no matter what it took. I noticed the tree's base shifting.

The vines surrounding it began to stir, their motion almost imperceptible at first. They twisted and curled, moving with an organic grace that seemed almost sentient.

Slowly, the tangled mass of greenery began to form a door, its shape emerging from the lattice of branches. The pattern was intricate, a labyrinth of intertwined vines that pulsed with a faint, otherworldly glow. The gentle, spectral light seemed to breathe, casting shifting shadows that danced across the ground. The air grew cooler as I approached, carrying a hint of earthy musk mixed with a whisper of something metallic. I could hear the soft rustling of the vines as they settled into place, their movement creating a subtle sound of creaks and sighs. Despite the door's beauty, I felt a pressing urgency, a need to move forward that tugged insistently at my core.

I stepped through the threshold with a deep breath that seemed to fill my lungs with both fear and resolve. The moment I crossed the barrier, the world around me shifted dramatically. It felt like I was being enveloped by a soft, enveloping mist that gradually cleared to reveal a new space. I found myself in a room overflowing with treasures—jewelry, trinkets, and artifacts of every conceivable kind. The air was thick with the scent of aged wood and a faint, sweet aroma reminiscent of old books. Tiny specks of dust floated in the beams of light that filtered through unseen windows, casting a warm, golden glow over the myriad of objects. Each item was a unique relic, their surfaces gleaming or tarnished with the passage of time. The sheer volume of treasures made it difficult to discern the boundaries of the room. The walls were obscured, hidden behind the sheer density of the collection. Every object seemed to have a story, its presence adding to the rich tapestry of this unexpected trove. The room felt alive with history and mystery; each artifact oozed a quiet allure, beckoning me to explore further. It was a sensory overload—visually captivating, rich with textures and scents, and imbued with a palpable sense of wonder.

I wandered through the room, my fingers grazing over the various items. Each piece seemed to hum with an energy. There were ornate necklaces, delicate porcelain figurines, and ancient coins, all in a beautiful yet chaotic display. As I moved deeper into the room, I noticed a small, intricately carved wooden box on a dusty shelf. Its craftsmanship was exquisite, and it called out to me. Carefully, I opened the box, revealing a delicate locket inside. The locket was adorned with intricate engravings, and inside was a tiny, faded photograph of a young woman and a child. The image was of my mother and me, my heart skipped a beat at the image bringing back the feeling of longing. Closing the locket, I held it tightly in my hand. I continued exploring the room. Heading over to a small table nestled by a large window, I moved cautiously, the soft creak of the wooden floorboards beneath my feet punctuating the quiet. I reached out and picked up the old rustic hand mirror, feeling the slightly rough texture of its frame against my fingers. The mirror's handle was decorated with intricate, swirling patterns that seemed to dance with a life of their own under the filtered sunlight. As I raised the mirror, its surface caught the light, reflecting a warm, golden glow that seemed to beckon me. I held it up to my face, and the moment my eyes met my reflection, the room around me seemed to dissolve. The mirror's surface shimmered and rippled like a tranquil pond disturbed by a sudden breeze.

Suddenly, I was no longer looking at my own image. Instead, the glass transformed, presenting a familiar scene from the past. It was as though the mirror had become a window into a long-forgotten moment. The boundary between the past and present blurred as I gazed deeper into the mirror. I felt myself being lured into the reflection, sinking into the moment as if it were a part of my reality. I watched as Luke and I sat at our worn-out kitchen table, its surface scarred and stained from years of use.

The table was strewn with a chaotic array of bills and bank statements, each one a reminder of our financial struggles. The papers were disorganized, some crumpled and others spread out in haphazard piles, their edges frayed and yellowed with age. The sight of the overdue notices, their red ink demanding immediate attention, was a cruel reminder of the mounting pressure we faced. The tension in the room was suffocating. Luke's face was etched with deep lines of worry, his brow furrowed and his eyes reflecting the same anxiety I felt inside. His fingers drummed nervously on the edge of the table, a silent testament to his stress and frustration.

"We can't keep going like this, Dee," Luke said, his voice heavy with frustration as he buried his head in his hands. "We've cut back on everything we can, but it's still not enough."

I reached across the table and took his hand, squeezing it gently. "We'll figure it out, Luke. We always do." I leaned in closer, trying to offer some comfort. I can pick up some extra shifts at work, or we can try to sell some things we don't need.

He sighed, rubbing his temples. "It's just… it feels like we're drowning. I hate seeing you work so hard and still struggle." My days blurred together in a whirlwind of writing sessions, research, and correspondence with publishers. Despite the grueling schedule and relentless push to produce my best work, the financial rewards seemed to be perpetually out of reach. Each rejection letter or low royalty statement felt like a personal defeat, magnifying the sense of struggle despite my relentless hard work.

I squeezed his hand, determination burning in my chest. "We'll get through this together. We'll find a way."

The memory faded, leaving me standing with the mirror still in my hand. I shifted my attention to a different item on the table- a small, intricately brooch. As I ran my thumb across its surface, the sensation was soothing, yet it triggered another wave of memories that engulfed me. In an instant, I was transported to our old living room, tThe furniture was a mismatched assortment: a tattered sofa with faded floral upholstery, a creaky wooden armchair with peeling varnish, and a coffee table with scratches revealing its past. The carpet, once perhaps a vibrant shade, had dulled to a tired beige, stained in places by years of use. Luke's restless pacing disturbed the quiet, his footsteps soft yet insistent on the frayed carpet. He clutched his hair as if seeking ease in its tangles, his fingers tugging at the strands as though trying to pull together his thoughts. His face, etched with worry, was lit in sharp relief by the lamp's glow, emphasizing the deep lines around his eyes and the tight set of his jaw. The atmosphere was thick with tension, the air heavy and still, punctuated only by the soft shuffle of his steps and the strained quality of his voice.

"Maybe we can take out a loan," he suggested, his voice tinged with desperation.

I shook my head. "Another loan will only put us deeper in debt, Luke. We need to find another solution."

He stopped pacing and looked at me, his eyes filled with worry. "What if we sell the car? We can use public transport or walk for a while. It'll be tough, but it might help us get back on our feet."

I considered his suggestion, weighing the pros and cons. "It's a sacrifice, but it might be worth it. We can save on insurance and petrol too. It's not forever, just until we get things under control."

Luke nodded, relief washing over his face. "You're right. It's just temporary. We'll make it work."

Once again, the memory dissolved like mist, and I found myself back in the present moment. The brooch was still warm in my hand. These memories, though painful, also reminded me of how supportive we were of each other. I continued to touch various objects and being transported to moments of our past. Each memory was a window into the times Luke and I had faced financial hardship together, always finding a way to move forward despite the odds. I was transported to my most recent memory as I touched the last trinket, a small, worn-out coin.

****

We sat in the park, the cool breeze rustling the leaves above us. Luke was holding my hand, his eyes filled with hope and exhaustion. "I know things have been tough, Dee, but I believe in us. We'll find a way like we always do."

I nodded, tears welling up in my eyes. "I believe in us too, Luke. As long as we're together, we can face anything."

He kissed my forehead, his touch gentle and comforting. "I love you, Dee. More than anything."

"I love you too, Luke. Always."

Standing back in the present, I clutched the coin tightly, the weight of all those memories settling in my heart. Despite the struggles, Luke and I always found a way to keep moving forward. I knew I had to fight for the future I wanted. I would keep going for Evie, Atlas, Luke, and myself, no matter how hard it got. With a deep breath, I looked around the room one last time. I was drawn to a giant golden mirror mounted on the far wall as I scanned the room. Its surface began to shimmer, undulating in mesmerizing waves of liquid gold that seemed to breathe with a life of their own. Each ripple caught the light, casting golden sparkles that danced across the room, making the air feel electric and charged with anticipation. The mirror's glow grew stronger as I approached. It radiated a gentle warmth that embraced me, pulling me closer with a captivating magnetism. The light it emitted was soft but intense, bathing the room in a golden hue that felt both inviting and surreal. Reaching out with tentative fingers, I touched the mirror's surface. It was a sensation unlike any other—smooth and cool beneath my fingertips, like gliding your hand over a calm, undisturbed pool of water. The coolness was soothing, and as my hand sank into the shimmering surface, it felt like I was reaching into a hidden world, beckoning me to step through.

Bravely, I stepped through the mirror and was immediately enveloped in a swirl of shifting colors and light. The world around me twisted and blurred, a whirlpool of motion that left me feeling as though I were floating in mid-air. There was a peculiar sensation of weightlessness as if gravity had momentarily lost its grip. The sensation was disorienting, a dizzying freedom that made my heart race and my stomach flutter. As I emerged from the mirror's embrace, I was plunged into a dense darkness that pressed in on all sides. I stood still, the silence heavy and my senses straining to grasp my new surroundings. Gradually, my eyes adjusted to the dimness, revealing a scene both haunting and majestic. I was in the heart of a neglected castle. Nature's relentless advance now swallowed the once-imposing grandeur of the structure. Gnarled trees and dense vines had taken over, their branches stretching through shattered windows and weaving a tangled canopy across the broken ceiling. Once smooth and pristine, the stone walls were now mottled with moss and creeping ivy. Sparse beams of weak light filtered through the overgrown foliage, casting shadows that had a life of their own, flickering and dancing on the cold, uneven stone floor. The air was thick with the musty smell of damp earth and decay, mingling with the faint scent of mildew. Each breath seemed to draw in the castle's forgotten history, a blend of desolation and silent grandeur that whispered through the stillness. The overwhelming sense of abandonment and the sheer scale of the ruin made me feel small and insignificant, a lone observer in a forgotten world.

I took a hesitant step forward, the cold bite of the stone floor seeping through my feet, sending goosebumps up my bare legs. Each footfall echoed softly in the vast, silent space, my breath forming brief, misty clouds in the dim light. As I moved, several torches embedded in the walls flared to life, their flickering flames casting a warm, amber glow that slowly pushed back the encroaching darkness. Turning back to the mirror, I was struck by its stark and out-of-place presence amidst the ruins. It was as if an artifact from a different world had been carelessly dropped into this forsaken realm. While the rest of the castle was cloaked in shadows and grime, the mirror stood untouched. Overtaken by the beauty around me, I jumped at the sudden sound of shouting. The voices echoed through the empty halls, their tones sharp with disagreement. They sounded familiar. As the torches lit up the space, casting dancing shadows on the walls, I saw the remnants of my past. There were echoes of Luke and me darting around the empty castle as we argued. The scenes played out like ghostly apparitions, fragmented but vivid.

I watched as a younger version of me gestured animatedly, my face twisted in frustration. Luke stood with his arms crossed, his expression equally stubborn.

"You never listen to me, Luke!" my past self shouted, her voice sharp with exasperation. "You're always so wrapped up in your world, and I feel invisible!"

"That's not fair, Dee! You know I've been dealing with a lot. It's not like I'm ignoring you on purpose." Luke's ghost shot back, his tone defensive.

"Not on purpose?" I scoffed, throwing my hands up in the air. "You might as well be! It's like talking to a wall. Do you even see me anymore? Do you even care?"

Luke's face softened for a moment, but his stubbornness quickly returned. "Of course, I care, but you don't understand the pressure I'm under. It's not always about you, Dee."

My past self stepped closer to him, her eyes filled with hurt. "I know it's not always about me, Luke. But it shouldn't always be about you, either. Relationships are supposed to be a two-way street, but with us, it feels like I'm the only one putting in any effort."

Luke's jaw clenched, and he looked away. "I... I just don't know how to balance everything. It's like I'm drowning."

"And what about me?" I demanded, my voice trembling with emotion. "Do you think it's easy for me? I'm drowning, too, Luke. But instead of reaching out to me, you push me away. It's like I don't even exist to you anymore."

He finally looked at me, his eyes filled with guilt and frustration. "I never wanted to make you feel that way. I'm just... I'm struggling too."

"I get that you're struggling," I said softly, the anger giving way to sadness. "But shutting me out isn't the answer. I want to be there for you, but you have to let me in. We're supposed to be a team, remember?"

Luke sighed, running a hand through his hair. "I do remember. I just... I don't know how to fix this. I don't want to burden you with my problems, Dee."

My past self looked at him, her eyes softening with empathy and determination. "Burden me? Luke, that's not how this works. We're supposed to share our burdens to help balance each other out. You don't have to carry everything on your own."

He looked down, his voice barely above a whisper. "I don't want you to feel like you have to take on my struggles. It's not fair to you."

I stepped closer, placing a hand on his arm. "Luke, it's not about fairness. It's about partnership. When you shut me out, it makes me feel like you don't trust or believe in us. I want to help you because I love you. That's what we do for each other—we take on each other's problems so neither of us feels alone."

Luke's eyes met mine, filled with gratitude and uncertainty. "But what if my problems are too much for you? I don't want to drag you down."

"You won't drag me down," I said firmly. "We'll lift each other up. We are stronger together than apart. I know it's hard, and I know it's scary, but we have to lean on each other. That's the only way we'll get through this."

He took a deep breath, his shoulders relaxing slightly. "You really think we can do this? Fix things, I mean?"

"I do," I replied, squeezing his arm gently. "But it starts with being open and honest. No more shutting each other out. We face everything together, no matter how tough it gets."

Luke nodded slowly, a small smile tugging at the corners of his mouth. "Okay. Together, then."

"Together," I echoed, feeling a glimmer of hope. "Always."

As the apparitions faded, I felt a pang of nostalgia. We had tried to mend the rift between us over and over again, but the journey had been far from easy. I strolled towards another apparition, drawn to the pieces of our past. Their voices grew louder and more apparent as if the castle replayed the memories.

"This isn't just about us. It's about everyone!" my past self shouted, her voice ringing with exasperation.

Luke's apparition responded, his tone equally heated. "And you think I don't know that? But running away isn't the solution!"

I winced, remembering the intensity of our arguments. We had both been so passionate and so sure of our perspectives. As I moved closer, the apparitions dissolved into the mist, leaving me solitary in the grand hall. The torches cast flickering shadows on the ancient stone walls, their warm light dancing across the intricately carved woodwork and towering columns. The grand staircase, a magnificent centerpiece, rose majestically in the middle of the hall. Its polished mahogany balustrades gleamed with a rich, deep hue, catching the flickering torchlight and casting a golden glow. The walls seemed to whisper our past disagreements, the painful moments we had endured together. "You never listen to me," "I feel invisible," "Why won't you let me in?"—the words surrounded me. Sharing the times we had failed to see eye to eye and the pain we had caused each other.

I felt acceptance as I walked along, reading the words etched into the stone. Each argument, each hurtful word, had been a part of our journey. The castle held our story within its walls in its decay and beauty, a tale of love and struggle. It was a reminder of the lessons we had learned and the growth we had achieved together. Surrounded by the remnants of our past conflicts. The walls might be covered in the scars of our arguments, but they also bore witness to our commitment to each other. It was a story of endurance, and I was ready to continue writing it with all its complexities and challenges. With each step I ascended the grand staircase, the air grew cooler, carrying the faint, musty scent of old wood and forgotten secrets. The rich, polished mahogany beneath my feet felt solid and reassuring, its surface warm from the torchlight. As I climbed higher, the apparitions of Luke and me, locked in passionate arguments, materialized once more. Though their ghostly forms flickered like shadows in the dancing torchlight, they no longer stirred unease. Instead, they were reminders of deeply intertwined love. Each flicker of their presence, framed by the ornate ironwork of the staircase and the grandeur of the hall, echoed the intense emotions we once shared, now softened into bittersweet reflections as I continued upward. After all, if you don't argue in a relationship, how do you show your commitment to fight for your love? Though painful, these moments were proof of our willingness to work through our differences.

As I continued exploring the decaying castle, the crumbling walls seemed to shiver with time. Around me, shadows deepened and shifted, gradually taking on a more defined shape. From my vantage point on the upper landing, I could see the grand hall below me starting to stir with spectral activity. The apparitions of Luke and me materialized amidst the wealthy, yet fading, splendor of the hall. The echoes of our voices filled the space, bringing a tense and familiar scene to life. Luke's face was a mask of concern and frustration, his hands clenched into fists at his sides. "Dee, you have to understand," he said, his voice tinged with desperation. "I'm not trying to be controlling. I just can't bear the thought of something happening to you."

My apparition, equally agitated, crossed her arms defensively. "Luke, I know you care, but you can't keep treating me like I'm fragile. I need to live my life, make my own choices."

He took a step closer, his eyes burning with intensity. "It's not about treating you like you're fragile. It's about how much you mean to me. You're everything to me, Dee. I can't lose you."

I watched as my past self softened slightly, the anger giving way to a flicker of understanding. "I know, Luke."

Luke's expression hardened momentarily before softening with vulnerability and fierce determination. His eyes locked onto mine with an intensity that sent a thrill through me. "I love you, Dee," he said, his voice dropping to a low, seductive murmur. "You are mine. And I'm yours. I need to keep you safe. I can't help it. I don't want anyone else to have you." The raw intensity of his words sent an electric jolt through me, causing an involuntary shiver along my spine. Even in the vision. I saw myself flustered, a mixture of emotions playing across my face. The possessiveness in his declaration was both overwhelming and deeply moving.

"Luke," my apparition whispered, her voice breathless as she pulled away, "I love you too, but we must find a balance. I need to feel like you trust me to care for myself."

Luke's gaze intensified, his vulnerability melting into a raw passion. He took a step closer, closing the distance between us. "I do trust you, Dee. But my love for you is so strong that it scares me. I'll work on it, I promise. Just... don't push me away."

Before I could speak, Luke closed the distance between us with a swift, decisive movement. His strong arms encircled me, lifting me effortlessly off the ground. I felt a rush of warmth and exhilaration as my legs instinctively wrapped around his waist, drawing me closer. The solid strength of his arms held me securely by my thighs, and the heat of his touch seemed to seep through the fabric of my clothes, igniting a tingling warmth against my skin. The world around us faded into a blur as our bodies pressed together. His breath, warm and ragged, mingled with mine, creating a sensation that was both intensely intimate and electrifying. His fierce and unyielding gaze burned into mine with an intensity that was both commanding and pleading.

"I trust you, Dee," he murmured, his voice thick with emotion. "I just ask that you don't push me away this time."

He pressed his lips to mine, the kiss igniting a fire within me. The intensity of his affection left me breathless, my body responding to his every touch. Our kiss deepened, and I could feel the desperation and love pouring from him, matching the rhythm of my own heart. As the vision disappeared, I felt the weight of his words and the depth of his love within me. Luke's passion and protectiveness were undeniable, and I understood the fierce devotion that drove him.

****

At the end of the corridor I discovered withered doors decaying along with the castle. The air was thick with the scent of damp wood and earth, and I could hear the faint rustling of leaves through the broken windows. As I walked along, the air was thick with the earthy scent of damp moss and decaying leaves, remnants of the plant life that had slowly claimed this castle. Each step I took on the ancient stone pathway was met with a soft, hollow echo, adding to the somber ambience of the once-grand place. I glanced down at the center of the castle where I had just stood, imagining its former splendor—an expanse of polished marble floors and vibrant tapestries, now swallowed by nature's relentless encroachment. A glimmer caught my eye, sharp and fleeting, compelling me to shift my gaze.

There, partially obscured by the encroaching vines, stood a set of double doors. Their dark wood was rich and polished; The doors were crafted with intricate metalwork that seemed to pulse with a life of its own. As I drew nearer, the brilliance behind the doors intensified, a warm, throbbing glow that promised secrets and wonders waiting just beyond the threshold. The light seemed to beckon, casting a golden halo around the edges and drawing me inexorably forward, filling me with a sense of intrigue and wonder. My pulse quickened with each step toward the glowing metalwork. I reached out, fingers grazing the intricate patterns that seemed to hum beneath my touch, a rhythmic vibration syncing with my heartbeat. I drew a deep breath, then heaved the heavy doors open. They groaned and protested, their ancient hinges straining against the weight of years.

As the doors parted, a warm, golden light poured into the corridor, casting long shadows and brightening the path ahead. I moved forward, drawn by the inviting radiance, curiosity propelling me through the threshold. As I crossed the threshold, I was swept away by the transformation before me. The castle, once shadowed and desolate, now shimmered with renewed splendor. Sunlight streamed through towering arched windows, warming the polished marble floors and highlighting the intricate floral decorations that adorned the walls. In front of me, a grand arched window framed a breathtaking view of a verdant forest, its trees standing tall and proud. The room was awash in the rich scent of roses, their petals carefully arranged to create an air of romance and elegance. A soft hum of life filled the space, mingling with the distant melody of birds serenading the occasion.

At the heart of this enchanting scene, a man and a woman stood poised beneath the golden light streaming through the window. The gentleman's polished suit and confident stance contrasted beautifully with the gentle grace of the woman beside him, her eyes reflecting a deep affection. The scene was unmistakably one of celebration, a moment of union and joy captured in every detail. The woman beside him wore a gorgeous wedding dress. The gown had a breathtaking open back decorated with intricate lace details. The delicate lace flowed seamlessly from the shoulders to the small of the back, adding an elegant and romantic touch to the gown. It was Luke and me on our wedding day. The memory was so real that I felt like I could reach out and touch it. I watched as we exchanged vows, our voices filled with emotion, our promises to each other echoing.

Luke took a deep breath, his eyes locking onto mine, filled with love and sincerity. "Dee, from the moment I met you, I knew my life had changed forever. You brought light into my world, a light I didn't know I was missing. Today, I promise to always cherish that light, to protect it, and to nurture it. I vow to be your rock, to stand by your side through every storm and every sunny day. I promise to listen, to understand, and to grow with you. You are my heart, my soul, and my home. We can face anything together, and I am forever grateful to call you my wife, best friend, and soulmate."

Tears slid down my face as I watched, my heart filled with joy. When it was my turn, I took his hands in mine, my voice trembling. "Luke, you are my guiding star, the one who makes my heart sing and my spirit soar. From the moment you walked into my life, I knew I had found my other half. Today, I vow to be your constant support, biggest cheerleader, and your partner for life. I promise to share in your dreams and to help carry your burdens, to laugh with you in times of joy, and to hold you close in times of sorrow. I vow to always see you, to always hear you, and to always love you. You are my forever, and I am so blessed to be yours. Together, we are unstoppable, and I can't wait to see where this journey takes us."

As the younger versions of us stood before the altar, fingers trembling slightly, the shimmering rings exchanged hands and our lips met in a soft, earnest kiss. The image of that moment unfurled before me like a vivid dream—brimming with the raw passion and earnest promise we had shared. I could almost hear the murmurs of heartfelt promises and feel the weight of that profound commitment. The sight of our younger selves, so full of hope and certainty, reignited the fire of our vows, casting a glowing light on the foundation of our love.

It was as if the very essence of those promises wrapped around us once more, reaffirming the strength of our bond and the journey we had embraced together. The memory faded, leaving me standing in the warmth of our vows lingering in the air. Our love, forged in the fire of happiness and hardship, was unbreakable. We had faced darkness together, and we would continue to walk hand in hand into the light. Our arguments and struggles were all part of that journey, but they did not define us. What defined us was our determination to stay together, no matter what fate threw at us. I felt a pain in my chest, a deep yearning to be with Luke, knowing that everything we had been through was proof enough that we would reunite soon. The path forward was clear, and I knew our story was far from over. We would continue to write it together, one chapter at a time, with the strength of our love guiding us.

As I stood there, the glowing orb's light enveloping me, I felt a stirring in the air—a promise that our next chapter would begin. I just had to get back to Luke first.

Hall of Emotions

Determination was an understatement; at this point, I was becoming desperate to find my way back to Luke. As I turned to leave the vow room behind, I encountered a new door. It was markedly different from the previous one: dark brown, worn with age, and marked by deep scratches. Soft candlelight flickered at its base, casting a warm glow against the rough wood. Carved into the door was a simple yet poignant note: "You are my forever." Steeling myself, I pushed open the door and stepped through. The transition was abrupt yet subtle. As I entered the next room, its serene beauty struck me. Large latticed windows lined one wall, their intricate patterns casting soft shadows across the floor.

A tranquil symphony immediately enveloped my senses. The cool water brushed against my submerged ankles, each step I took caused a delicate ripple, disturbing the stillness only briefly. My eyes were drawn to the hundreds of tea light candles gently floating on the water's surface. Their flames flickered softly, casting dancing shadows that wavered and intertwined on the water and walls. The scent of wax and a faint hint of incense mingled in the air, grounding me in this serene environment. The soft glow of the candles, both the floating ones and the larger church candles mounted on the stone tables along the walls, bathed the room in a warm, steady light. It defied the passage of time, creating an atmosphere of calm that felt both expansive and intimate. The light filtering through the latticed windows projected delicate patterns onto the walls and water, adding to the room's hypnotic effect. The floating candles, the soft light, and the water lapping gently at my ankles created a sanctuary from the outside world. In this refuge, I could gather my thoughts and strengthen my resolve. Drawn to the flickering flames, I reached down and picked up one of the tea-light candles. As soon as my fingers brushed the delicate flame, the room around me shifted and blurred. A new scene unfolded, vivid and clear, like a living memory. Luke stood in a spacious, well-lit mechanic's garage, the walls adorned with vintage automotive posters and framed certificates of achievement. The air was filled with the scent of oil and gasoline.

"This promotion is a once-in-a-lifetime opportunity, Luke," Bill, his boss, said.

"Relocating to the Manchester office will put you at the forefront of our biggest projects. You will be working firsthand with the biggest brand in car history. Think about the impact you could make."

Luke's face was tense, his eyes flickering with conflict. "I understand, and I appreciate the offer. But my decision isn't just about my career. It's about my life with Dee. She has her own goals and her own path. Moving to Manchester would mean asking her to give up everything she's worked for."

Bill's expression softened slightly, but he pressed on. "Sometimes sacrifices are necessary for greatness, Luke. I am sure she would understand."

Luke shook his head, his resolve hardening. "Dee is everything. Our life together is what matters most to me. I can't ask her to sacrifice her dreams for mine."

Bill looked him in the eye and replied, "And you should?"

The memory faded, leaving me in the candlelit room once more. My cheeks were damp with tears as I absorbed the weight of Luke's sacrifice. He had turned down an incredible opportunity, choosing our life together over his professional advancement. His love for me and his commitment to our partnership had been his guiding star. As I stood there, my mind raced to make sense of the situation. *He had never told me about this,* I thought, my confusion deepening. *Why am I suddenly seeing Luke's memories?* This was all so unexpected and disorienting. The images and scenes unfolding before me felt intimate and foreign, and I struggled to understand what had prompted this revealing of his past. *What did this mean for me, and why now?*

I reached for another candle, the flame flickering as I lifted it from the water. Once again, the room transformed, and I was brought into another memory. This time, I was in our cozy living room. Luke sat at the dining table, its surface cluttered with a stack of papers, pens, and a few neatly arranged checks. He was hunched over the paperwork, his brow furrowed in concentration, each furrow deepening with the weight of his task. The quiet rustle of paper and the occasional scratch of his pen against the surface created a steady rhythm. The weight of his actions evident in his furrowed brow.

"Are you sure about this, Luke?" Liam asked, sitting across from him. "This is a significant amount of money. You could invest it or put it into savings."

Luke glanced at the papers, then looked up with a soft but resolute expression. "I am sure. Dee's dream has always been to publish her book. She's worked so hard on it and I believe in her. This is her chance to shine and I want to support her, no matter the cost."

Liam leaned back, still skeptical. "It's a huge risk, you know. What if it doesn't work out?"

Luke smiled, his eyes filled with unwavering confidence. "I have faith in Dee. She's talented and passionate. Investing in her dreams is the best decision I could make. We're partners, and her success is my success. If I can help her achieve her dreams, every penny is worth it."

As the memory faded, A swell of emotions surged through me, my chest tightening as a sense of wonder spread through my heart. My eyes prickled with warmth, and my throat tightened as if something precious was caught just beneath the surface. The corners of my mouth curled into a soft, involuntary smile, and my hands trembled slightly, the sensation of gratitude and love mingling in the pit of my stomach, creating a bittersweet ache. Luke had never told me about this financial sacrifice. He had used his savings, money he could have invested for our future, to help me get my book self-published. His belief in me and willingness to put my dreams ahead of his financial security were humbling. I wondered why Liam never mentioned anything like this. I placed the candle back into the water, the flame dancing among the floating leaves.

As I moved through the room, the water swirling around my ankles created a soothing, gentle sound, echoing against the walls and filling the space with a calming presence.

With its light glowing steadily, a red candle bobbed gently on the water's surface, its flame burning steadily amidst the scattered leaves. I reached out and lifted it, its wax cool and slightly damp against my fingers. As I held it, the scene around me shifted like a ripple, and suddenly, I was transported to a vivid memory. I found myself back in our living room, the air charged with tension. My younger self was pacing frenetically, my hands gesturing wildly as I spoke. My voice, raised and sharp, cut through the thick silence, and I could see the frustration etched deeply into my face. Luke stood nearby, his expression a mixture of anger and confusion as we clashed in a storm of emotions. The room felt small and suffocating, every detail sharp and vivid against the backdrop of our heated argument.

"I just don't understand why you can't see it from my perspective, Luke!" my past self exclaimed, exasperated. "It's like you don't even care!"

Luke stood calmly, his face a mask of patience and understanding. "Dee, I do care. But we have to find a way to meet in the middle. This isn't just about one of us; it's about us together."

"Meet in the middle?" my past self scoffed, crossing her arms. "It always feels like I'm the one sacrificing. Why can't you ever bend for once?"

Luke took a deep breath, his voice steady and soft. "Dee, I bend for you more than you realize. I try to be here for you and support you, even when it means putting my needs aside. I would do anything for you."

Watching the scene unfold, I felt a pang of guilt. I remembered this argument, but seeing it from this perspective, I could see how unreasonable and selfish I had been. Luke had demonstrated such patience, and his love for me was evident in his calm and forgiving demeanor, even in the face of my harsh words. The brightness of the candle intensified, my eyes squinting and becoming increasingly sensitive to the searing glow. I instinctively raised my hands to shield my eyes, but the light pierced through my fingers, sharp and blinding. Caught off guard, I fumbled with the candle. The sensation of its heat was overwhelming, and the intensity of the flame made me drop it in a reflexive, startled movement. My heart pounded fiercely, a relentless drumbeat in my chest, echoing the rising panic that twisted my insides. The peaceful calm that had enveloped the space moments before dissolved into a swirling maelstrom of confusion and fear. I struggled to find my footing, the serene atmosphere of the room slipping away and leaving me disoriented in its wake. My foot caught on something without warning, and I lost my balance. I tumbled backwards, hitting the water with a splash. But instead of landing in a shallow puddle, I felt myself sinking, entirely submerged in cool, enveloping water. I thrashed instinctively, my body reacting to the sudden immersion.

When I opened my eyes, an endless expanse of deep blue enveloped me. I was submerged, the candles and the room above had vanished entirely, replaced by the serene embrace of water. The cool liquid brushed against my skin, its gentle current playfully tugging at my dress and hair, creating a soft, swirling motion around me. The taste of saltwater lingered on my lips, sharp and briny, a stark reminder of my new environment. As the initial panic began to subside, a surreal calmness settled over me. I floated effortlessly, suspended in this underwater realm where the dim, blue-tinted light filtered through the water, casting an ethereal glow.

I noticed there was no clear sense of up or down, no discernible direction, just an infinite space of tranquil blue. The silence was profound, a deep, enveloping quiet that contrasted sharply with the chaos above. As I adjusted to this new reality, I discovered with a start that I could breathe normally, the water not impeding my breaths in the slightest. A thought surfaced through the peaceful fog in my mind: *Was this another challenge, another test of my resolve to reunite with Luke?"* The realization dawned slowly, adding a layer of contemplation to the calm, underwater expanse surrounding me. I began to swim, not knowing which direction to go towards. Each stroke was deliberate, pushing me through the water with purpose. As I swam, I felt the water around me pulse. I paused, feeling the gentle pull of the current around me. As I floated in the tranquil blue expanse, a vision coalesced in the depths. The water around me shimmered and distorted, the once-clear surface now rippling with an almost liquid light, images started to materialize and I saw myself sitting at my desk, completely absorbed in my writing.

The soft glow of the desk lamp illuminated my focused expression, and the pen moved swiftly across the paper. My round glasses sat on my face, and a crease formed between my eyebrows as I concentrated. From the depths of the water, I could hear Luke's thoughts echoing clearly, reverberating with deep admiration. As he leant on the door frame of my office, watching with an unwavering sense of pride. *She's so talented*, his thoughts began, filled with warmth and pride. *Every word she types brings her closer to realizing her dream.* The vision provided a different perspective, allowing me to see myself through Luke's eyes. His admiration was noticeable, and his love intertwined with deep respect. It was as if the water carried his emotions to me, wrapping me in a comforting blanket. I watched as Luke observed me with a gentle smile. He didn't interrupt, understanding how much my writing meant to me. His silent support was proof of his belief in my abilities and dreams. Seeing this, I realized how much he cherished these moments and how proud he was of my dedication and passion. The vision faded, taken away by the current, leaving me surrounded by the cool, embracing water. Before I started swimming, another vision began to form in the water drawing me deeper into Luke's memories. This time, it was more intimate, more personal. I could feel his emotions vividly.

In the vivid memory, I watched as Luke's lips traced a path up my legs. Each kiss left a lingering, sweet taste on his lips, a tactile sensation that seemed to resonate through the water. He took his time, savoring every inch of my exposed skin. I could sense the warmth of his breath and the deliberate, tender pressure of his touch, feeling the way my body reacted and shifted beneath his caress. When he reached between my legs, there was no hesitation. His touch was direct and purposeful, exploring my most sensitive areas with practiced skill. The memory was alive with the soft, rhythmic sounds of pleasure, a symphony of moans and gasps that echoed through the water. I could almost hear Luke's thoughts intertwining with these sounds: *I love how she responds to me,* he mused. *Her taste is intoxicating.* His thoughts reverberated with a deep sense of longing and satisfaction, blending seamlessly with the sensory overload of the memory. As the visions faded, I found myself again in the endless stretch of water, but now, I felt an overwhelming sense of purpose and strength.

Reflecting on Luke's thoughts and memories, I began to grasp the depth of his devotion and my impact on his life. This realization inspired me to acknowledge my own self-worth.

****

In the pool of emotions, another vision began to form around me. This time, I was seeing through Luke's eyes. The surroundings shifted, and I found myself in our old apartment. It was late at night, and the room was dimly lit by the soft glow of a single lamp. From Luke's perspective, I watched myself asleep on the couch, a book on my chest. Luke entered the room quietly, his footsteps soft as he approached me. His gaze was filled with fierce tenderness and possessive protectiveness, and I could feel the intensity of his emotions as if they were mine. He knelt beside the couch, carefully lifting the book and placing it on the coffee table. With a tender touch, he removed my reading glasses and set them gently aside. He brushed a strand of hair away from my face, his fingers lingering momentarily as if he couldn't bear to let go.

She's been working so hard, Luke's thoughts echoed, *I need to make sure she takes care of herself.* With a gentle yet firm grip, Luke scooped me into his arms, cradling me against his chest as he carried me to our bed. His touch was both tender and protective, a silent vow to always be there for me. The scene shifted again. We were at a crowded party, the noise and energy of the room buzzing around us. I was engaged in a lively conversation with friends, unaware of Luke standing a few feet away. His eyes never left me. He was constantly scanning the room, alert for any sign of discomfort or danger. Suddenly, someone bumped into me, causing me to stumble. Before I could react, Luke was by my side, his grip tight with tension, a mixture of worry and protectiveness etched on his furrowed brow. As he tensed, preparing to confront the person who had caused my stumble, I instinctively stepped before him, placing a gentle hand on his chest. *I'm gonna kill him; he knocked her over. Not even an apology. I'll make him apologize.*

"Luke, calm down," I urged my voice steady despite the adrenaline coursing through me. "I'm fine, really."

He hesitated, his jaw still clenched with tension, but the urgency in my voice seemed to break through his protective instincts. Slowly, he released the tension in his muscles, his gaze softening as he looked down at me.

"Okay," he murmured, his voice filled with relief and gratitude. "I just...I can't stand the thought of anyone hurting you." His thumb gently brushed against my lip as he placed his other hand on my face, his touch both soothing and possessive. Slowly, he leaned in, his eyes searching mine for a heartbeat before he pressed his lips to mine in a kiss that was both tender and fervent. The vision diminished, I began to swim again, each stroke filled with a sense of purpose. Our story was far from over, and our connection felt stronger with each stroke. I was no longer just searching for Luke; I was securing our bond through all our challenges and victories. The water around me started to swirl and shift, creating a whirlpool beneath my feet; I felt a powerful tug pulling me downward. Helpless against its force, I was sucked into the vortex, feeling as if I were being drawn into another dimension. The world around me blurred and twisted, colors and shapes blending into a dizzying whirl.

Suddenly, as abruptly as it had begun, the chaos subsided. I found myself standing in the hallway of my childhood home. I glanced down at my dress, expecting to see it clinging damply to my skin, but it fell smoothly over me, untouched by water. The fabric, light and dry, fluttered softly with each step I took. I ran my fingers through my hair, half-expecting to feel it matted and wet, but it fell freely around my shoulders, perfectly dry and impeccably in place. The strange dryness contrasted sharply with the lingering sensation of water against my skin, leaving me disoriented. The walls, lined with picture frames, seemed almost too vivid, each snapshot brimming with memories that felt both distant and immediate. Birthdays, school achievements, family vacations—every frame held a moment frozen in time, yet as I walked by, they seemed to shimmer and pulse with life. In each frame, I saw myself at different stages of life, reliving the highs and lows, the laughter and tears. But among these cherished moments, I noticed a recurring theme—my parents' gradual drifting apart. In some frames, their smiles seemed strained, their embraces less frequent. A pang of sadness tugged at my heart as I realized how their relationship had evolved.

As I gazed at the photograph, the world around me began to blur and fade. A sudden, tingling sensation swept over me, and before I could fully grasp what was happening, I felt a force gently tugging me forward. The picture's edges seemed to ripple like water, drawing me into the frame. The colors shifted, and I returned to that warm, sunny afternoon. The air was thick with the sweet aroma of chocolate cake and the slightly artificial scent of balloons. I heard the cheerful chatter of children mingling with the clinking of cutlery on paper plates. The melody of "Happy Birthday" filled the room, its notes bouncing off the colorful streamers and the glimmering foil of the decorations hanging from the ceiling. The walls were adorned with vibrant, hand-drawn banners that read "Happy Birthday" in bright, crayon-like letters. The table was festooned with a cheerful pink tablecloth, and the centerpiece was a cake crowned with five flickering candles. I watched my younger self, eyes sparkling with delight, as I blew out the candles amidst a chorus of applause and laughter from the small but lively group of friends. The joy of being the center of attention made me feel unique and loved, as the memories came flooding back with an intensity that was both nostalgic and exhilarating. But as the memory continued, it took a darker turn. The scene shifted to later that night. I found myself standing, shivering slightly, behind the door frame of the living room. The warmth of the birthday party had receded, replaced by an unsettling chill that made me draw my arms closer to my body. I watched my parents argue in hushed but intense voices. I couldn't distinguish all the words, but I caught enough—money troubles and my name being mentioned repeatedly. My mother's face was etched with worry, my father's with frustration.

"We can't keep spending like this, John," my mother said, her voice tight with anxiety.

"Well, what do you want me to do, Michele?" my father snapped back, barely keeping his voice down.

"Do you think I'm not trying? Everything is so expensive, and we have Dee to think about."

"Don't you dare put this on her," my mother replied, her tone softer but no less intense. "She deserves a normal childhood, even if things are tough."

I felt a lump in my throat, a mixture of sadness and guilt, as if, somehow, their problems were my fault. My small hands gripped the door frame as I stood there, unseen, absorbing the weight of their words.

"Maybe we should cut back on the activities," my father suggested, exasperatingly lacing his words. "She doesn't need all those dance classes."

My mother sighed deeply, her worry evident in her eyes. "She's just a child, John. She doesn't need to know any of this. We have to find a way to make it work."

The emotions of that night rushed back to me in the present, filling me with a profound sense of sadness and anger. I watched the scene unfold with a heavy heart until, abruptly, I was pulled out of the memory and back into the hallway. I paused at a frame showing my graduation day. I stood proudly in my cap and gown, the weight of the past few years finally lifting off my shoulders. Beside me, Luke grinned, his arm draped casually around my shoulders, the promise of support. My mum stood on my other side, her eyes shimmering with unshed tears, her smile radiant and proud.

But my father's absence was a dark cloud over an otherwise perfect day. He had left us years before, a ghost of the man he once was, disappearing without explanation. The pain of his absence had dulled over time, but on that day, it flared up anew, sharp and biting. I had always dreamed of sharing that moment with him, of seeing him in the crowd, clapping and cheering for me. As I looked at the photo, anger and sadness washed over me. Why hadn't he been there? Why hadn't he cared enough to stay? I clenched my fists, feeling the familiar burn of resentment. It wasn't fair that he had missed such an important milestone in my life, leaving a void that could never be filled. Luke must have sensed my struggle even then. He squeezed my shoulder gently, drawing me back to the present. "You did it, Dee," he whispered, his voice steady and reassuring. And we're so proud of you."

My mum echoed his sentiments, pulling me into a tight hug. "Your father doesn't know what he's missing," she said softly, her voice tinged with sorrow and defiance. "But we're here, and we couldn't be prouder."

Their words had been a balm to my aching heart, but the wound of my father's absence had still throbbed beneath the surface. I had plastered a smile on my face, trying to focus on the joy of the moment, on the achievement I had worked so hard for. But inside, I had felt hollow, the shadow of my father's absence casting a long, dark shadow over the day. I stared at the photo, the weight of it all pressed heavily on me. In a sudden burst of frustration, I swung my fist at the frame. The impact was sharp, the sound of shattering glass echoing in the small space. Splinters of wood and shards of glass rained down, landing in a crumpled heap on the floor. The force of the blow left my knuckles stinging, but the physical pain was a fleeting distraction compared to the storm of emotions surging through me. The frame lay there, its contents scattered, a tangible reflection of the chaos that had erupted inside me.

Looking at the photo, I could see the strain in my smile and the forced cheerfulness in my eyes. It hurt to remember, to feel the old wounds reopening through the cracks of the glass. But it also reminded me of how far I had come, of the strength I had found in myself and in the people who had stood by me. The past was painful but also a part of me, shaping who I had become. And while my father's absence still hurt. I had built a life of love and support and tried not to let his memory overshadow that. The soft crackle of the match as it ignited the wick filled the silence, and I turned instinctively toward the sound. In the dim glow, I saw the candle's flame dancing midair, casting shadows that wavered against the walls. Curiosity tugged at me, urging me to follow the floating candle as it drifted down the hallway. The candle's soft, flickering light left a trail of shimmering reflections on the worn wooden floorboards, guiding my path. With each step I took, the creak of the floor seemed to join in a gentle symphony with the candle's quiet flame. The walls of my childhood home seemed to be melting away into shadows as the candle's faint light flickered desperately against the encroaching darkness. The room, once so familiar and comforting, was retreating, giving in to the all-consuming blackness that was slowly swallowing it whole. With each hesitant step, the darkness pressed in closer, almost as if it were a living thing, wrapping around me and consuming the space. The candle's light, my only source of illumination, flickered more erratically, casting fleeting reflections that barely held back the encroaching blackness. The room's edges vanished, replaced by a shifting abyss. The darkness surged around me, as if it were a sentient entity, moving and twisting in response to my presence. The candle's flame seemed like a fragile beacon offering only a brief escape from the overwhelming void that threatened to engulf everything.

Shadows swirled, merging into shapes that seemed almost human. As they circled me, One shadow whispered to me, its voice insidious and cold. "Look at you," it sneered. "You're nothing but a burden with your fibromyalgia. How long before it takes over completely?"

A third shadow loomed larger, whispering fears of losing the ones I loved. "You'll end up alone, just like before. Everyone you care about will leave you."

The room appeared to expand around me, the walls stretching as if they were made of elastic, distorting and warping as shadows crept upward, becoming taller and more menacing. The familiar silhouettes of the space seemed to stretch into an infinite distance, leaving me feeling increasingly insignificant within its vast, distorted expanse. The walls, once close and comforting, now felt miles away, and the dark tendrils of shadow pressed in on me from every angle, squeezing and constricting my sense of space. It was as though the room was an ever-expanding maw, and I was trapped inside, unable to escape. Each brush of the shadows against my skin felt like a cold, invisible hand, their touch sending involuntary shudders through my body. My limbs felt heavy and unresponsive, paralyzed by a growing sense of dread. The oppressive darkness seemed to press in on all sides, suffocating and consuming, leaving me frozen in place, overwhelmed by the fear of what might emerge from the ever-expanding blackness that surrounded me. I pressed my hands tightly against my ears, fingers digging into my scalp, desperate to block out the clamor that roared around me. The relentless and insistent voices seeped through my attempts at silence, growing louder and more chaotic until they felt like a swarm of angry bees buzzing and gnawing at my mind.

The darkness seemed to grow thicker, a weight that pressed down on my shoulders, making each breath feel like a monumental effort. My chest tightened with the crushing pressure of my insecurities, the feeling almost like a vise squeezing my rib cage. Each inhale came in sharp, ragged gasps, and my heartbeat pounded frantically, a frantic rhythm against the suffocating gloom. As the room seemed to shrink around me, I could feel the walls closing in, my space collapsing into an ever-tightening cocoon of fear. I curled inward, my body trembling uncontrollably, the chill of abandonment seeping into my bones. The sensation of being utterly alone was overwhelming, like an invisible hand gripping my heart, squeezing it tightly until I felt a deep, gnawing emptiness. I was lost, drowning in a sea of overwhelming shadows and fears, with nothing but the oppressive silence after the voices to amplify my isolation. The silence pressed against me like a cold, unfeeling presence, intensifying the loneliness and despair that wrapped around me like a suffocating shroud.

But then, a thought pierced through the suffocating fog of fear. *I made it this far. I had faced my darkest memories, relieved the pain, and still stood strong. These twisted shadows wouldn't be the ones to bring me down.* I opened my eyes and straightened my spine, lifting my chin. With a sudden burst of courage, I exclaimed, "Enough," my voice shaking but resolute. "I am better than this. I am stronger than this."

The shadows hesitated, their whispers faltering. I took a deep breath, feeling the strength within me grow. "I have faced worse than you," I continued, my voice gaining confidence. "I have survived pain, loss, and fear. I will not let you control me." The shadows recoiled, their forms beginning to dissolve. I took another step forward, the warmth of my resolve pushing back the darkness. "You don't define me," I said firmly. "I define myself. I am not my insecurities. I am not my fears. I am more than my illness."

The room began to change. Once stretching and oppressive, the walls seemed to draw closer, the space becoming more intimate and less intimidating. The shadows continued to retreat, their whispers fading into the ether. The room was becoming brighter.

"I am worthy of love and happiness," I declared, my voice echoing with conviction. "I am capable and will not be diminished by your lies."

As I yelled at the last shadow, my voice echoing sharply in the oppressive silence, I swiped at it with a desperate motion. The shadow dissipated into a swirl of dark mist. In the vanishing darkness, I felt something solid materialize in my hand. I looked down, my heart racing, and opened my palm to reveal an unexpected discovery—a key. The key was surprisingly warm against my skin. I ran my fingers over its surface, feeling the intricate handle shaped like intertwining vines. The delicate tendrils of the design curled and twisted, their fine details brushing gently against my fingertips, creating an intricate and alive sensation.

The key's metal was worn smooth in places, with tiny scratches and grooves that hinted at its long history and countless past uses. Its weight was solid and reassuring in my hand, grounding me amid the swirling uncertainty. The key's presence felt oddly powerful, like a talisman imbued with significance, and it seemed to offer a glimmer of hope and control during the encroaching darkness.

The room was suddenly bathed in a warm, golden light spilling across every surface. The overpowering chill that had clung to my skin like an icy shroud lifted, replaced by a soothing warmth that enveloped me in a comforting embrace. The warmth seeped into my bones, a gentle, nurturing presence that felt like the embrace of a long-lost friend. I noticed a small door at the far end of the room, previously hidden by the encroaching shadows. It now stood illuminated by the golden light, its surface gleaming softly. I walked toward the small door, the key in my hand warm and solid, symbolizing my reclaimed power. Its intricate design pulsed with the same golden light that now filled the room. I approached the door and noticed that the patterns on the key echoed the elaborate patterns now visible on the door. Turning the key, I felt a satisfying click and heard the gentle creak of the door opening. As it swung wide, a path revealed itself, bathed in the same radiant light that now enveloped the room. As I stepped through the threshold, my senses were immediately engulfed in a symphony of beauty and serenity. The grand hall before me stretched into a mesmerizing expanse, where cascading waterfalls adorned every wall, their glittering streams dancing in the soft, ambient light.

The sight was nothing short of magical—each waterfall's delicate curtain shimmered like liquid crystal, refracting beams of light into a dazzling array of rainbows that played across the floor and walls. The visual splendor was enhanced by the rhythmic flow of the water, which created a soothing, melodic patter as each drop joined the pool below with a gentle, almost musical splash.

The air was filled with a tranquil ambiance, as if the hall itself breathed in harmony with the waterfalls. The sound was an enchanting, continuous murmur, a gentle lullaby that resonated through the space and wrapped around me like a warm embrace. It was as if the water's soft whispers were communicating secrets of calm and relaxation, washing away the noise of the outside world. As I reached out to touch the flowing water, a cool, refreshing sensation met my fingertips. The water's touch was like a delicate caress, a crisp yet gentle embrace that left a fine, damp trail on my skin. The sensation was invigorating and soothing, a tactile reminder of nature's graceful power. The droplets seemed to linger for a moment, leaving a faint, pleasant chill that contrasted beautifully with the warmth of the surrounding atmosphere, drawing me further into the tranquil enchantment of the hall. As I approached the cascading waterfalls, something unusual captured my attention. At first, it was a subtle, almost invisible shift in the water's gleaming surface. But as I drew nearer, the mesmerizing flow of the waterfalls seemed to ripple and undulate in a way that revealed fleeting glimpses of a different reality. The shimmering curtain of water began to transform before my eyes. Each cascading stream momentarily parted to unveil fleeting images, like delicate, transparent veils hanging in mid-air.

These images, bathed in the soft, golden glow of the ambient light, floated through the water's flow, shimmering like reflections on a pond.

****

I sat at my desk, my heart racing with nerves and excitement. The laptop before me displayed the final confirmation screen for publishing my book online. Beside me, Luke stood, his hand gently holding mine in a reassuring grip. The room was filled with suspense as if the walls held their breath for this moment.

"Okay, here goes nothing."

I clicked the 'Publish' button, and a jolt of energy surged through me. The screen blinked with a confirmation message, and I felt my breath catch as I turned to Luke. My eyes, now glistening, met his with a mix of astonishment and elation, a smile spreading across my face that spoke louder than any words could.

He smiles warmly, "You did it, Dee. You officially published your book." with a tender kiss, he seals his words, his joy and pride evident in the gentle touch of his lips.

"I did… I actually did it." I said as my voice trembled,

Luke pulled me into a tight embrace, "I'm so proud of you, Dee. You've worked incredibly hard for this moment."

"Thank you, Luke. I couldn't have done it without you." I said as tears formed in my eyes,

"It feels surreal," I said as I stared at my published book on the laptop,

Luke gently wiped away my tears with a tender touch. "You deserve every bit of this, Dee," he murmured, his voice filled with warmth. "Every page you've written, every hurdle you've overcome—it's all right here, a testament to your incredible talent and determination."

A smile broke through my tears as I looked up at him. "I feel happy, Luke. Truly happy."

He brushed a soft kiss against my forehead, his touch both soothing and celebratory. "As you should be," he whispered, his words enveloping me in a cocoon of love and pride.

Yet, the water shifted, revealing the setbacks of my past. I saw myself facing rejection from publishers; their words cut deep as they told me my story wasn't what people wanted. They urged me to compromise my vision, demanding more violence or explicit scenes. Each rejection threatened to extinguish my spirit, but always, always, Luke was there, holding my hand, reminding me of my worth.

"They...they have turned me down," I murmured, my voice barely above a whisper, "They said because I didn't change the ending, they are no longer interested," I watched as Luke walked in wearing his work overalls, his face etched with fatigue. Without a word, he crossed the room and sank beside me, his presence a comforting balm.

Luke's hand tightened around mine, reassuring me I wasn't alone in this recollection. "That's okay, there are others out there," he said softly, his gaze filled with belief. "You will find someone, and your book will be out there, "You believe in your vision; don't give up." As he pulled me close, his warmth and steady heartbeat against my side offered a quiet strength, reminding me that, together, we would face every challenge.

I nodded, remembering the temptation to compromise, to mold my story into something more marketable. But Luke had been there, a beacon of steadfast support. "It's tempting, though," I admitted, "to give in, to change everything just to please them."

"But you didn't," Luke affirmed, his voice unwavering. "You stayed true to yourself, even when it was the hardest thing to do."

Emotions brimmed in my eyes as I looked at him, overwhelmed by deep love and motivation.

"Because you believe in me," I whispered, "when everyone else doubted, you are there."

He pulled away slightly, lifting my chin with gentle fingers, his gaze filled with love and pride. His expression softened, each gesture a testament to his unwavering support. "I know your story was worth telling, Dee," he said gently. "It's about more than just pleasing others—about staying true to yourself."

A small smile tugged at the corners of my lips, a glimmer of happiness amidst the memories. "Thank you, Luke," I said, my voice catching with emotion, "for never letting me forget."

"You're stronger than any rejection, Dee," he murmured against my hair. "Look how far you've come." I closed my eyes, leaning into his chest, listening to his steady heartbeat, finding reassurance in his tireless belief.

"With you by my side," I whispered, "I can overcome anything."

In that small moment, surrounded by the warmth of Luke's love. I saw moments where I faltered, where self-doubt clouded my beliefs. Yet, these moments were not failures but lessons, each showing me my confidence in myself and trusting my instincts. Water began to drip down from the ceiling in the grand hall; I stood there, feeling its cool touch on my skin. The trickles turned into streams, then torrents, as the ceiling buckled under the pressure. The once distant waterfall now roared closer, its thunderous crash deafening, and the entire room shuddered as the water surged forward. Plumes of mist and spray filled the air, drenching everything in its path, as the mighty cascade relentlessly advanced, tearing through the hall with unstoppable force.

This time, my heart remained steady. With my hand outstretched to the side, I welcomed the water as it enveloped me. The cool liquid wrapped around me like a familiar embrace, each droplet whispering tales of triumphs and trials. The water flowed over my skin, carrying with it the echoes of my past, mingling the warmth of hard-won victories with the sting of old wounds. As the water washed over me, I felt a transformation within. Each drop seemed to carry away my doubts and fears, leaving behind only strength and understanding. The gentle pressure of the water massaged my skin, soothing away tension. My heart lightened with each passing second. I closed my eyes, surrendering to the sensation, feeling a deep, purifying cleanse that touched both body and soul. Each breath I took felt lighter, each heartbeat steadier. The noise of the waterfall began to fade, replaced by a serene silence that enveloped me.

When I opened my eyes again, I found myself in a different room far from the waterfall. This space was a serene haven filled with delicate pink blossoms and expansive windows stretched from floor to ceiling, revealing an endless sky where clouds drifted lazily without a trace of land in sight. In the center of the room was a freestanding bathtub bathed in soft natural light. Its elegant design was complemented by the surrounding floor of water, shimmering like a serene bath mat. The scent of blossoms and a hint of lavender created an intoxicating aroma that tugged at my senses. My gaze was drawn to the bathtub, its elegance beckoning me closer, the water inside mirroring the tranquility of the sky beyond the windows. This room reminded me of the moments of beauty I had found amidst the chaos of my journey. The gentle fragrance brought back memories of Luke's warm embrace, his cologne always laced with a similar floral note. The sunlight streaming through the expansive windows mirrored the golden hue of his eyes, and the tranquil atmosphere of the room echoed the peace I felt in his presence. I took a deep breath, feeling the cool water beneath my feet, and imagined Luke's hand in mine. Every detail of the room, from the delicate pink blossoms to the tranquil bathtub, whispered his name, reminding me of the quiet strength and unwavering support he always provided. My yearning for Luke grew with each passing moment, an intense desire to feel his presence again. Though I knew thinking he could be here was irrational, the room's calm and beauty made it almost seem possible.

As I stepped closer, a hazy image began to form in the tub, and my breath caught in my throat. Amid the floating blossoms, I saw Luke sitting there with a calm expression; his eyes closed as if lost in a peaceful reverie. He was bare-chested, the gentle curve of his shoulders and the smooth line of his chest glistening faintly in the ambient light. The sight was a gut-wrenching blend of hope and disbelief, each detail piercing through the fog of my thoughts. My heart hammered against my ribs, each beat echoing in the quiet room.

The scent of blossoms grew more intense, filling my senses and wrapping around my chest like a gentle but unyielding vice. My heart raced, its frantic rhythm echoing in my ears as the boundaries between reality and illusion began to blur. The once-clear outlines of the bathtub, the floating petals, and Luke's vision seemed to meld into a single, shimmering, captivating scene. The gentle ripples in the water distorted his image, creating a mesmerizing dance of light and shadow that made it hard to discern what was real and what was a haunting mirage. His eyes fluttered open, revealing the familiar warmth and depth I had missed so dearly. For a brief moment, our gazes locked. His eyes, filled with an earnest, inviting light, softened as they met mine. He raised a hand slowly, his fingers beckoning toward me with a gentle, almost imperceptible motion. The water around him seemed to ripple in response, creating a path that shimmered with an ethereal glow. His lips curved into a soft, reassuring smile, and the calm expression on his face seemed to promise a sanctuary from my turmoil.

With trembling fingers, I reached for the straps of my dress, the fabric whispering softly as it slid down my shoulders and pooled around my feet. The sound was faint, like a sigh that echoed the flutter of my heart. When the dress fell to the floor in a soft heap, the cool air brushed against my naked skin, sending a cold tremor along my spine. The allure of the bathtub, with its promise of peace and connection with Luke, tugged insistently at my senses. Each step I took forward was hesitant yet eager. My bare feet brushed against the water's edge, the cool liquid seeping into my toes with a surprising, refreshing chill. With a deep breath, I sank into the tub, the water rising to gently embrace me. The cool liquid enveloped me, and the delicate petals floating on the surface brushed against my skin, their touch like a caress. Each blossom, with its delicate pink hue, spun in a slow, hypnotic dance, creating a mesmerizing pattern that swirled around me. The petals formed a cocoon of soft color and texture, cradling me in their gentle hold. The sight of them drifting serenely in the water was almost surreal, their delicate movement a soothing rhythm that seemed to sync with the pounding of my heart. The vision of Luke grew stronger.

His presence felt so real that I could almost hear his voice and feel the warmth of his touch. I reached out, my fingers trailing through the water, but the vision began to fade, his form dissipating like mist under the morning sun. The petals around me seemed to thicken, their soft rustling a whisper in my ears. They danced and swirled; suddenly, the room around me blurred and the petals, which had seemed so light and harmless, started to cling to my skin, pulling me down with a surprising strength. I tried to brush them away, but their grip tightened, wrapping around my limbs like tiny, persistent fingers. Panic set in as I struggled against the weightless yet unyielding force dragging me under. The water, once clear and inviting, now felt like a suffocating trap. Every time I tried to push myself up, more blossoms swarmed around me, their beauty becoming a deceptive snare. My heart pounded, and my breath quickened, the serene moment turning into a disorienting battle against the floral tide. I could feel the petals wrapping around me, pulling me deeper, the weight of their delicate forms paradoxically heavy.

The boundaries between the present and the past blurred into a dreamlike haze. The petals continued their gentle, hypnotic dance, their soft rustling like a lullaby wrapped around me, drawing me deeper into a cocoon of longing and memory. The serene haven of blossoms began to waver and dissolve, their delicate hues fading as the room around me started to distort and swirl. The tranquil scent of flowers grew faint, replaced by the heavy, steamy aroma of a small, cramped bathroom. I found myself no longer surrounded by the gentle embrace of the bathtub but standing in a dimly lit bathroom, the walls closing in with their grimy tiles and the pervasive scent of soap. My past self sat in the corner of the shower, huddled beneath the cascading water that fell like a curtain of consolation.

I heard Luke lightly knock on the door, "Dee, are you okay?" his voice filled with concern as he asked to come in. There was no answer; the only sound was my quiet, choked sobs, bouncing off the tiled walls and merging with the rushing water from the showerhead. The door creaked open, and Luke stepped in, his clothes clinging to him as he stepped through the thin veil of steam. Without a word, he stepped into the shower, fully dressed. The water streamed off his clothes, drenching him as he wrapped his arms around me. He shifted slightly, reaching behind him to turn off the faucet, and the steady rush of water ceased. His arms felt even more secure in the sudden silence, holding me close as if to shield me from the grief that had taken over."

"I thought... I thought this time was going to be different," my voice cracked, barely above a whisper, my words catching in the thick silence.

He drew me closer, his arms wrapping around me with a comforting but shaky grip. "I know," he murmured, his voice trembling. "I thought so, too. I was so sure this time..."

I lifted my tear-streaked face to his, my eyes swollen and heavy with a deep, anguished resignation. "How many times... how many times do we have to endure this?" I asked, my voice cracking under the weight of my plea. My gaze fell to the ultrasound photo I clutched tightly in my damp hands, the image now smeared and curling from the shower's relentless spray. Each drop of water on the photo felt like another layer of our loss, blurring the hopeful image that had once brought us so much anticipation.

He swallowed hard, and the lump in his throat made speaking difficult. "I don't know," he managed, his voice barely audible. I looked away, unable to meet his eyes, and wiped away the tears that had begun to streak my face. The silence between us grew heavy and suffocating, punctuated only by the quiet, sorrowful sniffles that seemed to linger in the stillness of the room.

Luke held me close, his arms strong and secure around my trembling form. The fabric of his soaked clothes pressed against my bare skin, cold and clammy yet somehow comforting. He gently lifted me from the wet floor of the shower, the tiled surface slick beneath us. The cold air outside the shower caused goosebumps to rise on my damp skin. With careful, deliberate steps, he carried me to our bed. Each movement was measured as if he feared I might shatter. The scent of his wet clothes mingled with the faint aroma of our bed linens, a familiar blend of lavender and clean cotton that brought a small measure of comfort. As he laid me down, the soft fabric of the sheets caressed my skin. Luke's touch was tender, his fingers brushing hair away from my face. Each kiss he pressed against my forehead and cheeks was like a whisper of warmth, his lips soft and gentle. They carried his reassurance like a lifeline, a silent promise that we would endure this pain together. His love and support enveloped me, a steady presence in the midst of my turmoil. The bed creaked slightly as he settled beside me, his body heat radiating through the blanket. The distant hum of the house marked the quiet of the room, the rhythmic ticking of a clock, and the sound of our mingled breaths.

"It's not your fault, Dee," Luke murmured, his voice a soothing balm against the ache in my heart. "I love you," he continued, each word a promise etched in the air around us. He began to kiss my bare, naked body, showing me the passion in his words; every time his lips touched my skin, a fire burned within me, wanting more. His kisses trailed down my neck, the warmth of his breath sending shivers through me. His hands roamed gently, his tentative and reassuring touch grounding me in the present moment. I could feel the rough texture of his wet clothes against my skin, a reminder of our shared vulnerability.

Luke's lips continued their journey, each kiss igniting a spark that spread warmth through my body. He kissed the curve of my shoulder and the hollow of my collarbone. His warm and even breath was a steady rhythm against the hurried thrum of my heart. As he moved lower, his hands caressed my sides, fingertips grazing my ribs, sending waves of anticipation through me. The fire within me grew, stoked by the gentle, insistent pressure of his lips and the slow, deliberate pace of his movements.

He paused for a moment, his gaze meeting mine, eyes filled with love and desire. "You are everything to me, Dee," he whispered, his voice thick with emotion. "We'll get through this together." His words, filled with sincerity and passion, cradled me. I reached up, my fingers tangling in his hair, pulling him closer. With each kiss, each touch, Luke reminded me of the strength we shared, the love that bound us together. Our movements became more urgent and insistent. As the night wore on, we found comfort in the intimacy, each caress and whispered words a balm to our wounded hearts. The pain of our loss began to fade, replaced by the gentle, enduring flame of our connection.

As I emerged from the water, petals clinging to my soaked skin, the cool air hit me like a jolt. My heart ached with an insistent pull, a desperate need to return to the moments when Luke's touch had felt so real. The scent of the blossoms around me, mixed with the lingering traces of his cologne in my memory, made the present moment feel empty and hollow. Without giving myself time to fully grasp the scenes playing out in my mind, I sank back into the bathtub, the water closing over my head. The water rippled and cleared, revealing a vivid scene of our bedroom. The familiar scent of coconut oil filled the air, sweet and tropical, instantly calming. I saw my younger self resting on my stomach, the cool, crisp sheets beneath me contrasting with the warmth radiating from Luke's hands. His presence was palpable, a reassuring weight next to me as he delicately spread the warm oil over my skin. Each touch was deliberate, his fingers gliding smoothly with the aid of the fragrant oil. The warmth seeped into my muscles, relaxing them under his practiced grace. The soft glow of the bedside lamp cast a gentle light, highlighting the sheen of the oil on my skin and the careful movements of his hands.

Luke's fingers kneaded and soothed, working out knots of tension I hadn't even realized were there. His touch brought a tenderness and care that words could never fully express. The rhythmic motion of his hands created a sense of safety and peace, each stroke a silent promise of his love and support. The coconut scent, combined with the warmth and intimacy of the moment, enveloped me in a cocoon of tranquility, making it easy to forget the world outside our haven.

"You seem tense," he murmured, his hands working magic on my shoulders. I melted into his touch, grateful for the relief as my fibro had flared up earlier that week. I hadn't wanted to worry Luke by mentioning it.

"Oh, really?" I replied playfully, trying to hide my discomfort.

"You know, Dee, you can tell me anything on your mind," he said softly, pausing in his ministrations. I hesitated, unsure whether to confess to him. After a moment, he turned me around, his eyes filled with concern and desire as he gazed at me.

"Maybe I should focus on your front," he suggested, his tone becoming more seductive. I bit my lip, feeling a rush of anticipation as he released a soft sigh.

"Maybe you should," I whispered, unable to resist. He wasted no time in savoring every moment of touching my body.

In one swift, fluid motion, he flipped me over, my back pressing into the cool sheets. The sudden movement left me breathless, my heart pounding with a mix of excitement and desire. As he settled above me, his eyes roamed over my bare body, darkening with a hungry intensity that sent a thrill through me. The coconut scent mingled with the musky aroma of our shared desire, creating a heady atmosphere that heightened every sensation. His fingers brushed along my collarbone, tracing a slow, deliberate path down to my breasts. Each touch was like a spark, igniting a trail of heat that spread through my entire being.

"You're so beautiful," he murmured, his voice thick with emotion. His eyes never left mine, even as his hands continued their explorations. He leaned in, his lips capturing mine in a kiss that was both tender and urgent. I felt the warmth of his breath against my skin, the gentle press of his body against mine. His hands moved lower, caressing my stomach, hips, and thighs with a reverence that made my heart ache with love and longing.

His fingers danced over my skin, exploring every curve and contour as if committing them to memory. I arched into his touch, my body responding to his with an almost overwhelming need. When he finally settled between my legs, his eyes met mine once more, filled with a blend of love and raw desire. "Tell me what you need, Dee," he whispered, his voice a low rumble that sent shivers down my spine.

"I need you," I breathed, my voice trembling with the intensity of my emotions. "I need you more than anything."

He smiled, a slow, seductive curve of his lips that promised everything I longed for. "I'm yours," he replied.

Returning to the reality of the blossom-filled chamber, I shivered as the warmth of Luke's touch faded. Wanting to climb out, I settled not to torment myself with these bittersweet memories any longer. All I wanted was Luke.

Emerging from the bath, I paused to absorb the room's beauty again, letting the serene ambience wash over me. My heart ached for him, longing to be closer again. I reached for my dress and draped it over my damp skin, feeling the weight of the fabric against me. With a deep breath, I walked toward the door.

"I'm coming, Luke."

The Power of Choice

As I exited the blossom-filled room, a strange sense of calm washed over me. The delicate petals and gentle fragrance had been a welcome salvation. I turned back for a final glance, the door softly closing behind me with a quiet click. The hallway stretched endlessly before me again, but as I walked, a curious transformation began. With each step I took, the vibrant colors of the doors seemed to fade, and the intricate patterns started to blur. I stopped in my tracks, observing with awe and confusion. The doors, each holding a fragment of my past, were now starting to vanish. The wooden panels that had seemed so important and daunting were dissolving into nothing, leaving only the smooth, bare walls behind. It was as if they were melting away, their significance diminishing as I confronted and overcame the inner conflicts they symbolized.

It dawned on me that the vanishing doors were more than just physical changes—they were symbols of my progress. Each time I walked through one and faced what lay beyond it, each challenge I overcame or emotion I resolved seemed to strip away another layer of my inner barriers.

The doors were not just barriers but markers of my journey, each representing a part of myself that I had faced and understood. As I passed a door, an unsettling sensation prickled at the back of my neck. My senses sharpened, facing the door, and my breath caught in my throat. Unlike any other door I had seen before, this one was made entirely from a dense, impenetrable darkness. The door wasn't merely covered in shadows; it was as if the darkness itself had been forged into a solid form. Its surface was a void so profound that it seemed to absorb all light and color, creating an unsettling void that seemed to pulse with an eerie, rhythmic energy. I glanced toward the darkness that seemed to pulse with a life of its own. The air grew cold, and an eerie silence fell over the corridor.

Suddenly, an unseen force gripped my arms with a vise-like intensity, dragging me toward a door that I had not noticed before. I fought desperately against the force pulling me, my fingers scrabbling at the door frame as if it were my last lifeline. My nails scraped against the rough wood, and my breaths came in panicked, ragged gasps. The door creaked open with a groan that seemed to reverberate through my very bones, the sound echoing like a dirge in the oppressive silence. In a heartbeat, I was yanked through the threshold. The world around me shifted violently. The corridor I had been in dissolved into a vortex of darkness, the very air vibrating with an eerie hum. Tendrils of shadowy forms coiled around me, their presence palpable and suffocating. They swirled ominously, their undulating movements creating a disorienting spiral that tugged at my sanity. I tried to scream for help, but my voice was swallowed by the darkness, rendering my cries mere whispers against the all-consuming void.

Twisted shapes loomed around me, their forms ever-shifting and barely discernible in the gloom. Eerie whispers wove through the air, their hissing voices merging into a cacophony of dread. The whispers seemed to speak of my fears, echoing my anxieties in a language I could almost understand but not quite grasp. The sensation of being engulfed by this realm of shadows was overwhelming. It felt as though the darkness was closing in, tightening around me like a suffocating shroud. The fear was visceral, a tangible force that wrapped itself around my chest, making each breath a struggle. My heartbeat pounded in my ears, a frantic rhythm that seemed to sync with the throbbing darkness around me.

"Fuck!" I exclaimed, my voice trembling as I fought to push back the rising tide of panic. "What is this place? I can't... I can't see anything!"

A tentacle of darkness brushed against me, and the sensation was immediately unsettling—a cold, fluid touch that seemed to seep through my skin and into my very soul. In an instant, the surrounding shadows seemed to ripple and shift, merging into a haunting vision that materialized from the darkness. The cold, oppressive weight of the tentacle pressed down on me, and the scene began to unfold before my eyes. It was as if the darkness itself had become a canvas, and I was forced to watch a scene from my past being projected in vivid, unsettling clarity. The shadows revealed a haunting vision—a memory I had long buried. I saw my father, distant and cold, leaving me behind in a haze of abandonment. The pain of that moment surged through me, raw and overwhelming, as if I were reliving it all over again.

"Dad," the teenage version of myself called out as I watched my father climb into the car without glancing at me. Where are you going? Why is Mum crying?" I called out, but he just closed the door. "No, Daddy, please don't leave me! I need you!" I yelled out despite tears blurring my vision as I began to chase the car down the street.

The vision disappeared like smoke. A sharp pain formed in my chest as though an unseen hand had tightened its grip around my heart. My fingers dug into my palms, the pressure so intense that my knuckles whitened, and the creases of my skin turned white. The vision of my father, distant and cold, still lingered in my mind, the raw pain of that moment echoing like a constant drumbeat. My vision blurred as I fought to hold back the tears, my lashes brushing against my cheeks with each shaky blink. I pressed the heels of my hands to my eyes, trying to block out the overwhelming sting that threatened to break free. The darkness around me seemed to pulse, its cold tendrils wrapping tighter around my heart. The air was thick and heavy, like a great weight was pressing down on my shoulders, pulling me deeper into a chasm of sorrow. My body trembled uncontrollably, the weight of the despair anchoring me in place, making every breath a struggle against the suffocating gloom that enveloped me.

Did I push him away? Was it my fault he had retreated into himself, leaving me alone in the void he had created? The guilt was a searing pain that intertwined with the grief, making my thoughts churn with relentless self-blame. The absence of my father in those crucial moments of my life had been like a gaping hole, a missing piece that left me feeling incomplete and lost.

"Why do you keep showing me these memories?" I pleaded, my words echoing softly in the void. The shadow remained silent, a looming presence that seemed to absorb my words without response.

"He left. Why does he matter?" My voice cracked with emotion, and my hands clenched into fists. I searched the darkness for answers, but only the unsettling quiet greeted me.

Instead of answering me, the formless darkness began solidifying, and through the swirling obscurity emerged a figure that I could no longer ignore. The shadows took on a familiar shape, merging into my father's stern, distant visage. His eyes, cold and unreadable, locked onto mine with an unsettling intensity. The ghostly figure seemed to mirror my anguish, its presence a haunting reflection of the pain and abandonment I had felt. I stared at the indistinct figure resembling my father; fear tightened its grip around my heart. "Are you going to leave too?" I whispered, my voice barely audible amidst the swirling darkness. The shadowy figure remained silent, its form wavering as if contemplating the question. It seemed to embody all my fears of abandonment, bringing back memories of my father's distant departure and the ache of loneliness that followed.

"Leave!" I screamed, my voice echoing off the walls of the empty room, the sound reverberating through the cavernous space like a desperate cry for relief. The figure remained motionless, an oppressive presence that refused to dissipate, its form a haunting reminder of all the pain and disappointment it had caused.

"I was never enough for you!" I continued, my voice cracking with raw emotion. "You left me feeling like I was nothing but a burden, just a speck of dirt you couldn't be bothered to clean off your shoe. Your absence was like a gaping wound that never healed, making me doubt everything about myself."

The anger surged through me, a searing heat that boiled my blood and made my hands tremble. "You never cared about me or Mom; it was always about you and your needs and desires. We were just collateral damage in your self-centered world."

I felt a wave of despair crash over me as the weight of my words hung heavy in the air. "Because of you, I almost lost the love of my life. I was so consumed by your ghost, by the shadow of your absence, that I nearly drove away the one person who made me feel whole. And now? Now, I'm left feeling like I'm nothing, unworthy of love and happiness because of the void you left behind." My knees gave way, and I collapsed to the floor in front of this shadowy presence.

I felt a weight settle upon my shoulders, the weight of unanswered questions and unresolved emotions. The darkness around me pressed closer, enveloping me in a suffocating embrace of uncertainty and fear. Every victory I had achieved, every triumph I had celebrated in the rooms before now seemed to evaporate into insignificance. The courage I had summoned, the battles I had fought, and the progress I had made were overshadowed by the relentless flood of doubt that now engulfed me. Yet, despite the overwhelming presence of my anxieties manifested in the shadow form, a flicker of determination sparked within me. I thought of Luke, the love and support he had given me through my darkest moments. His presence was a reminder of why I couldn't give up. The memory of his smile, the strength of his embrace, and the kindness in his eyes fueled a resolve that refused to be extinguished.

I inhaled deeply, summoning all my strength as I pushed myself to my feet, steeling myself against the onslaught of memories and fears that threatened to overwhelm me.

"I won't let you consume me," I whispered defiantly to the shadow, a quiet resolve strengthening my voice. With each word, I felt a glimmer of courage flicker within me, pushing back against the shadows that sought to trap me in their grasp. I ignited a strength I had forgotten I possessed. Drawing on this inner power, I could feel the heat building inside me, growing brighter and more intense with every breath. The shadows wavered, their hold loosening as the light within me swelled.

A sudden, blinding burst of radiant light erupted from the core of my being, a fierce and uncontainable brilliance that seemed to tear through the fabric of darkness surrounding me. The light surged outward in a brilliant explosion, casting stark shadows and making the oppressive gloom recoil as if scorched by its intensity. The room was bathed in an ethereal glow, the walls and floor shimmering with an almost tangible luminescence that felt both exhilarating and overwhelming. The brilliance was so intense that it felt like a physical force, pressing against my skin and saturating my senses with its searing energy. My eyes stung from the sheer radiance, the light so dazzling it left trails of afterimages dancing behind my closed eyelids. It was as though the very essence of the light had seeped into every pore, making me feel simultaneously weightless and anchored by its profound clarity. As the light stabilized, the harsh, blinding brilliance softened into a warm, soothing glow. I took a deep breath, feeling the cool, refreshing air fill my lungs, carrying with it a sense of serenity and renewal. The room, now bathed in a gentle, calming illumination, seemed to exhale with me, its once oppressive atmosphere now replaced by an inviting tranquility. The memories and traumas that had haunted me for so long felt like distant echoes, their presence still there but now muted and less insistent. The darkness that had once seemed all-encompassing was now reduced to mere shadows, fading into the periphery of my mind. It was as if the light had not only dispelled the physical gloom but had also created a buffer, a protective barrier that allowed me to see my past with a new perspective. I was no longer entangled in the suffocating grip of my past; the overwhelming weight had lifted, replaced by a sense of acceptance and understanding. The light had not erased my memories but had given me the space and clarity to confront them on my own terms.

"I won't let you belittle me," I murmured to the lingering shadow, now mere wisps of darkness at the edges of my consciousness. "You weren't there when it mattered, so why should you matter now?"

As the intense burst of light gradually faded, its searing brilliance softened into a warm, gentle radiance that lingered in the air. The blinding glare diminished, and with it, the room around me seemed to dissolve, melting away like mist in the morning sun. I found myself standing once again in the vast, sprawling hallway. The transition was almost invisible, like waking from a vivid dream into a reality that felt equally surreal. Suddenly, a new presence caught my eye: a door. It was situated slightly off-center, drawing my attention. It was framed by intricate carvings that seemed to writhe and shift subtly, their complex patterns mesmerizing. The wood was dark and polished, with a deep, rich hue that absorbed the surrounding light, making it appear almost as if it were emerging from the shadows rather than part of the corridor. The ornate handle was cold, its metalwork finely detailed with delicate spirals and geometric patterns. I turned it slowly.

On the other side of the door, I was greeted by a breathtaking and baffling sight that took my breath away. The space before me was a vast expanse of intertwined staircases, a labyrinth of reflective surfaces that twisted and spiraled in every direction. The staircases seemed to float in an endless, shimmering void, their polished surfaces catching and scattering the ambient light into a thousand dazzling fragments. The intricate design created a dizzying visual effect, with steps ascending and descending in a seemingly chaotic dance, merging seamlessly into one another. The stairs were composed entirely of mirrors, their reflective quality amplifying the sense of boundlessness. As I gazed at the intricate display, I saw countless versions of myself and the world mirrored infinitely into the distance. The reflections multiplied, creating overwhelming images that shifted and blended with each movement.

With awe and worry, I stepped onto the mirrored staircase. The sensation beneath my feet was oddly smooth and slightly cool, the surface giving way just enough to feel both solid and supernatural. The mirrors beneath me rippled as my weight pressed down, creating a wave-like distortion that flowed outwards, causing the reflections to shimmer and warp. Each step I took brought with it a flood of shifting images. The mirrors reacted dynamically to my movement, reflecting not just my current self but also vivid snapshots of my past. I saw fragmented scenes play out before me, each step triggering a new memory. One particular image emerged as I reached a new part of the staircase: my mother lying in a hospital bed, her once-vibrant face now pale and weary from illness. The beeping of medical equipment and the distant murmur of doctors and nurses felt real, as if I could hear them despite the absence of sound. The reflection of her pain struck me like a physical blow, gripping my heart with a renewed ache. It was as though the mirrors had pulled the raw, unhealed fragments of that memory to the surface, forcing me to confront the agony of watching her slowly succumb to her illness. The sensation was bare as if the mirrors were not just reflecting but reliving the pain, making it impossible to ignore. Another step showed my friend dying in front of my eyes, the helplessness and grief consuming me anew. I could still see her, crumpled and lifeless, the vibrant spark that once defined Evie extinguished in an instant. The sight hit me like a punch to the gut, and I was overwhelmed by a wave of helplessness and grief. My legs felt as if they were sinking into the staircase, immobilized by the weight of my sorrow. I stood there, paralyzed, unable to move or even cry out. My voice was trapped in my throat, and tears, though ready to fall, stayed stubbornly hidden. All I could do was watch as my world seemed to shatter around me.

These events created a ripple that would never cease to spread. It altered the very fabric of my existence. The mirrors continued to reveal the abandonment by my father, the deep scars his departure left behind. Each memory played out in the mirrors—Luke and our life together, the love and challenges we faced. I saw my rejections from publishing companies, each a blow to my dreams and a source of solidity. The constant battle with fibromyalgia, the pain, and fatigue, but also the strength it had forged within me. The mirrored staircases required careful attention. The paths twisted unpredictably, some ascending while others looped back, creating a dizzying effect. The mirrors, flawlessly polished, reflected every movement, their surfaces shimmering and shifting with each step. My footsteps echoed softly, adding to the disorienting experience. Despite the confusion, a subtle sense of purpose guided me. Each step seemed to vibrate with quiet assurance, leading me toward understanding and resolution. The shifting reflections provided both a challenge and a beacon, suggesting that a path to inner peace was within reach despite the chaos. With each memory and reflection, I realized how every choice and experience had shaped who I was in this present moment. The pain, the joy, the love, and the loss intertwined to form my life.

As I climbed higher, I noticed a faint, ethereal glow emanating from a distant point above. I pressed forward the intricate staircases with increasing confidence. The mirrored surfaces no longer felt like obstacles but rather like a reflection of my journey—complex, multifaceted, and ultimately leading me toward clarity. As I reached the top of the mirrored staircases, the shimmering reflections around me began to warp and twist. The air grew colder, and a sense of unease settled in my chest. The last step was unlike the others; instead of leading to another level of the reflective maze, it seemed to dissolve beneath my feet. For a moment, I was suspended in a void, weightless and adrift. Then, with a jolt, I found myself standing on a narrow path, the oppressive darkness pressing in from all sides. The mirrors were gone, replaced by an abyss that seemed to swallow the faint light from the path beneath me. I took a cautious step forward. My foot almost slipped, and I had to catch myself, realizing that the path was a narrow stretch with a long drop to nothing on either side. The ground was unstable, the width of the path barely enough to keep my balance. The rest of the room was swallowed by darkness, an inky void that seemed to pulse with an eerie silence.

Fear struck me like a sudden chill, seizing my senses with an icy grip. My breaths quickened, each inhale shallow and sharp as though the air itself had become a constricting force. I spun around, my movements frantic, eyes darting desperately for the familiar comfort of the room I had just left; there was no way back. I took a hesitant step forward, the path seemed to extend endlessly, a dizzying expanse with sheer drops on either side. Each step felt precarious, a delicate balance on the edge of the abyss. The air grew heavy, thick with tension pressed against my chest with each labored breath. The oppressive silence enveloped me, a deafening absence of sound that only heightened my isolation. Each step tested my will, the ground beneath me a constant reminder of the problematic drop. The rooms from before were nothing but a distant memory. All that was left was the path, the darkness, and the whisper of something unknown waiting at the end. I looked ahead, but there was nothing but dark space and the narrow path stretching into the void. I wondered where this path led, but with limited options, I had to trust that this place, my mind, this limbo, was on my side.

I tried to steady myself as I moved forward, my steps cautious and deliberate. The air around me was thick with a dense mist, swirling in shades of grey and black. Each breath I took was tinged with a damp, musty chill, carrying the faint scent of decay and forgotten places. The shadows below began to writhe and twist, taking on a life of their own. Slowly, the shadows merged into a scene, and I realized they formed a memory. I watched as the memory played out beneath me. It was a familiar scene, one that I had already been shown before. I saw myself, younger and full of warmth, tending to a little boy who had fallen off his bike. He was crying, a scrape on his knee, and I gently cleaned the wound, offering comforting words.

"What's your name?" my past self asked.

The boy sniffled, wiping his tears. "Luke," he replied in a small, shaky voice.

Hearing his name sent a jolt through me. Could this little boy be the same Luke I knew in the present? The coincidence was too striking to ignore.

As I watched, my younger self introduced herself, and a sense of familiarity and connection filled the memory.

"Nice to meet you, Luke. I'm Dee. Don't worry, you'll be just fine."

The memory faded, and I was left standing on the narrow path, the darkness around me seeming even more oppressive. A jolt of shock coursed through me, and my steps faltered. My eyes widened, straining to reconcile the swirling shadows beneath my feet with the surprising vision of a little boy who resembled Luke. *If this little boy was indeed the Luke I knew, had fate been guiding us together from the beginning? Were we always meant to be a part of each other's lives?* I took another cautious step forward, the shadows beneath me now a mix of comforting memories and haunting doubts. My heart ached with the possibility that Luke and I were destined to be together, yet I felt trapped in this limbo, unsure if I would ever return to him. *But if that were true, where did that leave me now? Would I ever make it back to him, or was this journey through my memories a cruel game that fate was playing?* The uncertainty gnawed at me, making me question everything I thought I knew.

As I continued down the path, the questions and fears lingered, but so did a glimmer of hope. If fate had brought us together once, it could do so again. I just had to keep moving, trusting that this journey had a purpose and that I would find my way back to him. Suddenly, a loud thump reverberated from the end of the narrow path, jolting me out of my thoughts. The sound was like a loud drumbeat; I strained to see through the now-deepening shadows, and a brief, flickering light cut through the darkness, casting eerie, shifting patterns on the walls. My heart raced, each beat pounding in my chest like a drum. Without a second thought to the dangerous drop that loomed on either side, my survival instincts kicked in. I dashed toward the flickering light with a burst of adrenaline, my steps hurried and frantic. The path felt like it was closing in around me, but the promise of the light ahead was a beacon I couldn't ignore.

I fueled each step with pure determination and trust in myself. The light ahead seemed to beckon me, a beacon of hope in all the uncertainty. But as I ran, the light remained still, not growing closer despite my efforts. Panic surged in my chest, a tight, choking sensation that made each breath come in ragged gasps, but I pushed forward, refusing to give in to despair. The path felt endless, the darkness closing in around me. *Was this another cruel trick of fate, teasing me with a glimpse of salvation I could never reach?*

As I ran, my thoughts raced. *I have to find Luke.* The thought of reuniting with him was the only thing driving me forward. *If there's even a chance, I can't let it slip away.* Doubts and exhaustion swirled around me, but the image of his face kept me going. *Is this the right path?* I pushed the question aside. *I need to keep moving.* The light ahead, no matter how distant, was my only hope. *I have to believe it's leading me back to him.* But as I continued to run toward the elusive light, frustration and anger began to well up inside me. Why was this journey so difficult? Why couldn't fate show me a clear path forward? I threatened to break through the determination that had sustained me thus far.

With each step, the ground beneath me seemed to grow more treacherous. Loose gravel and jagged edges made every stride perilous. My breath came in ragged gasps as I pushed myself harder, desperate to reach the light that remained stubbornly distant. The thumping sound grew louder as I continued forward, echoing in my ears like a heartbeat, urging me forward with a relentless rhythm. I focused all my energy on chasing that sound, willing myself to ignore the doubts and exhaustion that threatened to overwhelm me. But as the thumping intensified, so did my frustration and impatience. Anger simmered just beneath the surface, fueled by the relentless pursuit of something I couldn't quite grasp

And then, in my haste and frustration, I slipped.

Time seemed to slow as I fell, the narrow path offering no grip to halt my descent. Panic surged through me, my hands clawing desperately at the empty air. The darkness closed in, a suffocating shroud that swallowed my cries and left me tumbling through an endless void.

Are You Ready?

I landed abruptly on a hard surface, the impact jolting my already frayed nerves. My breath came in ragged gasps as I struggled to calm the lingering panic from the fall. The room was icy, the polished, glass-like floor radiating a sharp, biting chill that seeped through my clothes and numbed my skin. Confusion swirled around me, blending with the remnants of my fear. "What the hell?" I muttered aloud, my voice trembling as I tried to make sense of the stark, unfamiliar surroundings. Before my eyes, the entire room began to transform, shifting with a disorienting fluidity. The walls, floor, and ceiling melted into a seamless expanse of mirrors, each surface reflecting my startled face from every angle. The room became a labyrinth of endless reflections, where my confusion and fear seemed to multiply in infinite directions. The air was unnervingly sterile, carrying a faint, sharp scent of freshly cleaned glass that stung my nostrils. The polished surfaces caught and amplified every sound, the faint echo of my own breathing reverberating off the endless mirrors like a haunting chorus.

"Mirrors again," I sighed, recognizing the bizarre recurrence of these reflective surfaces in my journey.

I pushed myself up on shaky legs, the cold, hard surface beneath me feeling like a thin layer of ice. Each step was precarious, the floor's fragility evident with every movement. I stumbled forward, the sensation of instability making my legs tremble as I approached the nearest mirror wall. The glassy surface reflected my hesitant steps, the mirrored expanse amplifying my uncertainty and fear. The glass was cold and smooth under my fingers, but then, with a sudden crack, it began to fracture.When my hand touched the glass, a spiderweb of cracks spread out from the point of contact, splintering in all directions. The room around me shimmered and dissolved like a glitching simulation. As the mirrored fragments fell away, a scene emerged through the web of cracks.

I found myself standing in a memory, both disconnected and vividly present. I saw myself sitting on a weathered bench in a secluded part of the woods. The air was crisp, each breath stinging with the bite of winter. The trees stood bare against a gray sky, their skeletal branches reaching out like dark, twisted fingers. The ground was frosty, crunching underfoot as I moved closer. I remembered this day—it was the day my mother had passed away. My younger self sat on the bench, shoulders slumped and eyes vacant, a picture of utter desolation. The numbness I had felt then returned in a rush, an emptiness so profound it seemed to swallow everything else. My past self sat there, staring blankly ahead, lost in grief. I watched as Luke approached quietly and sat down beside me. He offered me his coat even though I didn't feel the cold. His presence was a silent comfort, a gesture of understanding in a moment of profound loss.

"Hey," Luke said softly, his voice barely audible above the leaves rustling in the winter breeze.

Silence hung between us, heavy and laden with unspoken emotions. I remained motionless, my gaze fixed on a point in the distance, lost in thoughts too heavy to bear.

"I know there are no words that can make this better. But I'm here if you need anything," Luke said gently, struggling to find the right words to say. I knew he was trying his hardest to provide comfort in his way. Luke placed the coat around me, ensuring I didn't get cold. My past self finally turned to look at Luke, my eyes red-rimmed and distant, reflecting the pain I felt inside.

"I don't understand, Luke" I whispered, my voice barely a murmur in the stillness of the woods. My words seemed to hang in the air, mingling with the soft rustling of the bare branches. "Why did this have to happen? Why did my mother have to die?" The cold seemed to press in on me, intensifying the weight of my grief. I struggled to grasp the reality of her absence. Each breath I took felt like a struggle, the crisp winter air stinging my lungs as if it were a physical manifestation of my sorrow. "How can I make sense of losing her?" I continued, my voice trembling as it cut through the silence. "Why did she have to go? I can't understand why she was taken from me."

"I wish I had answers for you. Sometimes, life is just cruel," Luke replied quietly, his voice filled with empathy.

I blinked rapidly, fighting to keep the tears at bay despite the emotional storm raging inside me. "I feel like I should be doing something... but I don't know what."

Luke reached out tentatively, placing his arm over my shoulder and pulling me in. "You don't have to do anything right now. Just let yourself feel. It's okay to be lost."

I nodded slightly, acknowledging Luke's presence and words and grateful for his support.

"Your mom... she loved you so much. That's something you'll always carry with you," Luke continued, his voice gentle yet firm.

"I miss her so much..." I choked out.

"I know. And that's okay," Luke murmured, his words a balm to my wounded heart. He leaned in, pressing a tender kiss to the side of my head, the softness of his lips a small but profound comfort. His hand began to rub my arm in slow, deliberate circles, his touch warm and reassuring against the biting chill of the winter air. We sit in silence for a while longer, the weight of grief hanging heavily between us. Luke remains steadfast beside me, offering silent support amid profound loss. I watched with sorrow and appreciation. Luke's simple act of kindness had meant more to me than words could express at the time. Moments like these proved to me that Luke was my soulmate and that he would be there no matter what.

As the spider web of cracks in the mirror began to shift and fade, the memory they revealed slowly receded. The vivid scene of the woods and the bench melted away, but the emotional impact lingered intensely. Tears welled up in my eyes, blurring my vision as the flood of emotions surged within me. My breath hitched, and I pressed a trembling hand to my mouth, trying to stifle the sobs that threatened to escape. The walls of mirrors around me seemed to ripple with the intensity of my feelings, each reflection capturing the raw ache in my chest.

Just as the last traces of the previous memory began to evaporate, a new crack appeared on the far side of the room. It spread slowly across one of the mirror panels, its jagged lines slicing through the glass with a faint, metallic whisper. The crack grew, and as it did, the mirrors around it started to warp and twist, distorting the reflections and creating an eerie, undulating effect. Through the widening fissure, another scene emerged. This time, I was seated at the familiar corner coffee shop. On this very spot, a car tragically hit Evie. It was a haunting memory etched deeply in my mind.

Across from me was my past self, who sat unmoving and vacant-eyed at one of the outdoor tables. I watched her gaze fixedly at the empty spot where Evie had lost her life, her expression devoid of any emotion. The constant buzzing of her phone broke the silence. Still, she seemed oblivious, lost in the torment of reliving that fateful moment. I reached out instinctively, wanting to shake her out of the haunting memory that held her captive. But I knew I was merely an observer now, unable to change the course of events that had already unfolded. The phone continued to ring, displaying Luke's name repeatedly. Each missed call was a reminder of the support and love he had tried to offer during those dark days. But my past self remained detached, trapped in the overwhelming grief and guilt that had consumed her after Evie's death. I felt an intense wave of frustration and helplessness as I reached out, my fingers straining toward her. I wanted to shake her, to pull her out of the suffocating grief that kept her captive. My hand passed through the air, an ineffectual gesture in the face of her emotional paralysis. The phone's vibrations intensified, each buzz a painful echo of the support she was ignoring.

"Answer the phone!" I shouted, my voice breaking through the stagnant air, but it felt like shouting into a void. "Luke is trying to reach you!" My frustration mounted as I watched her, unseeing and unmoved by the phone's persistent calls. "Don't shut him out! He's here for you, and you need him. You don't have to face this alone!" My pleas grew desperate, mingling with the phone's incessant ringing. Tears stung my eyes as I watched the scene unfold, knowing the pain and isolation my past self was experiencing. Knowing I had distanced myself from those who cared most about me. The phone continued to ring, creating a rift that had grown between Luke and me during those dark days. His name flashed on the screen.

"Please," I pleaded, my voice cracking. "Pick up the phone."

But my past self remained motionless. I swallowed hard. *How could I have let things unravel like this? How could I have shut out those who cared about me the most?* And then, as abruptly as I had arrived, the scene began to fade. The coffee shop dissolved around me, its edges curling and distorting like an old film reel catching fire. Colours bled together, and the once vivid images flickered and warped before disintegrating into a hazy, ethereal mist. I closed my eyes, trying to steady myself against the onslaught of emotions that threatened to overwhelm me. I closed my eyes, feeling my chest tighten as a wave of frustration and anger rose within me. My past self selfishness was like a slap in the face, a stark reminder of how she had shut out those who cared. The journey through my mind proved more challenging than anticipated, each memory a sharp reminder of my vulnerabilities and mistakes.

I had to keep going.

****

Trying to steady my racing heart, I took slow, deliberate breaths, pushing back against the gush of emotions and memories threatening to engulf me. I had to regain control and reclaim the person I was before this explosive journey began. I focused on the mirror's reflective surface, and I noticed something shifting before my eyes. Once a cold, unyielding barrier, the mirror started to shimmer and ripple, like water disturbed by a sudden breeze. The smooth, glassy surface quivered and twisted, transforming before me. The ripples grew more intense, spreading outward with a mesmerizing fluidity. My gaze was drawn to a deep, verdant green that seeped through the undulating surface. Gradually, the shimmering formed into the shape of a door. It emerged from the mirror like a ghost from a fog, its edges solidifying and taking on a rich, intricate texture. The door was an ancient, weathered wooden structure with ornate carvings and brass fixtures. The deep green shade of the door seemed almost out of place, a relic of a bygone era intruding into the present. The soft creak of old wood mingled with the quiet hum of the room. My heartbeat steadied, and a sense of cautious anticipation filled the space between the past and the future, signaling a new path to explore.

Feeling a mixture of wonder and determination, I reached for the green wooden door, its surface cool and textured under my fingertips. The wood, worn smooth from years of use, was intricately carved with delicate mushroom shapes, each one seeming to rise from the surface like a small, fantastical forest. Embedded within the door were etched glass panels, their dark, phoenix silhouettes glowing faintly in the dim light. Beyond the threshold, the world unfolded into a realm of pure fantasy. Mushroom-shaped trees, their caps swollen and variegated in shades of lavender, teal, and gold, rose majestically from the forest floor. The trunks were thick and deformed, covered in soft, luminescent moss that glowed faintly in the light. The ground was a vibrant tapestry of flowers in hues that seemed almost surreal, their petals glistening with dew that caught the light like tiny prisms. The air was rich with the intoxicating aroma of blooming flora, a heady blend of sweet nectar and subtle hints of earthiness that teased my senses with every breath. Each inhalation felt like a sip of something pure and refreshing, invigorating my spirit. As I ventured deeper into this enchanted forest, the phoenix birds drifted overhead, their feathers aflame with crimson, gold, and orange shades. Their majestic, powerful and smooth wings cut through the air with a gentle whoosh, sending down a cascade of sparkling embers. These glowing trails danced in the air, leaving a shimmering light that flickered like fireflies, adding to the ethereal quality of the landscape. The phoenixes' soft cries, melodic and distant, blended harmoniously with the rustling of the giant mushroom caps and the whisper of the gentle breeze. Their fiery glow created a warm, comforting illumination, transforming the forest into a living, breathing painting of wonder.

The path beneath my feet was a plush carpet of moss and flower petals, yielding softly with each step. As I walked, the vibrant flowers seemed to lean aside, parting like a living pathway to guide me forward. The scenery became more enchanting, and my journey felt increasingly like an exploration of my own inner landscape rather than just a physical path. I reached a clearing where the towering mushroom trees arched inward, their caps forming a natural, protective circle. In the center stood a majestic ancient tree, a striking contrast to the others. Its bark was a deep emerald green, textured and rugged, while its roots were festooned with blossoms in an astonishing array of colors—pinks, blues, and golds—each flower delicate and vibrant, adding an almost magical aura to the tree.

The grand tree beckoned to me with a nearly magnetic allure, suggesting it held the essence and secrets of the entire forest. As I placed my hand on the tree's rough bark, a wave of warmth surged through me. The sensation spread from my fingertips, radiating outward and enveloping my whole body in a comforting embrace. The warmth seemed to pulse with a gentle rhythm, synchronizing with the steady beat of my heart, filling me with a sense of profound connection and peace.

Suddenly, a gentle voice whispered, "You are stronger than you know." I jumped, my heart pounding. It was not my own voice but seemed to emanate from the ancient tree itself. "Embrace your strength and let go of your fears. This world is yours to shape."

I looked around the clearing, noticing a path leading further into the forest. "Thank you," I whispered to the tree, feeling a sense of gratitude for its wisdom and comfort. I turned and began walking down the path. A phoenix bird flew overhead, its brilliant feathers leaving a trail of sparks in the air. I watched in awe as it circled above me. As it soared higher, a single feather detached and drifted slowly down towards me. I reached out and caught the feather.

The moment it touched my hand, it burst into flames. Panic surged through me, my heart racing, but the fire didn't burn. Instead, it felt warm and comforting, like a gentle embrace. The flames spread, enveloping my entire body, and I stood there, paralyzed with surprise. As the fire consumed me, I felt an overwhelming sense of release and surrender. The blaze transported me to a place within my mind—a realm of memories. The fire around me transformed into scenes from my past. The vivid images of loss emerged from the flames, each one hitting me like a wave: I saw my mother in her hospital bed, her life slipping away with each labored breath. The helplessness I felt then resurfaced, gripping my heart once more. Next, Evie's lifeless form appeared, crumpled and still, the vibrant spark that once defined her extinguished in an instant. Then, the memory of my father walking away, his back turned, leaving me lost and alone. Each painful memory struck with the same intensity as the day it happened. The pain was real, sharp, and unrelenting as if I were reliving these moments all over again. My heart throbbed with pain as tears flowed freely, blending with the gentle warmth of the fire. But as quickly as the painful memories appeared, they faded, replaced by images of my achievements.

I saw myself at graduations, standing on stage with a diploma in hand. I saw promotions, moments of recognition, and accomplishments that should have filled me with pride. Yet, each one left me feeling hollow. Despite the outward signs of triumph, a nagging feeling of incompleteness had always shadowed these moments. The flames around me flickered and danced, their warmth both comforting and intense. They seemed to be more than just fire; they were purifying, burning away the lingering pain and emptiness. Each flicker of flame symbolized a step in my transformation, a cleansing of my soul. As I stood in the blaze, I felt a shift within me. The fire, far from consuming me, was revealing the core of who I was. It was stripping away the layers of grief, loss, and self-doubt, leaving only clarity and understanding behind. The realization dawned on me that my past, with all its pain and triumphs, had shaped me but did not define me. I embraced the flames, surrendering to their warmth and letting go of my fears. The fire symbolized my inner strength and resilience, illuminating the path to my true self. I was no longer a prisoner of my past but a phoenix rising from the ashes, ready to shape my own destiny. As the fire began to dampen,

"You cannot change the past," the gentle voice from the ancient tree whispered in my mind. "But you can shape your future. Embrace your strength, and let go of your fears."

The flames finally extinguished, and I found myself back on the path in the forest. The phoenix feather that was in my hand crumbled like ash to the floor, but its warmth lingered in my heart. I looked around, the forest seeming even more vibrant and alive. I took a deep breath, feeling lighter and more determined than ever. The path ahead was still uncertain, but I was ready to face whatever came my way. With renewed purpose, I continued walking, knowing that this journey was just the beginning of something extraordinary.

As I moved forward, the forest began to shift around me. The once vibrant colors of the mushroom-shaped trees dulled, and the sky overhead turned dark and gray. The air grew colder, and my breath came out in shaky puffs. My heart pounded louder with each step, the vibrant hues now muted, replaced by shadows and whispers. Suddenly, tall walls of ivy and thorns erupted from the ground, enclosing me in an endless maze. An icy tremor rippled through my spine, and my stomach coiled with a blend of fear and steely determination. The silence pressed in, broken only by the distant rustling of leaves and my own unsteady breathing. This maze was a challenge, a test of my willpower. I had to confront how I felt and face the emotions and memories that had held me captive for so long. It wasn't enough to believe I had faced them; I also needed to accept them. Taking a deep breath, I stepped into the maze, each footfall a defiant beat in the oppressive quiet.

A periwinkle flower blossomed beside the path as I pushed through the maze. Its delicate petals released a cloud of white powder, drifting through the air like pollen. The sweet, heady scent of periwinkle filled my senses, and I was suddenly transported back to a vivid memory. The walls of ivy shimmered and reshaped, and I found myself reliving the traumatic moment of Evie's death. The scene unfolded with brutal clarity, the pain and sorrow hitting me like a tidal wave. I clenched my fists, the anguish almost too much to bear, and shouted into the memory, "It won't work this time." Determined to move on, I forced myself away from the painful vision and sought another exit. My heart raced and my breath quickened, each step through the maze a testament to my resolve to confront and overcome the shadows of my past. After what felt like an eternity, I reached another dead end. As I stood there, the air was filled with the cloying scent of lilies, their fragrance weaving through the cold air like a ghost from the past. The scent triggered a rush of memories, and the ivy wall before me shimmered and transformed, revealing a different scene.Evie's mother appeared, her face twisted with grief and anger, her eyes burning with an accusation that cut deep.

"You," she spat, her voice trembling with emotion. "You were supposed to look after her. How could you let this happen?"

I took a step back, my heart aching at the sight of her. "I didn't mean for any of it to happen," I said, my voice barely above a whisper. "I loved Evie too."

"Don't you dare say her name!" she shouted, her eyes narrowing. "You don't deserve to speak about her. She trusted you, and you let her down."

Tears welled in my eyes, but I fought to keep my composure. "I did everything I could. It was an accident."

"An accident?" She spat the words with venom. "You were selfish, always dragging Evie into your petty dramas. Because of you, her son is left without a mother."

"I know," I replied, my voice breaking. "I miss her just as much as you do but it wasn't my fault."

"You don't understand," she said, shaking her head. "You have no idea what it's like to lose a child. I loved you like my own, but now all I see is the person who took my daughter away from me."

The pain in her words sliced through me, each accusation a jagged shard. My chest tightened the familiar sting of guilt searing through my veins. I looked down, my hands trembling uncontrollably, and the ground beneath me seemed to shift and tilt as if rejecting my presence. "I never wanted to hurt anyone," I murmured, my voice barely more than a whisper, heavy with the weight of my self-loathing. My heart ached with a relentless, throbbing ache as if it were being crushed under the weight of my remorse. "I would give anything to bring her back." My words faltered, my gaze falling to the floor.

"Then do us all a favor and stay away," she said coldly. "You've done enough damage."

As the memory began to dissolve, the scene around me shifted back to the maze. I found myself standing alone among the twisting walls of ivy, the harsh echo of her words still ringing in my ears. The tears I had been holding back finally spilt over, and I sank to my knees, feeling the full force of my guilt and sorrow. But then, a voice inside me whispered, "No, I am better than this. It wasn't my fault." I wiped away my tears and stood up my resolve hardening. I couldn't let this memory control me any longer. I was determined to find my way out of the maze. I continued on my path, ready to face whatever came next.

My pace quickened, and each step felt heavier. Soon, I reached another dead end. The ivy wall projected another painful memory—voices telling me over and over again that I wasn't worth it, that I would never be good enough. The voices echoed, growing louder and more insistent, filling me with self-doubt. I felt the words pressing down on me, but then I thought of Luke, Evie, and my mom. Their love and support had always been my anchor. Drawing strength from their memories, I silenced the voices with a determined shout, "I am worth it!"

The echoes of self-doubt gradually diminished, their once oppressive weight dissipating like mist in the morning sun. Once towering and foreboding, the maze walls began to crumble away in slow, deliberate chunks. Each fragment fell to the ground with a soft, echoing thud reverberating through the now-quiet space. Dust floated in the air, shimmering in the light that started to filter through the clearing cracks. I stood tall, feeling a surge of empowerment. The darkness receded, and the sky lightened. The maze that had once seemed endless now felt like just another obstacle I had overcome. As the maze disintegrated into rubble, I saw the forest beyond coming into view.

****

I made my way back towards the ancient tree, carrying the weight of the memories and challenges I had faced. As I approached, something unusual caught my eye. The tree's surface, once rough and gnarled, seemed to be shifting as if it had been waiting for me all along. Weathered by time and trials, the tree's massive trunk began to transform before my eyes. Its bark, aged and textured, parted slowly to reveal an intricately carved door hidden within its core. The door, framed by the tree's sturdy branches, was adorned with delicate pink roses embedded into the wood, their petals sculpted with such precision that they seemed almost alive. The roses were intertwined with the branches, creating a natural yet enchanting entrance. Stepping through the door, I was enveloped in a warmly lit living room that seemed to pulse with a golden glow. The room exuded a comforting familiarity—plush rugs, soft shades, and a gentle, crackling fire in the corner. An inviting armchair sat in the center of the room, and there, nestled in its embrace, was my mother. She sat peacefully, sipping tea from a delicate porcelain cup, her movements slow and deliberate, as though savoring each moment. A plate of golden-brown biscuits rested on her lap, the aroma of butter and sweetness mingling with the faint scent of chamomile rising from her cup. Her smile was gentle, the kind that had always been a balm to my restless heart.

I stood there, my feet rooted to the spot, unable to move. The room's warmth felt suddenly stifling. The world seemed to blur at the edges as my eyes filled with tears. I blinked rapidly, hoping the vision before me would clarify, but instead, it only intensified. My throat tightened, a lump forming as I struggled to breathe through the surge of emotion. The corners of my vision darkened. I could feel the painful conflict between this tender illusion and the reality I knew to be true. The sight of her, so vividly real yet painfully unattainable, was like a cruel echo of what I had lost.

"Mum?" I whispered, my voice trembling.

There she was, full of life and glowing with health, a far cry from the fragile, unconscious figure I had seen lying in the hospital bed. Her face lit up with a gentle smile, and she set down her tea cup as if nothing had ever been wrong. "Hello, Dee," she said softly, her voice warm and welcoming. "I've been waiting for you."

I rushed towards her, my heart pounding like it used to when I'd run into her arms after a long day. As I collapsed into her embrace, I clung to her, my voice trembling with disbelief. "But... how? I thought..." The world around me seemed to blur, and for a moment, I was that child again, wrapped in her love and protection.

Her arms wrapped around me, comforting and familiar. "Sometimes, we find ourselves where we need to be the most," she murmured, stroking my hair soothingly.

I buried my face in her shoulder, overwhelmed by the warmth and love surrounding me. "I miss you," I whispered, tears streaming down my cheeks.

"I know, sweetheart," she whispered, holding me close. "I'm always with you, no matter where life takes you." As we sat together in that cozy living room, time seemed to stand still. The weight of my journey, the challenges, and the revelations seemed to fade away in the comfort of her presence.

After a while, I pulled back slightly, gazing into her eyes. "I don't understand..." My voice faltered, the words barely escaping as my brow furrowed and my eyes darted between her serene face and the space around us, struggling to piece together how this impossible moment was unfolding.

"You don't have to," she said gently, brushing a tear from my cheek. "Just know that everything happens for a reason, and you're exactly where you must be right now." My mother reached out, her fingers gently brushing my cheek and tucking a stray strand of hair behind my ear. The touch was tender and reassuring, grounding me amidst the whirlwind of emotions. She smiled, her eyes radiating pride and warmth. "I've been watching you, Dee," she said softly. "I've seen you grow into a beautiful, strong, resilient young woman. I am so proud of you."

Her words brought fresh tears to my eyes, but this time, they were tears of happiness. "I miss you so much, Mum," I whispered.

"I know, sweetheart," she replied, her voice tinged with sadness. "I'm so sorry to hear about Evie. I wish I could have been there for you during that time."

"It was so hard," I said, my voice breaking. "I didn't know how to cope."

She nodded, her expression understanding. "But Luke has been an amazing support, hasn't he?"

I smiled through my tears, thinking of Luke and the unwavering strength and love he had shown me. "Yes, he has. I don't know what I would have done without him."

"He's a good man, Dee. Hold on to him. Your journey is far from over, and more challenges will be ahead. But remember, you have the strength within you to overcome anything. Believe in yourself and the love you share with Luke, you are meant to find him."

I took a deep breath, her words filling me with a sense of resolve. "I will, Mum. I promise."

She reached out and took my hands, her touch warm and reassuring. "This is only the beginning, Dee. There is still so much for you to face and experience. Trust in yourself and the people who love you. You are stronger than you know and will find your way."

"I'll do my best," I said, my voice steady.

"I know you will," she said, smiling. "Remember, I'll always be with you, in your heart and memories. You are never alone."

I clung to her with all my might, my arms wrapped around her as if I could somehow merge us together. Every second felt precious, and I buried my face in her shoulder, taking in the scent and warmth that had always made me feel safe. "Thank you, Mum. I love you so much,"

"I love you too, Dee. More than words can say."

The room around me started to dissolve, the vibrant colors and warmth melting into a gentle haze. The comforting scent of her perfume lingered in the air, a reminder of her presence. Before I knew it, I found myself standing at the base of the tree arch once more. The once bustling and vivid scene had vanished, leaving only the arch's ancient branches arching above me. The branches shifted and swayed, gradually returning to their natural state.

I looked up at the tree, and I discovered that I was exactly where I needed to be.

Nostalgia Rising

The forest around me transformed as the sky darkened, its tranquil green giving way to a deep, twilight blue that wrapped the world in a velvety, calming embrace. The tree arch above me shimmered and blurred, and stars started to pierce the darkness. Their distant twinkling created a celestial backdrop that flickered with soft, silvery light. From this cosmic canvas, a flock of phoenix birds emerged, their feathers blazing with a supernatural fire. As they soared and circled, their wings produced a whooshing sound that was both soothing and exhilarating, like the soft, steady beat of a distant drum.

The flames the phoenixes conjured spiraled around me in a mesmerizing dance, their light flickering like a thousand tiny stars caught in a whirl of radiant motion. Even as the flames roared and swirled with an intensity that would normally be searing, there was no sting or discomfort. Instead, the flames felt like a warm, velvety embrace. They enveloped me with a gentle heat that was more comforting than burning. The flames grew brighter and more vivid, I sensed my body and spirit shedding their old layers. In this otherworldly space, I felt as if I were being reborn, the transformative power of the fire wrapping around me, cleansing the old and igniting the new.

As the cocoon of fire intensified, it lifted me off the ground with an almost imperceptible force. The sensation was akin to floating in a gentle current of light and heat. The phoenixes' circles tightened, their fiery vortex growing more focused. The world below seemed to drift away, replaced by the dazzling spectacle of the phoenixes' dance and the enveloping, protective cocoon of radiant fire. As the flames receded, the scene around me transformed seamlessly. I found myself standing in a beautifully illuminated outdoor setting. The canopy of fairy lights overhead twinkled like stars, casting a soft, enchanting glow across the area. A large picnic bench decorated with a spread of mouth-watering home-cooked dishes came into view. Each dish was lovingly prepared, a testament to family traditions and warmth. The table overflowed with a ton of food, reflecting a sense of home and celebration.

A wave of nostalgia washed over me. This was something we used to do back when life was simple. The scent of homemade dishes wafted through the air, rich with the savory aromas of roasting meats, freshly baked bread, and the sweet undertones of desserts cooling in the evening breeze. My family would gather around the large picnic bench, the surface covered in various colorful dishes. Each plate was a masterpiece, steaming and inviting, laden with the flavors of love and tradition. The sound of laughter echoed around me, voices mingled, rising and falling with animated stories and playful banter. This setting was more than just a gathering; it was a celebration of togetherness, a sanctuary of shared history and love. I walked towards the table, memories flooding back with each step. I could almost hear the echoes of conversations, the clinking of glasses, and the joyous laughter of loved ones. As I approached, I was greeted with warm smiles and welcoming embraces.

My uncle, his face lined with the years but eyes still twinkling with mischief, raised his glass. "Dee! Just in time for the toast!" he called out, his voice rich with affection.

My cousin, who was always the life of the party, winked at me as she handed over a plate heaped with food. "We saved you the best spot, right next to me," she teased, her grin infectious.

My mother's voice, so familiar and comforting, drifted to me from across the table. "Remember the time we tried to make Grandma's famous pie and ended up with a kitchen disaster?" she said, laughter bubbling up in her words.

I laughed, the sound blending with the chorus of voices around me. "How could I forget? We ended up ordering pizza instead!"

I reached out and picked up a plate of my grandmother's famous lasagna. The taste was just as I remembered – rich, comforting, and filled with love. As I took a bite, I felt a warmth spread through me, not just from the food but from the memories it carried. Suddenly, the space around me began to change. All the familiar faces of my family appeared, their smiles lighting up the scene. My cousins were joking around as they tended to the BBQ, their laughter infectious. My mum and Evie sat at the table with my aunts, engaging in animated conversation. I saw Luke and me huddled in the corner, sharing a quiet moment of togetherness. We looked so content, so at peace. It was a snapshot of pure happiness, a moment I wanted to be stuck in forever. But deep down, I knew that wasn't possible. As we exchanged whispers and soft laughter, Evie's voice suddenly cut through the air, loud and playful. "Hey, you two! Get a room!" she shouted, her grin wide and mischievous.

Luke and I laughed, looking up to see her standing there with her hands on her hips, pretending to scold us. The warmth of the moment spread through me, and I couldn't help but smile at the scene unfolding before me. Evie shook her head, her eyes twinkling with affection. "Seriously, you two are adorable, but you're making the rest of us look bad," she teased, her voice filled with mock exasperation.

Luke chuckled and pulled me closer. "Sorry, Evie. We'll try to tone it down," he said with a wink.

Evie rolled her eyes but couldn't hide her own smile. "Yeah, yeah. Just make sure you save some of that sweetness for the rest of us, okay?"

The scene was a perfect setting of joy and connection. I wandered through it, savoring each detail. The sizzle of the BBQ, the clinking of glasses, the murmur of voices, and the warm summer breeze that carried the scent of grilled food and blooming flowers created a perfect summer evening. It was as if time had stood still, preserving this precious memory for me to revisit. Walking closer to the table, I heard my mother's laughter, which always made me feel safe and loved. She looked over at me, her eyes twinkling with pride and joy. "Dee, come sit with us," she called, her voice warm and inviting.

I made my way over, the familiar warmth of the setting wrapping around me like a comforting blanket. As I approached, my mother turned to my aunts, a proud smile on her face. "I was just telling them about your book, Dee," she said, her voice filled with admiration. One of my aunts, her eyes wide with interest, leaned forward. "Really? You've written a book? That's wonderful, Dee! What's it about?"

My fingers twisting the hem of my sleeve. My gaze flickered to the floor as my heartbeat quickened. Sensing my discomfort, Evie quickly jumped in to change the subject. Evie smiled at me, her eyes sparkling with mischief. "Remember when we used to sneak extra desserts when no one was looking?" she teased, nudging me playfully.

I laughed, the sound echoing through the clearing. "How could I forget? We thought we were so clever."

The tension in my shoulders eased as I glanced at my mother and aunts. They were now chuckling, the focus shifting away from my book. My mother shook her head, smiling. "You two were always up to something," she said, her tone fond and nostalgic.

One of my aunts chimed in, "Oh, I remember that! You'd come back with chocolate all over your faces, trying to act innocent."

Evie's grin widened. "And we never got caught, did we, Dee?"

"Not once," I agreed, the warmth of shared memories wrapping around me. "But I think everyone knew anyway."

The conversation flowed into a series of lighthearted anecdotes, the weight of the earlier questions lifting from my shoulders. I stole a grateful glance at Evie, who winked back at me, her mischief now replaced with understanding. I wanted to stay, I knew I couldn't. I looked at Luke and smiled. The scene around me began to fade, and the voices grew softer. I took one last look at the table and at the people I loved and whispered, "Thank you."

The space around me shifted once more, time seemed to flutter, casting people into different corners of the space but there were new faces this time. Atlas, Evie's son, played with my cousins near the BBQ. Theo, Evie's husband, was laughing and chatting with my aunts. My mum was also present, but she was coughing a lot. Despite everyone's concern, she brushed it off with a wave of her hand and a reassuring smile.

She coughed again. "I'm fine, Dee. Just a tickle in my throat," she said, her voice still warm but a bit strained.

"Atlas, be careful near the grill!" Theo called out warmly as he turned back to my aunts. "He's growing up so fast."

My aunt Clara nodded, glancing fondly at Atlas. "He's got Evie's spirit. Always full of energy."

My mum's cough interrupted the conversation, and everyone turned to look at her with concern. "Mum, are you okay?" I asked, stepping closer.

She waved her hand dismissively. "I'm fine, sweetheart. Just a tickle in my throat."

Evie frowned, not convinced. "Are you sure, Mum? Maybe you should sit down and rest."

"I'm fine, really," Mum insisted, forcing a smile. "I'm not missing out on this family time. We don't get together like this often enough."

Theo handed her a glass of water. "At least drink this, then. We all worry about you."

Mum took the glass gratefully. "Thank you, Theo. You all fuss too much." She murmured a quick excuse and slipped away from the group, her steps hurried and unsteady. I followed her with my eyes as she moved toward the edge of the garden, her hand fishing out a small handkerchief. She brought it to her mouth, and her body shook with a silent cough. When she pulled the hanky away, crimson dots marred the pristine white cloth. My breath hitched, my hand flying to cover my mouth. Eyes wide and heart pounding, I turned to my mum, fear etched across my face.

The scene began to morph once more, the familiar sensation of change washing over me like a tidal wave. A soft breeze swept through, carrying away the laughter and chatter like sand slipping through fingers. The vibrant colors of the garden dulled, the cheerful ambiance evaporating into a heavy, sorrowful air. My chest tightened as I scanned the faces around me, the stark absence of my mum piercing through the growing gloom. A hollow ache settled in as the reality hit: this was the year she was no longer with us.

Despite the sorrow, my family still gathered. Conversations were softer, words barely more than whispers as they floated on the breeze. "Do you remember when…" someone began, but the sentence trailed off into nothingness, the weight of memory too heavy to complete the thought. Hugs were tighter, an unspoken attempt to bridge the chasm left by our loss. My Auntie's, once full of chatter and warmth, now wore somber expressions, their usual joviality replaced by a heavy quiet. Laughter, when it came, was tinged with sadness, a fragile echo of happier times. Atlas sat quietly beside Theo, who had a distant look in his eyes, staring into the void as if searching for something lost. Evie caught my gaze, her eyes reflecting my grief and determination. The absence of my mum was a never ending void, but we were there for each other, holding on to the threads of our family bond even as the world seemed to crumble around us.

Luke was by my side, his hand reassuringly in mine. His presence was a steadying force, a reminder of my support.

He squeezed my hand gently, and I felt a surge of gratitude for his unwavering support.

"We have to keep doing this," Evie said, sensing my thoughts. "For Mum. For all of us."

I nodded, swallowing the lump in my throat. "I know."

As I watched the memory fade away, I acknowledged that I needed to cherish every moment, no matter how small, because each one was important. Every smile, every shared laugh, every touch of a hand—it all mattered. These moments wove together the fabric of our lives, creating a story of love, loss, and everything in between.

An owl perched above, its feathers shimmering with an indecent glow that shifted with the moonlight, A spine-tingling sensation swept through me. Its eyes, wide and deep like pools of starlight, seemed to pierce through the darkness with an almost otherworldly gaze. The haunting hoot it released was a distant whisper, conveying ancient wisdom and melancholy. Suddenly, as if responding to the owl's eerie call, the fairy lights flickered once and then extinguished, plunging the garden into silence. Undeterred by the sudden change, the owl flapped its wings and took flight, its silhouette briefly outlined against the darkened sky. Driven by a mix of curiosity and a sense of urgent need, I followed it. The owl glided gracefully through the night, its glowing feathers cutting through the darkness with a spectral light. I walked silently, the path twisting and turning until it opened into a hidden nook. Before me lay a small, gorgeous garden, its beauty breathtaking and serene. In one corner, a garden recliner was nestled among the blooming flowers, its woven wicker frame adorned with soft, plush cushions that seemed to invite me to rest. I eased into the recliner, sinking into its cool, velvety fabric. The cushion beneath me was soft and yielding, cradling my body with a gentle, comforting embrace. As I lay back, I felt the subtle rustling of the leaves and the faint, sweet scent of blooming jasmine wafting around me. Above, the stars twinkled like tiny diamonds scattered across a velvet sky, their light casting a delicate, ethereal glow over the garden. It almost looked real, but I knew it wasn't. The more I looked, the more the stars appeared to be alive, moving slowly in a beautiful dance that changed and sparkled, creating a stunning performance against the dark sky.

"It's beautiful," I murmured to myself, "Thank you for this, I couldn't do this without these memories." I whispered to the night sky, my voice barely above a whisper.

I sank further back into the chair, letting the stars' movement lull me into calm. Each twinkle and swirl told a story, weaving a narrative of resilience and hope. As I gazed up, the stars began to form constellations, their shapes becoming more distinct.

One constellation caught my eye, its stars aligning to form a perfect heart against the night sky. Slowly, they morphed and shifted, transforming into a vivid scene from my past. They had woven together an image of a bustling fun fair, where vibrant lights danced across colorful rides. Brightly lit booths and carousels whirled in an enchanting display, their colors blurring into a carousel of reds, blues, and greens. I watched with a mix of nostalgia and wonder as a younger version of myself appeared, walking hand in hand with Luke. Our faces, illuminated by the festive lights, were full of joy and laughter.

The memory played out vividly. We spent the day enjoying the rides and games. The memory unfolded before me. I could almost see Luke's face, a deep flush spreading across his cheeks as he fidgeted with the edge of his jacket. He kept glancing away, his eyes darting nervously around, avoiding mine with a sheepish grin. His mouth moved in hesitant, stammering motions, trying to find the right words but falling short. The scene played out with all the clumsy charm of that moment. I couldn't help but smile as I watched, knowing the familiar sequence that would follow. Summoning every ounce of courage, I leaned in, the space between us shrinking until I could feel the warmth of his breath. My lips brushed against his in a soft, tentative kiss, a delicate touch that sent a jolt through my chest. For a heartbeat, time seemed to pause. Luke's eyes flew open in surprise, his gaze locking with mine before slowly drifting shut. The initial stiffness in his posture melted away as he responded, his lips moving gently against mine. The kiss deepened, each touch and brush of our lips blending into a rhythm of its own.

I pulled back just enough to keep our faces inches apart and, with a playful glint in my eye, whispered, "I figured I'd give you a hand since you looked like you were about to burst from all that nervous energy."

Luke chuckled, his eyes sparkling. "Nervous? Me? Never."

"Sure," I teased, brushing a strand of hair away from his forehead. "Your face was practically the color of that cotton candy."

He grinned, his hand gently cupping my cheek. "Well, I guess you saved me then. Mind if I return the favor?"

Before I could respond, he leaned in and kissed me again more confidently. He looked at me with a mischievous glint when we finally pulled apart.

"So," he said, his voice low and playful, "do I get to take you on the ferris wheel, or was that your grand finale?"

I laughed, feeling a rush of excitement. "Depends. Are you going to hold my hand this time?"

Luke squeezed my hand gently, his thumb tracing circles on my skin. "Oh, I'll do more than that. Just wait and see."

With a playful tug, he led me toward the Ferris wheel, our laughter echoing through the night. As I watched the memory replay, a gentle warmth began to spread within me. It was as if a soft, golden light had spread from the center of my chest, radiating outward. The scene of our first kiss seemed to glow brighter in my mind, like an old photograph slowly coming into focus. The realization settled over me like a comforting embrace—Luke and I had come so far since that tentative kiss. Each memory we had created together, from the laughter and adventures to the quiet, tender moments, stacked upon that initial spark. The stars shimmered and began to shift, their gentle glow transforming into a more intimate scene.

Luke paused, looking at me with a mix of nerves and tenderness. "Are you sure about this?"

"Yes, I am. Are you?" I smiled softly, nodding,

Luke took a deep breath. "Yeah, I am. It's just I want it to be perfect."

I touched his hand, "It doesn't have to be perfect. We're in this together, right?"

Luke nodded and squeezed my hand, "Right."

Inside the bedroom, the atmosphere is tense yet filled with anticipation. Luke and I stand close to each other, our gazes locked in a mix of nervousness and desire.

Luke leans in, his voice barely above a whisper. "Should we…?"

"Yeah, let's," I said, my voice barely a whisper.

We move closer, our movements hesitant but determined. As we fumbled to remove each other's clothes, the task proved more challenging than anticipated. My earring snagged on the fabric of my shirt, and in the struggle to free it, my elbow accidentally knocked into Luke's eye. We both winced at the awkward clumsiness of it all, our laughter mingling with the slight discomfort. His breath hitched, and I could feel the heat radiating from his body, a reminder of the closeness between us. The gentle rustle of fabric and the muted thud of clothes hitting the floor filled the silence, punctuated by our shallow, uneven breaths. Our palms were sweaty, slick with the mix of excitement and nerves, and I could see the goosebumps forming on Luke's skin as his body responded to the charged atmosphere.

I giggled softly, breaking the silence, "I'm sorry, I'm just… really nervous."

Luke smiled and brushed a strand of hair away from my face. "Me too. But it's okay. We'll figure it out together."

We continue, maneuvering through the awkwardness with patience and tenderness. Despite the initial clumsiness with my earring and the nervous giggles, Luke remains understanding and gentle, his touch reassuring as we explore this new intimacy together. Finally, once we were both completely naked, the initial awkwardness began to melt away, replaced by a more raw, unfiltered connection. The cool air of the room brushed against our exposed skin, heightening the sensation of every touch.

My fingers grazed his skin, sending shivers down both our spines. I couldn't resist the pull any longer, the magnetic draw of our bodies overcoming the remaining hesitancy. With each tentative touch and shared moment, our bond deepened. As our fingers intertwined, the warmth of his skin against mine created a comforting heat that eased the tension between us. We gazed into each other's eyes, the soft, flickering light of the bedside lamps reflecting in our shared gaze. It was a vulnerable experience, yet a sense of trust and closeness grew between us. The initial nervousness disappeared into a shared sense of comfort and connection, creating a moment of unexpected bliss amidst the awkwardness.

As we lay naked on his bed, I turned to look up at him with affection. "Thank you for being patient with me," I whispered.

"Always," Luke replied, his voice tender as he caressed my cheek with gentle fingertips. He pressed a soft kiss to my forehead, his lips lingering for a moment as if to imprint his promise with an affectionate seal. His touch sent warmth through me, reassuring me in ways words couldn't express.

Our laughter mingling with newfound intimacy, we knew this moment, imperfect as it may be, was a significant step in our journey together. Now, back in the present, my gaze on the vast expanse of stars. The memory of our first intimate moment slowly faded. It was a moment of vulnerability and closeness that I knew I would cherish forever. These first moments with Luke were precious, filled with nerves, laughter, and gentle caresses.

They marked the beginning of something deeper between us, a bond that grew stronger with each new experience. The vast expanse above felt distant and cold, a hollow ache that pulsed with every beat of my heart. Each throb was a reminder of the void left in Luke's absence, as though a piece of my soul had been wrenched away. The ache was so palpable that it almost felt like a physical weight, pressing down on me. The stars blinked indifferently, their twinkle seeming to amplify my longing. I could almost feel the void between us stretching, a gap that yearned to be filled with his presence.

Every beat of my heart felt like a silent plea to find him, to bridge the space that separated us. The desire to reach out and hold him, to bury my face in his chest and whisper my appreciation, was overwhelming. It was as if the night itself was echoing my deep need to convey how profoundly his patience, understanding, and love had touched me.

9

Fragments

I lay there under the canopy of twinkling stars, thinking of Luke and the warmth he brought me—their distant light offering a sense of calm in the stillness. Once lively and comforting, the sounds from the garden had dwindled to a faint, distant hum. Dark clouds began to roll across the sky, the familiar comfort of the recliner seemed to dissolve away, the once-supportive cushions slipping through my fingers like fine sand. A silvery mist began to curl around my feet, cool and otherworldly, curling and undulating like ghostly tendrils.

I attempted to rise, but the air around me grew heavy and thick with a suffocating stillness that pressed down on my chest. My movements felt sluggish, each step forward as if I were wading through a dense, viscous swamp. The mist clung to my legs, and the ground beneath me transformed from the soft embrace of the recliner to the cold, unyielding surface of stone. I landed with a thud, the shock of the icy stone against my skin sharp and disorienting.

When I managed to steady myself and look around, I found myself in an unfamiliar realm that defied conventional space. The floor, though solid beneath my feet, was obscured by a dense, swirling mist that appeared to hover and shift with each movement. It felt as though I was walking on an invisible, solid surface cloaked in a shifting veil of fog. The mist was thick, curling around my ankles with a soft, damp pressure that made every step feel like wading through a heavy, suffocating shroud. The walls were nowhere to be seen; the mist extended endlessly in all directions, erasing any boundaries and leaving me in an open, disorienting void. The air was thick and oppressive, pressing down on me with a stifling weight that made each breath feel labored and difficult. It was as though the very air was laden with a heavy, invisible burden, similar to the deep-seated ache of my fibromyalgia that tugged at my muscles and joints.

When I managed to steady myself and look around, I found myself in an unfamiliar realm that defied conventional space. Though solid beneath my feet, the floor was obscured by a dense, swirling mist that appeared to hover and shift with each movement. It felt as though I was walking on an invisible, solid surface cloaked in a shifting veil of fog. The mist was thick, curling around my ankles with a soft, damp pressure that made every step feel like wading through a heavy, suffocating shroud. The walls were nowhere to be seen; the mist extended endlessly in all directions, erasing any boundaries and leaving me in an open, disorienting void. The air was thick and oppressive, pressing down on me with a stifling weight that made each breath feel labored and difficult.

It was as though the very air was laden with a heavy, invisible burden, similar to the deep-seated ache of my fibromyalgia that tugged at my muscles and joints. Faint echoes of voices flitted through the dense fog, their sounds distorted and fragmented. The echoes seemed to weave in and out of the mist, adding to the eerie confusion and disorientation that engulfed me. My steps felt slow and unsteady; the fog seemed to close in around me, heightening my panic and making the unfamiliar terrain feel even more treacherous. My heart raced, and a cold sweat clung to my skin as I fought to steady my breathing against the suffocating air. Despite the overwhelming sense of dread and confusion, the urgent need to find Luke burned within me, a beacon of familiarity in this bizarre and unsettling place. I clung desperately to his memory, hoping that it would guide me through the fog and lead me to answers.

As the mist began to solidify, it formed vivid scenes, like a ghostly movie screen. The first image that emerged was my mother in our kitchen, tears streaming down her face as I shouted at her. The kitchen's details—worn linoleum and chipped countertops—were rendered with unsettling clarity. The mist softened my mother's figure, her sorrowful expression and glistening tears vividly apparent. My raised voice cut through the thick air, harsh and jagged, contrasting with her muffled sobs.

"I don't need your help, Mom! You never understand anything!" I screamed, slamming the door behind me.

I remembered the moment vividly. It was soon after my father had left, and the pain in her eyes showed the emotional upheaval in our family. I reached out to apologize, but my hand passed through the mist, and the scene changed to a new, unresolved image.

This time, it was Luke. We stood in the park where we used to go on lazy Sunday afternoons. His expression was a mixture of frustration and sadness as I accused him of being unattenitive.

"Why do you even bother if you won't put in any effort? Maybe you don't care as much as you say you do," I had said, my voice laced with bitterness.

I saw the pain in his eyes, a pain that I had caused. It was after Evie had died, and I had taken my sadness out on Luke, unfairly directing my grief and frustration towards him. I regretted my actions deeply. I wished I could go back and stop myself from hurting Luke, to make myself realize how much he cared and how hard he was trying to be there for me despite my harshness. But as I reached out in desperation, the mist shifted, and the park scene faded away, leaving me with only the sting of my own past mistakes. Next I was shown Evie. She was crying, clutching a birthday gift she had given me, which I had dismissed thoughtlessly.

"Evie, I told you I don't need anything from you. Stop trying to fix everything," I had snapped, the words sharper than I intended.

I remember how deeply her pained and betrayed expression affected me. It was a time after my mother had passed away, and I had unfairly taken out my grief on Evie, even though she was dealing with her own pain. Seeing her so hurt made me feel overwhelmed with guilt and shame. I didn't mean to hurt her; I just wanted her to understand that I was struggling with my own issues. But instead, I ended up hurting her deeply, and it made me feel like I had failed. Back in the room of swirling mist, the air felt impossibly dense and suffocating. I felt a crushing weight on my chest as if the very air was pressing down on me. Each memory that flickered through the mist was like a dagger, piercing my heart with sharp reminders of my past mistakes. The cold, eerie atmosphere seemed to seep into my very bones, making me shiver uncontrollably. The mist around me felt icy and oppressive, wrapping me in a chilling embrace that matched the weight of my remorse. My breathing came in heavy, ragged gasps, each inhalation laborious as I struggled against the suffocating air. Every regret felt like a heavy chain, pulling me deeper into a pit of despair. I was overwhelmed by a desperate longing to undo every hurtful word and thoughtless action, wishing I could rewrite the past and ease the burden of my guilt.

"I'm sorry," I whispered, choking back tears. "I'm so sorry. I never meant any of it. I just… I just didn't know how to handle my own pain. I hope you all know that. I miss you all so much."

Suddenly, a memory began to unfold before me, vivid and raw. I saw my older self standing face-to-face with my father. He looked older and more worn than I remembered, his face etched with the lines of time and regret. Behind me, Luke stood as a supportive presence, his jaw was set tight, and his shoulders were tense, reflecting his concern and the emotional strain of witnessing my suffering.

"Why are you here?" I shouted, my voice echoing with years of built-up anger. "You left us! You left me! You're a selfish coward!"

He flinched at my words, but I was too consumed by rage to care. "Do you have any idea what you put us through? Do you even care? Mom is dead because of you! I wish it was you dead instead of her! It would have been better if you were never around at all!" Luke gently placed a hand on my shoulder, but I shrugged it off roughly, rejecting his attempt to comfort me. In a fit of frustration, I stormed out of the room, slamming the door behind me with a deafening crash, the echo reverberating through the heavy mist.

As I watched this painful memory play out, I felt the old anger and hurt bubbling up inside me again. My father's face, twisted with regret and pain, was a mirror of my own torment. Tears welled up in his eyes, reflecting the depth of his sorrow and remorse., leaving him standing there, broken and alone. The guilt and shame were suffocating. I fell to my knees, overwhelmed by the intensity of my emotions. My harsh words echoed in my mind, a constant reminder of the hurt I had caused. Even though my dad had done some terrible things, he was still my dad in the end. I needed to accept that nobody is perfect and that everyone has their own struggles.

"I'm sorry," I whispered into the misty room, my voice trembling and echoing softly through the dense fog. "I'm so sorry, Dad. I didn't mean it. I was just so angry."

****

I closed my eyes, taking a deep breath. The weight of my anger and guilt was still there, but it had eased. I understood my struggles and knew I needed to let go. Mistakes had been made—by me, by others; I realized they were what made us human. The imperfections and the missteps were all part of the journey, each teaching us and shaping us. I opened my eyes again. My breath was the only sound around me, steady and grounding; the world blurred, the mist thickening, swallowing the edges of my vision. Suddenly, a sharp smash echoed through the air, cutting through the silence. The noise was ear-splitting, causing the mist to retreat rapidly, swirling away like a curtain being pulled back. As it cleared, I could see the floor beneath me, a rugged expanse of block stone, rough and uneven underfoot.

Shards of glass rained down from above, glinting sinisterly as they caught the dim light, though the room lacked any ceiling. I darted my eyes upward, searching for a source, but found only an infinite void. Instinctively, I moved to dodge the falling fragments, but my movements were too slow. A sharp piece slashed across my shoulder. A searing pain shot through me, and I clutched my shoulder, feeling the warm blood seep through my fingers and stain my dress a deep crimson. The sting was all too real, compared to the surreal surroundings. My mind whirled with confusion and fear. *If this was my own limbo, how could I feel such real suffering?*

Darting and dashing to find a way out, a piece of glass shattered before me. Reacting swiftly, I sidestepped another glass fragment as it hurtled towards the ground. As I jumped to the floor to avoid the glass, I landed hard on my shoulder. Pain jolted through me, making me wince. Among the shards scattered across the ground, a piece of the mirror caught my eye. Its shattered webs reflected a small, romantic moment with Luke. My chest tightened, and I bit my lip, wishing I had savored those little moments more. In the memory, the scene unfolded like a cherished film reel. Luke and I were at home, wrapped in the comfort of our pajamas, nestled together on the couch.

Luke's smile was tender, his eyes reflecting affection as he gazed down at me. His voice was a soft murmur in the quiet room. "I love nights like these, just the two of us."

I nestled even closer, feeling the reassuring warmth of his embrace. "Me too," I whispered back, my heart swelling with the simplicity and warmth of the moment.

His touch was gentle as he brushed a stray strand of hair away from my face, his thumb tracing a tender path. "You know," he murmured, "I could stay like this forever."

As I watched the memory through the fractured reflections of the shattered mirror, a deep longing stirred within me—a yearning for the intimacy and peace of those simple, cherished moments. The awareness of their fleeting nature weighed heavily on my heart, but alongside it, a newfound determination took root, like a seed sprouting in the spring. I knew then, with a resolute certainty, that I had to find Luke, to reclaim what we once had and cherish it more deeply than ever before. I rolled over, gritting my teeth against the pain, and pushed myself up. As I did, a door slowly materialized before me. I sprinted toward the door, weaving through the lethal rain of glass shards that fell like deadly confetti. The room was transformed into a treacherous maze, the floor littered with glittering fragments, each piece a potential hazard. The shards caught the dim light, gleaming dangerously as they tumbled through the air. The sharp clinks and clashes of glass hitting the ground echoed around me, creating a bluster of danger that made each step a calculated gamble. My rapid movements sliced through the rushing air, each swerve and dodge a desperate bid for survival. The sound of falling glass was disorienting, a constant barrage that seemed to grow louder and more chaotic as I neared the door. My heartbeat pounded like a war drum in my ears, each thud a frenzied beat of adrenaline. Every near-miss sent a surge of electricity through my veins, my breath coming in quick, ragged bursts. A shard of glass sliced across my cheek, its sharp bite a stinging, instant reminder of the danger that pressed in from all sides. I gritted my teeth, the pain a fierce, burning edge that only drove me harder. My gaze locked on the door ahead, a beacon of urgency through the storm of falling glass, pushing me to close the distance before the deadly rain could claim its next victim.

Finally, after dodging and weaving through the rain of deadly shards, I reached the door. It was smaller than the other looming doors, almost dwarfed by their imposing size. Above it, a flickering red and blue light creates an unsettling, strobe-like effect. A small, foggy glass window in the door, smeared and clouded, made it impossible to see through clearly. An antiseptic smell emanated from the door, sharp and clinical. In the distance, faint sirens wailed, their eerie, distant cries adding to the growing sense of urgency. Smashing glass grew louder, reminding me of the danger closing in. The flickering lights and the oppressive smell heightened my unease, but the increasing noise made me take action. I pushed through the door. I was no longer in the room with falling glass. Instead, I found myself looking down at my own unconscious body, lying on a gurney. The scene was dark and unsettling, with the broken wreckage of our car visible in the background and crowds of concerned people gathered around, their faces tense with worry. My heart sank as I searched desperately for any sign of Luke.

I didn't see him anywhere, but I clung to the belief that he was okay and had to be okay. Breathing heavily, I watched in a state of mounting dread as the paramedics moved my unconscious body into the back of the ambulance. The sterile scent of antiseptic filled the cramped space, mixing with the tang of sweat and fear. The hum of the ambulance's engine droned in the background, a monotonous sound that seemed to amplify the scene's urgency. The paramedics worked with swift precision, their movements a blur of practiced efficiency. One paramedic, a woman with sharp eyes and steady hands, shouted over the beeping machines and the rhythmic hiss of the oxygen mask, "We need to get her stabilized! Start chest compressions—now!"

Another paramedic, a tall man with a grim expression, nodded and positioned himself. "Chest compressions, 30 to 2. Make sure they're deep and fast." He pressed down firmly, his arms working methodically as he counted, "One, two, three, four…"

The woman adjusted the defibrillator, her face set in determined lines. "Prepare for a shock. Clear the area!" She glanced up at her colleague. "We've got to hope she responds. We're losing precious time."

The tall man finished the cycle of compressions and stepped back, sweat beading on his forehead. "Ready for the charge."

"Clear!" The woman called out, stepping back as she activated the defibrillator. A jolt of electricity surged through the body, and the machine's beep changed pitch.

The man took a breath, his eyes scanning the monitor. "No response yet. Let's continue with CPR. We can't afford to slow down."

As the paramedics continued their relentless efforts, the woman wiped her brow, her voice a mix of determination and fatigue. "Keep pushing. We're not giving up on her." I felt the weight of fear and desperation tighten around me, my attempts to grasp the reality of the situation intensifying. My hands clenched into fists, knuckles white as I fought the urge to reach out, to shake someone, to scream. Each breath felt like a heavy weight pressing down on my chest, my ribs aching with the effort to breathe. The realization of my helplessness seemed to close in on me, suffocating and relentless.

I could feel my heart race, the rapid thudding syncing with the mechanical beeps and hisses of the equipment. My legs felt weak, trembling as if they might collapse under the strain of the scene unfolding before me. I squeezed my eyes shut for a moment, trying to push away the crushing fear that gripped me. When I opened them, the desperation was still there, a raw, gnawing urge to do something—anything—to wrest back some semblance of control. I willed myself to remain focused, to cling to the slim thread of hope that maybe, just maybe, there was still a chance. The paramedics' urgent voices sliced through the chaos, their commands sharp and punctuated. I wanted to fight alongside them, to be part of the battle for the life that hung precariously in the balance. With a stubborn grip, I yanked open the ambulance doors, the cold metal biting into my palms. The sudden rush of air hit me like a wall, sharp and frigid, stealing my breath in a frantic gasp. My chest tightened, each inhalation coming in shallow, desperate bursts as the pressure of the scene inside overwhelmed me. I was airborne, flung out into the sky. The ground vanished beneath me, leaving nothing but open air as I plummeted headfirst into the unknown. The colors outside swirled together in a chaotic blur, a dizzying whirl of dark hues and fleeting lights. Panic surged through me, a tight knot of fear constricting my throat and making each breath a labored effort. Gradually, the chaos of swirling colors began to merge into a discernible shape. The vibrant blur of green emerged from the void, transforming into an expanse of lush foliage stretching endlessly below me. As I hurtled toward it, the greenery became more defined and vivid, a dense carpet of leaves and branches unfurling with each fleeting second. Fear tightened its grip around my chest, each beat of my heart echoing the rush of my descent. The once distant foliage now loomed large, its intricate details sharp and overwhelming. I instinctively raised my arms to shield my face, bracing for the impact.

****

But nothing happened. Slowly, cautiously, I opened my eyes. I was lying on my back among a wild tangle of overgrown plants. Tall stalks and thick vines twisted around me, forming a natural labyrinth that seemed to go on forever. The air was thick with the scent of earth and vegetation, rich and heady. Sunlight filtered through the dense canopy above, casting dotted patterns on the forest floor like a patchwork quilt of light and shadow. I sat up slowly, taking in my surroundings. The oppressive weight of the ambulance scene seemed worlds away now. I noticed, with a start, that my white dress was no longer covered in blood, and the cut on my shoulder had vanished without a trace.

I stood up, shaking off the dirt and leaves that clung to my dress. My fingers brushed over the spot where the cut had been, but now the skin was smooth and unscarred. The forest hummed with life—the rustle of leaves, the distant call of birds, and the gentle buzz of insects filled the air. Each step I took stirred the rich, loamy soil beneath my feet, releasing a fresh wave of earthy scent. Sunlight filtered through the trees above, dotting the ground with light and shadow. My eyes darted wide and alert, drinking in the vibrant greens and the intricate tangle of plants that stretched endlessly around me. A mix of awe and trepidation quickened my breath as I ventured deeper, senses heightened by the vivid, pulsing life all around me.

As I moved through the tangled undergrowth, bright blue thorns hanging from an overgrown hedge caught my eye. Their vibrant color stood out starkly against the green foliage, mesmerizing me. Without thinking, I reached out and touched one. The thorn pricked my skin with a sharp, stinging sensation, like a tiny needle piercing my fingertip. The pain shot up my arm in a swift, electrifying jolt, causing me to gasp. My breath hitched, and my eyes widened in shock. The initial sting deepened, sending waves of tingling discomfort through my hand, making my fingers twitch. Gradually, my vision began to blur at the edges. The rustling leaves, and distant bird calls faded, their sounds muffled as if wrapped in cotton. My surroundings dissolved into a haze, the vibrant greens and browns of the forest melting into indistinct shapes. My eyes glazed over, the trance-like state drawing me in deeper.

The forest around me vanished entirely, replaced by the sharp clarity of a vivid memory, pulling me away from the present and back into a moment from my past. I watched my past self sit in a cozy corner of a travel agency, surrounded by glossy brochures depicting exotic destinations. The air was filled with the scent of fresh ink and the promise of adventure. I could almost hear the soft murmur of the agent flipping through pages, discussing itineraries and possibilities. The gentle hum of an old ceiling fan mixed with the distant buzz of a phone ringing occasionally. The muted chatter of other customers blended into a comforting background noise. Sunlight streamed through large windows, casting warm, golden patches on the polished wooden floor. The cool, crisp pages of the brochures under my fingertips felt smooth and inviting.

"I've always wanted to travel the world," I heard myself saying, my voice tinged with wistfulness. "To see places I've only read about, experience cultures completely different from mine."

"You can do it, you know," she said gently, her voice carrying a hint of encouragement. "There are so many possibilities out there. From exploring the ancient wonders of Machu Picchu in Peru to sailing through the breathtaking fjords of Norway or wandering the bustling markets of Marrakech in Morocco. Each journey offers a glimpse into a different world, a chance to experience something unforgettable."

She flipped through the pages of brochures with practiced ease, each depicting vibrant landscapes and enticing adventures. "Whether you dream of immersing yourself in the rich history of Europe, trekking through the wild jungles of Southeast Asia, or simply lounging on a pristine beach in the Caribbean, the world is yours to explore." Her words sparked excitement, reigniting the dormant embers of my passion for travel. The thought of embarking on such journeys, stepping outside my comfort zone, and embracing the unknown felt daunting and exhilarating.

"I get it," she said gently. "Sometimes the world seems too big, and our dreams too far-fetched. But remember, sometimes the biggest adventures start with a leap of faith."

I nodded, grateful for her understanding, yet still feeling the weight of doubt pressing down on me. "I'm sorry," I apologized quietly, pushing my chair back to stand. "Thank you for your time."

As the memory faded, my eyes, which had once been glazed over, regained their focus, though a hollow ache remained. I had talked myself out of pursuing my dream of traveling the world, convincing myself it was impractical and out of reach. Now, confronted with this forgotten desire, I felt a pang of missed opportunities for letting fear and doubt hold me back. I looked at the wild, untamed landscape before me. The blue thorn in my hand gleamed brightly, catching the light like a hidden gem, reminding me of the dreams I had buried deep within myself. Here, in this surreal realm, the overgrown garden seemed to whisper promises of rediscovery, a chance to rewrite the narrative and bring those dreams to life. I wandered further into the tangled greenery, and a soft shade of orange caught my eye. It was another thorn, glowing gently amidst the vibrant foliage. Mesmerized, I reached out and touched it. The moment my fingers made contact with its delicate surface, a jolt of electricity surged through me, tingling from head to toe. My vision blurred, and my eyes glazed over as a vivid memory surged, overwhelming my senses. The garden faded and I stood in a retro, sunlit space with shelves lined with books of every genre imaginable. The scent of paper and ink enveloped me, and the soft murmur of customers browsing added a comforting rhythm to the air. It was the bookstore I had once dreamed of owning—a sanctuary where book lovers could lose themselves in stories and ideas. I was filled with a sense of purpose and excitement in the memory. I envisioned cozy reading nooks, author signings, and community events celebrating literature and creativity. I had innovative ideas to blend digital and physical experiences, create themed reading spaces, and host workshops to inspire a love of reading. But as quickly as the vision came, so did the doubts. Practical considerations and the fear of failure loomed large. *How would I fund the venture? Could I compete with larger chains and online retailers? What if my ideas didn't resonate with customers?*

I had let those doubts silence my passion, burying the dream beneath the weight of practicality and uncertainty. Yet, surrounded by a landscape of possibility, I felt a flicker of hope reignite within me. Closing my eyes, I clung to the memory, savoring the warmth it evoked. This magical realm allowed me to confront my fears and explore what could have been and perhaps still could be. With each step forward, I vowed to embrace the challenges ahead and uncover the courage to pursue my dreams, one thorn at a time…

10

Tides of Time

When I finally opened my eyes, the overgrown forest had vanished, revealing a breathtaking expanse of boundless ocean stretching endlessly in every direction. The lush foliage and tangled vines of the garden slowly melted away like wisps of smoke dissipating in the wind. Before me lay a slender ribbon of land, seemingly conjured from the sea itself. The supple sand beneath my feet shifted gently with each wave, which lapped against the shore with a soothing rhythm. The ocean, a vast, hypnotic expanse, stretched out under a sky awash in shifting shades of gray.

A soft breeze drifted from the ocean, carrying the faint, salty scent of seaweed and the cool tang of saltwater. The sound of waves rolling in and withdrawing was a comforting, gentle lullaby, a soothing rhythm punctuated by seabirds' distant, faint cries. Each wave approached with a rhythmic, caressing embrace, then retreated with a whispering sigh, leaving delicate patterns of foam and scattered shells on the sand. As I walked carefully along the narrow strip of land, the water's edge was a cool, refreshing touch against my toes, vitalizing and soothing all at once. The serenity of the ocean and the calm, rhythmic dance of the waves offered a tranquil contrast to the chaotic memories I had just relived, drawing me deeper into the ocean's embrace.

I felt free.

As I reached the end of the strip of land, the tide reached its peak, and with a gentle whisper, it began to ripple. A memory surged forth as it did, pulling me into its depths. I found myself with Evie, her laughter echoing around us as we danced in the kitchen, our friendship symbolizing joy and light. The waves moved and a memory disappeared like a withering flower in the water, and suddenly, the crushing grief enveloped me, my shoulders slumped forward, the weight of loss pressing heavily on my frame. My hands trembled, fingers curling into tight fists at my sides as if trying to hold onto something that had slipped away. Another wave crashed onto the shore, washing away the crushing grief and revealing a new vision. My mother's face appeared, glowing and joyful, as she tucked me into bed, read me stories, and gently kissed my forehead.

The scene darkened, showing the sorrowful days after her death. My childhood home felt emptier without her warm, comforting presence. Every room reflected memories of her laughter, guidance, and tireless love. The emptiness that followed her passing was more than just physical; it was a gaping hole in my heart, an emptiness that no one else could fill. I reached for the phone to call her, only to remember she was no longer there to answer. I barely had time to catch my breath before the tide rolled in again, revealing Luke. My heart swelled at the sight of him, at the memories of our joyful moments—picnics in the park, late-night conversations, and the warmth of his embrace. But the scene turned somber, replaying the moments of our arguments, the tension that had built up before the crash. The impact of the collision reverberated through me, a jarring reminder of the fragility of life. As the tide pulled away, I began to understand. The flow and movement of the water mirrored the process of grief. It declined and flowed, sometimes gentle, sometimes overwhelming, but always moving, constantly changing. Acceptance of this natural rhythm only came with time and the willingness to let the tide take its course. Standing at the water's edge, I felt a sense of truce wash over me. I had been carried through the highs and lows, the joys and sorrows, and now, I could see the beauty in the balance. Grief was a part of the journey, a legacy of the love and connections I had experienced. Taking in the sight before me, I embraced the lessons of the tide. I knew that I had the strength to guide the waters of my own grief, to find happiness in the memories, and to move forward with a heart that had been shaped by both love and loss.

As I watched the ocean stretch before me, its surface mirroring the ever-changing colors of the sky, the narrow strip of land beneath my feet began to crumble and fragment. The crumbling earth fell away in sharp, jagged pieces, each section breaking apart with a dramatic urgency that sent a jolt of panic through me. I struggled to maintain my balance as the ground vanished. Still, before I could react, an invisible force drew me downward. A stream of liquid starlight swiftly enveloped me, its ethereal glow casting a mesmerizing light that danced across my surroundings. The starlight felt cool and refreshing against my skin, its gentle and invigorating touch as it carried me effortlessly through the realms. The sound of rushing water accompanied my descent. This soothing symphony blended with the faint echoes of distant memories and experiences from each realm I traversed. The enchanted garden flashed by, its vibrant colors and exotic flora vivid against the darkness of my journey, a sight that would leave any onlooker in awe. I then sped through the heartbreak room, where sad hues and reflective surfaces seemed to whisper the sorrows I had faced, a place that would stir the curiosity of even the most indifferent. The starry dreamscape followed, shimmering with constellations and nebulae that added a touch of celestial wonder to my passage, a sight that would inspire a sense of marvel in anyone who beheld it. As I passed through the realms, a faint, proud smile tugged at the corners of my mouth. The soft, harmonious hum of the starlight and the echoes of distant challenges blended into a symphony of triumphs and growth, creating a palpable aura of achievement that seemed to shimmer in the very air around me.

I realized then that this limbo was vast and beyond my understanding. It was a realm of endless possibilities where my subconscious fears and desires were brought to life. Instead of fighting against the current, I decided to relax and enjoy the journey, trusting that this liquid starlight would lead me closer to finding Luke. The ride was exhilarating and soothing all at once. The starlight flowed like a river, carrying me through cosmic landscapes and fantastical vistas. I felt a sense of acceptance wash over me as I surrendered to the flow, knowing that every twist and turn was a step closer to my destination.

****

Finally, the starlight faded, and I found myself in my old flat. The room was cluttered with various items, each a relic infused with sentimental value. Sunlight filtered through the windows, casting warm, dappled patterns across the worn carpet and illuminating the dust particles that floated lazily in the air. The furniture, marked by signs of wear and tear, told stories of countless moments lived and shared. I took a hesitant step forward, my feet sinking slightly into the soft, familiar texture of the carpet, which offered a comforting, grounding sensation. My fingers brushed over the surfaces of nearby objects: the polished wood of an old bookshelf, the rough fabric of a faded armchair, and the cool, smooth metal of a picture frame. Each texture evoked a different fragment of my past, a tangible connection to days gone by.

The room was filled with the gentle hum of a distant appliance and the faint, persistent murmur of the city beyond the windows. As I explored the room, a wave of nostalgia washed over me, mingling with curiosity and a tinge of melancholy. Each item, each scent, and each sound stirred up a rush of emotions, highlighting how much had changed since I last stood in this space.

As I approached the coffee table, my gaze was drawn to a letter lying there, its edges curling up like the petals of a long-forgotten flower. I picked it up, feeling the weight of its significance in my hands. The paper was yellowed with age, its once-crisp surface now soft and worn from repeated handling. The corners were crumpled and slightly torn, evidence of countless readings and the tender care with which it had been cherished. Luke's handwriting, though slightly faded, remained readable. The letter felt smooth yet brittle beneath my fingertips. As I unfolded the paper, a faint scent of ink and aged paper wafted up.

My Dearest Dee,

As I sit here under the expansive sky, with stars twinkling above and the hum of the camp around me, my thoughts are only filled with you. The distance between us feels immense, but my love for you bridges every mile. I can almost feel your warmth next to me, hear your laughter, and see your beautiful smile.

Life here is tough, and there are moments when the weight of my responsibilities bears down on me. But thinking of you, of us, gives me the strength to keep going. You are my anchor, my reason for pushing through the hard days. I want you to know how much you mean to me and how your love is my guiding light in this challenging journey.

I miss the little things the most: the way you make coffee in the morning, your comforting presence beside me, and the way you scrunch your nose when thinking hard about something. Those moments are etched in my heart, and I carry them wherever I go.

I know this separation is demanding on both of us, and there are days when it feels unbearable. But I believe in us, our love, and the future we are building together. Every challenge we face has strengthened of our bond. I dream of the day I can hold you again, of the nights we'll spend talking about everything and nothing, of the life we'll build together. Until then, know that you are always in my thoughts and prayers. Your love is my fortress, my sanctuary amidst the chaos. Stay strong for me, as I stay strong for you.

With all my love, now and always,

Luke

Tears welled up, threatening to spill over as I finished reading the letter. Luke's words were a reminder of the deep connection we shared. His love felt as real and powerful as ever across the distance and time. But over time, the distance and the demands of life caused us to grow apart. Once filled with passion and longing, the love letters became echoes of a connection that wasn't enough to keep us together. I carefully placed the letter back and walked over to the kitchen counter. I found it tucked away in an old keepsake box—the token from our first date at the funfair. It's a small, silver disc, smooth to the touch and slightly worn around the edges as if it has been cherished for years. On one side, a colorful carousel spins in intricate detail, its horses frozen mid-gallop, adorned with tiny stars that glint in the light. The name of the fair is elegantly engraved around the edge, a reminder of that enchanting night. Flipping it over, the numeral "1" was stamped clearly, marking its value in rides or games.

Holding it in my palm, I traced the faded carnival logo with my fingers, and the world around me began to dissolve. It was a warm summer evening at the funfair, the air filled with the scent of popcorn and the sounds of laughter and carnival rides. Luke and I had spent the night wandering hand in hand, playing games, and riding the Ferris wheel. As the night drew closer, we found ourselves at a small booth filled with trinkets and souvenirs. Luke picked up a small token, its bright colors catching the light.

"This is for you," he said, slipping the token into my hand. His eyes sparkled with mischief and affection. "A keepsake from tonight."

I laughed, feeling a flutter of joy in my chest. "You're not supposed to take those, you know."

"Consider it a token of my love," he grins. "And a promise. Tonight was just the first of many dates we'll share."

I looked at him, my heart swelling with affection. "Promise?"

He took my hand, his grip warm and reassuring. "Promise. I'll always find a way to make you smile, Dee. No matter where life takes us, we'll have many more nights like this."

We stood there, bathed in the glow of the carnival lights, the world around us fading away. At that moment, his promise felt like a lifeline, a guarantee that we would face challenges together no matter the challenges.

****

As the carnival lights and laughter faded, the world slowly sharpened back into focus. I swayed slightly, my head still caught in the gentle spin of the Ferris wheel ride. I looked down at the token in my hand, its surface rough and familiar. It felt like a heavy treasure against my palm, a small, precious relic of our time together. The token, so small and seemingly insignificant to anyone else, held an entire universe of promises and love between us. Though life had taken unexpected turns and we had faced our share of challenges, that night and his promise remained etched in my heart. I held onto that, knowing his love was always with me, no matter where he was.

I turned and saw my engagement ring sitting next to the kitchen sink. It was a striking piece of jewelry, unlike any traditional ring. The band was crafted from a delicate yet durable silver, intricately designed to resemble intertwining thorny vines. The thorns were subtle, etched with meticulous precision, adding an element of wild beauty and resilience. At the center of the ring was an emerald diamond, its vibrant green hue catching the light and casting a mesmerizing glow. The emerald was set in a way that made it look like a delicate bloom amidst the thorns, symbolizing how love and beauty can thrive despite challenges. How the emerald sparkled reminded me of the depth and intensity of Luke's eyes, a reflection of our shared dreams and promises. I picked it up, remembering how many times we had to resize it and how Luke made it his mission to ensure it fit perfectly. I kissed the ring, then slipped it onto my finger, feeling warmth and connection.

I stood in the flat, my gaze sweeping over the familiar scene. Every detail seemed to hold a piece of our shared past. My fingers traced the edge of the wooden table where we had spent countless evenings, and the faint scent of his cologne—woody and warm—drifted through the air, a subtle reminder of his presence. Closing my eyes, I let the flood of memories envelop me. It was as though the past wrapped around me like an embrace, and I could almost feel his hand in mine, offering the reassurance that he was still near. I sighed softly, taking in the photographs and mementos scattered around the room. Each object felt like an anchor to the moments we had shared. Though he was not physically here, the love and memories we built together were woven into every corner of this flat, comforting me with the knowledge that he was always a part of my heart. A soft knock at the door broke through my thoughts. Curious, I opened it, expecting another part of this strange journey to unfold. Instead, I found myself staring into the vast hallway again. As I stepped out, I caught a glimpse of something that made my breath freeze. My eyes widened, the world seeming to slow down for a moment. Luke was leaning against the wall, his posture relaxed and effortless. The corners of his mouth lifted into that unmistakable, familiar smile as his gaze met mine. My heart raced, and the scene before me felt like a dream I was struggling to wake from.

"Hey, stranger," he said, his voice warm and inviting.

I bolted toward him, my legs almost betraying me as they carried me in a frenzied rush. My heart pounded like a drum, each beat echoing in my ears, a chaotic symphony of joy and disbelief. When I reached him, I launched myself into his arms, the warmth of his embrace enveloped me, sending tremors through my entire being. For a fleeting moment, the world outside dissolved, and all that existed was the solidity of his arms around me, grounding me in the incredible reality of his presence. He gently put me down, his hands cradling my face as he looked deeply into my eyes. I hadn't even realized tears were streaming down my cheeks until he gently wiped them away with his thumbs. The intensity of his gaze made the hairs on my arm stand up. Slowly, he leaned in and pressed his lips to mine in a slow, passionate kiss that seemed to meld our souls together.

My voice quivered when we finally pulled apart, "I miss you."

His thumb brushed my cheek tenderly. "I miss you too, Dee."

I took in his presence, savoring the feel of him, the reality of him. "How are you here?" I whispered, unable to control my emotion.

He smiled, a mix of sadness and love in his eyes. "Sometimes love finds a way, even across the boundaries of life and death. I'm here because you needed me. After all, I needed to see you."

I clung to him, afraid he might disappear if I let go. "I don't want to lose you again," I confessed, my voice breaking.

He held me tighter, his breath warm against my hair. "You never lost me, Dee. I've always been with you. I've been right there in every memory, moment of joy and sorrow."

A surge of panic welled up inside me as the reality of our situation hit me. "But the car crashed… Luke, I don't know if we're dead or alive. I just want to go home with you. I want us to be together."

His arms tightened around me, pulling me closer against his chest. I could feel the steady rhythm of his heartbeat beneath my cheek. He pressed his lips to my forehead, his breath warm and soothing. "Shh, it's okay," he murmured softly, his voice a calm balm to my frayed nerves. "Breathe, Dee. Just breathe." His hand gently stroked my back in a slow, deliberate rhythm, guiding me back to steady breaths as I nestled into his embrace.

Tears continued to fall down my face as I looked up at him. "I can't do this without you. What if I never wake up? What if I'm stuck here forever?"

Luke cupped my face in his hands, his thumbs gently wiping away my tears. "Listen to me, Dee. You are stronger than you know. This place, this limbo, it's a part of your journey, but it doesn't control you. You have the power to find your way back."

I shook my head, feeling lost. "But I don't know how. I just want to be with you."

He smiled, his eyes a mix of heartache and encouragement. "Everything will work out, but the choice is up to you. You have to believe in yourself and in your strength. You can do this, Dee."

"But what if I make the wrong choice?" I whispered, fear gripping my heart.

Luke leaned in, his forehead resting against mine. "There are no wrong choices, only paths that lead us to where we need to be. Trust yourself, and trust the journey. I'll be with you, always, no matter what."

We stood there, wrapped in each other's arms, time seemingly standing still. The hallway, the mist, and everything else faded into the background as we shared this precious moment. Despite the uncertainty of our futures hanging in the balance, I knew this was a gift, a chance to hold onto the love that had shaped my life and given me strength.

After a long, tender silence, Luke pulled back slightly, looking into my eyes with a gentle but determined expression. "Promise me you will keep going, you have to find your way back to me. There's still so much for us to do; I'll be with you every step of the way."

I nodded, feeling resolve settle over me. "I promise," I said, my voice steady. "I'll keep going for us."

He smiled, his eyes shining with pride and love. He kissed my forehead gently. "That's all I ask. Remember, I'll be with you every step of the way." With our hands linked, he brought my hand to his lips and kissed it gently, his touch both reassuring and intimate. We held each other one last time; I felt a sense of closure and understanding. When I finally let go, Luke's form began to fade; I clung to the memory of his touch and words, wondering how I would ever find the strength to carry on without him. I had to promise myself that this wasn't goodbye.

11

Oasis

A sharp whooshing noise echoed through the corridor, jolting me from my thoughts and a shudder rippled through me. The sound was followed by a loud thump that thundered through the hallway. Startled, I turned towards the source of the disturbance and quickened my pace down the hall, my footsteps quick and uneven. Before me stood a door, slightly ajar, its presence both strangely inviting and suspicious. The door looked constructed from weathered, salt-stained wood, its surface marred with cracks and splinters. Frosted glass panels, clouded and uneven, revealed only faint, turbulent shadows dancing behind them. The hinges and handle were coated in a layer of rust, and the door exhaled a faint, mournful whistling sound as though it were breathing in the chill of the corridor.

I reached out hesitantly, my fingers brushing against the cold, damp surface of the door. It was unyielding, the wood splintered in places, and the dampness seeped through to my touch, sending an uneasy chill up my arm. I pushed the door open. Further, the rusty hinges groaned softly in protest, and I stepped inside cautiously, each creak and shiver of the door amplifying my growing sense of unease.

The room had a narrow passage encased by towering glass walls on either side, their surfaces slick with moisture. A door stood on the other side as the gray sea, churning and tumultuous, heaved violently against the glass, its waves rising and crashing with thunderous force. Each impact sent a shudder through the floor, the tremors vibrating up through my feet. The relentless crashing of the waves against the glass walls created a deafening roar that rumbled through the confined space. The sound echoed off the walls and amplified the sense of entrapment. As I stepped further into the passage, the room was momentarily plunged into darkness, the glass walls barely visible, and the sea's fury obscured all light. This brief, stifling darkness only added to the growing sense of claustrophobia, the narrow confines of the passage feeling increasingly suffocating as the sea's power surged around us. The sea both fascinated and terrified me. I felt an urgent need to escape the narrow passage that seemed at risk of being overwhelmed by the relentless sea.

I approached cautiously, mesmerized by the intensity of the room before me. The water seemed alive, a pulsating mass of raw power and emotion. It reminded me of my turbulent emotions since Luke's departure. I watched as the waves pounded against the glass and a strange sense of familiarity washed over me. It was as if the stormy sea mirrored the storm within my heart, echoing the grief, the longing, and the uncertainty that had consumed me. Taking a deep breath, I pressed my palm against the cool glass, feeling the vibrations of each wave reverberate through me. The sea was daunting and mesmerizing, a reminder of the challenges I had faced and those yet to come.

As I stood there, lost in the rhythm of the crashing waves, I began to hear muffled voices, faint and distorted as if they were underwater. Gradually, the waves flattened out, their violent motion calming momentarily. Through the glass walls, a clear but shifting image emerged in the stilling water. I could see a vivid reflection of a memory: the last goodbye Luke and I shared before the car crash. In this surreal projection, I saw us standing together, exchanging hurried "I love yous" amidst our busy lives. The image captured that heartfelt farewell, but as I looked back, those words felt hollow, diminished by their repetition and the passage of time. The memory on the water's surface felt both haunting and poignant. Our repeated goodbyes and the cold, distant reality of the scene before me made the memory feel less deep. I watched, feeling the weight of missed opportunities and unspoken words. The glass beneath my palm felt cool and unyielding, starkly contrasting the warmth of Luke's embrace I longed for. Suddenly, the scene changed, and I watched the memory play out in front of me again, but this time it was different.

"I love you, Luke," I said softly, my voice filled with longing.

"I love you too, Dee," Luke replied, his smile warm and reassuring.

In the memory, I hesitated before speaking again, my brow furrowed with regret. "I wish... I wish I had said more."

Luke reached out and gently touched my cheek, his touch tender and filled with love. "Hey, it's okay," he reassured me, his eyes steady and kind. "You've always shown me how much you care. Words are just words."

I shook my head slightly, looking down as tears welled in my eyes. "But they felt... empty, Luke," I confessed, feeling the weight of missed opportunities.

Luke pulled me into a comforting embrace, holding me close. I felt the warmth of his body against mine, grounding me in the moment. "Dee, you're my everything," Luke whispered softly into my ear. "I know you love me, just as I love you. We don't need to say it every moment. Our love speaks through every smile and every touch."

I closed my eyes, savoring the feeling of being in his arms, the sound of his heartbeat steady and comforting. The memory faded, but the sense of his presence remained, filling me with a renewed sense of peace and understanding. I watched the waves hit the glass. Luke's words echoed in my mind, his embrace lingering like a fleeting dream.

I pressed my forehead against the cold, damp glass, feeling the slight tremors of the waves through the pane. "Why did you show me this?" I whispered, my voice barely audible over the roar of the sea. "Why now, after all this time?" Lifting my head, I began searching the waves for answers that seemed to slip through my grasp like sand.

"I've never allowed myself to dream of changing moments like this," I admitted, my tone growing firmer with each word. "Why now? What are you trying to tell me?"

The waves grew more violent, their rhythm shifting from a gentle ebb and flow to a relentless assault. Each crash against the glass was heavier and more forceful, the impacts vibrating through the pane and jolting up my arms. The water churned and thrashed with angry energy as if the sea itself was reacting to my questions with increasing impatience. Withdrawing my hand from the glass, I aggressively wiped away the tears that stained my face, feeling a sense of clearness over me. The memories and emotions were all pieces of a puzzle I was beginning to understand. I dashed across the room, my heart pounding against my chest like a drum. Each step grew heavier as I approached the door on the far side. The door loomed ahead, its details becoming more apparent with every stride. Made of aged, weather-beaten wood, it was marked by deep grooves and cracks that spoke of years of exposure to the elements. Brass fittings, tarnished with time, gleamed dimly in the faint light, their once-polished surface now dulled and pitted. A pair of small porthole windows, set into the door, framed darkened glimpses of the tempest outside.

Without pausing to reconsider, I grasped the cold, brass handle, its surface rough under my fingers. With a decisive pull, I swung the door open. A gust of pungent, salty wind slammed into me, as if the sea itself was trying to force its way in. The ocean's roar filled my ears, drowning out any other sound and amplifying the sensation of being on the edge of something vast and uncontrollable. Blinking against the force of the wind, I glimpsed a towering lighthouse perched on jagged rocks, its beacon slicing through the stormy night with unwavering determination. I pushed myself forward, battling the wind that threatened to push me back. Step by step, I guided through the treacherous path to the lighthouse door. With each step, images of Luke flooded my mind—his smile, his laugh, the warmth of his embrace. They surged with a determination to move forward.

Finally reaching the door to the lighthouse, I took in its weathered appearance. The door was cloaked in chipped, peeling paint; the once-bright colors now faded and flaked away to reveal the timeworn wood beneath. The porthole windows, small and round, were framed by the door's rough surface, their glass speckled with grime and sea salt. I gripped the sturdy rope handle, its texture rough and coarse against my palm, and the fibers worn smoothly from years of use. Pulling the door open, I stepped inside, leaving the storm's chaos behind. The sheltered silence of the lighthouse's interior enveloped me, a stark contrast to the raging tempest outside. The only sounds were the soft hum of the generator and the occasional creak of the wooden stairs leading upward; each groan a reminder of the lighthouse's enduring presence against the storm.

Ignoring the fatigue that threatened to weigh me down, I began my ascent up the spiral staircase, my hand gripping the iron railing for support. The stairs painted a weathered black, wound upwards, their surface gritty with accumulated salt and sand. As I climbed, the rhythmic echo of my footsteps echoed off the metal steps, blending with the faint, distant crash of waves that filtered through the narrow, tall windows lining the walls. Occasionally, a low, resonant foghorn sounded, its deep tone vibrating through the structure and mingling with the subtle creaking of the aged stairs. A faint, musty aroma of old, damp wood also lingered, adding to the lighthouse's distinct character. The iron railing felt warm and slightly rough under my fingers, worn smooth in places by countless hands over the years. At last, I reached the top, where the warm, constant light of the beacon enveloped me in a reassuring glow.

Standing before the towering lighthouse beacon, I turned to gaze out at the vast, rough expanse of the aggressive ocean. The waves crashed against the rocks below with relentless fury. The salt air stung my face, carrying with it the faint, earthy aroma of seaweed and the persistent scent of weathered metal from the balcony railings. The lighthouse beam, an intense and powerful slice of light, cut through the darkness with a mesmerizing, rotating brilliance. Each beam rotation was so intense that as the light swept over me, I could feel the warmth on my skin, a reminder of its strength against the cold, biting wind that tugged relentlessly at my clothes and hair. Its brilliance momentarily blinded me before being transported into a vivid memory.

****

Suddenly, I found myself seated at the familiar kitchen table of my childhood home. Everything around me seemed to have shifted; I was no longer an adult but had been transported back to a younger version of myself. The comforting aroma of freshly baked cookies filled the air, mingling with the sound of my mother's voice. She appeared younger too, her eyes filled with love and concern as she spoke to me with gentle reassurance. In this moment, I was enveloped in the warmth of my past, seeing and feeling everything through the eyes of my younger self.

"Sweetheart," my mother began, her voice soft yet firm. Life is so fragile. We often take it for granted, thinking we have all the time in the world. But the truth is, every moment counts—every single one."

I looked at her, feeling the weight of her words sink in. She reached across the table, taking my hand in hers. Her touch was warm, grounding me in the moment.

"When I was your age," she continued, "I used to think that life would go on forever, that there would always be time to do the things I wanted, to say the things I needed to say. But then I learned, sometimes the hard way, that we don't always get a second chance."

I could see in her eyes, the pain of lost opportunities, and the joy of seizing precious moments. "It's important to cherish the people you love," she said. "Tell them what they mean to you. Don't wait for the 'right' moment because sometimes it never comes." Her words reminded me of many times I had held back and the moments I had let slip away. She squeezed my hand, pulling me from my thoughts.

"Dee, you have so much ahead of you, but it's up to you to make the most of it. Don't let fear or doubt hold you back. Embrace every moment, even the difficult ones, because they shape who you are and who you will become." I nodded, absorbing the wisdom she was sharing.

"Remember," she said, her voice filled with emotion, "life is not just about the big milestones. It's about the little moments, too. The laughter, the tears, the simple joys. They all matter. They all count." The memory began to dissolve, the comforting scene of the kitchen melting away as the intense beam of the lighthouse flickered on. With each pulse of the light, I was pulled from the warmth of my childhood home and thrust back into the present. As the beam swept across the darkness, it carried me upward, back to the top of the lighthouse. Each flicker of the lighthouse's light was like a thread unraveling the memory, stitching me back into the present moment. Another vivid memory surged to the forefront of my mind. I sat on a weathered park bench beside Evie, the crisp, earthy scent of autumn leaves swirling around us. We watched Atlas, her little boy, as he soared back and forth on the swings, his gleeful laughter ringing out like a through the park. The vibrant colors of fall—the deep oranges and rich reds of the leaves—danced in the gentle breeze.

Evie turned to me, her eyes soft with delight. "These moments," she said, a gentle smile playing on her lips, "are blissful. Watching Atlas grow is scary, but It's all I live for."

Her words struck a chord deep within me. I admired her and the way she found endless joy in the simple act of being present for her son. Evie had always been like that—grounded, patient, and full of quiet wisdom. She reached over and squeezed my hand, her gaze steady and reassuring. "I know you and Luke are trying for a baby," she said softly, "but some things can't be rushed. Enjoy each other first. Savor your time together because those moments are precious, too."

There had been so much pressure, longing, and worry in our attempts to start a family. But Evie's words brought a sense of transparency, a reminder that the journey was just as important as the destination.

"Luke loves you," she continued, her voice filled with warmth. "And you love him. Let that be enough for now. Trust that the right time will come."

I nodded, unsure of what to say. Atlas ran towards us, his face alight with joy. This moment—sitting here with Evie, watching her son—was a gift. The memory began to dissolve, blending into the steady pulse of the lighthouse beacon. I was back at the top. I stood there, listening to the crashing of waves beneath me. Life was unpredictable, and every moment counted. I took a deep breath, the salty sea air filling my lungs. The storm outside still raged, but inside, I could feel a shift happening—not just within myself but also in this place.

Suddenly, the blaring sound of the lighthouse horn pierced the air, pulling me into yet another memory. This time, I found myself in a cozy bookshop, the familiar scent of old pages mingling with the rich aroma of freshly brewed coffee. Soft light filtered through the windows, glowing warmly on the shelves lined with well-loved books. Liam sat across from me at a small, round table. Normally relaxed and easygoing, he seemed different today—tense, almost anxious. His fingers drummed lightly on the table, a subtle sign of his unease. His warm eyes, usually sparkling with mischief or calm assurance, were now filled with a deeper sincerity, a hint of concern lurking behind his gaze.

"Dee," Liam said, leaning forward across the small table, his expression severe yet compassionate, "staying true to yourself is crucial. Never let doubts cloud your understanding of how remarkable you are." I nodded thoughtfully, my gaze fixed on Liam's earnest eyes. He reached across the table, his hand extending slowly until it found mine. His touch was warm and comforting, yet there was a hint of hesitation in how he made contact as if he were gauging my reaction.

"Be kind to yourself," he continued, his voice softening. "And remember, everyone fights their own battles internally. Some struggles are more visible than others, but each person's journey is uniquely theirs. No one is flawless, so there's no need to strive for perfection. Instead, embrace who you are and explore every aspect of yourself."

I felt a lump form in my throat, moved by Liam's sincerity. His words seemed to carry a weight beyond our conversation as if he spoke from personal experience. "Sometimes," Liam added, his tone taking on a hint of introspection, "discovering who you are means confronting parts of yourself that you've kept hidden. It's about acceptance and learning to love every part of your identity."

As he spoke, I noticed a fleeting shadow pass over Liam's eyes, a moment of vulnerability that spoke volumes. Memories flashed in my mind of times when Liam had seemed distant or contemplative, moments that hinted at a deeper internal struggle he hadn't fully shared with me As we sat there, the comforting hum of the bookshop around us and Liam's advice reminded me to embrace my true self and to steer life's challenges with compassion and understanding—both for myself and others. The memory dissolves into the steady pulse of the lighthouse beacon. The horn still echoes in my ears.

A sharp, intense pain burned through my head as another memory surged forward. Gripping the railing, I found myself at my mother's funeral. The overcast sky was a blanket of gray, mirroring the somber mood. The air was heavy with the scent of rain and freshly turned earth. Standing among the mourners, I felt the dampness seeping through my shoes and the chill wind brushing against my skin. The quiet murmurs and occasional sobs of family and friends punctuated the heavy silence. My heart ached with the loss of my mother, each beat a painful reminder of her absence. Luke was by my side, his hand firmly holding mine, offering silent support. I saw my father standing by the casket, his face etched with lines of regret and sorrow. He looked older, more fragile than I had ever seen him. His eyes, usually so distant, were now filled with a depth of emotion that mirrored my own grief. As the service ended and people began to disperse, my father approached me. I felt Luke tense beside me, his protective instincts kicking in. My father's steps were heavy, each seeming to carry the weight of his regrets.

"Dee," my father began, his voice breaking slightly, "I know I wasn't there for you and your mother. I made mistakes... so many mistakes."

Luke's grip on my hand tightened, his eyes narrowing as he watched my father with suspicion and anger. I gently squeezed Luke's hand, silently reassuring him that I was okay.

My father's eyes searched mine, pleading for understanding and forgiveness. I could see the weight of his regrets, the years of absence that now seemed to crush him.

"I thought I had all the time in the world," he continued, his voice barely above a whisper. "Thinking I'd make it up to you later. But later never came."

My vision blurred, and a lump rose in my throat. Sorrow mingled with a newfound empathy for the man who had always kept his emotions hidden, making my chest tighten.

I blinked rapidly, trying to clear the tears that threatened to spill, each breath becoming a struggle against the wave of emotions crashing over me.

"Your mother... she was always there for you, for both of us. She knew what was important," he said, his voice trembling. "Being present for your family, truly being there, is what matters most. I learned that too late."

He took a hesitant step closer, and Luke moved slightly before me, his protective stance clear. I placed a hand on Luke's arm, signaling him to let my father speak.

"Don't make the same mistakes I did, Dee. Cherish the ones you love. Be present in their lives every moment you can. That's what your mother would want." His words cut through the fog of my grief, embedding themselves deep in my heart. His voice softened, and he added, "I'm proud of you, Dee. More than you know."

My vision blurred, a lump rising in my throat as tears streamed down my face. I blinked rapidly, trying to clear the tears that threatened to spill, each breath becoming a struggle against the wave of emotions crashing over me. I nodded, feeling a strange sense of connection with my father that I had never felt before. The memory began to dissolve, the cemetery fading into the warm glow of the lighthouse beacon. The storm was still fierce, but I felt a calm determination taking root inside. Without having time to think, the lighthouse beacon pulled me into another memory.

This time, I found myself in our bedroom, standing in front of the mirror. Tears streamed down my face, blurring my reflection. The harsh light from the overhead fixture accentuated every flaw, every imperfection I had convinced myself existed. A deep, aching pain radiated through my body, a constant reminder of my struggle with fibromyalgia. My muscles throbbed with an unrelenting soreness, making even the act of standing feel like a battle. "I hate how I look," I cried, my voice breaking. "I'm so tired of feeling like this. I'm so tired of the pain."

Luke was there; he wrapped his arms around me, the warmth of his embrace seeping into my cold, aching skin. His steady heartbeat against my back was a comforting anchor amidst my self-doubt and physical pain. The scent of his cologne mixed with the faint aroma of our bedding, a familiar and soothing blend. His breath was warm against my ear as he whispered, ""Dee, stop,"" his words were encouraging against the harsh self-criticism I faced in the mirror and the constant discomfort of my condition. "You are beautiful to me," he said softly but firmly, turning me to face him. "You're gorgeous the way you are. You need to start believing that."

I shook my head, unable to meet his eyes, my tears blurring around the room. "I don't feel beautiful. I feel…"

"Beauty is many things," he interrupted gently, lifting my chin with a firm grip so I had no choice but to look at him. "But perfect isn't always one of them. You need to get out of your head and see yourself the way I see you. You're hurting yourself with these thoughts." His words were a cure for my wounded self-esteem, each one laced with genuine love and concern. Luke had always been my rock, always there to lift me up when I couldn't stand alone.

"You are captivating, Dee. Inside and out. And I need you to believe that because I hate seeing you like this. You deserve to be happy with who you are."

I searched his eyes, seeing sincerity and love reflected back at me. Slowly, I felt the tension in my chest begin to ease, the harsh self-criticism melting away under the warmth of his words.

"Promise me you'll try," he whispered, his forehead resting against mine. "Promise me you'll start seeing what I see." Luke smiled softly and kissed my forehead, then gently guided me to the bed. His hands were tender but firm, easing me down onto the soft mattress. He knelt beside me, his eyes never leaving mine as he spoke. "I love every part of you," he murmured, his voice a soothing balm. "Especially your thighs."

He began to kiss my thighs, each kiss a gentle promise of his words. The warmth of his lips against my skin sent shivers through me, not of pain but of love and reassurance. His touch was deliberate, reverent, making me feel cherished and beautiful. "You see these?" he said between kisses. "These are a part of you, and I love them. I love how strong they are, how they carry you through every day despite the pain you endure." His hands roamed gently, his kisses growing more passionate as they traveled upwards. "And these," he whispered, his lips brushing over my hips and stomach. "I love how they curve, how they hold so much strength and grace."

He continued his journey, his hands and lips worshiping every inch of my skin. "Your breasts," he said softly, cupping them with reverence. "I love their softness, their warmth. They are a part of you, and that makes them perfect." His kisses moved to my collarbone, each touch a promise of his unwavering love. "And your arms," he continued, tracing the lines of my arms with his fingertips. "They hold me close, they comfort and protect. I love them."His eyes locked with mine, filled with an intensity that made my heart swell. "You are beautiful, Dee. Every inch of you."

With each kiss, each touch, I felt my self-doubt and pain begin to melt away. Luke's words and actions lifted the weight of my insecurities. The harsh light that once exposed my perceived flaws now illuminated the love and acceptance in his eyes. "Promise me," he whispered again, his lips trailing up to my neck. "Promise me you'll see yourself the way I see you."

"I promise," I whispered back, my voice stronger this time, filled with a newfound conviction. I reached out, running my fingers through his hair, feeling a deep connection and a profound sense of healing.

With the memory now gone, Luke's touch still lingered on my skin, a comforting reminder of his presence. Bathed in the lighthouse's steady light, I felt irresistibly drawn toward the beacon, like a moth to a flame. The world around me began to dissolve into the darkness, the lighthouse beam slicing through it with mesmerizing precision. A magnetic force seemed to pull me forward, its gentle and unyielding grip. The pulsating glow of the lighthouse beacon grew brighter with each step, the light wrapping around me in a warm, hypnotic embrace. The boundaries between reality and the surreal blurred, the edges of the world around me softening and fading away. With each pulse of the light, I felt a sensation of movement, as if I were being gently lifted and carried away from where I stood. The cool night air mixed with the faint scent of salt and seaweed, the wind brushing against my face as the light swirled around me. The rhythmic sound of the rotating beam and the distant crashing waves blended into a symphony of sensory experiences. The stark contrast between light and shadow, the warmth of the beam, and the chill of the night air all mingled, creating a surreal dance of sensations. The lighthouse's glow became my entire world, the pulse of the light like a heartbeat, guiding me forward until I felt completely enveloped by the luminous glow.

The change was both exhilarating and disorienting. The familiar surroundings of the lighthouse and stormy seas dissolved into a swirling haze, replaced by a new realm unlike anything I had ever seen. Instead of trees with traditional bark, towering structures surrounded me, their surfaces reflective like mirrors, casting eerie glimmers in the shifting light. A mixture of awe and apprehension coursed through me as I took in this strange new world. My heart pounded with a mix of excitement and anxiety, each step forward feeling both thrilling and unnerving. Drawn by curiosity, I walked towards one of these reflective trees, my mind racing to understand the surreal transformation. As I approached, my image emerged from the mirrored surface, staring back at me. The reflection felt eerily familiar, yet something was distinctly different. My face, while recognizable, bore a weight of wisdom and stability that seemed foreign and profound. I couldn't shake the feeling that this reflection was showing me a version of myself I didn't fully understand—one that seemed both distant and intimately connected to who I am. A wave of confusion washed over me. *Why does my reflection look so different?* I thought, my mind struggling to reconcile the image before me with the person I know myself to be. I reached up to touch my cheek, feeling the smooth texture of my skin, and watched as the mirrored version of myself mimicked the movement with eerie precision. The glassy surface of the tree shimmered with each shift, creating ripples that danced across the reflective surface.

As I extended my hand to touch the tree, the surface rippled under my fingertips like water disturbed by a gentle breeze. Startled, I jumped back, my heart racing with wonder and fear. *Is this a part of me or something entirely separate?* I wondered, feeling both captivated and unsettled. The shimmering, liquid-like movement of the tree's surface left me feeling like the fabric of reality was bending around me. I was caught in a liminal space between the familiar and the unknown. Being in a place where the rules of nature seemed to be rewritten filled me with a deep, unsettled curiosity and a yearning to understand what this strange, reflective world might reveal about myself and my journey.

The ripples gradually settled, forming a clear image. The scene materialized around me, plunging me into a vivid memory. I was brought back to the tin can alley, I watched as we laughed and teased each other. From Luke's perspective, I watched as he deliberately missed his shots, a mischievous glint in my eyes as I glanced over at my younger-self. I could see the smile spread across my face when she offered to take a turn, catching the hint of awkwardness in our interaction. I looked at her, younger and nervous, during our first date at the fun fair. The fairgrounds buzzed with life around us, vibrant and energetic, filling the scene with their sights and sounds. With the perspective shift, I could feel his intentions. He wanted to break the ice, make me laugh, and ease the nervous tension. He had lost on purpose, creating a moment for me to shine, share a laugh, and bridge the gap of unfamiliarity. I stepped closer to the mirrored tree, my hand hovering over its shimmering surface as I watched the memory play out. Even then, the joy in Luke's eyes sparkled with happiness as his genuine affection warmed me. The reflective surface rippled again as the memory faded, returning to its original state. I stepped back, my thoughts filled with Luke. *I never knew Luke had let me win that night. I thought my aim had just miraculously improved. He was always looking out for me, even in the smallest ways. He wanted to see me smile, to make our first date special. I never realized how much thought he put into those moments.*

Curiosity led me to the next tree, eager to understand how Luke perceived our relationship. I reached out, my hand lightly brushing its reflective surface. As my touch disturbed the mirror-like sheen, the reflection rippled like water, revealing another scene from Luke's point of view. This time I was shown a chaotic base camp, the air was thick with urgency and tension. Soldiers' boots crunched on gravel, mingling with the low, constant murmur of voices and the occasional sharp shout. The metallic clatter of equipment and the distant rumble of machinery created a continuous backdrop of noise punctuated by the distant thud of artillery.

Luke sat on his bunk; a bead of sweat trickled down his temple as he focused intently on a piece of paper before him. His firm grip on the pen created a scratching sound as it moved swiftly yet carefully across the page. The paper crinkled slightly under his touch while his brow remained furrowed in concentration. Despite the chaotic atmosphere of the camp, marked by the rough textures and constant sounds, Luke's eyes were filled with resolve and longing. His calm focus during the clamor highlighted the importance of the letter he was writing—my letter. When he finished writing, Luke paused momentarily, reading over his words. A soft smile touched his lips, and he pressed the letter to them, giving it a brief kiss. The tender gesture was full of longing and love.

"Hey, Romeo, what's with the love letter?" one of his army mates called out, as he settled down on the bunk beside Luke .

Luke's eyes narrowed slightly as he folded the letter with deliberate care. "It's for Dee," he replied, his voice steady and defensive.

The soldier chuckled, not sensing the shift in Luke's demeanor. "Didn't know you were such a romantic."

"Yeah, well," Luke said, standing up and meeting his friend's gaze, "when you have someone worth writing to, it changes things."

The playful teasing halted as the other soldier nodded in understanding, revealing their camaraderie and respect. Luke tucked the letter into his jacket, his eyes distant and I could feel his thoughts were of me. The image rippled and faded, dissolving into the rough bark of the tree. As I stepped back, the trees around me seemed to undulate and shift, their once-ordinary surfaces now mirroring back fractured images of myself. Each reflection moved with a curious autonomy, gesturing in unison, urging me to advance. My heart raced with a mix of intrigue and unease as I cautiously proceeded, my eyes darting to the shifting mirrored figures that seemed to beckon me forward. With every step deeper into the forest, the reflective trees grew more dazzling. The light, fractured into a thousand tiny prisms, danced and sparkled around me, creating an almost blinding brilliance. The forest's once-muted hues exploded into vibrant, dazzling colors that seemed to pulse with each beat of my heart. The light cascaded like a torrent, overwhelming my senses. I raised one hand to shield my eyes from the intense glare, feeling the warmth of the light even through my closed eyelids.

The forest, now a prism of shifting reflections and blinding radiance, felt both mesmerizing and disorienting. I raised my hand instinctively, squinting through the dazzling brilliance that seemed to seep into every corner of my vision. The intensity of the light was almost tangible, pressing against my eyes like a tangible force. My hand shielded my face, but the glow still seeped through my fingers, turning the world into a blur of intense, radiant colors. The forest felt like it was pulsating with a frenetic energy, its beauty so overwhelming that it left me both entranced and momentarily lost. With my sight impaired, I abruptly felt the sensation under my feet change. Instead of the soft grass I had grown accustomed to, I felt something rough and granular shifting between my toes. Peeking through my fingers, I saw the familiar texture of sand unfolding before me. My heart raced with curiosity and fear as I took hesitant steps forward, lowering my hand, the gentle crunch of sand beneath my feet echoing in the quiet surroundings.

****

I lifted my gaze and found myself abruptly transported from the mirror forest to an endless expanse of golden sand. The expansive desert stretched infinitely, its undulating dunes forming a sea of shimmering gold that seemed to ripple in the heat. The sun hung mercilessly high in the sky, casting a blinding glare that made the sand appear as if it were aflame. Each grain of sand glistened like tiny shards of sunlight, creating a dazzling, almost hypnotic effect that made it hard to discern where the sky ended and the earth began. A searing heat radiated up from the dunes, wrapping around me like an oppressive blanket. The air felt thick and dry, each breath drawing in the arid, sun-baked aroma of the desert. The silence was profound, broken only by the occasional whisper of wind shifting the sand in soft, sighing gusts. My footsteps sank into the powdery surface, leaving faint, transient imprints that were quickly swallowed by the shifting sands.

Dread washed over me, heavy and suffocating. There was no sign of the forest's reflective allure—just the relentless expanse of golden dunes stretching endlessly. The oppressive vastness bore down on me, offering no sanctuary or direction, only an unbroken horizon and the stark realization that there was no visible escape, no doorway or path to return to the place I had left behind. The enormity of the desert, combined with its blinding brilliance and desolate silence, created an overwhelming sense of isolation and helplessness. A wave of anxiety hit me as I began walking. The sand shifted beneath my feet, each step dragging like a slog through thick mud. The sun blazed persistently overhead, its scorching heat searing my skin and draining my energy. With every step, my feet sank into the hot sand, emerging blistered and sore. The vast stretch of sand seemed to taunt me, endless and unyielding. As I walked, time felt meaningless. What felt like hours might have been minutes, and the empty desert prolonged endlessly in every direction. The unchanging landscape made me feel more isolated with each step, and the sun's punishing heat left me dehydrated and disoriented. My vision blurred from the heat and exhaustion.

The desert shimmered, and distant shapes flickered in and out of focus. At first, I thought they were just tricks of the light. But the shapes grew more apparent, and I saw Luke standing on a far-off dune. His figure stood out sharply against the bright sky, giving me hope. I called out his name and hurried towards him with all the energy I could muster, but as I got closer, the image vanished, leaving just empty sand. Determined, I kept going, but Luke's ghostly presence kept appearing. Sometimes, he was closer, reaching out to me, his face full of concern. I tried to grab his hand, but he vanished like smoke. His image appeared in different places—sitting on the sand with his familiar smile, walking beside me, or laughing joyfully like we were at the fair. Each time, I felt comforted momentarily before the illusion disappeared, deepening my sense of loss. The mirages grew more vivid. I heard Luke's voice telling me I could do it and that I had the strength to keep going. But every vision only made my longing sharper. My feet were bleeding and raw, each step a test of my resolve. The desert seemed never-ending, and the line between reality and illusion blurred. I felt like I was on the brink of madness, but I kept moving, hoping that somewhere beyond the dunes, there would be an end.

My shoulders sagged under an invisible burden, each step sinking deeper into the scorching sand. The horizon stretched endlessly before me, a vast, unbroken expanse of golden dunes that seemed to mock my every effort. My legs felt like lead, dragging through the gritty sand, each movement sapping the last reserves of my strength. My breath came in ragged, shallow gasps, the oppressive heat pressing down on me like the unrelenting weight of fibromyalgia pain, making every inhale feel labored and every exhale a struggle.

Mistrust gnawed at the edges of my mind. The endless sea of dunes felt like a labyrinth with no exit, and the relentless sun overhead offered no solace. The silence around me was heavy, broken only by the whisper of the wind as it shifted the sand in subtle, mocking ripples. The vast emptiness seemed to swallow my footsteps, erasing any evidence of my progress and amplifying the isolation that wrapped around me like a shroud. Each time I glanced at the endless stretch of sand, the oppressive feeling grew stronger, whispering that I was trapped in a never-ending desert with no direction, no guide, and no hope of escape. But as my thoughts churned, I thought back on what I had learned. My mother's wisdom about cherishing each moment, Evie's reminder to enjoy the journey, Liam's advice on staying true to myself, my father's plea to be present, and Luke's belief in me—all these pieces of wisdom fueled my determination.

I took a deep inhale, feeling the sting of the hot air in my lungs causing me to cough, and kept moving forward. Even when my feet ached, and my spirit felt broken, I pressed on, knowing that every step was part of my journey. As I climbed another sand hill, my heart leapt at the sight of a small oasis in the hollow below. I ran towards the oasis, my legs trembling and unsteady, each step sending a jarring echo through the still desert air. The shimmering mirage in the distance seemed almost too good to be true, but with every stride, the vivid sight of sparkling blue water became more evident. I stumbled, tripping over the uneven, golden sand, the rough texture scraping my palms as I fell. My heart raced, and my muscles burned with fatigue, but I refused to stop. As I collapsed at the edge of the oasis, my hands plunged into the cool, inviting water. The refreshing liquid offered immediate relief, its purity a sharp contrast to the dry, dusty taste of the desert that had clung to my mouth for days. I drank deeply, the water soothing my parched throat with its life-giving essence. The coolness of the water on my face was refreshing, washing away the grit and exhaustion that had accumulated. I splashed water onto my face, feeling the oasis's relief and cool embrace.

The water began to shimmer under the sun's harsh rays, I hesitated, uncertain if this was another cruel trick of the desert. But as I stared, the surface of the oasis transformed, showing me another memory. Suddenly, I was back at my mother's funeral. Only this time I saw myself standing at the podium, my voice steady despite the heaviness in my heart. I watched myself with a new perspective. I saw strength in my posture, a resolve not to break in the face of overwhelming grief. My words were a tribute to my mother's life; each sentence proved the love and lessons she had imparted. Luke stood nearby, watching supportively, his presence a steady anchor in my sea of emotions.

"Thank you all for gathering today to celebrate the remarkable life of my mother. She was a woman of grace, wisdom, and boundless love, touching the lives of everyone she met. One of the most profound lessons she taught me was the importance of living fully in every moment and embracing opportunities without hesitation. I cherish countless afternoons spent with her, where she would pause to admire a breathtaking sunset, listen intently to children's laughter echoing through the park, or simply savor the quiet joy of being surrounded by loved ones. These moments, she would say, are the essence of life—the small, beautiful fragments that define our existence.

"Her life exemplified seizing opportunities and finding joy in the present. She encouraged me to pursue my dreams boldly, reminding me never to let fear hold me back. I recall a specific instance when she urged me to take a chance on a new path, assuring me that every moment is an opportunity to learn, grow, and connect with others. Even in her final days, she remained a beacon of strength and positivity, teaching us all to find joy and gratitude in the simplest of things. Her unwavering spirit in the face of adversity showed us that even amidst challenges, there are moments of profound beauty and love. Today, as we honor my mother's memory, let us carry forward her legacy by living as she did—fully present, embracing every opportunity, and finding joy in the everyday moments. Her spirit will continue to guide us through the love and memories we share. Thank you, Mom, for teaching us the true meaning of life. Your lessons and love will forever resonate in our hearts. I love you, Mom."

The water shifted, to manifest a memory of me and Atlas, sitting at the kitchen table. He looked up at me, his innocent eyes filled with curiosity and longing as he asked about his mother. I hesitated, feeling the weight of the past pressing down on me, but I knew I had to be strong—for both of us.

A smile tugged at my lips as I told him the tales of our escapades together. "Well, there was this one time when we decided to sneak out past curfew to explore the abandoned amusement park at the edge of town. Your mom, always fearless, led the way through overgrown paths and broken fences like she owned the place."

Atlas chuckled, clearly captivated by the stories of his adventurous mother. "What happened next?"

"We ended up climbing onto the old roller coaster tracks," I continued, my voice full of excitement reliving those moments. "I dared your mum to ride the frail coaster cart down the first hill. Of course, She couldn't back down from a challenge, so she did it!"

Atlas grinned, imagining the scene vividly. "Wow, Mom was brave!"

"She was," I affirmed warmly, my heart swelling with love and pride for Evie. "And she had a way of turning ordinary days into unforgettable adventures. Like the time we got lost in the woods during a camping trip and ended up making friends with a family of squirrels."

Atlas laughed, clearly entertained by the image of his mom surrounded by woodland creatures. "That sounds like something she'd do."

I nodded, tears pricking the corners of my eyes from laughter as I continued. "Your mom had a spirit that couldn't be contained. She taught me so much about embracing life's surprises and finding joy in every moment, no matter how small."

Atlas leaned closer, absorbing every word with rapt attention. "Thank you, Auntie Dee. I feel closer to mum."

"You're welcome, Atlas," I replied softly, feeling a deep connection as we reminisced.

"Do you think my mummy is in heaven?" he asked quietly.

The question caught me off guard, and for a moment, I was at a loss for words. I took a deep breath, searching for the right words to ease his tender heart. "Of course," I began gently, reaching out to place a comforting hand over his small, earnest heart. "I believe she is watching over you right now. Even though you can't see her, she is here." I pointed softly to his chest. "She's always with you, in here."

Atlas looked down, his gaze lingering on where my hand rested, as if trying to feel the truth of my words.

"If we carry on the stories of her, if we remember them and keep their memory alive, they will live on forever," I continued, hoping my words would bring him some comfort. "Every time you remember her, every time you tell her stories, it's like she is right here with us."

Atlas's eyes filled with a mixture of hope and understanding. "So, she knows everything that's happening with me?"

I nodded, offering him a reassuring smile. "Yes, Atlas. She knows and she cares. She would be so proud of you, and she would love to see the person you're becoming."

The moon hung high, casting a silvery glow over the landscape. The gentle breeze carried the scent of blooming jasmine and freshly cut grass, mingling with the faint, earthy aroma of the evening dew. The sound of crickets chirping created a soothing backdrop, their rhythmic symphony blending with the occasional rustle of leaves in the breeze. I could feel the smooth texture of the wooden porch beneath me, its surface slightly worn from years of use but still warm from the day's sun. The night's chill brushed against my skin, a pleasant contrast to the lingering warmth of the day. I glanced at Luke.

I sighed softly, my gaze drifting out into the night as Luke's quiet voice called my name.

"Dee…"

I turned towards him, my heart heavy with both sadness and determination. "Luke, we need to talk."

He nodded slowly, his eyes reflecting the emotions swirling within him. "I know."

Swallowing the lump in my throat, I gathered my thoughts. "This distance… It's been so hard on both of us."

Luke hesitated, then withdrew his hand after reaching out briefly. "I never wanted it to be like this."

Taking a deep breath to steady myself, I looked out at the familiar porch where we'd shared so many moments. "Neither did I. But I also don't want to hold you back from chasing your dreams, Luke. If the army is what you want to do, I won't stand in your way."

His nod was filled with understanding, his gaze steady on mine. "I miss you, Dee. Every day."

Tears threatened to spill from my eyes, but I fought to keep them in check. "I miss you too, Luke. But…" I hesitated, struggling to find the right words. "…but maybe this isn't the right time for us. Not now."

Luke looked down, his expression tinged with sadness. "I understand. But that doesn't make it any easier."

I shook my head, trying to hold back the lump in my throat. "It's not just about what's easier. It's about what's right. And as much as it hurts to say this, maybe breaking up is the best decision for us right now."

He looked up at me, his eyes reflecting a mix of hope and heartbreak. "But I wish you'd fight for us, Dee. I wish you'd tell me you want me to stay."

I took a deep breath, feeling the weight of my conflicted heart. "I do want you to stay, Luke. I want us to be together. But I also want you to follow your dreams, even if it means going separate ways for a while. It's so hard because I want both— for you to be with me and for you to be true to yourself."

Luke's eyes softened, and he took a step closer, his voice barely above a whisper. "So what does that mean for us?"

Reaching out, I gently took his hand, holding it with tenderness and sorrow. "It means that we need to figure things out. We need to find ourselves again, separately, before we can see if we can come back together. This doesn't mean it's over forever. It just means... we need time."

He squeezed my hand gently, his eyes filled with love and acceptance. "I know. And I'm willing to wait. For however long it takes. I'll be here, working on my dreams, and hoping that maybe, someday, we'll find our way back to each other."

I nodded, tears finally slipping down my cheeks. "Thank you, Luke. That means more to me than you know. And no matter where we go from here, I'll always cherish what we had and hope for what might be."

Luke leaned forward, brushing a tear from my cheek with his thumb. "I love you, Dee. Always."

I whispered softly, my voice breaking with emotion, "I love you too, Luke. Always."

The soft glow from the porch light cast a warm, golden hue around us, contrasting sharply with the cold, creeping night air. Luke's thumb gently brushed against the back of my hand, a soothing, rhythmic gesture that spoke volumes about his care and affection. I could feel the warmth of his skin, a welcome reprieve from the cool night. I squeezed his hand, trying to convey all the words I couldn't find. My heart ached with the realization that this was the end of a chapter, but not the end of the story we had begun together. The silence between us was heavy, filled with the weight of unspoken thoughts and the echoes of what-ifs. Luke leaned back against the wooden porch railing, staring at the star-studded sky. The stars seemed to twinkle with a melancholy brilliance, their distant light a metaphor for the hope we both clung to despite our separation.

"I'm going to miss this," he finally said, his voice low and reflective. "Miss sitting here with you, talking about everything and nothing, sharing the quiet moments."

I nodded, unable to speak for a moment. I fought to keep the tears at bay, taking in the familiar sounds of the night that had once been a backdrop to our shared memories. "Me too," I managed to say, my voice catching slightly. "I'll miss how you always knew how to make me laugh, even when I didn't feel like smiling."

He turned to look at me, his eyes glistening with unshed tears. "And I'll miss how you always made me feel like everything was going to be okay, no matter what was happening."

We both took a deep breath, letting the cool night air fill our lungs. The tension in our bodies eased slightly as if the simple act of holding hands was enough to calm the storm raging within us.

"I guess this is what it feels like to let go," Luke said quietly, his fingers brushing a stray strand of hair from my face. "It's hard, but maybe it's what we need right now."

I nodded, trying to muster a brave smile through my tears. "Yeah, it's hard. But maybe it's also the right thing. We need to find out who we are on our own before we can truly be together again."

As I sat at the edge of the oasis, a disturbing shift began beneath me. The sand felt alive, slipping through my fingers like quicksilver, while the once-clear water became a jagged, shimmering expanse. The surface of the water churned violently, its calm ripples now a chaotic swirl, pulling everything into a dark, swirling abyss.

12

Fireflies

The oasis began to sink into the swirling abyss; panic surged through me, causing my legs to falter. I stumbled backwards, my heart hammering so violently it felt like it might burst from my chest. The sand around me followed suit, its surface rippling and plunging into the mysterious void that seemed to stretch endlessly downward. Desperation clawed at me as I scrambled on all fours, my hands scrabbling futilely at the disintegrating ground. Each tremor beneath me echoed the rising dread inside, making my entire body quake with fear. A chill crept up my spine as the oasis dissolved into the dark maw below. The once vibrant landscape dissolved into a shadowy emptiness, leaving only the haunting memory of its beauty behind. The intense pull of gravity seemed to grow stronger with each passing moment, an evil force threatening to drag me into the abyss alongside it. I could feel the icy grip of terror tightening around my chest.

My breath came in ragged gasps, my throat tightening as the edge of the collapsing sand drew closer. I squeezed my eyes shut, bracing for the inevitable plunge into darkness. But an odd sensation of weightlessness enveloped me instead of the anticipated fall. Trembling, I slowly opened my eyes. To my astonishment, I sat on a narrow glass bridge suspended high above an endless expanse of clouds. The sky stretched infinitely around me, its serene blue blending seamlessly with the distant horizon. The cool, smooth glass beneath me sent a shiver through my limbs, contrasting sharply with the terror that had just gripped me. The bridge swayed gently, adding to the disorienting sensation of floating weightlessly.

   A soft, cool breeze caressed my face, carrying a whispering symphony that mingled with the breathtaking panorama before me. My dress fluttered around me, its fabric billowing in response to the playful wind. The sensation of the glass against my bare feet was both soothing and surreal, an odd comfort amidst the strangeness of my situation. Looking down, I saw only a thick, fluffy blanket of clouds below, as if I had ascended to a realm untouched by earthly concerns. As I rose from the bridge floor, a part of me tensed, half-expecting the fragile structure to shatter under my weight. But the cool glass beneath my soles held firm, grounding me in this new reality. Each step I took was accompanied by a thrilling rush of exhilaration, a sense of liberation that defied all logic and expectation. With every movement, a wave of reflection washed over me. The trials of the desert had not merely been physical challenges; they had been a deep journey into my history. Each obstacle overcome, each struggle faced, had molded me into who I had become. The desert had tested my limits and reshaped my understanding of myself and the world. A sense of peace settled within me as I paused, taking in the boundless sky.

   The fear and uncertainty that had once gripped me dissipated, replaced by a quiet confidence born from my journey. I inhaled deeply, feeling a serene calm as I approached the edge of the bridge. My fingers curled around the rail, the smooth, cool glass offering a reassuring touch. Below me, the clouds began to swirl and form a vortex, their movements hypnotic. Drawn in by the mesmerizing display, I leaned closer. The swirling clouds parted, unveiling a vivid scene from my past. I saw myself standing in a cozy bookshop, the sign above the door reading "The Reading Nook." The rich aroma of freshly brewed coffee that wafted from a quaint café area tucked at the back of the store enhanced the shop's inviting warmth.

The soft murmur of conversation and the clink of mugs added to the shop's comforting ambience. I was browsing the shelves, lost in the quest for my next adventure. The gentle doorbell chime interrupted my reverie, and I looked up, my heart skipping a beat. There stood Luke, his weary eyes meeting mine with a flicker of recognition. Despite the fatigue etched into his features and the guarded distance that now marked his demeanor, a fragment of his old warmth shone through in his smile as he approached me.

"Dee," he said, his voice tinged with relief.

Overcome by astonishment, I stumbled over to him, my steps shaky. My voice quivered as I spoke, my pulse quickening with a mix of disbelief and excitement. "Luke," I managed to say, my words coming out in a stammer. We stood there, suspended in a moment of uncertainty, the air thick with the weight of unspoken emotions. "What are you doing here? I thought you were still on tour."

"I'm back." he said with a smile, "Evie told me I could find you here, but I had to come and see you. Can I get you a coffee?" Luke suggested, nodding towards the small café section at the back of the shop. His smile hit me like a wave of warmth, and I couldn't help but notice the way his dimples appeared with that familiar curve of his lips. It had been too long since I'd seen that smile, and suddenly, I realized how much I'd missed it. His smile was like a beacon that drew me in, and the sight of it made me ache with a longing I hadn't expected.

"Sure, I would love a coffee." I agreed, leading the way. We settled into a corner booth, the familiar scent of coffee and old books enveloping us.

"How have you been?" I asked, trying to sound casual. Rubbing my sweaty palms against my jeans.

He hesitated for a moment before answering. "I've been good. You?"

"Good," I echoed, my words as hollow as his. We both knew our answers had no truth, but neither pressed further. In the heavy silence that followed, I blurted out, "I've been writing again."

"That's great! I'm really happy for you," he said, his eyes lighting up and his smile stretching so wide it nearly reached his ears. He gave a soft chuckle, shaking his head slightly as if trying to contain his delight. I could see how genuinely thrilled he was for me. After a brief pause, his smile softened into something more tender, and he looked down, his voice barely above a whisper. "I missed you." The words lingered between us, his gaze meeting mine with a mixture of vulnerability and affection. I could see the sincerity in his eyes, the way they held a quiet, wistful longing that made my heart flutter.

"I missed you too," I confessed, feeling a lump in my throat. "It hasn't been the same without you."

Luke looked at me intently, searching for something in my eyes. "Are you seeing anyone?" he asked, his tone casual but his eyes betraying his genuine curiosity.

I shook my head. "No, I'm not."

A small smile tugged at the corners of his lips. "Good," he said softly, reaching across the table to take my hand. "I'm glad."

The clouds molded, and I found myself back on the sky bridge, gripping the rail tightly. I closed my eyes for a moment, savoring the warmth of our renewed connection. It felt like an old song had played again, and I was dancing to its familiar tune. I stood there, high above the clouds, and I understood the parallel paths we had been walking. Luke's war struggle was about survival, facing the horrors, and reclaiming a sense of normalcy. My struggle had been about finding my inner strength, standing tall in the face of adversity, and learning to trust myself. Like our connection, the glass bridge beneath me felt fragile and unbreakable. Each memory that resurfaced was a piece of our shared history. I continued to walk; the clouds swirled and shifted, exposing more memories. I saw us on a road trip, I could almost feel the sun-drenched breeze on my face, whipping through my hair as we sped down the highway. The sound of our laughter intertwined with the music blasting from the speakers, each note vibrating through the car's interior. The scent of pine and fresh asphalt mingled in the air, and the endless stretch of road ahead seemed to promise freedom, each mile unraveling the weight of our worries as we shared glances and smiles that spoke of pure, unburdened joy.

"Remember this song?" Luke shouted over the wind, his smile infectious.

"Of course! It's our song!" I replied, turning up the volume. We sang together, our voices loud and terrible. But we didn't care.

The clouds parted to reveal a sunlit summer festival bursting with color. We strolled among the lively stalls, the earthy aroma of popcorn and sweet, sugary treats mingling in the air. Our fingers brushed occasionally, and I could feel the warmth of Luke's hand clasped in mine. His face lit up like a child's at the sight of a vintage record player; his eyes sparkled with a deep, infectious excitement. The rich, mellow sound of old vinyl crackling from the player seemed to fill the air with an almost tangible warmth, a harmony that mirrored the sudden, vivid thrill that surged through me.

"Look at this beauty," he said, crouching down to examine the record player.

"You should get it," I encouraged, loving how his enthusiasm made his eyes shine.

"Only if you promise we'll dance to every record I play," As he spoke, he wrapped his arm around my waist, pulling me gently toward him.

"Deal," I laughed, sealing it with a kiss. Pushing him away.

****

The clouds unfolded to a rainy afternoon in a cozy café. We sat by the window, the world outside blurred by the falling rain. Luke had just returned from another tour, and his silence spoke volumes. I reached across the table, my hand finding his, offering silent support.

"Talk to me," I whispered, my eyes searching his. I reached out to grasp his hand.

"It's just… hard to switch off," he admitted, his voice thick with emotion.

"I'm here," I said simply, squeezing his hand. "For as long as it takes."

The memories continued to unfold. Later that night, we stayed up talking until dawn, sharing our fears and dreams. "I'm scared of the dark," he continued, his voice cracking, "it's like it's always waiting, lurking just beyond the edges of the light." His eyes, shadowed and distant, were haunted by unspoken fears, reflecting the turmoil that clung to him like a second skin. He shifted uncomfortably as if trying to shake off the lingering ghosts of his past.

"Me too," I admitted, my own fears bubbling to the surface.

"I just can't shake them sometimes," Luke admitted, his voice hushed as we sat in the quiet of our living room. "The images, the sounds... they follow me even when I'm awake."

I reached for his hand, offering what comfort I could. "You don't have to face them alone, Luke. I'm here for you, always."

He squeezed my hand gratefully, his eyes reflecting relief and lingering anguish. "Thank you, Dee. Knowing that you're here makes a world of difference."

The clouds rolled away to reveal the scene: Luke waking in the dead of night, drenched in a cold sweat that clung to his skin like a clammy shroud. His breaths came in jagged, frantic bursts, each inhale a sharp gasp that seemed to pierce through the oppressive silence of the room. The cool night air brushed against our skin, making the dampness on his forehead feel even colder. I could feel the rapid thrum of his heartbeat beneath my fingertips as I held him close, the steady pulse of his fear palpable against my chest. His breaths were hot against my neck, mingling with the scent of sweat and the faint tang of distress. I wrapped my arms around him, my touch gentle yet firm, trying to offer him a sense of stability.

"Stay with me," Luke pleaded, his arms tightening around me as if afraid I might slip away.

"I'm not going anywhere," I assured him, kissing his forehead gently. "You're safe now, with me."

As I stood on the glass bridge, lost in reflection, a faint crack caught my eye on the floor beneath me. It was barely noticeable at first, a thin line stretching across the transparent surface. My heart skipped a beat, a jolt of fear gripping me—*was the bridge giving way beneath me?* The crack widened suddenly, spreading like a spider's web across the glass, each new fracture a chilling sign of impending disaster. Panic surged through me as the bridge began to shatter into countless shards. The sound was deafening, a high-pitched shriek of breaking glass that reverberated in my ears as the structure splintered. Desperately, I tried to run, but the glass beneath my feet fractured completely, crumbling away with a thunderous crash. I felt myself falling, the world tilting and spinning as I plummeted into the vast expanse of clouds below.

The rush of air whipped fiercely against my face, tearing away my breath and gasping me. The sensation was disorienting, the cold wind mixing with the heat of panic. There was no time to scream; the sensation of falling deeper into the unknown consumed me. Shards of large, glistening crystals began to surround me as I tumbled. The fear of the drop below melted away as I embraced the air around me, letting go of my fear and uncertainty. I realized that this journey was not just about physical trials or emotional upheavals but about embracing the revelations and strength found within the chaos. I closed my eyes, bracing for impact. Yet, instead of the expected jolt, I felt the rushing air slow and soften around me. Something warm and comforting pressed against my back, cushioning my descent.

Slowly, cautiously, I opened my eyes.

****

Before me stretched a cave unlike any I had ever seen. The walls, instead of cold stone, were woven from the rough bark of old trees. The bark twisted and curved, forming a protective embrace that surrounded me—shafts of soft light filtered through the gaps, casting gentle patterns on the moss-covered ground. I blinked, trying to take in the strange beauty of my surroundings. Huge trees rose high above, their branches intertwining to form a natural roof. Sunlight trickled through the leaves, dappling the ground in a dance of light and shadow. The ground was covered in thick, green moss, which felt soft underfoot and smelled faintly of earth. The scene felt like a secret hideaway. The air was fresh and cool, with a gentle breeze carrying the soft sounds of distant birds. It was a peaceful, magical place, offering a quiet escape from the world outside.

As I stood up, a hush fell over the cavern, broken only by the soft fluttering of hundreds of fireflies. Their tiny bodies glowed with a warm, golden light, creating a shimmering ballet in the air. Each firefly's gentle, pulsating light wove intricate patterns—dancing spirals and graceful arcs—that bathed the cavern in an enchanting, magical glow. The air was alive with a symphony of soft sounds. I could hear the rustling of leaves high above, a soothing whisper that blended with the distant murmur of a babbling brook. I took a hesitant step forward, feeling the ground beneath my feet. It was soft and yielding, like walking on a bed of thick, plush moss that cushioned each step. With every movement, a wave of calm washed over me, soothing my senses and making me feel more at ease.

As I ventured deeper into the cavern, I noticed the bark of the living trees was etched with detailed marks—symbols and shapes that told a story of ancient wisdom. I reached out, my fingers brushing against the cool, rough texture of the carvings. Each touch sent a subtle, tingling sensation through my fingertips, making me feel a deep, profound connection to the timeless stories and hidden truths woven into the very fabric of the trees. The gentle glow of fireflies ahead steered me away from the carvings. Their soft, golden light created a mesmerizing display, dancing in intricate patterns that seemed to pulse with a life of their own. Each firefly floated and twirled through the air like tiny, living stars, their delicate light flickering and shimmering in the cool, still air.

Intrigued, I cautiously moved closer, stepping lightly as the fireflies' warm glow illuminated the path before me. Their tiny bodies drifted effortlessly, casting a dreamlike radiance over the surroundings. The light they emitted was soft and soothing, a gentle contrast to the cool shadows of the cavern. As I reached out with my hand, one firefly separated from the group. It descended slowly, its glow intensifying as it approached. It floated gracefully through the air, its light casting a soft, golden hue on my outstretched finger. The moment it landed, it felt like a delicate, warm tickle against my skin, and I could feel a subtle vibration as the firefly's tiny legs made contact. The gentle, fleeting touch was a calming sensation, adding to the sense of wonder and serenity that filled the cavern.

Its glow intensified suddenly, a burst of light that momentarily blinded me as if capturing a moment with a camera flash. Blinking against the brightness, I stood in a sunlit office, manuscript in hand, listening as the representatives of a traditional publishing house proposed extensive changes to my novel. Their vision was different from mine, altering the essence of my story. Doubt gnawed at me as I wrestled with their suggestions.

Luke sat beside me, "You know your story better than anyone else," he reminded me gently. "Trust your instincts, Dee. This is your dream."

With Luke's support, I made the courageous choice to self-publish. Fear clenched at my heart—I was stepping into unknown territory, unsure of the outcome. But with Luke by my side, I knew I was not alone. The thought of honoring the story I had poured my soul into gave me strength. The firefly flashed again, revealing another memory. Evie and I stood outside a boutique window, where a stunning black dress caught her eye. My gaze was drawn to the stunning black dress showcased inside. It hung on a sleek, modern mannequin, its fabric catching the ambient light and shimmering with a subtle, lustrous sheen.

"Dee, you have to try this on," Evie enthusiastically insisted.

I hesitated, glancing at the dress uncertainty. "Oh, Evie, I don't know… It's probably not my style, and they properly won't have my size," I replied, my voice tinged with self-consciousness.

Evie rolled her eyes playfully. "Dee, come on! You've got to stop hiding behind those baggy shirts and jeans. You have such a gorgeous figure, and this dress would look amazing on you."

I shifted uncomfortably, feeling exposed under Evie's unwavering gaze. "I just… I'm unsure if I can pull it off," I quietly admitted.

Evie's expression softened, her voice gentle. "Dee, trust me. You deserve to feel beautiful. Let's just try it on for fun, okay? No pressure."

The firefly on my finger lifted into the air, its gentle glow dimming as it fluttered away, leaving me in the soft, twilight embrace of the living tree sanctuary. I wiped a stray tear from my cheek, feeling the cool, damp touch of the tear against my skin. As I looked around, my gaze fell upon a door carved into the bark wall nearby. The door seemed to emerge naturally from the tree, its edges seamlessly integrated into the intricate patterns of the bark. The surface of the door was etched with delicate, winding designs that mirrored the organic shapes of the tree's growth, giving it an ancient, mystical quality. Standing before the door, I noticed there was no handle—just a smooth, continuous expanse of carved bark. A mix of hope and uncertainty fluttered in my chest as I placed my hand on its surface. My fingers traced the intricate patterns etched into the wood, feeling the cool, textured grain beneath my touch. With a deep breath, I gently pushed against the door. To my surprise, it swung open with a smooth, silent motion as if gliding on an invisible track. The soft, wooden creak was barely audible, and the door's movement was so fluid that it seemed almost magical.

As the door opened wider, a warm, inviting light spilt into the corridor, bathing the space beyond in a gentle, golden glow. Stepping through, I found myself in a vast, circular chamber. The air was crisp and carried the subtle, earthy aroma of the forest, mingling with a hint of pine and fresh moss. The chamber's floor was covered in a lush, deep green moss that felt springy and soft underfoot. From the center of the room, countless paths radiated outwards like the spokes of a giant wheel. Each path was lined with stones that glistened softly in the ambient light, their surfaces smooth and cool. The paths stretched out in different directions, weaving through the chamber like veins of an ancient, living organism.

The chamber walls were covered with glowing bioluminescent fungi, casting a soft, pulsating light that created shifting patterns of shadow and light across the space. The soft hum of the fungi added a calming background noise, like a distant lullaby. As I took in the scene, the sheer scale of the chamber and the multitude of paths leading from its center filled me with a sense of awe and wonder. Each pathway seemed to hold the promise of discovery, and the entire space exuded an atmosphere of mystery and endless possibility.

I stood at the edge of the chamber, my breath quickening and becoming shallow as I scanned my surroundings. The oppressive silence weighed heavily on me, making my chest tighten with an almost tangible pressure. "Which one?" I muttered to myself, my voice barely breaking the stillness and echoing softly in the vast, cavernous space. Decision came swiftly. With a mixture of anxiety and determination, I chose the path to the left. The moment my foot touched the aged stone, it responded with a sudden, warm glow, as though it had been roused from slumber by my presence. The illumination was both surprising and slightly comforting. As I stepped further, the stone path shimmered beneath me, casting a gentle, golden light that danced across the surrounding walls. The light revealed intricate patterns etched into the stone, ancient runes that seemed to come alive with each step I took. The stone felt cool and solid underfoot, its chill contrasting with the comforting warmth of the light it emitted. I could even feel a subtle vibration pulsing through it, as if the stone was alive and responsive to my presence.

"Well, that's a good sign," I whispered, a hint of relief and reassurance coloring my voice. The warmth and glow of the path provided a sense of direction and purpose, easing the earlier conflict and hesitation that had gripped me. I took each step cautiously. The path had no sides, just a dark gray mist below that seemed eager to swallow me whole. The cold stone beneath my feet felt reassuringly solid, but the emptiness on either side was unnerving. I had made it halfway down the illuminated path when a harsh breeze sliced through the chamber, catching me off guard. My arms flailed wildly as I fought to stay upright, but the force of the wind was too much. My feet slipped out from under me, and I crashed hard onto the stone, my knees slamming against the unforgiving surface with a jarring impact. The breath was knocked from my lungs, leaving me gasping on the cold, hard ground.

"Ugh," I groaned, trying to steady my breath as I lay there. The mist that clung to the floor began to churn and twist, rising in swirls around me. As the fog thickened, a distant, fragmented memory began to surface, slipping into focus through the haze.

I was little, clutching my mum's hand as we wove through the crowded shopping center. The air was alive with the murmur of conversations, a tapestry of voices blending together into a constant hum, punctuated by the faint strains of upbeat background music that drifted from overhead speakers. The bustling crowd moved around us, the clatter of footsteps and the rustle of shopping bags creating a rhythmic accompaniment. In a moment of wonder, I momentarily released her hand, drawn to a shop window where a dress sparkled under the store's lights. The fabric shimmered with a mesmerizing play of colors, reflecting hues of gold and silver that danced like tiny stars trapped within the material. My wide eyes were fixed on the dress, enchanted by its radiant allure and the delicate way it caught the light, making it seem almost magical amidst the busy world around me.

I spun around, my hand reaching instinctively for my mum's familiar grip, only to find nothing but empty space. My heart lurched, pounding furiously as my eyes darted frantically through the sea of faces. The vibrant chatter and the rhythmic hum of the shopping center seemed to swell into a chaotic blur, each passing stranger a potential obstacle in my desperate search. I felt a cold rush of panic clutch at my chest, squeezing tightly as I struggled to focus on any hint of her familiar figure in the undulating crowd.

"Mum?" I called out, my voice small and frightened. People walked by, paying no attention to the little girl lost in the sea of shoppers. Tears welled in my eyes as I moved through the throngs of people, feeling increasingly alone.

"Excuse me, have you seen my mum?" I asked a passerby, but they brushed past without a glance. I wandered, calling out for her, my voice growing hoarse. The crowd seemed to close in, and I felt a rising fear.

I reached a section of the shopping center at a crossroads. I stood there, trembling, trying to decide which way to go. Mum always told me to trust my instincts. Taking a deep breath, I chose the path to the left, even though it looked less familiar.

"Please, let this be the right way," I whispered, my tiny feet moving quickly over the polished tiles.

As I rounded a corner, I saw her. My mum was talking to a security guard, her face pale and eyes wide with panic.

"Mum!" I cried out, relief flooding through me.

She turned, her eyes locking onto mine. "Dee!" she shouted, running over and enveloping me in a tight embrace. I buried my face in her shoulder, the familiar scent of her perfume soothing my frayed nerves.

"Thank goodness, I was so worried!" she exclaimed, holding me close.

"I'm sorry, Mum," I mumbled into her shoulder. "I got lost."

She pulled back to look at me, her eyes softening. "It's alright, sweetie. You found your way back to me. That's what matters."

The mist divided, breaking up the memory I had just witnessed; I pushed myself up from the stone floor, wincing as my knees protested with a sharp, persistent ache. The familiar, nagging pain of fibromyalgia flare up, adding a dull throb to my already strained muscles. Each movement felt labored, a reminder of the invisible weight I carried. Despite the discomfort, my resolve solidified. "Alright, let's keep going," I said, my voice steadier now, though it wavered slightly with the effort. I pressed onward, my gaze fixed on the warm, inviting glow at the end of the path, each step a struggle but also a testament to my determination.

A faint hissing noise, like steam escaping, drifted up from the mist below, catching my attention. I leaned over the edge, peering into the swirling gray. As I watched, the mist started to gather and take shape, and another memory began to surface, wrapping around me like a shroud. I was in my twenties, standing in a small, box-like apartment that felt both new and confining. The walls were bare, their stark whiteness accentuating the emptiness of the space. Scattered around the floor were a jumble of boxes, their cardboard surfaces marked with hurriedly scrawled labels and creases from the move. The faint smell of new, untouched cardboard mingled with the lingering scent of packing tape.

The apartment, though modest, was distinctly mine, marked by the absence of familiar comforts. I felt a twinge of excitement mingled with a thread of trepidation as I surveyed my surroundings. The creaky floorboards beneath my feet seemed to echo with the promise of new beginnings, while the silence of the empty room was both liberating and a little lonely. The harsh overhead light cast sharp shadows, emphasizing the starkness of the space. In that moment, a blend of exhilaration and uncertainty settled in my chest, a tangible reminder of the leap I had taken away from home and toward the pursuit of my dreams.

"This is it," I whispered, a small smile tugging at my lips. "A fresh start."

I walked over to one of the boxes and pulled out a picture frame. It was a photo of my mum and me on my graduation day. I placed it on a small table by the window. Seeing it brought a pang of homesickness, but I knew I had made the right choice.

The phone rang, and I picked it up, hearing my mum's familiar voice on the other end. "Hi, Dee. How's the new place?"

"It's great, Mum," I replied, trying to sound more confident than I felt. "Just getting settled in."

As I surveyed the room, my phone buzzed with a call from my mum. I picked it up, and her voice came through warm and reassuring, though it was interrupted by a series of hacking coughs. "I'm so proud of you, sweetie," she managed between coughs, her tone comforting despite the raspiness. "I know it's a big step, but you're doing the right thing."

I took a deep breath, feeling the weight of her concern even through the phone. "I know," I said, trying to steady my voice. "I just want to make something of myself, you know? I want to grow and be independent."

"And you will," she assured me. "Remember, it's okay to be scared. Taking risks is part of the journey. Just trust yourself."

"I will, Mum," I promised, feeling a surge of determination.

The memory began to fade into the mist, and I returned to the familiar glowing path. As I neared the end of the path, the glow ahead grew brighter and more intense, casting an otherworldly light that bathed the chamber in a warm, golden hue. The illumination revealed an ornate door, its design intricately carved with motifs that hinted at secrets lying beyond. It was reminiscent of the one from my memory, a striking resemblance that quickened my heartbeat with a mix of anticipation and trepidation. Delicate, leaf-like patterns seemed to flutter across the door's surface, and faint, almost imperceptible footprints wove their way through the intricate carvings. The door stood as a mysterious threshold, promising the unknown. My fingers traced the cool, smooth surface of the door, feeling the subtle texture beneath my touch.

"Please open," I whispered, my voice tinged with hope. Gathering my courage, I took a deep breath and pushed gently. The door swung open effortlessly, revealing a world beyond that awaited me. As I stepped through, the sense of entering something both wondrous and enigmatic filled me, the door's promise of hidden marvels now poised to unfold.

16

Footprints of Destiny

I found myself in a mystical forest like no other. The trees stood tall and bare, their bark adorned with leaves shaped like vibrant green birds that blended seamlessly with the branches. The sky above was a stunning sunset of oranges and purples, illuminated by two delicate pink moons that cast a serene, otherworldly glow. The forest floor was alive with movement as flowers wandered on their stems, their petals fluttering shyly. The ground was soft and cushion-like, creating a gentle, living carpet underfoot. The air was crisp and cool, filled with the fresh scent of foliage and the faint, sweet fragrance of the wandering flowers. The forest was alive with a symphony of natural sounds: the rustling of leaves, soft chirps from the leaf birds, and the gentle creak of the swaying trees. This surreal scene evoked a sense of awe and wonder, blending tranquility with a touch of nervousness at the enchanting, dreamlike beauty around me.

As I gazed around in wonder, I noticed a single pair of footprints on the ground. They were unmistakably human, yet the glow emanating from them hinted at something otherworldly. The illumination swirled like ethereal smoke, casting a calming, ghostly aura around each print as I drew closer. The glow, delicate and translucent, shimmered like a gentle mist, undulating in soft patterns that danced across the surface. As I reached out to touch the glowing smoke, it felt strangely insubstantial, like mist that evaporates at the touch. Despite its lack of physicality, the sensation was soothing and reassuring, offering a strange comfort. A mix of curiosity and a sense of destiny stirred within me. I took a deep breath, feeling the cool, faintly sweet scent of the glowing smoke, and made a brave choice. With a tentative step, I placed my bare foot into the first footprint. As my skin made contact with the illuminated ground, a familiar voice echoed softly in my ears, adding a layer of mystery and connection to the surreal scene.

"Keep going, Dee. You're doing great," my mother's warm and encouraging voice whispered.

A surge of comfort filled me. I stepped forward, placing my foot in the next glowing footprint. This time, I heard Luke's voice, steady and reassuring. "You're stronger than you know; you just have to believe it."

Each step brought another whisper, each one a voice of a loved one, both alive and deceased. Liam's voice was next. "You've got this. Don't give up."

Atlas followed. "Go, Auntie Dee,"

Then I heard my father say, "I'm so proud of you, Dee. Keep moving forward."

Finally, as I placed my foot in another glowing print, I heard Evie, "I'm with you, always. You can face anything."

The glowing footprints, faint yet persistent, guided me deeper into the heart of the forest, where the shadows grew thicker and the air colder. My feet crunched softly on the carpet of fallen leaves and twigs beneath me. As the trail narrowed, the trees seemed to close in around me, their gnarled, skeletal branches reaching out like skeletal fingers, casting intricate, eerie patterns of shadow on the ground. The whisper of the wind through the branches was a constant, haunting murmur that mingled with the rustling of unseen creatures in the underbrush. The bushes ahead appeared like a dense, tangled mass, their leaves sharp and unforgiving. I braced myself as I pushed through, feeling the sting of the thorns and the scrape of twigs against my skin. The prickles were sharp and relentless, pulling at my dress and adding to the challenge of my progress. The damp earth beneath was uneven, causing me to stumble occasionally, and the scent of wet foliage mixed with the faint, earthy odor of rotting leaves filled the air.

I could hear my own labored breaths through the silence, each gasp sharp and ragged as my determination was tested. The muffled, encouraging echoes of my loved ones' voices reverberated in my mind, their words a faint yet fervent beacon of hope. Their encouragement seemed to meld with the sounds of the forest, driving me forward. With a final push, I forced through the thicket, the branches snapping back with a loud crack that echoed through the stillness. I stumbled into a clearing, I dusted myself off, I took in my surroundings. The room before me was a mesmerizing spectacle. Glowing strands cascaded from the ceiling, intertwining in intricate patterns that resembled a web of dazzling laser beams. The ethereal light they emitted danced across the room, creating a display that was both captivating and foreboding.

A chill of fear gripped me as I moved forward, acutely aware of the potential danger that lurked in this surreal space. The strands pulsed with an almost sentient rhythm, their light flickering like the breath of some unseen entity. Compelled by a mix of curiosity and trepidation, I reached out to touch one. But as my fingertips neared, the room shifted dramatically. The radiant strands vanished in an instant, leaving behind a blinding flash before an unseen force hurled me violently against the wall, my head spinning in a whirl of confusion. I crumpled to the floor, dazed and disoriented, as the remnants of the room's strange light faded into darkness. Groaning, I rubbed my head and slowly gained my composure. I looked around, finding myself in a dimly lit hall. The walls were covered in old tapestries, their fabric faded and worn. As I walked along, the tapestries began to come to life. At first, I felt uneasy, as if the eyes of the figures in the tapestries were watching me.

I came across one tapestry that stopped me in my tracks. It was a family photo, meticulously woven with rich, textured threads that gave it a lifelike quality. The fabric felt dense yet supple under my fingertips, each thread painstakingly chosen to capture the scene's essence. In the tapestry, I stood at ten, a younger version of myself with a bright smile, flanked by my mum and dad. The image was remarkably detailed, from the gentle curves of my mother's face to the reassuring strength in my father's gaze. The tapestry's texture brought their expressions to life, imbuing them with a warmth that almost made me expect them to speak. The sight struck a deep chord within me, and my heart began to pound with a tumultuous mix of nostalgia and dread. The memory seemed to envelop me in its embrace, the familiar sensations of the past flooding back with vivid clarity. My parents were locked in a heated argument, but this time, something was different. This wasn't a replay of my birthday; it was something else entirely, something sinister. I struggled to hear their words as my gaze was drawn to a shadowy figure lurking behind them. An icy grip of fear clenched around my heart, paralyzing me with a bone-deep dread.

The shadowy figure advanced slowly, its dark form spreading and deepening, casting an oppressive gloom over the scene. The figure's presence was real and menacing like a dark cloud suffocating the air. My parents continued their argument, oblivious to the encroaching darkness that seemed to seep into every corner of the room. The memory unfolded in an unsettling silence, punctuated only by the muffled sounds of their voices, as the shadow grew more defined and ominous with each passing moment. "What is this?" I whispered, my voice trembling. I wanted to look away, but I couldn't. The fear was too intense, paralyzing me completely. As I watched my parents argue. Their voices rose and fell like waves crashing against the shore, each word carrying a weight I couldn't fully comprehend. The shadowy figure lingered in the background, a silent observer of our family's turmoil.

My mother stood by the sink, her hands gripping the edge as she looked at my father with tear-filled eyes."John, we can't keep going like this," she pleaded, her voice trembling with worry and fear. "I don't know how long I can keep going."

My father, John, paced the worn floor, his footsteps echoing in the quiet kitchen. His face was etched with lines of stress and exhaustion, his brow furrowed with the weight of their financial burdens. He stopped abruptly, turning to face my mum, his hands clenched into fists at his sides.

"I've tried everything," he said, his voice heavy with frustration. "Therapy, medication… nothing seems to help. I can't stand the thought of dragging you both down with my struggles. I need to leave to keep you safe from my own pain, until I can figure things out."

My mum reached out to him, her voice softening with concern. "John, what about Dee?" she asked gently, referring to me, their daughter. "Are you going to say goodbye to her?"

My dad's shoulders sagged, a heavy sigh escaping his lips. He glanced towards the hallway to my room, where I was sleeping soundly. "It would be too hard," he whispered, his voice thick with emotion.

I listened, my heart sinking as the truth began to unfold. My father wasn't leaving out of choice or abandonment. His departure was a desperate attempt to shield us from the burden of his own inner darkness. Years of battling depression and PTSD, coupled with the crushing weight of financial strain, had led him to this heart-wrenching decision. A wave of guilt surged through me. In my younger years, I had often resented his extended hours and absences during crucial moments. Now, I saw the immense weight he carried, the emotional scars he bore, and the sacrifices he made in a bid to protect us.

"I'm sorry," I whispered, my voice barely audible in the charged silence. "I didn't understand."

The shadowy figure's presence was a haunting reminder of our challenges. My father's departure wasn't a betrayal but a sacrifice made out of love and a desperate desire to protect us from himself.

My mother reached out to him, her hand trembling as she touched his arm. "We can find a way through this," she pleaded, her voice filled with determination. "Please, John. Don't leave us to face this alone."

He looked at her, his eyes filled with sorrow and resignation. "I can't let our debts destroy us," he said softly, his voice cracking with emotion.

My tears felt like ice as I realized the depth of his sacrifice, the burden he had carried in silence for so long. The guilt gnawed at me, knowing that I had added to his pain during those tumultuous times. The figure reached out a shadowy hand, and just as it was about to touch my mum's shoulder, the tapestry went dark. I stumbled back, my breath coming in ragged gasps. The hall was silent again, the tapestries still and lifeless.

"What was that?" I said to myself, my voice echoing in the quiet hall. I forced myself to take a deep breath to shake off the fear. Whatever I had just witnessed, I knew it was a warning. A challenge I had yet to face. "What was that?" I muttered aloud, the words reverberating off the walls of the quiet hallway. The chill of fear pricked my skin, and I clenched my fists until my knuckles turned white, trying to squeeze out the tremor in my hands. The scene I had just witnessed felt like a warning, a harbinger of challenges I hadn't anticipated.

My mind raced with questions, but one emotion surged above all: anger. I was angry at my mother for not telling me anything, and I was angry at myself for not pushing harder or uncovering the truth sooner. Guilt gnawed at me like a relentless predator. I could have done better and been more persistent and intuitive. If only I had known the whole story from the beginning. *But why hadn't she told me? How could she keep something so significant hidden?* The foundation of trust I had built with my mother now felt shaky, cracked by the weight of withheld truths. I blamed her for my ignorance, the opportunities lost, and the pain that could have been prevented. As my anger simmered, I needed to confront her for answers, clarity, and closure. *But how could I when she was dead?* I couldn't continue stumbling through the darkness of half-truths and omissions. This was my life and future, and I no longer refused to be kept in the shadows. Taking another deep breath, I steadied myself. The hallway stretched out before me, its silence urging me forward. With each step, my resolve solidified. I would demand the truth, no matter how uncomfortable or painful. Ignoring the rich tapestries hanging on the walls, my focus narrowed, and the world around me blurred. My mind raced back to the burning questions within me. *Why hadn't Mom told me?* I was young, yes, but not incapable of understanding. A surge of resentment flared within me, white-hot and blinding, for shielding me from the truth, for assuming I couldn't handle it. The hall's beauty faded into insignificance as the need for answers drove me forward. Lost in my thoughts, I reached a door without realizing it. Absently, I pulled it open and stepped inside. The scene that greeted me snapped me out of my reverie like a splash of cold water.I found myself standing in my grandmother's house. The familiar scent of lavender and freshly baked cookies enveloped me, instantly transporting me back to my childhood. There she sat on the sofa, just as I remembered—small and frail, yet radiating an inner strength that belied her appearance.

Nan didn't look up as I entered. She continued knitting, the rhythmic click of her needles filling the room with a comforting, steady sound. It was as if she had been expecting me, as if she could sense the storm of emotions raging inside me. The soft, warm glow of the lamp cast gentle shadows, making the room feel both timeless and serene. The air was thick with the mingling scents of lavender and cookies, creating a cocoon of nostalgia. Her presence, though she had passed away years ago, felt tangible, a beacon of comfort and understanding in that moment. Her steady hands and the familiar sound of knitting needles were a silent reassurance, anchoring me amidst my turmoil.

"Nan," I said softly, my voice cracking with disbelief. She glanced up then, her eyes gentle and knowing, just as they had always been.

"Sit down, dear," she said, patting the space beside her on the sofa. I obeyed, sinking into the familiar comfort of her presence.

My voice quivered as I fought to steady it, feeling a lump form in my throat. "I found out something Mom never told me. About Dad. Why he left." Tears welled up in my eyes, threatening to spill over, as a whirlwind of emotions churned inside me—anger, betrayal, and a deep, aching sadness. My hands trembled, and I could feel my heartbeat pounding in my chest, each beat amplifying the confusion and hurt that gripped me. Nan's presence, steady and calming, felt like the only anchor in the storm of my emotions.

Nan nodded knowingly, her expression softening with empathy. "Your mother has always carried a heavy burden, dear. Sometimes, the duty of a parent is to protect the ones they love, no matter how difficult the truth may be."

"But I feel so angry," I admitted, tears growing. "And guilty. Guilty for not knowing about dad, for not understanding."

Nan reached out and gently wiped away a tear from my cheek. "Anger and guilt are natural reactions, my dear. But they can also blind us from our own happiness. Your dad had struggles and battles he had to face on his own. Sometimes, people like him need to go through their journey alone to protect the ones they love."

I looked into her wise, kind eyes, searching for some semblance of peace. She continued softly, "Letting go is crucial, even when it feels daunting. Remember, you possess great strength—more than you may recognize." Her words resonated deeply, offering a glimmer of understanding amidst the turmoil within me.

I nodded, "I just don't know how to forgive Mom right now."

Nan smiled gently, her eyes twinkling with a wisdom born of years. "Forgiveness takes time, Dee. But remember, not everything you've seen so far, including your mother and father, is in black and white. Sometimes, the hardest decisions are made out of love."

Her words felt like a puzzle. The complexity of human emotions, the shades of gray in life's choices—Nan reminded me of truths I had momentarily forgotten in my pain.

"Life is too short to be stuck in the past," Nan continued, her voice soft yet firm. "Forgive your mother, not because she deserves it now, but because someday you will understand."

I looked at Nan, her words sinking in with a quiet certainty. Her wink, almost mischievous yet filled with knowing, left me curious and hopeful.

"Thank you, Nan," I whispered, feeling a weight lift from my heart.

She squeezed my hand gently. "Anytime, my dear. Remember, you are never alone."

As Nan's hand slipped from mine, her presence seemed to waver like a mirage in the desert heat. A soft breeze whispered through the room, carrying a faint scent of lavender. Panic surged within me, realizing she was fading away.

"Nan?" My voice quivered, reaching out instinctively as her form blurred before me.

Her eyes twinkled with that familiar mischief, even as her figure became translucent. "Remember, my dear," she murmured, her voice fading with her image. "Strength comes from within. Embrace the pain."

I clasped my hands, trying to hold on to her vanishing essence. "But I still need you," I pleaded, the weight of her departure sinking in, heavier than ever.

Her wink remained etched in my mind, a comforting yet enigmatic gesture. "You have what you need," she assured me, her voice now barely a whisper.

And then she was gone, the room felt emptier, the air colder, as I stood there, grappling with the void her departure had created.

"Thank you, Nan," I whispered into the stillness, my eyes brimming with tears, a sense of gratitude mingled with the loss.

14

Nexus

As I wiped my eyes, a soft, almost imperceptible glow began to emanate from the far wall. The light grew brighter, outlining the edges of a door that hadn't been there moments before. The door was not made of wood but appeared to be composed of shimmering, electric currents, its surface crackling with energy. I hesitated, drawn to the hypnotic dance of blue and white sparks arcing across the door's surface. The intricate patterns, like veins of lightning, pulsed with rhythmic energy, creating a low, electric hum that filled the room. The air around it felt charged, making the tiny hairs on my arms stand on end. Raising a tentative hand, I inched closer, feeling the static prickle against my skin. The electric door exuded a sense of foreboding and promise as if it were a nexus to a place where answers lay hidden.

A gentle hum filled the air, the sound vibrating through my bones. The faint scent of lavender still lingered, mixing with an earthy, almost metallic tang. I took a deep breath, steeling myself for whatever lay beyond. With one final glance at the fading remnants of Nan's presence, I reached out, my fingers tingling as they neared the electric surface. The door seemed to respond to my touch, the sparks intensifying, illuminating the room with a brilliant, otherworldly light.

Stepping through the doorway, I was enveloped in a storm of lightning. Each flash illuminated the room with a stark, otherworldly brilliance, and the air around me crackled with raw energy. The electric charge was palpable, sending tingling sensations up my spine and making my hair stand on end. The sound of the storm reverberated through my bones, a deep, resonant hum that filled the space with an almost deafening intensity. The storm's power was overwhelming. Each burst of light made me jump, the sudden brightness searing my vision and leaving dancing afterimages in its wake. The accompanying thunderclaps were sharp and explosive, rattling through my chest and echoing in my ears.

The environment felt like a nexus, a point where different dimensions and energies converged. Swirling currents of light and shadow twisted together, creating a mesmerizing, chaotic vortex of power and possibility. The very air seemed alive, charged with potential and brimming with a sense of infinite pathways and uncharted realms. Each step I took felt like a leap into the unknown, the energy around me throbbing with anticipation and the promise of discovery. I steered through the chamber cautiously, careful not to stray into the path of the lightning bolts, which now seemed to have a life of their own. The walls, now bathed in their eerie glow between flashes, seemed to pulse with a strange, arcane energy. Every surface hummed faintly as if resonating with the same power that coursed through the storm outside. Despite the awe-inspiring spectacle, fear gripped me. I dared not touch anything, unsure of the consequences in this charged environment. Yet, a nagging feeling persisted—that there was a purpose to my presence here, a reason I had been drawn through that archway.

Not paying attention, I overlooked the impending danger until it was too late. With a deafening crack, a lightning bolt struck with pinpoint accuracy, sending searing pain coursing through my entire body. The sensation was beyond excruciating—fresh and raw, as if each nerve ending was laid bare, ignited by a fire unlike any I had ever felt. I screamed out in agony, my voice a raw echo in the tumultuous air. My muscles convulsed, and my vision blurred as the pain overwhelmed me. The air felt thick and suffocating, each breath a struggle as if I were inhaling smoke and electricity. My heart pounded furiously, matching the chaotic rhythm of the storm around me.

Just as suddenly as the pain had enveloped me, I was lifted off the ground by a strange, luminous force emanating from the lightning itself. Suspended in mid-air, the energy surged through me, simultaneously excruciating and strangely empowering. My limbs hung limp, yet I felt an odd sense of weightlessness as if the lightning had taken control of my body. Memories flickered within the bolts of light around me, snapshots of my life flashing before my eyes. Faces of loved ones and moments of joy and sorrow all danced in the electric storm. Confusion and fear gripped me, the intensity of the experience almost too much to bear. Yet, amidst the chaos, a strange clarity began to emerge, as if the lightning was not just a force of nature but a conduit to something deeper, a connection to the very essence of my being. I saw a vivid scene unfold—a memory from years ago, walking home from school with Evie. I called out to her, saying goodbye as she continued on her way. But the vision turned dark as I witnessed Evie arriving home to a hateful display—a door defaced with red paint and cruel words that cut deep.

'Go Back Home'

I watched as Evie headed through the front door and headed to the kitchen, where her father was filling up a bucket of water,

"They did it again, didn't they?" she asked, the frustration etched on his expression telling me everything.

As I hung suspended in the electric storm, the searing pain began to ebb away, replaced by a numbing chill that spread through my body like a cold, soothing balm. The sharpness of the lightning's strike faded into a deep, penetrating frost, easing the raw, fiery agony that had consumed me. I was gently lowered back to the ground, my descent smooth and almost tender, as if the luminous force that had lifted me was now cradling me softly. When my feet finally touched the floor, a profound sense of relief washed over me, mingling with the residual tremors of pain. I lay there trembling, the chill of the energy seeping into my bones, numbing the last vestiges of discomfort.

The chamber around me was now eerily still, the storm's fury reduced to a distant, muted rumble that seemed to recede into the background. The air, once crackling with tension, now felt calm and almost serene, allowing me to catch my breath and absorb the stillness of the aftermath. As I lay on the ground, trying to steady my breath amidst the lingering numbness, questions raced through my mind like frantic whispers in the aftermath of a storm. *Why had Evie never mentioned this incident before? How long had she carried this hurt in silence, hidden beneath the veneer of our everyday lives?* The chamber around me seemed to hold its breath, the walls pulsating softly with a calm glow that no longer felt menacing but rather contemplative. Once charged with volatile energy, the air felt strangely quiet, as if waiting for me to grasp the revelations it had unveiled. Slowly, I pushed myself into a sitting position, my hands trembling slightly. The memory of Evie's pain weighed heavily on my heart, mingling with my own anguish from the lightning strike. It was clear now that our friendship, though deep and enduring, had its hidden scars. I recalled when we shared laughter, dreams, and secrets—moments now tinged with unspoken sorrow. Had I been blind to Evie's struggles, or had she chosen to shield me from the ugliness that had stained her life? Before I could fully grasp the lingering relief, another lightning bolt struck, enveloping me in a blinding, searing light. The brilliance was so intense it felt like it was slicing through my very essence, reigniting the pain with a ferocious clarity. It surged through me, a sharp, intense agony that jolted my entire being, more overwhelming than before. Once again, I was lifted off the ground, the electric force propelling me upward with an unsettling, almost violent speed. The sensation of weightlessness combined with the renewed pain left me gasping, struggling to acclimate to the sudden shift. The lightning wrapped around me like tendrils of raw, pulsating energy, each spark and surge coiling around my body with a menacing grip. It dragged me into another storm of memories, their images flashing vividly in the searing light. These visions raced past my eyes—snapshots of the past, each one more vivid and emotionally charged than the last. The storm's fury surrounded me, making each memory feel like a tangible force pressing against my senses, amplifying the confusion and intensity of the moment.

This time, I stood on Evie's street, the scene unfolding cruelly before me. It was night, and under the dim streetlights, I saw neighbors defacing Evie's home. Red paint was splattered across the front door; graffiti scrawled with hateful messages that twisted my stomach. The words "Go back home" were scrawled across the house and her parents' car, the viciousness behind them palpable even through the haze of memory. As the memory continued to play out, a group of neighborhood kids appeared, throwing eggs at the house and shouting insults. Their taunts echoed in the air, each word dripping with venomous prejudice. The realization that this cruelty was born from nothing more than the color of their skin made my heart ache with deep, raw pain.

"Get out of here; you don't belong!" one kid yelled, hurling an egg that splattered against the front door.

"Go back to where you came from!" another shouted, his voice filled with spite.

Evie and her family huddled inside, trying to shut out the hateful words. Her father stood by the window, watching helplessly as the eggs hit their home. "Just ignore them," he muttered, more to himself than anyone else, his voice shaking with suppressed anger.

Evie clung to her mother, tears streaming down her face. "Why do they hate us so much, Mom?" she asked, her voice small and fearful.

Her mother stroked her hair, trying to soothe her. "They're just ignorant, sweetheart. They don't understand."

A particularly loud taunt rang out. "You're not wanted here! Go home!"

Evie's father clenched his fists, turning away from the window. "Enough is enough," he said quietly, but the frustration and pain were evident in his tone.

I stood there, watching the prejudice unfold, my heart breaking for Evie. *How had I never known? How had she kept this all inside?* I had been shielded by ignorance, failing to fully grasp the depth of Evie's pain and the pervasive nature of such prejudice. This scene forced me to confront my past blindness and recognize the deep, often unseen torment endured by others, urging me to face uncomfortable truths about empathy and understanding.

Suddenly, the electricity shifted, and I saw Evie in her room, listening quietly as I rambled on about my trivial problems. I could see now the weight she carried, the pain she never shared.

"Why didn't you tell me, Evie?" I whispered into the void, my voice drained and lifeless.

The electricity changed again, showing the day they moved away. Evie stood by the car, looking back at the house one last time. She saw me across the street and waved, forcing a smile. "Goodbye," she mouthed, the sadness in her eyes now painfully clear.

Her father loaded the last box into the car, his face etched with frustration and resignation. "Let's go," he said, his voice heavy with the unspoken reasons for their departure.

The memory faded, and I was left lying on the floor, tears streaming down my face. "I'm so sorry, Evie," I whispered. "I'm so sorry for not seeing what was going on, for not being there for you."

At the time, I didn't understand why they left so abruptly. Now, the reason was painfully clear. They had been driven away by the hate and bigotry, forced to seek safety and peace elsewhere. The chamber was silent, the lightning's rumble a distant echo. The shame bubbled inside me, a dark, churning mass of regret. As I lay helpless on the floor, I curled up into a ball, trying to shield myself from the crushing weight of my ignorance. *How had I missed the signs? How could I have been so blind to my best friend's pain?*

I wept with guilt, tears flowing freely as I realized the depth of my failure. My sobs echoed through the chamber. Evie had been my closest friend, yet I had failed to see her suffering and offer her the support she so desperately needed. The thought that I would never have the chance to tell her how sorry I was tore at my heart, making the ache of missing her even more unbearable. With a shuddering breath, I sobbed into the stillness, "I'm so sorry, Evie. I'm so sorry for not being there for you."

Suddenly, a sharp and commanding voice cut through the silence, slicing through the heavy, oppressive air. "Get up!" it shouted, the sound reverberating with a startling force that jolted me from my sorrow. My heart raced as I scanned the dimly lit chamber, my breath catching in my throat. The walls, cold and rough, seemed to pulse with the residual energy of the voice's command. The chamber remained empty, but the air felt taut with an invisible presence, making each echo of the voice seem even more intense and disorienting. Unsure of who or what had spoken, I forced myself to sit up, my body aching all over, almost a reminder of my fibromyalgia. Each movement sent a jolt of pain through my muscles and joints, a cruel echo of my physical suffering. I knew I couldn't stay on the floor any longer, though every inch of my body protested. As I struggled to my feet, the lightning had retreated towards the walls, its bolts crackling harmlessly against the stone, leaving only a dim glow that cast long shadows around the chamber.

Against one wall, the relentless lightning crackled and split the darkness, casting fleeting, jagged shadows that danced across the chamber. With each burst of light, the storm illuminated a previously hidden door. The door surface was a series of interlocking geometric shapes reminiscent of a mirror prism. The colorful patterns shimmered momentarily, hinting at secrets concealed behind its unassuming facade. Taking a deep breath, I straightened myself up and harshly wiped my face. "Let's go," I said aloud, my voice trembling as I tried to summon the courage that was close to slipping away. With a mix of determination and trepidation, I approached the door. The anticipation hung heavy in the air as I reached for the handle and slowly, deliberately opened it.

****

I stepped through the threshold, only to be engulfed in an overwhelming sea of mirrors. The endless maze of reflections stretched out in every direction, creating an infinite expanse of my own image, each one bending and fracturing into ever more distorted versions of myself. As I tried to steady myself, my hand reached out, desperately searching for something solid to lean on, but I found only cold, smooth glass that offered no comfort. The door behind me had disappeared, swallowed up by the mirrored labyrinth. My pulse quickened, each beat resonating with the rising dread that enveloped me. My breath came in shallow, uneven gasps, each inhalation a struggle against the tightening grip around my chest. It felt as though my lungs were being squeezed in a vice, making it increasingly difficult to pull in air. I felt a frantic surge of panic, a wave of fear crashing over me with overwhelming force. My heart thudded erratically, the rhythmic pounding in my chest like a relentless drum, each beat reverberating through the hollow space and amplifying my growing sense of entrapment. The mirrors seemed to close in around me, their relentless reflections morphing and warping as if mocking my distress. Desperation seized me as I spun around, my eyes darting across the countless, shifting reflections. Every angle showed a different version of myself, each one more disoriented and helpless than the last.

The distorted images twisted my features into grotesque caricatures of fear and confusion, their exaggerated forms a cruel reminder of my vulnerability. The glass walls shimmered and wavered, casting eerie, fractured light that seemed to pulsate in sync with my rapid heartbeat. I tried to find an escape, but every turn led me back to another reflection, each mirror amplifying the horror of being forever trapped in a nightmarish reflection of myself. The oppressive silence of the mirrored maze was occasionally broken by the soft, distorted echo of my own panicked breathing, a constant reminder of the overwhelming fear that gripped me. Sweat beaded on my forehead, quickly becoming rivulets that snaked down my temples. My hands shook so violently that they felt like they might detach from my arms. I blinked rapidly, but the edges of my vision swam in a haze of shimmering tears. The salty droplets splattered onto the icy floor, vanishing into the sea of reflections that surrounded me.

The mirrors seemed to press in, their glassy surfaces narrowing as if drawing closer with each frantic beat of my heart. My throat felt like it was closing up, constricting my airway until every breath came out as a ragged gasp. My chest tightened painfully, and I struggled to pull in the air, my lungs seeming to shrink with every inhale. The oppressive silence was occasionally pierced by the harsh rhythm of my own breathing, a syncopated drum that pounded in my ears. My pulse raced, a frantic cadence that seemed to vibrate through the glass, mingling with the distorted echoes of my own panicked breaths.

A wave of dizziness swept over me, making the world tilt and sway. I stumbled, my legs buckling beneath me, and reached out blindly. My hands met only the frigid, unyielding surface of the mirrors, offering no stability. I swayed on my feet, my vision narrowing to a tunnel of flickering reflections that mocked my desperation. I shut my eyes, but darkness offered no refuge. Instead, the cacophony of my fear grew louder—my breath came in short, irregular bursts, and the relentless pounding of my heart was like a drumbeat in a frantic parade. The swirling chaos of my thoughts clung to the edges of my consciousness, a maelstrom of despair that only deepened with each passing moment.

"No, no, no," I exclaimed, trying to calm myself down. I closed my eyes, hoping to shut out the overwhelming reflections, but the sense of entrapment only grew stronger.

Luke's voice echoed in my mind, urging me to find the strength to move forward. "My love, you are so much stronger than you realize. I believe in you, I know you can do this."

I clung to the words as if they were a lifeline, my fingers trembling slightly against the cool glass. I forced myself to inhale deeply, the air feeling thick and heavy as it filled my lungs. My chest expanded slowly, a slight shiver running through me with each deliberate breath. The rhythmic thud of my heartbeat became a focal point, each pulse a reassuring drumbeat amidst the chaos. With a whisper of encouragement, "You can do this," I opened my eyes, the tension in my brow easing just a fraction. My gaze shifted from the sea of mirrors to my own reflection, my eyes searching for a semblance of resolve amidst the swirling distortions. I shifted my weight, taking a tentative step forward. My footfall was careful and measured, each movement a conscious effort against the disorienting array of reflections. My fingers brushed lightly against the surface of the mirrors as I moved, feeling the cold smoothness beneath my fingertips—a stark contrast to the warmth pooling in my palms.

Another step followed, my body leaning slightly into the motion as if each advance carried the weight of my determination. The reflections twisted and warped, but I kept my focus steady. I drew a shaky breath, the exhale coming with a slight quiver, but I continued, step by deliberate step. Each movement, though small, felt like a victory. The panic was still present, a shadow at the edge of my thoughts, but with each step, the tremor in my limbs seemed to lessen. My resolve, though fragile, began to harden as I navigated the maze, each careful step grounding me further in my pursuit of escape. As I moved deeper into the maze, the mirrors began to change. The reflections shifted, showing no longer my panicked face but scenes from my past. Each mirror became a window into a moment I had endured, a piece of the puzzle that was my life since being stuck in this limbo.

One reflection showed me slumped against a wall, every muscle taut with invisible suffering. My face was a mask of anguish, eyes closed tightly, as if bracing against a storm that only I could feel. The glass distorted the agony into a grotesque, exaggerated form, my limbs seeming to twist and strain under the weight of an unseen burden. The shadows around me seemed to pulsate with a rhythmic throb, mirroring the relentless ache that seemed to pervade my being. My struggles with fibromyalgia. This relentless pain shadowed me every day. I saw the moments of self-doubt, the times I had broken down, feeling overwhelmed and helpless. But I also saw the times I had risen, pushing through the pain to be there for those I loved. The pain I dealt with every day didn't make me weak; it made me a warrior, someone who refused to break under pressure.

And then, in another mirror, I saw Luke. His eyes were a serene pool of love and understanding. They held a clarity that seemed to cut through the fog of my confusion and self-doubt. At that moment, his gaze was not just a reflection of him but of the beautiful life we had built together. I felt a lump rise in my throat as I took in the truth I had been avoiding. The mirror didn't just show Luke; it revealed the enduring strength of our relationship and the support he had always provided. It was as if his reflection was reaching out to remind me of who I was beneath the layers of self-criticism. Realizing the truth, I had been escaping. "I am a loving wife," I whispered, my voice trembling with emotion. "I am a beautiful person. I can't keep breaking myself down."

I drew in a deep breath, feeling a sense of self as I peered at my reflection, "I am strong," I continued, my voice growing steadier. "I have faced unimaginable pain and still found the strength to get up every morning. I am resilient. My challenges have only made me tougher, not weaker. I am kind," I said, "I have always been there for the ones I love and will continue to be. I am a force of nature, standing up for what I believe in.

The reflections around me shimmered, their surfaces rippling like liquid silver as if affirming my newfound understanding. The room was bathed in a soft, ethereal glow, with beams of light dancing across the mirrored walls. I could see the woman I was, not defined by my pain and struggles but by my strength, compassion, and unwavering spirit. My eyes, once shadowed with doubt, now sparkled with a renewed sense of purpose. The faint scent of jasmine filled the air, blending with the delicate sound of a distant chime, creating an atmosphere of serene clarity.

"I am a fibro warrior," I declared, my voice ringing with conviction. "Every day, I battle the pain and refuse to let it defeat me. I am a survivor and will not let my past dictate my future. And above all," I said softly, my gaze upon the election of Luke. "The love I share with you is proof of my ability to give and receive love, to build a life filled with joy and connection. I am deserving of that love, and I will cherish it."

"I am enough," I whispered, tears beginning to surface in my eyes, not from the feeling of acceptance. "I am enough just as I am. I am worthy of happiness, love, and respect. I need to stop running," I said, my voice firm. "I need to face the truth and embrace who I am."

A soft, cracking sound filled the air as the words left my lips, sharp and brittle like ice breaking underfoot. I looked around in alarm, but the fear that once paralyzed me was now a distant memory, replaced by a calm resolve. The mirrors surrounding me began to fracture, lines spreading across their surfaces like intricate spiderwebs. The delicate pattern of cracks expanded, each splinter resonating with a faint, musical chime. The glass splintered and shattered bit by bit, raining down in a dazzling cascade of light and reflection, each fragment catching and refracting the light into a myriad of sparkling colors. The sound of shattering glass was both violent and beautiful, a symphony of liberation echoing around me. The cool air stirred, carrying the scent of fresh rain and the promise of a new beginning, as the last remnants of the mirrors fell away, leaving me standing amidst a sea of shimmering shards.

****

In the middle of the chaos, I stood still, watching as the pieces of the mirror maze fell away. Each shard of glass descended like a sparkling curtain being drawn aside, revealing the world beyond. The tinkling of falling fragments was like delicate, crystalline music, each note dissolving a piece of my past. As the mirrors shattered around me, the air grew lighter, the oppressive weight of old fears and doubts lifting from my shoulders. The broken pieces caught the light, creating a dazzling display of reflections that danced around me before they settled on the ground. The mirrors shattered the illusions I had clung to for so long, their fragmented images refracting reality into a thousand glittering facets. With each fragment that broke free, I felt a part of my past dissolve, the old fears and doubts dissipating like mist in the morning sun.

As the last piece of glass fell, it landed with a final, resonant chime, leaving me standing in the center of open space. The gallery emerged from behind the shattered mirrors, revealed in a flood of natural light. The walls, adorned with vibrant art, came into view, each piece a testament to creativity and resilience. The air was filled with the subtle scent of fresh paint and polished wood, mingling with a faint echo of distant laughter and conversation. The transformation was complete, the curtain of glass having lifted to unveil a new beginning. The maze walls were gone, replaced by a tranquil gallery with large paintings. I realized that I was in a gallery of my life.

Confusion washed over me as I tried to gather my emotions. How had I ended up here? What did it all mean?

Slowly, I walked along the gallery, each step echoing softly in the stillness, my footsteps a gentle rhythm against the polished wooden floor. The walls were adorned with a myriad of vibrant paintings, each one capturing a moment in time. I stopped in front of a painting that caught my eye, its colors vivid and hauntingly familiar. In the center of the canvas, I saw myself crumpled on the floor, my body contorted in pain. The background muted, shadowy hues contrasted sharply with my form's raw, visceral detail. The brushstrokes were both delicate and intense, capturing the texture of my disheveled hair and the tension in my clenched fists. The pain etched on my face was unmistakable, each line and furrow telling a story of enduring agony. The scene brought back the memory with a rush of raw emotion, the dull, throbbing ache of a fibromyalgia flare-up echoing in my mind. I could almost feel the sting of tears and the heaviness in my limbs. The soft light from the gallery's ceiling cast a gentle glow on the painting, accentuating the contrast between the despair in my eyes and the faint glimmer of determination that lingered there. As I stood there, absorbing the scene, the memory washed over me, intense and unfiltered, yet tempered by the knowledge that I had emerged stronger.

"Luke," I called out, my voice trembling,

Luke rushed beside me, his movements hurried and almost frantic. His face, though tender, was etched with worry, his eyes wide and darting. He dropped to his knees, almost skidding on the floor, and scooped me into his arms with a quick yet careful motion. His hands trembled slightly as he fumbled in his pocket for the pain medication, the pills rattling against the plastic. He pressed them into my hand, his breath coming in short, rapid bursts. Despite his panic, his touch was gentle, his fingers brushing my skin with the lightest pressure. He leaned in close, his voice a soft murmur of soothing words, each one imbued with a desperate, loving urgency.

"Hey,… It's okay. I'm right here with you." His voice was a soothing murmur; I closed my eyes, letting his words wash over me.

"Just breathe, Dee. You're strong. You've got this." He cradled me gently, his touch a lifeline; his fingers traced calming circles on my back, grounding me in the present despite the pain. "I know it hurts, but I'm here. You're not alone in this," he whispered; tears welled in my eyes as I felt the weight of his presence. "You're the bravest person I know. We'll get through this together, okay?" he said as he brushed a strand of hair from my forehead. I nodded, unable to speak as the pain was unbearable.

"I love you, Dee. Always," he said, looking into my eyes, his gaze filled with love and reassurance.

It became clear to me that we were, indeed, soulmates. Despite the hardships, we had weathered storms together, always finding our way back to each other, stronger and more connected than before.

The Abyss

The walls around me shifted and transformed as I walked through the gallery. The serene scenes of my life morphed into something starkly familiar—a hospital hallway. Soft hues and peaceful paintings gave way to stark, sterile white walls under the harsh glare of flickering fluorescent lights. The calming artwork that once adorned the gallery now seemed a distant memory, replaced by a clinical, almost oppressive atmosphere. The sound of footsteps echoed differently in the hospital hallway, the noise amplified by the bare walls and floors. Each step seemed to resonate, bouncing off the stark surfaces, creating an eerie cadence that was both unsettling and disorienting. Faint murmurs of medical staff and the intermittent beeping of machines added to the ambient noise, heightening the sense of being in a hospital environment.

A distinct hospital scent permeated the air—antiseptic mixed with faint medicinal odors. It was a sharp, sterile smell that triggered a flood of memories and emotions. Each breath I took seemed to pull me further into the past, evoking associations with medical settings that I had long tried to forget.

Each step echoed softly in the stillness as I moved cautiously forward. Room numbers passed by—204, 205, 206—until I reached it: Room 209. Dread settled heavily in my chest as I recognized the number on the door. This was where my mother had spent her final days fighting a battle with cancer that neither of us could win. The hallway seemed to constrict around me, walls closing in with an oppressive weight. Each breath came shallow and quick, my pulse drumming in my ears. I hesitated for a moment, my fingers twitching, then curling into tight fists. The doorknob felt icy against my damp palm. Forcing my hand steady, I pushed open the door. Inside, the room was a ghostly echo of the past. The clinical sterility and the faint hum of medical equipment were all there, unchanged by time. On the bed lay my mother, her figure barely rising above the crisp, white sheets. The harsh fluorescent lights overhead cast a cold, clinical glow over her frail form, illuminating the hollow cheeks and thin, translucent skin. Her once vibrant presence was now reduced to a fragile, still silhouette, just as I remembered her from those final moments.

I moved closer, my heart thudding in my chest, each beat a reminder of the grief and guilt that clung to me. The floor beneath my feet was cold and unforgiving, and the faint rustle of my footsteps seemed unnervingly loud in the stillness. Sitting beside her, I reached out hesitantly, my fingers trembling as they brushed against her cold, lifeless hand. The touch was jarring, a stark contrast to the warm, familiar memories of her touch. The monitor beside her emitted a steady, rhythmic beep, its sound sharp and punctuating the quiet like a relentless metronome. It was a noise that had haunted my dreams, now painfully real, anchoring me to the somber reality of the moment.

"Mom," I gasped, my voice barely above a whisper, "I'm sorry. I'm sorry for the anger, for the resentment. I've come to understand why you couldn't tell me everything, why you shielded me from your pain. I was so focused on my hurt and confusion that I couldn't see beyond my perspective. I realize now how naive I was, how much I needed to see things from your point of view."

I paused, the weight of my words hanging heavy in the air. Memories of times when she had tried to protect me from the harsh realities of life flooded my mind—her gentle reassurances when things seemed uncertain, her quiet strength in the face of adversity. I saw now that her silence had been an act of love, a sacrifice to spare me from her suffering. I needed to let go.

"I forgive you," I continued, my voice steadier now, filled with sorrow and acceptance. "I know you did what you thought was best, even if it meant keeping secrets. I was hurt when you passed, Mom, because I felt like you left me. But I know you didn't leave me willingly. You were fighting a battle I couldn't fully understand." The monitor beside her bed beeped softly, a steady rhythm that underscored the finality of the moment. I gently squeezed her cold, lifeless hand, feeling the chill of her skin against mine. It was a stark reminder of life's frailty and how quickly everything could change.

"I wish I could have eased your pain and shared your burden. But I promise you, Mom, I will always carry your love with me. And I will learn from your strength and ability to face life's challenges gracefully." I whispered hoarsely as I kissed her cold hand. The room seemed to shimmer and blur. My mother's presence faded, leaving only an empty bed and an open door leading into darkness. I stood slowly, my emotions raw yet strangely peaceful. A voice, faint yet familiar, called out from beyond the room.

"Are you ready?" it asked, its tone gentle yet insistent. I knew instinctively where I needed to go next.

Leaving the room behind, I retraced my steps through the hospital corridor. The harsh, fluorescent lights flickered above, casting a cold, clinical glow on the pale, linoleum floor that seemed to stretch endlessly before me. The muted hum of distant machines and the soft scuff of my shoes against the tiles created a rhythmic backdrop to my thoughts. As I walked, the sterile environment began to blur, its clinical sterility dissolving into a distant memory. Gradually, the hallway's sterile whiteness gave way to the warm, enveloping darkness of the cave, where the blinding light at its center pulsed softly, a beacon of clarity and understanding.

As I approached, the shadowy figure from before emerged, its presence hidden in the eerie and menacing shadows. I confronted it, my voice steady despite the shock of recognition. "Who are you?" I asked the question hanging in the air between us. As the figure approached, the dim light revealed a haunting similarity—a distorted mirror of myself. Its hair was interwoven with tangled leaves, and slender vines coiled around its limbs like nature's embrace. The figure's eyes, deep and sorrowful, carried an emotional weight that tugged at my very core. Their gaze seemed to reach into the depths of my soul, unearthing a profound sadness that was both unsettling and familiar. As I locked eyes with this reflection, a wave of self-awareness surged through me, like a cold wind stirring dormant leaves.

The figure's voice, soft yet unmistakably clear, drifted through the air. "I am you," it murmured, its tone a haunting echo of my own. Its eyes, dark and intense, seemed to pull back layers of my defenses as it continued, "I am the part of you that you bury deep, the pain you refuse to face." As the words hung between us, the air felt heavy, charged with the unspoken truths and buried sorrows it revealed. "To understand this place," it said, its voice resonating with an eerie calm, "you must step into the light and confront the darkest corners of yourself."

The figure's gaze pierced through me, as if peeling back the veil that shrouded my heart. "Only by facing these shadows head-on will you begin to unravel the mysteries that bind you here. Your journey back to Luke, to the world you cherish, lies in confronting and embracing the parts of you that you have long avoided." A shiver ran through me, a mixture of dread and reluctant resolve. The figure's words were like a cold wind sweeping through a hidden chamber, stirring up the dust of forgotten pain. "The path forward is through this confrontation," it continued. "Understanding the depths of your own sorrow and accepting these fractured pieces of yourself will illuminate the way. Only then can you hope to return to the life you hold dear." As the figure's image flickered in and out of focus, I felt a surge of both fear and determination. Its haunting presence was a grim reminder of the journey ahead—one that required not just bravery, but an honest confrontation with the darkest parts of my own soul.

I met its gaze, finally understanding the journey I had embarked upon. This confrontation was not about defeating an enemy but embracing my own truths, accepting every part of myself—the light and the darkness.

With a deep breath, I nodded slowly. "I'm ready," I said firmly, my voice steady with resolve. "I'm ready to face myself, to embrace who I am."

****

I stepped into the blinding light; each memory unfolded like a dark prophecy, each a reminder of my deepest failures. The cave around me morphed into a battlefield, where shadows of my past sins rose to challenge me. These weren't mere reflections; they were evil specters, twisted versions of my family, each eager to drag me into the abyss of my own guilt. First came the phantom of betrayal, wearing Evie's face, her features twisted into a mask of ruthless fury. Her once warm and confident brown eyes were now blazing with the fire of deception, glowing with an intense, vicious light. Her dark skin, once radiant, now appeared ghostly and etched with dark, pulsating veins that seemed to writhe and twist with her every movement.

Her hair, once flowing and beautiful, now whipped around her like a dark storm, adding to her fearsome appearance. Her tattered and torn dress seemed to shimmer with spectral light as if woven from the shadows of our broken past. The air around her crackled with tension, the scent of bitterness filling my nostrils, mingling with the metallic tang of my own fear. Her voice was a dagger, each word piercing through the fragile defenses of my heart, dripping with venom and unyielding rage.

"I trusted you," she spat, her voice venomous and cold, echoing with the weight of her broken trust. "You shattered that trust, and now you will pay." She lunged at me with the speed of a striking cobra, her movements fluid and deadly. Now twisted into sharp, claw-like talons, her fingers slashed through the air with lethal precision. I barely evaded her attack, my heart pounding in my chest. Her claws grazed my skin, leaving burning trails of agony that flared with an excruciating intensity. Each wound was a testament to the hurt I had caused, the pain a searing reminder of my disloyalty.

"I'm sorry," I cried, tears mingling with blood as I blocked her next vicious blow. "I didn't understand the damage it would cause."

But there was no rest. The next opponent wore Luke's face, emerging like a specter from the depths of my remorse. His eyes, once warm pools of understanding, now blazed with the torment of my harsh words. They gleamed with an intensity that seemed to pierce through the very core of my being, each glance a searing reminder of the pain I had inflicted. His presence was a towering figure cloaked in rage and anguish. His posture was tense, every muscle coiled with a restrained fury that threatened to erupt like a storm. The air around him crackled with an electric tension; his features, typically gentle and caring, were now hardened with lines of stress and disappointment. His jaw set in a firm, unyielding line. His stance was confrontational. With shoulders squared and fists clenched, he advanced towards me. The ground seemed to tremble beneath his steps, echoing the explosive wrath within him.

"You said things that cut deeper than you know," he roared, his voice echoing a storm of pain. "I thought you understood me, but your words... tore us apart."

His attacks were relentless, each strike a hammer blow to my soul. I stumbled, barely managing to deflect his fury. Each swing of his spectral fists left me gasping, the weight of my remorse nearly crushing.

"I never meant to hurt you," I shouted, my voice cracking with remorse as I fought to stay upright. "I let my anger get the best of me, and I'm sorry for the pain I caused."

No sooner had I caught my breath, another specter loomed—my failure, a monstrous titan. Its presence was suffocating, each step sending tremors of self-doubt through the ground beneath me. Its form unfolded with unsettling familiarity—deep shadows and jagged lines marking essential moments where I faltered. Its eyes held a depth of disappointment. As it advanced, the ground quivered, amplifying the weight of self-doubt. Confronting this manifestation of my failures demanded more than acknowledging mistakes—it challenged me to find strength in forging a path forward despite the shadows of the past.

"I had dreams," I admitted, my voice barely whispering beneath the oppressive weight of fear. "But I was terrified of failing, of not being good enough."

The giant laughed, a deep, mocking sound that echoed like thunder. "You let fear hold you back," it jeered. "Now, face the paths you never took, the dreams you abandoned."

It swung a colossal fist at me. I barely dodged, feeling the ground shudder beneath its might. I could feel my fears clawing at my resolve, but I could not let them win. I charged the giant with a primal scream, striking with all the courage I could muster. The impact sent shockwaves through my body, but I stood my ground, refusing to be crushed by my doubts. Its form morphed, carved from ice, angular and sharp, devoid of warmth or empathy, with eyes that gleamed like shards of ice reflecting a harsh, unforgiving light. The shadow's features were a distorted mirror of my own, exaggerated in their self-serving intentions. Its posture exuded a sense of superiority as if it considered itself above reproach or consequence. Each movement it made seemed precise and calculated, designed to maximize personal gain at any cost.

The ground beneath its feet crackled with frost, echoing the frosty detachment that characterized its behavior. In this embodiment of selfishness, I faced not just a reflection but a reminder of the times I prioritized my desires over the needs of others. Its presence demanded recognition of the consequences of my actions, urging me to confront the shadows of my motivations and their impact on those around me.

"You did it for yourself," it sneered, circling me like a predator. "You took credit for others' work. You prioritized your own needs. But at what cost?"

It lunged with deadly precision, its attacks merciless. I dodged and countered, every move weighed down by the guilt of my actions. "I was wrong," I shouted, striking back with my confession. "I didn't consider the impact on others."

Each admission weakened the specter, its form flickering like a dying flame. But there was no end to this nightmarish gauntlet. My lies and neglect took shape, a hazy figure materializing before me. Its silhouette was jagged and unclear, shifting and swirling with the weight of broken promises and shattered trust. The air around it crackled with an atmosphere heavy with disappointment and betrayal, casting darkness that seemed to seep into the very fabric of the chamber. The figure's features were cloudy yet hauntingly familiar—reminders of the moments when I chose falsehoods over honesty and indifference over responsibility. Once trusting and hopeful, its eyes now glowed with a dull, accusatory light, reflecting the pain of those I had let down. As I faced this shadowy figure, I knew that confronting it meant more than mere acknowledgment—it demanded genuine remorse and a commitment to repair what had been broken. It challenged me to confront the shadows of my past actions and find a path toward redemption amidst the darkness I had created.

"I lied," I confessed, the weight of my deceit heavy on my chest. "I thought it wouldn't matter, but it only pushed people away."

The shadow's tendrils wrapped around me, squeezing the breath from my lungs. "Trust is fragile," it hissed. "And once broken, it takes more than words to mend." I struggled against the tightening bonds, feeling my life force diminishing. But I couldn't surrender. I tore through the darkness with a desperate surge, shattering the tendrils' grip.

The battle continued; my dependence on substances emerged as a looming figure, its form hidden by swirling shadows. The substance was a dark, swirling mist that enveloped the figure. Within its depths, it reflected the seductive promise of relief from the relentless pain of fibromyalgia. As the mist coiled and shifted, it oozed sweetness tinged with bitterness, reminiscent of the pills that had once been my refuge. Each swirl seemed to whisper promises of temporary ease. The air around it grew heavy with the weight of dependency, imbued with the lingering scent of pharmaceuticals and the faint echo of distant cries for help. The figure of substance moved with fluid grace. With every step it took closer, I felt the pull of familiarity and the pang of longing for relief.

"I sought escape through substances," I admitted, my voice strained with regret. "But it only masked the deeper issues."

The figure of addiction shifted, its silhouette contorting into a twisted reflection of my own. Its eyes, dark and hollow, bore into mine with a chilling intensity, echoing the void left by my attempts to numb the pain of fibromyalgia. "You think you can evade responsibility," the shadow hissed, reverberating with scorn. "But you only prolong the inevitable."

With determination, I squared my shoulders, bracing myself against the onslaught of accusations. I clenched my fists, summoning courage from the depths of my blame. As the shadow lunged forward, I met its attack head-on, a clash of wills and regrets echoing through the chamber. The impact reverberated through my bones as we grappled, its icy touch searing against my skin like a reminder of past mistakes. Each blow exchanged was proof of my internal struggle against my weaknesses. Gritting my teeth, I rebelled, refusing to yield with every ounce of strength; I fought to reclaim ground lost to addiction's grip. Sweat mingled with tears as I confronted the specter head-on, grappling with the harsh reality of my choices and the wounds they inflicted. I wrestled the specter to the ground, pinning it beneath the weight of my newfound resolve. The shadows wavered, their edges blurring as light pierced through the darkness that had clouded my judgment.

"My mistakes will not define me," I declared, my voice steady. "I will face the pain, confront my demons, and emerge stronger."

With a final surge of strength, I reached out, grasping at the misty tendrils that composed its shape. Each touch felt like a battle against my own urges and desires, a struggle against the lure of temporary relief. With a shout, I commanded the specter to dissipate. The mist shuddered and trembled under my touch, resisting at first before gradually yielding to my claim and watching as it dissolved into wisps of darkness scattered into the air. As the last shadow disintegrated, I stood, breathless yet victorious. The battlefield flooded with light, the echoes of my battles fading into silence. I was bruised and battered, but my spirit was unbroken. "I see it now," I spoke aloud, addressing the light and the weight of my own conscience. "I cannot change what I've done, but I can change how I move forward."

The light pulsed softly, a gentle glow of understanding. "I will no longer hide behind fear or convenience. I accept responsibility," I said, each word said with conviction. "For the pain I've caused and the opportunities I've missed, but I will not let my past define me." Like a cool breeze on a hot summer day, a wave of release washed over me, sweeping away the chains of guilt and regret that had bound me for so long. I felt lighter and freer, as if a heavy burden had been lifted, allowing me to stand taller and more confident. I embraced the complications of my humanity—the intertwining of light and darkness within my soul. I could feel the warmth of acceptance spreading through me like sunlight breaking through storm clouds.

"Forgiveness," I whispered, a tear rolled down my cheek, "begins with forgiving myself."

The light dimmed as I stood at the cave's threshold. A door waited for me; it was unlike any I had seen before. Its ancient wood was weathered and bore marks of countless journeys, scratches that hinted at trials endured and wisdom gained. The handle, wrought from tarnished brass, gleamed faintly in the cave's dim light. I knew my journey had just begun, and with newfound strength and determination coursing through my veins, I reached out to grasp the handle, ready to face whatever challenges lay beyond.

16

What If?

I walked into the vase hallway, and a wave of hope and relief washed over me. The corridor, once a chaotic maze cluttered with countless doors—each representing a past decision or regret—had transformed. As I faced my past and came to terms with it, many of those doors began to fade away. Now, only a few doors remained, each one spaced apart and standing as symbols of crucial moments or important lessons learned. This change symbolized my progress and the release of past burdens, revealing a clearer path forward.

My hands brushed against the empty spaces where doors had once stood, and I felt a light, almost electric sensation at my fingertips, as if the absence of the doors had released a current of liberation and freedom. The air around me seemed to breathe easier, carrying a faint, clean scent like the first breath of spring. With each step, the old, oppressive weight of my past seemed to dissolve, replaced by a crisp clarity that invigorated my senses. The smooth, cool floor beneath my feet felt firm and reassuring, guiding me steadily forward. As I moved deeper into the corridor, my footsteps echoed softly, drawing me closer to the end of this journey and the reconciliation with Luke that I longed for. Ahead, a single door stood out, adorned with three shimmering threads—gold, silver, and red—woven into a delicate pattern. Touching the threads, I felt a subtle, rhythmic hum, as if they were intertwining the strands of my past, present, and future. With a mix of anticipation and resolve, I turned the handle. The door creaked open to reveal a warm, golden light spilling into the corridor, leading to a serene meadow bathed in sunlight. The peaceful landscape filled me with hope and clarity, signaling that the path to Luke and the answers I sought was now within reach. Stepping into the room, I entered an average, small box room with no furniture. The room's stark emptiness was starkly contrasted by the three glowing threads positioned in the center. Each thread emitted a soft, pulsating light—one a warm amber, another a cool silver, and the third a vibrant crimson. The threads shimmered faintly, casting gentle, shifting hues across the room's bare walls. The faint glow of each thread created a mesmerizing dance of colors, as if they were alive with a subtle, otherworldly energy. I hesitated, my senses tingling with both curiosity and trepidation, unsure of what these threads might signify or what would unfold if I touched them. Taking a deep breath to steady myself, I reached out to the first thread, the warm amber one. The moment my fingers brushed against it, I felt a delicate, almost electric tingle run through my hand, spreading up my arm. The room around me began to dissolve, replaced by a rush of vivid imagery and sensations.

Suddenly, I was transported to a sunlit park from my childhood. The scene was bathed in golden light, and the air was filled with the joyous, carefree sounds of laughter. I saw myself as a child, giggling as I chased Evie through a field of emerald grass. The scent of freshly cut grass and the warmth of the sun on my skin were palpable, evoking a deep sense of nostalgia. The weight of the past seemed to lift, replaced by the pure, unburdened joy of those carefree days. As I released the thread, the warm, amber glow faded, and the room reappeared around me. A bittersweet smile tugged at my lips, touched by the simplicity and warmth of that cherished memory. As I grasped the central thread, the world around me abruptly shifted. The sterile, empty room dissolved into a chaotic blur, replaced by the harsh, bright lights of an emergency room. The sharp, metallic smell of antiseptic stung my nose, mingling with the acrid scent of sweat and fear. I was thrust into the heart of a frantic scene. The rhythmic beeping of monitors and the urgent shouts of paramedics filled my ears, creating a cacophony of distress. The defibrillator paddles pressed against my chest were cold and harsh, delivering a jolt that surged through my body like a lightning strike. The medics' strained, intense faces were a stark contrast to the calm that had preceded this moment. Their movements were quick and deliberate, their eyes locked in concentrated effort.

A surge of panic swept over me as I comprehended the gravity of the situation: I was reliving a moment of crisis, a life-or-death struggle. The urgency of the moment struck me with visceral force, intensifying my sense of dread. I needed to escape this scene and return to the present before it was too late. With a rush of fear and determination, I pulled away from the thread. The chaotic scene faded, and the room reformed around me. My mind raced, realizing that these threads were not merely symbolic but portals to different times in my life—past, present, and future. Gripping the last thread, a vibrant crimson one, I felt an overwhelming urgency. My heart pounded as I reached for it, desperate to glimpse what lay ahead. The thread's warmth seemed to promise revelations and the answers I so desperately sought, fueling my resolve to face whatever the future might hold.

Visions flooded my mind with overwhelming intensity. I was immersed in a cascade of vivid images and sensations, each one more poignant than the last. I saw myself, my belly rounded with a baby bump, standing beside Luke in a brightly lit hospital room. The sterile smell of antiseptic mingled with the warm, comforting scent of our shared anticipation. The moment of holding our baby for the first time was etched into my mind with breathtaking clarity. I could feel the soft, delicate weight of the newborn in my arms, the tiny, warm body nestled against me. The baby's first, tentative breaths and the gentle, rhythmic sound of their breathing filled me with an indescribable joy. I watched as our child took their first wobbly steps, their tiny feet making hesitant but determined progress across the floor. Each milestone was marked by a sweet, heartwarming resonance—a first word, a giggle, a proud moment of growth. The future was bathed in a golden light of love and happiness, a tapestry of shared moments that shimmered with authenticity.

Despite the beauty of the vision, a tension gripped me as I tried to pull away from the thread. My fingers clung desperately, unwilling to let go as the vibrant scenes played out in front of me. The edges of the vision seemed to blur and waver, as if resisting my attempt to escape. Tears welled up, hot and stinging, streaming unchecked down my cheeks. Each drop splashed onto the thread and the floor, mingling with the shifting, golden light of the future. My breath hitched and quickened, chest rising and falling unevenly, as the joy of the vision contrasted sharply with the cold reality of my grasp.

"Why?" The word escaped my lips in a strangled whisper, trembling like a leaf in a storm. My voice cracked, and the sound seemed to dissolve into the radiant glow around me. The vision remained tantalizingly close, shimmering with promise, but the gap between the dream and my present reality felt as vast as an unbridgeable chasm. My plea was for a simple answer, a guiding light to navigate the path toward this dream. I clung to the hope that the thread would offer a clue or direction to make this future a reality, desperate for any sign that would lead me there.

But the only answer I received was the opening of the door behind me. My shoulders sagged slightly, a physical manifestation of the disappointment that coiled tightly in my chest. The silence was not merely the absence of sound but a weight, pushing down on me, squeezing the breath from my lungs. I realized that life, whether in living or limbo, demanded hard work and endurance before good things could come to actuality. I had to earn the future I had seen. With a heart full of hope and determination, I left the room, carrying the visions with me. As I stepped out of the room, my senses were immediately enveloped by a new environment. I found myself in the grandeur of an auditorium, its sheer scale making me feel small yet exhilarated. The floor beneath me was cool and smooth, a stark contrast to the warmth of the room I had just left. My footsteps echoed softly, a rhythmic accompaniment to the murmurs of anticipation that seemed to hum through the space.

Rows upon rows of seats stretched out before me, each upholstered in deep, plush fabric that seemed to invite relaxation. The seats were arranged in a gentle curve around a stage that stood at the far end of the room, illuminated by a soft, inviting light. The stage was like a magnet, pulling my gaze forward, promising something both intriguing and unknown. I approached a seat in the middle and settled into it, feeling the cushioning mold to my form.

The fabric was cool against my skin, and as I leaned back, the gentle creak of the seat beneath me was a soothing sound that matched the quiet anticipation in the air. Tilting my head back, my eyes were drawn upwards to the ceiling, where a breathtaking display of stars twinkled above. The ceiling had been transformed into a vast, dark canvas, and the stars shimmered with a brilliance that seemed almost tangible. Each star was a tiny, flickering point of light, casting a soft, ethereal glow that danced across the dark expanse in intricate, mesmerizing patterns.

The stars seemed to sway and shift as if guided by an unseen hand, their light casting a subtle, silvery sheen across the ceiling. The patterns they formed were both familiar and foreign, evoking the grandeur of the cosmos and the mysteries of the universe. The sight was simultaneously enchanting and humbling, making me reflect on the boundless expanse above and the smaller, yet significant, journey I had navigated through my own experiences. The air in the auditorium was crisp and slightly cool, carrying with it the faint scent of polished wood and a hint of lavender, adding to the serene ambiance. I inhaled deeply, feeling a sense of calm as the soft, ambient light of the stars filled my vision, urging me to ponder the vastness of the universe and the experiences that had shaped my journey in limbo.

Why was this happening? What did all of it mean? Where was Luke?

As I sat there, gazing up at the constellation of stars, a subtle shift began. At first, the stars drifted lazily across the ceiling, their twinkle steady and calm. Gradually, their movement quickened, the stars swirling into a dynamic dance of light and shadow. The once serene patterns gave way to a more frantic, pulsating rhythm, their bright pinpricks merging and separating to form intricate shapes that seemed almost alive. The air around me grew cooler, and a faint hum, like the distant whisper of a cosmic wind, seemed to accompany the celestial display.

I could almost feel the soft, tingling sensation of the stars' light on my skin, a gentle reminder of the transformation occurring above me. Suddenly, the stars coalesced into a focused image, and the shimmering patterns began to resolve into a vivid, tangible memory. The scene shifted abruptly, and I found myself transported into a small, dimly lit doctor's office. The transformation was so complete that I could almost sense the change in temperature—the sterile chill of the medical environment contrasting sharply with the warmth of the auditorium. The walls of the office were lined with medical charts and anatomical posters, their edges slightly yellowed with age. The faint smell of antiseptic hung in the air, mingling with the subtle, earthy scent of old paper. The soft rustling of paper and the quiet ticking of a wall clock punctuated the silence, enhancing the sense of confinement and focus in the room.

Across from me, my mother and father sat in sturdy, straight-backed chairs. Their faces were illuminated by the dim light, etched with lines of concern and anticipation. I could see the tension in their posture, the way their hands rested nervously in their laps, and the faint creases on their brows. My father's fingers tapped rhythmically on the arm of his chair, while my mother's gaze shifted between him and the doctor, her lips pressed into a thin line of worry. The doctor, a kind-looking woman with glasses perched on the edge of her nose, spoke softly, her voice tinged with sorrow.

"I'm very sorry," the doctor said gently. "You've had a miscarriage."

The words seemed to hang in the air, heavy and painful. My mother's face crumpled as if the weight of those words had physically pressed down on her. Her hands flew to her face, fingers clutching at her cheeks as her breaths came in sharp, ragged gasps. Her entire body shook uncontrollably, the sobs escaping from her in harsh, stuttering waves that made her shoulders jerk with each cry. The muffled sounds of her grief seeped out between her fingers, filling the space with a palpable sense of despair. My father reached out, placing a comforting hand on her shoulder, his face a mask of stoic strength. He squeezed her shoulder gently, his touch conveying the support and love he couldn't quite put into words.

"Okay," my father began, his voice steady but strained, "what do we need to do to take care of her? What should we expect?"

The doctor leaned forward, her expression compassionate and understanding. "Physically, she'll need rest. The body needs time to recover from the loss. Emotionally, it's going to be a difficult journey. She'll need your support more than ever. It's important to be patient and understanding." She paused, ensuring that the weight of her words was sinking in. "In terms of medical care, there are a few key stages we should be aware of."

"First," the doctor continued, "we need to monitor her for any signs of complications. Even though the miscarriage was early, there can still be issues such as infection or excessive bleeding. It's crucial to keep an eye on her symptoms and report anything unusual, such as severe pain, heavy bleeding, or fever. Second," she said, "we'll schedule follow-up appointments to ensure her physical recovery is on track. Typically, this will involve a check-up in a week or so to make sure everything has returned to normal. We might also conduct an ultrasound to confirm that the uterus is clear."

She glanced at the concerned faces before her, giving them a reassuring nod. "Third, we'll provide guidance on emotional recovery. This includes offering counseling services or support groups if she finds them helpful. The emotional impact of a miscarriage can be profound, and it's important to have resources available for processing the grief."

"Lastly," the doctor said, "if you're considering future pregnancies, we'll discuss any necessary precautions or additional care to support a healthy outcome. It's important to allow time for physical and emotional healing before trying to conceive again, but we'll provide detailed advice tailored to her situation." She offered a gentle smile. "If you have any questions or concerns, don't hesitate to reach out. We're here to help every step of the way."

My mother lifted her tear-streaked face, her eyes red and puffy. "Why did this happen?" she choked out, her voice barely a whisper. "Was it something I did?"

The doctor shook her head, her gaze softening. "No, it's not your fault. Miscarriages happen for many reasons, and most of the time, it's something beyond anyone's control. Please don't blame yourself." She leaned forward, her eyes full of compassion. "Many women feel guilt or wonder if they did something wrong. But the reality is, miscarriages are usually caused by genetic factors or other issues that we cannot foresee or prevent. It's a natural part of many pregnancies, even though it's incredibly painful to experience."

Tears welled up in my mother's eyes as she listened, my father squeezing her hand gently. "But I was so careful," she whispered, her voice trembling. "I did everything right."

The doctor nodded understandingly. "I know you did. And that's exactly why you need to be kind to yourself. You did everything you could. Sometimes, despite our best efforts, nature has its own course. It's crucial to remember that this doesn't define you or your ability to have a healthy pregnancy in the future." She took a deep breath before continuing. "There's nothing you did to cause this, and there's nothing you could have done to prevent it. Allow yourself to grieve, and don't be afraid to lean on those around you. It's okay to feel a range of emotions—sadness, anger, confusion. All of these feelings are valid."

My father's grip on my mother's shoulder tightened, his eyes glistening with unshed tears. "How do we...how do we move forward from this?" he asked, his voice cracking slightly.

"Focus on healing," the doctor replied gently. "Both of you. Take the time you need to rest and process what's happened. Engage in activities that bring you comfort and peace. And if you ever feel overwhelmed, reach out for support, whether it's through friends, family, or professional help." She handed them a pamphlet. "This has information about local support groups and counseling services. Sometimes, talking to others who've been through similar experiences can be incredibly helpful. Remember, you're not alone in this."

My mother nodded slowly, her sobs quieting, but her pain was still palpable. "I just...I wanted this baby so much," she whispered, her voice breaking. "I wanted to be a mother."

My father wrapped his arm around her, pulling her close. "We'll get through this," he murmured, kissing her temple. "We'll try again when you're ready. We're in this together."

My mother leaned into him, drawing strength from his presence. "Thank you," she said, her voice trembling but filled with a tentative hope. "Thank you for being here."

As I watched this scene unfold, I felt a deep, aching sympathy for my parents. My mother's grief and my father's unwavering support were heart-wrenching to witness. As I watched this scene unfold, I felt a deep, aching sympathy for my parents. My mother's grief and my father's support were heart-wrenching to witness. I understood now why she had kept this part of her life from me. She had endured so much pain, and her silence was a shield to protect me from the heartache she had known. I knew all too well the heart-wrenching moment when something so precious dies inside you. The sudden, hollow realization that a part of you will never be, the dreams that evaporate instantly, leaving behind an emptiness that nothing can fill.

The physical pain, though intense, is nothing compared to the emotional agony. It's a loss that rips through your very soul, a grief that clings to you and becomes part of your daily existence. I had been through similar pain, and the realization that she had endured this silently made my heart ache with a newfound appreciation for her strength and resilience. I remembered the moment I had lost my own baby, the gut-wrenching despair that had consumed me. I had felt so alone, even with Luke by my side, because the pain was something so deeply personal, so profoundly isolating. The endless nights spent crying, the feeling of helplessness, and the question that haunted me: Why? It was a pain that felt insurmountable, and it had taken every ounce of strength to move forward. Knowing that my mother had gone through this same devastating experience, not just once but multiple times, and had still found the strength to raise me with love and patience filled me with an overwhelming sense of awe and respect. She had wanted to protect me from the heartache she knew all too well, sparing me from the burden of her grief while carrying it alone. Her silent suffering and quiet fortitude were proof of the depth of her love. The memory faded, and I was back in the auditorium, the stars resettling into their positions above me. My emotions were a mix of sorrow, understanding, and gratitude. My mother's silent suffering and my father's support had shaped our family in ways I had never fully understood

I sat there momentarily, absorbing what I had just seen. The stars above seemed to twinkle in response to my thoughts, their light offering a gentle reassurance. I realized then that I had to accept the flow of time to trust that everything would unfold as it should. It wasn't just about escaping limbo; it was about learning to trust in the process and to have faith that things would happen when they were meant to. I needed to let go of my fears and doubts to believe that the future held promise and hope. Standing up, I looked around the vast auditorium. It was empty, and the silence gave me a sense of purpose. I knew I had to keep moving forward, to face whatever challenges lay ahead with courage and determination. Walking down the aisle, thinking about the support my father had given my mum, I couldn't help but think of Luke. I missed him so much, and the thought of being with him again filled me with an almost unbearable longing. But I had to be strong. I had to find my way back, not just for myself but for him.

The doors at the end of the aisle stood closed, a barrier between me and the next part of my journey. It was a pair of large, ornate double doors, crafted from dark wood and adorned with intricate brass hardware. An overhanging sign above the door, reminiscent of theater marquees, was softly illuminated, casting a gentle glow that hinted at the significance beyond. Frosted glass panels in the doors displayed elegant etchings of theater masks and stars, suggesting an entrance to a place of dreams and stories. The brass handles felt cool and solid under my hand, their weight a reminder of the grandeur they guarded. On either side of the door, display frames showcased posters and playbills of past and upcoming performances, adding to the anticipation. A small red carpet led up to the door, its rich color contrasting with the polished wood floors and enhancing the feeling of stepping into a world apart. Sconce lights flanked the doorway, their soft light reminiscent of stage lighting, creating a warm and inviting ambiance. Decorative moldings framed the doors, their elaborate designs echoing the elegance of old movie palaces and playhouses.

I reached out, hesitating momentarily as doubt tried to creep in. But I couldn't let fear hold me back. I had come too far and faced too many truths to turn back now. With a deep breath, I pushed the door open.

17

Towards the Light

I stepped into a classic American theater, enveloped in the rich aroma of buttery popcorn that instantly transported me with nostalgia and comfort. The scent mingled with a faint hint of caramel, making my mouth water. As I made my way down the aisle, the plush red carpet beneath my bare feet absorbed the sound of my footsteps, its velvety texture a luxurious contrast to the smooth, cool marble of the lobby. The dim lighting cast a warm glow, highlighting the intricate gold leaf designs that adorned the ceiling and walls, their elegance reminiscent of a bygone era. I hesitated for a moment, then moved toward the screen room, the weight of curiosity and a tinge of apprehension guiding my steps. The heavy velvet curtains brushed against me as I pushed through, their thick fabric cool and smooth. Inside, rows of empty seats stretched out, all facing a large, glowing screen that cast a soft, dim light across the room, the illumination seeming to pulse with anticipation. I slipped into a seat in the middle, feeling the plush cushion give way slightly beneath me. My heart pounded, each beat a blend of excitement and nervousness, echoing in the quiet, almost expectant atmosphere of the theater.

The screen flickered to life with the characteristic hum and faint crackle of an old-school projector. Grainy, sepia-toned images filled the screen, jumping and settling into focus like an old home movie reel. To my astonishment, I saw different versions of myself from various stages of my life, each captured in the nostalgic, warm tones of vintage film. Each version of me looked vibrant, their faces illuminated with the lively hues of youth and energy, yet their eyes and postures carried the subtle weight of their experiences, each frame a testament to the passage of time.

They were all there—Childhood Me, Teenage Me, Adulthood Me, Pre-Miscarriage Me, Post-Miscarriage Me, and Present Me—lined up like a living timeline. Childhood Me, small and wide-eyed, was seated beside Teenage Me, who looked awkward yet earnest. Adulthood Me sat to the right, with a contemplative expression. Pre-Miscarriage Me and Post-Miscarriage Me were next, their faces reflecting profound changes, while Present Me occupied the end, observing the interactions with a mix of nostalgia and longing. As I watched, the different versions of myself began to engage with one another, their gestures and expressions shifting between familiarity and revelation, each exchanging words and looks imbued with wisdom I wished I had possessed in those moments. Childhood Me looked up at Teenage Me with wide eyes and an innocent smile. "What happens when we grow up?" she asked, her voice filled with wonder and a hint of fear.

Teenage Me sighed, a mixture of defiance and vulnerability in her eyes. "We face many challenges, but we also find strength we didn't know we had. Don't be afraid to make mistakes. They help us grow."

Early Adulthood Me, turned to Teenage Me. "I know you feel lost right now, but trust in yourself. Every decision, even the wrong ones, will lead you to where you need to be."

With a hopeful glow about her, Pre-Miscarriage Me looked at Early Adulthood Me. "I wish I could tell you to cherish every moment. Life changes so quickly, and sometimes, in ways you never expect. Hold on to hope, even when it seems impossible."

Post-Miscarriage Me, with shadows under her eyes yet an undeniable resilience, spoke next. "Grief is not a sign of weakness. It's okay to feel pain, but remember to let yourself heal. Surround yourself with love and never give up on the idea of happiness."

Watching this unfold, Present Me felt a deep connection to each version. I saw the changes in myself through the years—the growth, the setbacks, the strength that emerged from adversity. Each version of me carried vital lessons for the next stage of life. Present Me appeared as if she had just stumbled from a car crash. Her clothes were disheveled, a torn sleeve hanging loose. Her hair was matted and unkempt, and a bruise darkened one side of her face. The physical signs of a recent struggle were clear, but her eyes, though weary, held a deep and evolving understanding. I noticed a shift in their expressions. The younger versions started to look more hopeful, more assured. The older versions lightened as they imparted their wisdom, releasing the burden of their past mistakes and regrets. With a measured breath, I realized that this was the essence of my journey—understanding and accepting every part of myself, from childhood innocence to Adulthood's resilience. Each stage, each version of me, was crucial in shaping who I was and who I was becoming.

The image began to fade, and the versions of myself disappeared, leaving me alone in the empty theater. But I no longer felt alone. I felt a profound connection to my past, present, and future selves, a continuity that gave me strength and hope. As I stood up and walked back towards the door, Stepping out of the theater, I found myself in a corridor unlike any I had encountered before. The walls were made of shifting glass, each panel reflecting potential futures, teasing me with glimpses of what could be. The reflections were hauntingly vivid, each one tugging at my heartstrings with their stark portrayals of choices and consequences.

The first reflection showed a future where I didn't reunite with Luke. I saw myself standing alone at his grave, the sorrow etched deeply into every line of my face. The gravestone loomed before me, while my posture was slumped, shoulders heavy with a profound sense of loss. The ache in my chest was almost unbearable, a physical weight pressing down, making it hard to breathe. I had to force myself to look away from the haunting vision, the pain was too raw and intense to linger on. As I turned my gaze back to the grave, the real, cold stone beneath my fingertips grounded me in the present, a stark contrast to the aching void of that future reflection.

Moving forward, the glass shifted again, and another vision unfurled before me. This time, I was back among the living, but the absence of a baby was palpable. I saw myself seated on a park bench, my shoulders hunched as I struggled to hold back tears. Around me, children darted across the grass, their laughter ringing out like a cruel contrast to my silence. The sunlight danced off the swings and slides, casting long, shifting shadows that seemed to mock the emptiness within me. The air was filled with the sweet scent of blooming flowers and freshly cut grass, but these smells only heightened my sense of loss.

I could almost feel the weight of the dreams that might never be realized, pressing down on me, and making the emptiness suffocating. The longing in my eyes was a silent plea, an aching reminder of a future that might never come to be. The following vision was more disturbing than the last. I floated in a dark, empty void, the vast nothingness stretching endlessly around me. My life's moments flickered before me like a relentless projector—scenes of past mistakes and regrets replaying with cruel precision. The images looped endlessly, accompanied by the harsh, repetitive drone of my own voice, each word echoing with unsettling clarity. The relentless parade of failures weighed heavily on my chest, each cycle tightening like a vise. My breaths came in shallow, ragged bursts, each inhalation a struggle against the oppressive pressure of my past. The sense of being trapped in this unending cycle wrapped around me, a suffocating fog of dread that made escape seem utterly impossible.

The sights and sounds of my past surrounded me, suffocating me with their neverending presence. The air felt heavy and stale, and the echoes of my mistakes reverberated through my mind, creating an overwhelming sense of despair and hopelessness. The thought of never being able to escape this unending cycle sent shivers down my spine, leaving me feeling utterly helpless and lost. Every moment seemed to stretch on for an eternity, each misstep and missed opportunity etched into my consciousness like an unending nightmare. My heart pounded as I realized the time to choose was upon me. I had reached the end of my journey, and the weight of the decision pressed heavily on my shoulders. The corridor stretched ahead, the glass walls shimmering ominously as if mocking my indecision. Just then, a faint orange glow appeared ahead, gradually piercing the oppressive darkness of the corridor. Delicate paper lanterns began to float into view, their soft, warm light pushing back the shadows. Each lantern's gentle flicker cast soothing patterns on the walls, creating a luminous path that wound through the gloom. The lanterns' light shimmered like a tender embrace, their glow offering a fragile promise of solace. As I followed their path, the warmth of their illumination cut through the darkness, guiding me forward. The lanterns floated in a mesmerizing procession, leading me through the corridor with their flickering light, forming a clear, winding trail.

With every step, the darkness seemed to recede, revealing more of the path. As the lanterns' glow grew brighter, my initial fear began to dissipate, replaced by a growing sense of wonder and anticipation. The gentle light paved my way through the obscurity, calming my racing heart and filling me with cautious hope. As I moved deeper into the corridor, the lanterns continued to guide me, their light unveiling the end of the passageway. The cold, bare surfaces were gradually overtaken by a tapestry of vines, their emerald tendrils snaking up from the base and weaving across the walls in a mesmerizing dance.

Eventually, the path led me to a colossal tree. Its immense trunk, covered in deeply broken bark, seemed to breathe with the rhythm of ages past. As I stood before it, my fingertips pressed against the rough, weathered surface, the texture was both coarse and invigorating, carrying the cool, earthy scent of the forest and the rich aroma of damp moss. Above me, the sprawling branches stretched out like an intricate web of destiny, each limb twisting and diverging, leading to its own unique path. The soft rustling of the frosted glass leaves created a symphony of delicate, tinkling sounds as if the tree itself was whispering secrets of the universe.

Reaching up on my tiptoes, I carefully plucked a leaf from a low-hanging branch. The leaf, crafted from frosted glass, was smooth to the touch, yet surprisingly warm, as though it held a secret fire within its icy facade. It emitted a faint, sweet fragrance, akin to blooming lotus flowers mingled with a hint of winter's crispness, creating a scent that was both refreshing and soothing. As I held the leaf in my hand, its glow was mesmerizing—a soft, ethereal light that cast gentle reflections on the surrounding forest floor. The glass's translucent sheen revealed subtle shifts of color, from serene blues to glimmering silvers, each shade flowing seamlessly into the next. The leaf seemed to pulse with a life of its own, and as I clutched it, I felt a delicate warmth seeping through my fingers. With my eyes closed, I let myself be immersed in the memories of twenty-eight years that flashed through my mind. I saw the innocence of my childhood playing with Evie, our laughter echoing through sunlit afternoons. The sharp pain of my father's departure to the tender warmth of my first date with Luke, the nervous excitement palpable once more.

My mother's illness and eventual passing cast a shadow over the montage, her strength and love a beacon in the darkness. Evie's sudden departure left a void that still echoed in my heart, a reminder of the fragility of life and the depth of our bonds. The storm of emotions threatened to overwhelm me, but I clung to the leaf, its gentle glow anchoring me in the present. I opened my eyes, clarity washing over me like a cleansing wave. The decision, once clouded by uncertainty and fear, now felt clear. Before me, a door emerged from the base of the colossal tree, a gateway to the next phase of my journey. Crafted from deep mahogany with flecks of silver and gold, it featured intricate carvings of blossoming flowers and emerging butterflies. The door glowed softly, casting a warm, ethereal light and hinting at new beginnings. The handles, shaped like delicate butterflies with outstretched wings, were cool yet emanated a gentle warmth. As I touched them, a fresh, floral scent filled the air, accompanied by a faint, melodic chime. I glanced back at the tree, its glowing leaves and branching paths slowly fading from view. I stepped through the threshold, and darkness immediately enveloped me, a heavy void pressing in from all sides. The familiar world was gone, replaced by an endless black expanse.

Then, cutting through the silence, a clear, urgent voice rang out, piercing the darkness and urging me forward.

"Can you hear me?"

Index

As you follow Dee's journey, these symbols will reveal themselves, adding layers of meaning and depth to her story. Enjoy your adventure in "Soul."

Trees
- *Life and Growth:* Trees symbolize the cycle of life and the resilience found in nature.
- *Wisdom and Knowledge:* Representing deep roots and expansive branches, trees are symbols of profound wisdom.
- *Stability and Strength:* With their sturdy trunks and deep roots, trees embody stability and strength.

Mirrors
- *Self-Reflection and Truth*: Mirrors symbolize introspection and the revelation of one's true self.
- *Illusion and Deception*: They can also represent surface illusions and deceptive appearances.
- *Mystery and the Unconscious:* Mirrors often signify hidden realities and the unknown depths of the unconscious mind.

Phoenix
- *Rebirth and Renewal:* The mythical phoenix represents the cycle of rebirth, emerging anew from its ashes.
- *Transformation:* Signifying the ability to transform and grow stronger through adversity.

Water
- *Purity and Cleansing:* Water symbolizes the washing away of impurities and the renewal of spirit.
- *Life and Fertility*: Essential for life, water represents growth and the sustenance of living beings.
- *Change and Adaptability:* Reflecting its ever-changing forms, water embodies adaptability and the capacity to flow around obstacles.

Fire
- Passion and Desire: Fire often represents intense emotions, such as love, passion, and desire. Its burning nature reflects the fervent and consuming aspects of these feelings.
- Transformation and Renewal: Just as fire can destroy, it can also purify and transform. It symbolizes change, renewal, and the idea of something new emerging from the ashes of the old.

About The Author

At 27 years old, Georgia Spearing has crafted an electrifying new fantasy romance novel that promises to captivate readers with its tale of love, betrayal, and redemption. In her debut book, 'Soul,' she weaves a compelling story where a woman journeys between the realms of life and death in pursuit of her soulmate, encountering the best and worst of her existence in fantastical worlds. A spirited and resilient individual, Georgia is the proud mother of a beautiful baby girl named Iris. Despite living with fibromyalgia, a chronic pain disorder, for over a decade, she has never let it deter her from chasing her dreams. Her perseverance and dedication are evident in her writing journey.

Before stepping into the world of published fiction, Georgia honed her skills as a ghostwriter for Urban Writers, where she wrote 13 books across various genres in just a year. This extensive experience has sharpened her writing abilities and demonstrated her commitment to delivering quality work on time. Her passion, however, lies in the realm of romantic fantasy—a genre that has always provided her with an escape and a source of inspiration. Her life has been a fascinating adventure, from working security at high-class events in London, to transitioning to retail at New Look during the pandemic. The birth of her daughter marked a new chapter, prompting her to focus on her long-held dream of becoming a writer. Now, as a dedicated ghostwriter, she continues to produce high-quality work while aspiring to see her own stories in print.

'Soul' is not just a novel; it is a reflection of Georgia Spearing's life and experiences, offering relatable insights and emotions. Through her writing, she aims to convey to readers that it's okay not to have everything figured out and that the journey itself is where true growth and discovery lie.

@Authorgeorgiaspearing

Georgia Spearing

Book 2

The Soulbound Trilogy

Souls

Coming Soon